PENGUIN BOOKS

HANGWOMAN

K.R. Meera is a multi-award-winning writer and journalist. She has published short stories, novels and essays, and has won some of the most prestigious literary prizes including the Kerala Sahitya Akademi Award, the Vayalar Award and the Odakkuzhal Award. Most recently, she won the Kendra Sahitya Akademi Award for *Aarachar*, widely hailed as a contemporary classic and published by Penguin Books India as *Hangwoman*. She lives in Kottayam with her husband Dileep and daughter Shruthi.

A bilingual feminist scholar, J. Devika has translated Malayali women writers from the late nineteenth and early twentieth centuries, and contemporary authors like Sarah Joseph, Nalini Jameela, Anitha Thampi and V.M. Girija besides K.R. Meera.

PRAISE FOR THE BOOK

'Meera is at her best when she examines the lives of her women characters . . . . The writing is strong . . . An epic novel'—*Outlook*

'A daring book, for the panoramic sweep of its canvas, for the sheer audacity of its narrative logic . . . for its irreverent play with the paradoxes of life—Love and Death'—*The Hindu*

'This striking novel includes within its majestic sweep the enigmas of the human condition. . . . Stunning images bring out the depth and intensity of Chetna's spiritual development, and stand testimony to the author's consummate writing style'—*Deccan Herald*

'Meera achieves a vision of [Kolkata] that is both acutely observed, almost anthropological, in its minute detailing and, at the same time, mythic in its evocation of the city's decaying, decrepit majesty . . . . One of the most extraordinary accomplishments in recent Indian fiction'—*Indian Express*

'An absorbing novel'—*New Indian Express*

'One of the strongest voices in contemporary Malayalam literature . . . . Meera plays with the reader's anticipation masterfully . . . The novel is extremely atmospheric . . . Meera turns the entire city into a haunted house'—*Open*

'The book heaves with violence, is lush with metaphor and shocks with details. The reader can only gasp at the surgical precision with which Meera describes the act of hanging'—*The Hindu Business Line*

'An immense, intense coiled rope of a novel . . . There are chillingly clear-eyed vignettes and moments of razor-sharp dark humour . . . . If *Aarachar*, the original, was—plot, stock and barrel—"Malayalam's ultimate gift of love to Bengal," as its translator J. Devika puts it, its English translation is no less a bonus for showing us, its non-Malayali, non-Bengali readership, the dazzling interstices of her story, instantly recognisable across time and space'—*India Today*

'An incisive critique of the barbarism of the death penalty . . . [The book] gives us a glimpse into the inner lives of those who have been deputed to execute it through generations . . . A vast and riveting sweep of time, locked into the gritty interstices of the contemporary—a pastiche made of fact and fiction, news bulletins and nightmares'—*Mint*

'Stunning . . . Meera weaves history, romance and the politics of the present together into a narrative of incredible complexity . . . . J. Devika's translation is superb, and she captures the rich detail of Meera's Malayalam: descriptive, textured and evocative . . . Reading Meera, in Devika's meticulous and inspired translation, we experience the author's spectacular ventriloquism. And we are also reminded of the tradition that Meera comes from, which she has burnished and transcended with her epic novel'—*Caravan*

Hangwoman

K.R. MEERA

Translated from the Malayalam by J. Devika

PENGUIN BOOKS

An imprint of Penguin Random House

PENGUIN BOOKS

USA | Canada | UK | Ireland | Australia
New Zealand | India | South Africa | China

Penguin Books is part of the Penguin Random House group of companies
whose addresses can be found at global.penguinrandomhouse.com

Published by Penguin Random House India Pvt. Ltd
7th Floor, Infinity Tower C, DLF Cyber City,
Gurgaon 122 002, Haryana, India

Penguin
Random House
India

First published in Malayalam as *Aarachar* by DeeCee Books, Kottayam, 2012
First published in English in Hamish Hamilton by Penguin Books India 2014
Published in Penguin Books 2015

ISBN 9780143424697

Typeset in Dante MT Std by R. Ajith Kumar, New Delhi
Printed at Repro Knowledgecast Limited, India

www.penguin.co.in

1

When we first heard the news on TV that the governor had rejected Jatindranath Banerjee's mercy petition, the first hearse of the day had just rolled towards Nimtala Ghat. It passed by our house—in which huddle together a hairdressing salon, a dirty single-room shrine and a tea shop lined with small earthen cups—on Strand Road. Chitpur, where our house stands, was always of the black folk. We have been here for ever so long—long before the Europeans divided Kolkata into White and Black towns, before the Basaks and Seths set up villages besides the Hooghly. Though cramped, grimy and smothered by moss today, the heart of Chitpur lies in Rabindranath Thakur's family home, Jorasanko Thakurbari. If you start from Lal Bazar and walk along Rabindra Sarani on which the trams crawl, past the printing presses, the knife sellers and the tabla shops on Madan Chatterjee Lane, you come across Jatrapara, the offices of the drama troupes. Straight ahead are the red-lit streets of Sonagachi and Kumortuli, where idols of gods and goddesses are sold. Turn right, and you will find Macchua Bazar, which sells fruit but no fish. Turn left along Nimtala Ghat Road towards Strand Road, and you will reach the ancient burning ghat of Nimtala beside the Ganga, where all end their journeys. The tea shop facing north, and the salon and shrine to the east, which made up our sphere of existence, lay on the three-way junction on the turn from Strand Road into the lane towards the cremation ground. Night and day, the road in front of our house bustled with mourners, loaders, barbers, cobblers, ear cleaners, vendors and beggars, pushing and shoving in the flow towards Nimtala Ghat. Motor vehicles, pushcarts, horse carts, the bells ringing in wayside shrines and the bleating of sacrificial animals created a din louder than the circular trains. The mingled scents of sweetmeats cooking in ghee and sunflower oil, and corpses burning on pyres enveloped us.

A group of sannyasis singing *Hare Rama* walked behind the hearse. Most of them were young men in saffron robes, fair, bony, bearded. As they walked along taking in streetside sights, chanting, chatting with each other, joking and laughing, a stern-faced sannyasi with a greying beard and thick glasses stood up beside the saffron-shrouded corpse in the saffron-covered hearse, which had Om written on all its four sides. Shaking off the lather from the washing on my hands, I wondered which one was *really* the corpse—the one that reclined or the other which stood up straight? It was just then that Uncle Sukhdev, whom I call Kaku, and others Sudev, ran up from the salon, face beaming, to give us the news that the mercy petition had been rejected. Seeing him laugh, Phanibhushan Grddha Mullick, whom I call Baba, growled in anger: 'Chi! Beast! To be a man you need some tact . . .'

That blew into a fight. So, coming over to give the glad news when a job had surfaced after ten or twelve years is a big crime, grumbled Kaku. Brainless oaf, Father put him down. Hearing the squabble, my grandmother, whom I call Thakuma, pulled the tattered pallu of her sari over her head and hobbled in. Bhuvaneswari Devi, my father's mother, was over a hundred years old, and so shrivelled that she seemed no bigger than Father's arm. I continued washing Ramu da's clothes on the washing stone in the moss-covered and crumbling little courtyard shared by our rooms. When Kaku returned to his salon, Father stroked his grey-tinged handlebar moustache and smiled to himself. It was then that I realized that I had, in that little interval, tied a noose with the hanging end of my dupatta. The dupatta was old and frayed, but the noose was perfect. Even the infants born in our family could tie a perfect noose. It is the very first thing we Grddha Mullicks learn to do with our hands.

That was the eighteenth of May. The whiteness of the clouds had begun to dim and the faint rumblings of thunder now and then reminded us that the monsoon was on its way. Thunder rang—as if a cellar, way beyond the skies, was being thrown open. It made me hope for hailstones. When we were children, Ramu da and I used to run into the street to gather the hailstones. The last time it hailed, large hailstones fell which looked like tiles of the sky's glass roof. By then I had grown up so I could only stand leaning against the wall, making a noose with my dupatta and watching them melt. In the skies that day, the crows had flown twisting, flailing, screaming desperately. A lapwing had fallen, hit by a hailstone before my eyes; it thrashed about on the ground. The hailstones lay melting leisurely in the dim light upon the battered road from which the concrete had loosened. The first hearse that rolled over them after the rain was an expensive, fancily decorated one, with wreaths and roses and all. But there was no one to accompany it, weeping or otherwise. I stepped out to catch another glimpse of the vehicle which looked as if it was studded with gold and silver. A woman in a red kasi silk sari lay stiff and very straight upon the flowers, her hands placed lightly on her chest, impatience and defiance upon her face. A woman as tall as me, her face smooth-skinned. As the hearse passed, her pallid feet—their toes tied together—pressed against the glass window through the lilies. That whole night the thought that my toes had broken off left me panicstricken.

The truth was that from the time I was in my mother's womb, I was already tied up in the umbilical cord. My mother's belly had to be cut open so I could be taken out. Thakuma bragged that the noose I'd tied even as a foetus was a faultless one. That would always drive my mother, the fair, thin Sachinamayi Devi, sindoor liberally strewn in the parting of her white hair, into a fury. 'Born to her old man all right! And she put it on her own neck!'

Hey, you donkey, go and ask the Sarkar of this land what the Grddha Mullick is worth, challenged Thakuma. Then as usual, Ma, with her sunken eyes and dried-up high nose, would pull out her ace: 'Go and ask the whores of Sonagachi what he's worth . . . And even they weren't enough, it looks like—made me carry this load again . . .'

Ma was alluding to the story of how, twenty-three years ago, Father had spawned me the day he had hanged a serial killer who had snuffed out seven lives. After finishing his work at dawn he had drunk through the day, and then at noon, he grabbed Ma while she was buying vegetables in the market and tried to fuck her in full public view. He was sixty-five then. Mother had me at forty-five. Father was called to duty only a few times after that. But I learned by seeing. Before I was five, I could fashion a noose on my own. I also learned how to fix it on the human neck—tested it on the child next door. That's an interesting story, for later.

After Kaku retreated, I hung the washing to dry in front of the salon and the shrine. Inside, the sound of Ma and Thakuma bickering. Maybe the corpse of the sannyasi that passed by was burning; the air was filled with a foul stench. Somebody else's relatives streamed into the tea shop, their clothes wet from the dip in the Ganga after the cremation. As always, Father sat behind the cash counter proudly, head held high. Behind him, on a rusted iron bar hung the framed page of the *Statesman* which had published the very first news item on him in 1960. When that piece of paper had yellowed with age, and the picture of Father as a very young man with the noose had faded, he hung below it yet another news item about him that had appeared fifteen years ago in an English magazine. This was a colour picture. Sometimes customers cast their eyes on the wall, forgetting the pain of loss and the fatigue of the funeral. Father pounced on them and asked, 'Why, Dada, can't you read?'

Then he would call me or Ramu da. 'Child, read it out for them . . .'

We, Ramu da or I, would read aloud for them, 'All Set for Hanging: Grddha Mullick', or 'Hanging Is No Child's Play, Says Grddha Mullick'. It was Father who explained it in Bangla. Ramu da and I learned our English reading news articles about him. That's how Father learned English too.

Sometimes people looked deep into the tea cup and stayed downcast. Father caught their attention by banging on the table and saying: 'Brother, death is a timeless truth. Someone dear to you has passed away, isn't it? But it is time for him to go. Who are we to stop him? Look, as a hangman who has sent off four hundred and fifty-one people, let me tell you—pay heed—death is never in our hands.'

Every single person who heard it jumped in shock. So dramatically did he utter the word 'hangman'. When they raised their eyes to the picture on the wall, Father would stroke his greying handlebar moustache and roll his round eyes with the same dramatic effect as in his jatra performances. 'Not one, not two, all of four hundred and fifty-one . . .'

On the day Jatindranath Banerjee's mercy petition was rejected, however, Father sat with a grave face, silent, head high; he did not look at anyone who came in for tea, nor did he say anything to them. Pushing back the red-and-green checked gamchha which lay on his left shoulder and tightening the strap of the ancient steel wristwatch which kept coming loose, he seemed lost in thought. Once or twice he went into the inner room and sipped from the bottle tucked away behind the framed picture of Ma Kali. And smoked cigarette after cigarette. That day was busier than usual at the shop. Ma and Syamili Devi, Kaku's wife, whom I call Kakima, were taking turns at making the tea. The earthen tea cups were being flung out into the front of the shop, sometimes broken, sometimes not. I was pouring some water for Ramu da when the black telephone in Father's room rang—*tr . . . ing . . . tr . . . ing*. Father ran in to pick it up. Recognizing the voice on the other side, he drew the unlit cigarette away from his lips. That was a sign of respect. For he was easily capable of even bellowing with it resting on his lips.

'Babu, yes, Babu . . . But will anything really happen, Babu? Or will the crow snatch it away like in 1990?'

Kaku, who had scampered in from the saloon upon hearing the exchange, whispered to me that the voice was on the other side was either that of the jail superintendent or the DGP. Though he carried a lot of flab, Kaku is puny compared to Father, who is six feet and two inches tall, swarthy and strong. But they share the same dark complexion and protruding eyes. We have been known as Grddha Mullick from the days of royalty for those bulging eyes that reflect the hunger of vultures.

Father continued, paying no attention to us. 'Ah . . . what are you saying, Babu? Bhagawan Maheswar be my witness . . . I am sick of this sin . . . I am an artiste, Babu, an artiste . . . but this is the government's affair . . . our family profession too . . . If twenty thousand rupees and a job for my daughter is too big a demand, do find someone else, Babu . . . I am eighty-eight years old now. If I were to collapse today, there is no male who can shoulder the burden of my family . . . and I don't have to tell you again and again how that happened . . . May Bhagawan Mahadev bless you . . .'

As he talked, that right hand which had fastened the fatal noose on four hundred and fifty-one necks wiped off the sweat with the gamchha, still holding the cigarette between the index and middle fingers.

'Is money the only consideration in this affair, Babu? I'll give you one lakh rupees, Babu, will you do this job? Just involves pulling a lever? Babu, when I reach the other world, God will ask, Phani, why did you murder a fellow who did you no harm at all? Why didn't you say no? Don't I need a reply for that, Babu? Bhagawan, to give my girl who's grown so full-bodied that she fills the house a life; to get medicines for my loving, aged mother; to give my son medical treatment; to buy my dear wife food and clothing—I did it for all this. What other excuse do I have? Yes, Babu, yes. I will come over . . .'

Then, without even moving his head, Father raised his voice like an actor: 'Arre, Sudev, come here . . . Tomorrow morning we've to see Chakrabarty babu. Don't forget to get ready early! All right then, Babu. Let's decide when we will meet . . .'

He noticed Kaku only when he turned around. But ignoring that awkward moment, face expressionless, he smoothed his moustache and grimaced at us: '"Grddha, is money the most important thing in the world?" Indeed! Sounds as if fellows like him pay the government every month so that they can serve the people . . . such crooks!'

I stood there, looking at Father. As always, I felt uncertain about him but also proud. I have never seen an anchor on a TV show like him. Never seen a character like him in the movies or in the theatre. No one has ever been able to predict his words. But one thing is clear: Father's words are always extraordinarily precise. On every occasion, he says precisely what everyone longs to hear. Later, whenever I have had to speak, I have always racked my brains, trying to recreate in my mind what he would have said in my place.

I sat in the red plastic chair, so worn that it was nearly white now, near Ramu da's cot and flipped casually through the English textbook that Kaku's daughter Rari had studied last year. I was reluctant to look at Ramu da's face. In the past there were days on which the house overflowed with happiness. Once hangings became rare our source of income dried up. A high-pitched wail rang outside; I got up and peeped out through the door. One after the other, four or five hearses were passing by; the first two were fancy ones. Well-fed, fair-skinned men in gold-rimmed glasses and women in silk saris and sleeveless blouses walked behind them silently. It was a young girl of ten or twelve who belonged to the middle-class family that followed the high-class mourners who had let out that heart-rending cry for her father. Seeing the older people hold her as she walked, I became gloomy.

'Good business today, it seems—' Ramu da murmured, his eyes still shut.

It was a very hot day. The clothes hanging outside dried quickly. The bells rang in the Kali temple two houses away.

'The whole of last night, vehicles were passing this way,' Ramu da spoke again.

The flow of vehicles on Strand Road will cease only if there are no more deaths. In my twenty-two-year-old memory the road has never been free of funeral corteges. It was either motor vehicles that sped down the road falling into ancient potholes and dents, disturbing us with their rattling, or handcarts, which were less noisy. The bodies of the really poor arrived in handcarts and waste collectors' carts. When we needed more money, Ma and Kakima sold tea the whole night through. But such occasions were rare. 'I'm not loose in the head to keep making money so that the Sonagachi whores get some extra,' was Ma's stance. Sonagachi was just two turns down the road. Past the vegetable market and the street where sweetmeats were sold in shops on both sides of the road, the lanes of Sonagachi began. Like the droplets of water in the Ganga which gush towards the ocean, every extra coin that appeared in our family flowed towards Sonagachi and found its rest.

The twelve-fifteen train to Prinsep Ghat had just passed by; it was then that someone from the office of the IG, Correctional Services, Ajoy Chakrabarty, came looking for my father. When the police jeep rattled up to the house through the crowds and the hearses, Father stepped out of the shop with a smile of triumph. As the policemen waited, causing traffic jams on three roads, Father put on his white kurta and dhoti, and fastened the black leather belt that was almost as broad as his palm over them. Kaku hurried from the next house, rolling the sleeves of his checked shirt and trying to catch up with Father. I stood leaning against the wall, tying and untying a noose with my dupatta. Thakuma chanted Nama Shivaaya, hands folded in prayer. In the inner room Ramu da lay with his face to the wall, eyes shut. It was searing hot outside; the sun glowered. Sweat poured down. A feeling as persistent as hot steam building up within a tightly shut kitchen-pot seethed in my heart and body.

Before Father returned, the first newspaper man was at our doorstep. Narendra Choudhuri, local correspondent of the *Anandabazar Patrika*. I stepped out when I saw him. When I passed the Plus Two exams, he had reported it: 'Hangman's daughter scores high distinction in Plus Two exams'. But Father did not let him print my photo even with that news.

'Baba has been sent for from the jail, Babu.' I went up to him respectfully.

'Ah, he is going to be busy now . . . eh, so you didn't continue your studies?'

I smiled and shook my head, no, I didn't.

He looked at me with sympathy. 'You were working at a press?'

'I am not going anywhere now, Babu,' I told him.

As he left on his scooter through the hustle and bustle, I recalled my job as a proofreader in Anjaneya Prasad Yadav's Sri Maruti Press on Madan Chatterjee Lane when I was just out of Plus Two. The salary was fifty rupees. I was barely there for two weeks, but on my way to work I really enjoyed walking past the bookshops in front of Thakurbari, taking in their scent.

I was sitting on a wooden chair near a barred window in a small room of a two-hundred-year-old building, the lime peeling off its walls, comparing the written draft with the first proof on the writing board. I was correcting the errors in '*Ekla chalo, ekla chalo, ekla chalo, ekla chalo re . . .*' when two hands slid under my armpits and spread themselves on my breasts. Because the stink of paan and the reek of sweat invaded my nostrils suddenly, I knew it was Maruti Prasad, Anjaneya's son, without even looking. I turned around calmly and gazed into his eyes. I was neither fearful nor nervous. Instead, laughter bubbled up in me. Setting aside the writing board, I stood up. Like all the other Grddha Mullicks, I too am unusually tall, and have a strong, well-built frame. He was a couple of inches shorter than me when I stood up. Very slowly, I took the dupatta off my chest. He gawked greedily at my breasts. I tied a noose in the bat of an eyelid and, smiling at him, put it around his neck like a marriage garland. Before he could pull me closer, I had tightened the noose, passing the other end of the dupatta through the window bars and pulling it tight. His mouth gaped open. His eyes popped. His tongue protruded and paan juice flowed from it like blood. He struggled hard. But I took all that force on my left arm. He thrashed about desperately, his eyeballs bulged and his tongue hung close to his chin. Slowly, I eased my grip. He collapsed, panting, barely conscious. As I helped him sit against the wall, I remembered Father. Whenever he had to answer questions posed by journalists, Father would ask afterwards: 'Isn't that one thumping line?' I too felt like pitching one. So I said to him: 'The hangman's rope is not meant to tie the cow.' He looked at me, opening his drooping eyelids. Weak, they closed again. As I untied the noose from his neck and shook it to make a dupatta again, I also let him know: 'To kill a cock, you don't need a hangman.'

That was a terribly hot summer. The sun blazed at forty-five degree Celsius or more. The heat and the summer did not affect me. But, as I walked from the press to the bus stop and got on to bus no. 22, a tightened noose hung from my neck. I was afraid to look at my own hands. I had not realized that my hands were so strong, so rough. I had Ma's fair skin and her thick curly hair. But that moment I yearned for her short, frail figure too.

Thakuma was at the Kali temple as usual when I reached home. Ma had gone to Dum Dum to see her niece's baby. When Ramu da inquired with his eyes why I was home early, I told him, 'I proved that I am Grddha Mullick's daughter.'

Hearing me, Father came in from the other room. I had to tell him that Maruti Prasad had tried to molest me. He didn't believe me. Red and yellow hues flashed on his dark face. Then his eyes filled with tears. He went out of the room as if to calm the storm within. Ramu da looked at me, deep sympathy in his eyes. After some time, Father returned. 'How did you make that noose?'

His normally resonant voice sounded weary. I looked at Ramu da, picked up my dupatta again and tied a noose. Father took it in his hand and gave it a good look. Surprise dawned in his red bulging eyes. I put it around my neck. When he pulled its tail, it tightened. I leapt up, writhing. A smile spread across Father's face. He let go of the tail.

'Yadav's tongue must have stuck out?' he asked.

I rubbed my neck and nodded, still panting. It was then that Father put his tobacco-stained index finger on the point below the chin and above the depression in my neck and showed me the correct spot.

'This . . . this is its spot. If it moves up or down, the condemned will die flailing and thrashing. That's disgraceful for a hangman.'

He loosened the noose from my neck and threw the dupatta at me. Anyway, my employment ended that day. Father did not allow me to go out alone after that. On that day, 18 May, when Father returned at sundown in the police jeep, I realized that I was wearing the same dupatta that had tightened around Maruti Prasad's neck. In the past five years, I had been able to buy just one or two new sets of clothes.

Father came in looking vexed and tired. And fully drunk. He picked a fight quite unnecessarily with Ma, and retired to his room. It is the very room that you have seen in a couple of documentaries and the many TV programmes that came later. Asbestos-covered roof, unplastered laterite walls, garlanded pictures of Mahadeva and Ma Kali, and also Grandfather, on the stand nailed to the western wall. On all the other walls, framed news items about Father. An iron bar that supported the walls crossed the room; Father's old gamchha and shirt hung on it. As he stretched out on the narrow wooden cot in his threadbare lungi, Father looked as if he was wearing a white vest because all his body hair had turned white.

'Can't believe those deceitful fellows; don't touch even the water they offer! No rule indeed that hangmen's children should be given jobs . . . Uh-uh . . . playing around with Grddha Mullick?' Father raged.

I switched on the television, pretending not to hear. Sonia Gandhi had declared that she did not want to become prime minister. A woman with a big bindi on her forehead lamented to the newsreader that the country did not have the good fortune to have another woman prime minister. Everyone who appeared on TV was white-skinned, pinkish. Before I could get a good look at them, Kaku called from the salon on the other side, across the wall.

'O . . . Chetu!'

I went outside. Two cats had snuggled up in the cool wetness beside the washing stone. It was that moment, the one in which I stepped over the cats into the still glowering, reddish-hued summer evening, that my life turned upside down. Soon enough, I had to go to Alipore Central Jail.

A man led me into a strange cremation ground in a hearse of flowers with the toes of my feet tied together. From my life thus far, I can say this much: on this earth, only love is more uncertain than death.

2

Ours has been a family of famous hangmen for very long, right from the times when the Nanda kings ruled the land. Our roots sink deep, to four hundred and twenty years before Christ. Ramu da's teasing banter that the only events which our family members hadn't seen with their own eyes were Shiva's all-consuming tandava with the body of Sati—who had immolated herself in Daksha's sacrificial altar—and Vishnu's splitting of her body into pieces with his Sudarsana Chakra, with the pieces scattering over eighteen places sent Thakuma into a fit. But she had a swift reply to that. 'Get lost, you fellow! Kalighat is the place where Devi Sati's right toe fell when Bhagawan Mahavishnu cut up the body with his Chakra. Who do you think were the first inhabitants of this Kalighat?'

That was long before the White and Black towns came up. Thakuma took pride in the fact that even the chaturvaranya had taken shape much later. Before Bharat became Bharat, before three villages between the swamp and the forest beside the Hooghly became Kolkata, there was power and crime and death penalty in the country. The very first hangman in our family was Radharaman Mullick. He was the palace doctor. That great-great-great-great-great-great-great grandfather fell madly in love with a woman who came to him with a fever. She was the beloved of the prince, the true heir to the kingdom. Thakuma said that our forefather of yore became a hangman so that he could possess her. All the grandmothers' tales we heard as children were of death, of some sort.

That Grandfather Hangman's house stood in a large yard full of portia trees in full bloom. He was rich and handsome. Still, he did not win the woman's heart. When King Mahanandin passed away, Mahapadma

11

Nanda, his son by a dasi, threw out the true heir to the throne. A war followed. The wounded prince went to our illustrious primogenitor to be healed. Radharaman healed the prince but then handed him over to Mahapadma Nanda. The new king ordered the prince's public execution. Radharaman Mullick went to the court begging to be allowed to perform the hanging. He was the first person to go there asking for the job of his own free will. The king granted him his desire. The first time, the prince struggled and flailed as the noose tightened but nothing more happened. My ancestor brought him down. The second time he fastened the noose in the precise fashion which our family continues to follow: between the third and fourth vertebrae. This time his neck broke as easily as a portia flower from its stem, with a single pull of the cord. As he ascended the gallows for a second time, the man stared at our forefather and gritted his teeth: 'You will never possess her.' But just the opposite was to happen. When the king asked him about his reward, Grandfather Radharaman asked for that woman. And got her. But because of the precision with which that hanging was carried out, he had to work as a hangman for the rest of his life. Those days hangings were almost a daily affair. He would return home at night with swollen hands. That woman, Chinmayi Devi, bore all his ten children.

The night Thakuma told us that story, Ramu da, who was just twelve at the time, said to me as we lay on the soiled old mat, ready to fall asleep, 'I will never love a woman when I become big.' 'Me too,' I intoned. That was the time when the jingle 'One day I will grow and be like my big brother' was always playing on TV. In those days, when watching TV at Bhupen Chakrabarty's house next door cost ten paisa, that song re-echoed from not just my lips, but my very heart.

Thakuma never thought that hanging was vile. She was the daughter of my great-grandfather's sister. She told us that her prayer as a child was to marry a hangman. She reminded us: 'That is our profession, we kill for the sake of justice. When Grandfather Radharaman was a doctor, he saved the prince's life. When he became the hangman, he executed him. The doctor's job is to heal even the foe who appears before him seeking a cure. The hangman's job is to kill even his own son if he is the wrongdoer. No work is low. No work makes you a sinner. Then, as far as performing this task is concerned . . .' Pride swelled in Thakuma's voice: 'No ordinary person can do it. The mind must be firm, the hand must be strong and you've got to have brains.'

'Brains to kill, Thakuma?' I asked.

She laughed aloud. 'You think this is a simple matter? My grandfather's father, that is, your great-grandfather's mother's older brother, Yogendra Mullick used to say, "Work out at one glance the weight of the condemned's body. Then measure the hollow in his neck."'

'For what, Thakuma?'

'The life breath is in that hollow, girl. There are many types of men . . . some have strong bones there . . . won't break soon . . . so the noose has to be fastened correctly.'

Thakuma spoke as if she had done it a hundred times. As she retold the stories of hangings, Thakuma's hands knotted and loosened a noose on an imaginary cord. That was a habit common to all the women of our family. While we spoke, we obsessively made and unmade nooses with the ends of our garments, be it a sari or a dupatta. That must have been a psychological necessity. Only once did a woman from our family accept the job of the hangman. Hard to believe, but she had demanded the job.

On the nights Thakuma told us tales of the family, I went to bed thinking of the big mansion in the yard amidst the blooming portia trees with pride and the pain of loss. In class four, we were taken to Thakurbari on a tour. That is the biggest house I have ever set foot in. As I walked along Madan Chatterjee Lane, one in a line of children clad in grimy frayed uniforms, ancient houses of uncut red stone appeared in front of my eyes. In my desire-tinged imagination, I wished: If only Grandfather Radharaman's house were like Thakurbari. It was a happy pastime to imagine Ramu da and me playing hide-and-seek behind the pillars that lined the cemented central courtyard, almost as big as a football field. In my mind's eye, I stood on the terrace of the house and gazed at the road. Golden tram cars flashing their blood-red lights crawled over silver tracks in front of the house. Reality, at that age, is like the noose fastened on the hollow of the neck. From the shiny reddish floors of Thakurbari, I had to inevitably wake up below Thakuma's coir cot in our rathole of a home. Our home was dilapidated enough to look ancient too, as though it might tumble down any moment. It was one

13

of the oldest buildings on Strand Road. We were living in the cowshed of the house that her great-grandfather built so that he could bathe in the Ganga every day, sighed Thakuma.

Our house was like a narrow box with just three sides. All rooms opened into the small courtyard where only one person could stand. The tea shop, the salon and the kitchen had wooden false ceilings. The other rooms had asbestos roofs. Only the tea shop and the salon next to it could be seen from outside, and they jutted into the road. Father's room shared walls with them. Right in front of it was the drain in which we washed clothes and dishes. After Father's room came the room that Ramu da, Thakuma and I shared. It had doors that opened into Father's room, the yard and the kitchen next to it. Opposite the kitchen was Kaku's room. All the rooms had disfigured walls and cement-bordered apertures instead of windows. The kitchen floor lay cracked and broken for many years.

The rooms fought a losing battle against the dirty drain that flowed past the quarters of the Port Trust workers just a wall away. At night, when we went to bed, the ground shook with the electric train's *kata-kata-kata*. Hari da's bhelpuri shop where packets of Maharani paan hung like decorations was just next door. The walls echoed the cusswords of some drunkard high on the arrack secretly sold there at night, and the piercing cries of sacrificial animals from Hemant Mullick's Kali temple. When that happened, I always shut my eyes and calmed myself, kindling in my mind's eye the image of Thakurbari and Grandfather Radharaman with a long beard and gown that fell right down to his feet.

When I stepped outside at Kaku's call that 18 May, I was thinking of Grandfather Radharaman. That was because the news of the appointment of a special officer who would break open the lock of the strongroom at Thakurbari and make an inventory of the articles kept there had just been announced on TV. The Nobel medal and citation had been stolen from Uttarayan, at Santiniketan. Deep in thought, I did not notice the vehicle parked among the hearses and the ambulances in that narrow street; it looked just like them. Kaku was standing on the road in front of the salon. When the crowd passed us and moved towards the Ghat, I asked him why he had called me. He gave me a sly smile and, taking a ten-rupee note out of his pocket, asked me to go get some paan. That was unusual. Though surprised, I obeyed when he pressed me to go. To reach the paan shop just opposite the Ghat, you turn to the right from the house and walk past Thakuma's Shiva shrine and Hemant Mullick's Kali temple. But when I set off, Kaku stopped me. He told me not to turn right but to walk down the road to Hari da's bhelpuri shop and get it from there. I, with all the innocence of a twenty-two-year-old girl who had never been caught in love, walked merrily to Hari da's shop and back, swinging my arms, folding and unfolding them. I did not sense the danger I was in till I saw a handsome young man holding a mike against the backdrop of a funeral procession on the seven o'clock news. The story came just after the Muslim leaders' accusation that Mamata Banerjee's praise of Narendra Modi had caused the party's seats to be reduced to just one in the upcoming elections. Father laughed heartily when the house and its surroundings, and 'Vote for Avinash Chatterjee' in indigo on the wall appeared on TV. I, however, was sick and tired of it. 'Look, look,' he called us happily. I figured out only then why Father had been sitting rooted in front of CNC since six o'clock.

'Jatindranath Banerjee's hanging will be the first to happen in India in thirteen years. But after hangman Phanibhushan Grddha Mullick made it clear that he will not work unless his demands have been met, plans for Jatindranath's execution take a new turn.' The handsome young man looked into my eyes and announced this.

Then it was Father's face on TV. Smoothing down the ample grey moustache that grew almost on to his bulging cheeks, Father began to speak, holding an unlit cigarette between his index and middle fingers.

'In 1982, they had given this to me in writing when they decided to execute Jabbar Singh. Government jobs for my children . . . but later, when my son Ramdev Mullick was seriously injured . . . then they conveniently forgot the promise. How did he suffer that injury? The government ought to have had a care. I have sacrificed my life and my family's too, for the sake of this country. Doesn't the government have any obligation towards me? This business of hanging, is it a picnic? Babu, we don't tie the noose around the neck of a hen or a snake. We tie it around a human being's neck. Here, pinch me, and see for yourself, I am no block of iron or stone. A man, just like you. I too have a family. A wife. Mother. Brother. Children. He, the condemned man I am to hang, is not even my son's age. I am ending his life. Is that like smoking this cigarette? No, brother, no . . .'

Father lit his cigarette and let out a puff of smoke. When the camera panned sideways, Alipore Central Jail appeared. Father was coming out after seeing the Inspector General. He struck a jatra pose, gazing reverentially at something in the distance and folding his hands in salutation. Then he continued: 'I am a person who calls to God every day. I don't know what lies ahead of this life. I have hung four hundred and fifty-one people with these hands . . . not even one of those four hundred and fifty-one has returned to tell me what death is like and what lies beyond. Look here, you, I am an old man. May leave any time . . . if I leave and reach there, will the four hundred and fifty-one people be waiting for me? I don't know. Will they fry me in oil? That, too, I don't know . . . Everything ends after death, scientists say. But to know if it is really like that, we have to go by ourselves.'

'Do you believe in life after death?'

'No, brother, that is not the issue. The issue is the big risk I have taken. Risk, Babu, risk . . .'

Father pointed the cigarette at the camera and puffed hard once more. He wiped the sweat with his gamchha.

'Till which class did you study?'

'See? This is the problem with you. Why do you worry about the class up to which I have studied? Isn't it enough to ask how much I know? I know enough to read an English newspaper. To make sense of it. I know enough of maths and chemistry and physics and everything else to do my job. Why, won't that do?'

Father raised his eyebrows and laughed mockingly. His face really looked like that of a vulture.

'Are you saying that the government must compensate you for the torture you may have to undergo in the afterlife?'

'I said I know nothing of afterlife . . . there is risk even in life till death.'

'What risk do you face?'

'My son Ramdev . . . my son was cut down by the father of Amartya Ghosh whom I hanged at the gallows in 1990 . . .'

Father pulled hard on the burning cigarette. Suddenly my heart fell. We never spoke of that day. In 1990, Ramu da had been my age, twenty-two. Father's height, luxuriant hair and moustache, and Ma's fair complexion and gentle eyes made him handsome. All the girls in the neighbourhood were fastening nooses around his neck, I would tease; they threw look after look in longing. He was a good student. And reluctant to become a hangman. He argued with Father over it all night sometimes.

Those days, there were no twenty-four-hour channels. That was the heyday of newspapers. The news of Amartya Ghosh's execution continued to appear. Our family was all agog, having got a job after two or three years. But two days later, Ramu da, who was returning from college, was attacked by Amartya's aged father. The old man hacked off his fair, slender, delicate limbs.

'Didn't the government offer compensation for the injuries Ramdev suffered?' The young man continued to question Father.

'They gave fifteen hundred rupees then . . . and now a pension for the disabled . . .'

The image of Father flinging away the cigarette butt appeared on the screen.

I thought it would end there. But the young man's voice rang again. 'Only your son is disabled. You still have a healthy daughter. Are you not keen to hand over your job to her?'

I was stunned. Father too looked somewhat startled.

'I haven't ever thought of that . . .'

Father took out another cigarette, lit it, took a drag and continued without wasting any time. 'Uh-uh . . . why not? She can easily do it. But, brother, that is not for me to decide. It is for the government, right?'

Ma, Ramu da and I sat transfixed as Father turned around and looked at us with a smile. The scenes that followed were these: the young man's face appeared. 'Grddha Mullick made it clear that unless his daughter is granted a government job, he will not accept the court order and perform the hanging. While committed to the position that the children of a hangman may be given the same job, law minister Pallav Dasgupta

17

announced that Grddha Mullick's demand that his job be given to his daughter is unacceptable.'

Followed by the minister's face: 'No, no, no . . . this is not a job a woman can do . . . it requires a lot of strength . . . of mind and body . . .'

The young man's face: 'Do you mean to say that women lack in strength of mind and body?'

The minister: 'No, not that . . . but this is not a job like any other.'

Now the young man's face, again. 'This is not just a matter of the conduct of justice any more. The question of whether a woman has the right to work as a hangman cannot simply be denied, given the backdrop of arguments in favour of women's reservation. And at a time where the death penalty is being abolished in many nations of the world. This is the topic of debate today in CNC's *Face to Face*. Viewers may take part in the live discussion. This is the question: Can women be appointed executioners to hang criminals? To voice your views, call us on . . .'

I was deeply shocked. Still, I thought it would end there. It didn't.

'When we reached the house of the country's most famous hangman, Grddha Mullick, his first condition was that no images of his family members be made public. But CNC received images of his daughter secretly. Eighty-eight-year-old Phanibhushan now bargains with the government to make the life of this young woman secure—she who passed the Plus Two examination with very high marks but was unable to continue her studies because of financial problems.'

Footage of me began to roll on screen. Me about to turn right after taking money from Kaku. Then turning left. Walking towards the camera. Passing by the camera, swinging my arms merrily. The camera stays on my back till I reach Hari da's shop. As I return, my faded and tattered dupatta and the breasts it does not fully cover appear on the screen. Then my face comes into view on the screen, magnified. I saw the small wart on the left side of my nose, the smooth shiny hair of my eyebrows, and the bulging eyes, the same as Father's. This is how others see my face—now I saw too.

As I sat there dazed, the young man concluded: 'From Bhavanipore, for CNC, along with cameraman Atul Kishore Chandra, this is Sanjeev Kumar Mitra.'

'Sanjeev Kumar Mitra!' Father jumped up, furious. 'I'll finish him with my bare hands!'

Father was wrong. He was to die by my hands. That's why I was attracted to him from that very moment. He was special, with his exceptional height, thick straight hair, long straight nose. It took me much longer to be convinced that the feeling I had for him was what people call love. The kinds of love that the likes of us experienced were all like the noose fixed between the third and fourth vertebrae. Either the noose tightened and the person died, or the cord broke and the person escaped. But even those who broke the cord could never completely untie the noose from their necks. Like Chinmayi Devi who married Radharaman Mullick, we writhed and flailed without breath, all our lives.

3

I actually believed that Sanjeev Kumar Mitra was handsome only when I saw him on the morning news, reporting the CPM violence at Purbasthali against a rally organized by the Trinamool Congress in which two people had been killed. He had a fine high nose, curved eyebrows and a broad forehead. His glasses were dark-tinted; his eyes eluded me. He alone appeared in my thoughts. That he was so close at hand sent a thrill through my heart. I was up early at dawn and had turned on the TV by the time the flower-laden carts from the Mullick Ghat flower market hurried over Strand Road towards the shops in front of the cremation ground. As if answering my prayer, his image popped up during the news. Nothing that he said sank in, but his voice made me feel weak; I longed to see him in flesh and blood. My heart whispered what I wanted to tell him. My body now knew how it felt to sprout; to break through the skin of the seed. All this was utterly new to me. When his report was over, I switched off the TV, sighing. Pankaj Mullick's *Aayi bahaar aaj* . . . blared from a passing vehicle. Ramu da shook his head to the rhythm without opening his eyes. My hands reached out again towards the TV. Happiness was making me restless. It was that very moment when a roar sounded from outside.

'Grddha da, are you crazy?'

I went into the kitchen and looked out through the window. There stood the editor of the hundred-and-twenty-year-old *Bhavishyat*, Manavendra Bose. Whenever I saw him, my heart filled with awe and admiration.

'She is a young girl! You shouldn't have got her into such a fix.'

He kept scolding Father in a voice that rang and echoed like the roar of a tiger trapped in a well. The *Bhavishyat* office was on Chitpur Road, behind the percussion instruments shop just next to Thakurbari. When I worked at Maruti Prasad Yadav's press, I used to linger in front of it, munching a phuluri or piyanji from the nearby shop. I would try to peep into the inner rooms of the old British-style building stuffed with newsprint, past the iron handrails and grilles. Bose babu had a long white beard on his fair-skinned face. He bustled about inside, dragging his right leg which the police had broken during the Emergency; it was quite a sight. He used to come every month to Kaku's salon for a haircut. Strands of his thick, silver locks stood out with a special gleam in the heap of cut hair that Kaku swept out.

'Bose babu, do the gallows know the difference between old and young, male and female? What is it to the condemned anyway?'

The sound of Father flipping a page. Father was done with his morning tea and was now reading his papers and smoking a cigarette. He never stopped getting the newspapers even in our direst days. Not the English papers, though. Those, the agent gave him—the previous day's unsold papers. Father returned them in perfect condition after reading them.

'The hands and legs of the condemned have to be tied securely. Then the head must be covered. And then the noose. Bose babu, Sudev can do all this. The only thing the hangman does is check whether the noose is in the correct spot or not . . . Then what else, just pull the lever—that any small child can do. When my dadu began to work under the British, he was just eleven years old, did you know? Kalicharan Mullick . . . big artist. Did you know? People used to call him Maha Mullick as a mark of respect.'

'But still! How bright she is! Grddha, you should not have sacrificed her to this kind of job.'

'Babu, our line has always been brave and strong. There's nothing to fear—this is our mission. She is my daughter, she too has the courage which runs in my blood and that of my forefathers, and Ma Kali's blessings as well . . .'

I expected Father to ask immediately, isn't that a thumping line? After a second, he said, 'Nothing to fear if the Sarkar appoints her; I am here for now. She needs to come as a formality, that's all. And then, what is the guarantee that there will be another hanging soon? Isn't everyone against hanging criminals? It is against human rights, indeed! Uh-uh . . . what human rights do murderers have, that the butchered do not? Threw a cockroach into the hangmen's food for nothing! There used to be twenty or twenty-five hangings a month, and now . . .'

Father did not complete the sentence. I felt Ma's scared eyes staring at me when I turned around.

'Your old man's never had a heart, ever. If he did, would he even think of dispatching our only daughter to such a job? To go to a jail full of thieves and murderers, to hang them! Won't you be scared, my girl? Is this child's play?'

Ma vented her sorrow. I sighed heavily. Ma has never known much about me. But that May morning, her question did make me think. Was hanging a person at the gallows child's play? Sitting with my back against the wall, I tried to imagine the procedure that I had heard about umpteen times from Thakuma and read about in Father's words as printed in newspapers. I had watched with my own eyes Father and Kaku bidding us goodbye and departing at night after the puja. I had seen pictures of Alipore Central Jail only in the pages of newspapers and on TV. High red walls topped with barbed wire. Bright streetlights all around. Somewhere inside, the gallows built of sturdy rosewood. The rope that fell from the tall mast. The black planks on which a white circle was drawn. The lever, rendered smooth from my father's and forefathers' touch over the centuries. When pulled, it drew the planks apart with a massive sound, revealing a gaping dark cellar beneath. The sound of the pulled lever would reverberate everywhere in the prison like the boom of a battle drum. It was the sound of death. I imagined

21

for a moment how I would execute a condemned person. My hand jerked and trembled.

The most famous hangman in our family was Grandfather Dharmaraja Mullick. Local folk used to call him Mosh Grddha Mullick. His build reminded one of the wild buffalo. But no one in our family was as inclined to charity as he had been. He was witness to five different dynasties of kings in his lifetime. Each hanging was rewarded with considerable generosity in those times; he would distribute that money among the poor and the orphaned. Finishing this work early in the morning, he would return, have a bath, worship Maheshwara and Ma Kali, pick up his shovel and be off to the fields. He prayed fervently for the condemned before leaving for his duties at the gallows. Before putting the hood on the condemned's face, he would caress and kiss him on the forehead. He would then place his hand on the condemned's head and whisper: 'Son, do not fear.'

Lovingly, caringly, allaying fears, he would lead the condemned towards the doors of death as if he were taking his little son to school for the first time. Do not fear, he assured the condemned as he mounted the wooden planks, I am by your side. Lord, do not make your son weep, he would pray, as he placed the noose on his neck. Grandfather Mosh hanged a thousand and one people at the gallows. His fame spread far and wide. Many times, he was invited to other lands to execute notorious criminals. In those days, criminals believed that it was a great honour to die by his hands. Because he would give away all that he received as reward, the Raja of Gwalior rebuilt his house and gave Grandmother a hundred bags full of gold coins. Thakuma still had one of those coins. She kept it safe in her betel box, its shine dulled by specks of tobacco and opium. The truth is that it was the only bit of evidence in our house of all our two-thousand-year-old family traditions.

Manavendra Bose took his leave when a vehicle belonging to a women's organization which we knew of from the Bangla papers drew up near our house. I was lost in thought then, wondering if I, like Grandfather Mosh, could make the condemned man feel better.

The leader of that organization, Sumati Singh, spoke in Hindi. She said in a loud voice: 'Grddhaji, you must file a case. The Constitution promises equal opportunities to women and men. Don't let this pass.'

Sumati Singh had flown down hurriedly from Delhi. I, who was peeping out of the kitchen, really liked her expensive cotton sari, the wooden ornaments that went with it, and her flowing hair.

'Ah, Madam, we have no money for all that. She wishes to continue in the family profession . . . and that too, only if the good people of this land allow. It is God who settles birth and death, Madam. It is that Big Hangman who decides who is to die by whose hands and who must kill whom.'

Father raised his hands to the heavens dramatically.

'But Chetna must not lose this opportunity just because she is a girl.'

'All that God decides, Madam. If it is written in her fate everything will work out well . . . if not, it will not . . . everything that happens is for the good . . . everything that does not happen is also for the good.'

Father had reached top form rather quickly.

'No father will ever want his daughter's hands to pull the lever of the gallows, Madam. But if my daughter decides to do so, I cannot stop her. Look, in a father's eyes, his daughter's hands will always be tender . . . but she has to decide herself, as a person. She told me, Baba, my hands are strong, I can do this work. Yes, my daughter, as you wish, I told her, in this land women have the democratic right to equal opportunity.'

'We are willing to arrange a lawyer for Chetna. Our leader in Delhi is taking a keen interest in this.'

'No, no case, Madam. If you have money to help us fight this case, give it to us directly. I'll use it for her wedding.'

'Grddhaji, a girl's life does not end with marriage!'

'Madam, it begins only then. I am not going to make her sign on any piece of paper . . .'

They went on talking. I suddenly noticed that I had made yet another noose with my dupatta. Small but perfect.

'They want to see you.'

Father came in. He wiped his naked chest and back once more with the checked gamchha he had on his shoulder. It was another very hot day. He came near me and put his hand on my shoulder with rare tenderness. 'Chetu, putting a noose on someone up on the gallows isn't like putting one around Maruti Prasad's neck.'

Father looked deep into my eyes. I knew what that meant. It was easy to put a noose around Maruti Prasad's neck. Because the moment he gasped and struggled and his tongue stuck out, I could ease my grip. That wouldn't be possible in Alipore Jail. If a noose was made there, the lever would have to be pulled. And if it was pulled, the man would have to die.

I got up, opened the door and went out. People had gathered outside our tea shop. In front of them, three well-dressed, well-groomed, sweet-smelling pretty women sat, as if on a podium.

'Chetna Mullick, do you wish to work as a hangwoman?' Sumati Singh with her long nose, high forehead and red lips asked me.

'I have neither a wish nor a non-wish . . .'

'Is your father putting pressure on you?'

'It is no use putting any pressure on me if it is something I can't do. Isn't that so?'

They looked at each other, surprised. It was clear that they did not expect such answers from the daughter of an uneducated hangman.

'Do you know that according to the Constitution you cannot be denied a job?'

'Yes . . .'

I was not driven by the right and the wrong in my words, but by the fact that I had a chance to speak like Father. It made me giddy with excitement. The women whispered something among themselves. Sumati Singh got up and came to me.

'Chetna, we are the biggest women's organization in India. Do you know which one I'm referring to?'

'I do watch TV.'

'All right. We have decided to intervene on your behalf. If the government takes a favourable decision, you will be the first and only woman to work as an executioner.'

'There was a woman before me in our family who worked as a hangwoman.'

The women looked at each other, greatly surprised.

'Anyway, in no country in the world do they have a woman

executioner now. So your appointment would be a landmark. Our view is that you should not step back from this decision, because it is a matter of the pride of all women. It's our chance to declare to the world that there is no work that women can't do.'

I did not respond. A crowd slowly encroached into the little space of the tea shop. The TV cameras and reporters surrounded Sumati Singh and her colleagues as they got up to leave.

'Madam, are you supporting the death penalty?'

'Never. We are only supporting equal opportunities for women.'

'What is your view on abolishing the death penalty?'

'That is not the topic of the present discussion.'

Once Sumati Singh and her friends departed, the crowd turned towards me. Cameras, TV cameras and mikes stretched towards me. I faced them like a terrorist hemmed in by gun-toting commandos.

'Will your hand not tremble when you hang Jatindranath at the gallows?'

'My hand will not . . . but my heart surely will, thinking of that wasted life.'

'Do you know he has a wife and four children?'

'*He* should have remembered that.'

'Are you supporting the death penalty?'

'No, I am not. Two people were killed in last night's demonstration, right? I do not approve of that. I don't approve of those who attacked the demonstration either. Nor do I approve of the demonstration itself.'

It was the victory procession to celebrate a lost election that was attacked; a demonstration held to celebrate a minor gain, that of 2377 votes by the Trinamool Congress candidate in the Nadanghat assembly constituency. Indeed, this candidate had lost in the parliamentary constituency by 1,43,349 votes. The attackers who had targeted the demonstration shot at and stabbed twenty-five-year-old Buttu Sheikh and his twenty-six-year-old brother Sahedul Sheikh, killing both. Both were illiterate poor men. So were their killers.

'Why then should you apply for a hangman's job?'

'Because such a job exists.'

'Great, so you think you can live by killing another?'

'I am not killing anyone, the government is . . . I am only an instrument.'

They all fell silent soon. It was then that Sanjeev Kumar Mitra shot a question from behind.

'One can make a living from many other trades in this land.'

I would recognize that voice anywhere. It rendered me silent for a moment. Within my heart a bird shook its wings, wild and desperate. And so I replied as calmly as I could, 'Give me some land first . . .'

By then Father and Kaku had pulled me back and moved up front. The press fussed around them like crows cawing around a dead rat. One by one, all of them left. Only Sanjeev Kumar Mitra remained. I looked at him through the kitchen window. He was more handsome than I had thought. I yearned to see his eyes emerge from behind those dark glasses. I inscribed in my heart his smile, his speech, the way his wayward locks fell upon his forehead when he laughed. A noose of sheer happiness tightened around my neck. There was another noose at its tail. And another person too. A hangman's rope with two nooses! I caressed my neck in pleasure.

He went into Father's room and shut the door, but I continued to hang around. Father came out of the room a few times asking for fish or groundnuts. No unpleasant smells wafted from the room, so I guessed the liquor was of the expensive sort. When it was really dark Sanjeev Kumar stepped out, closing the door softly. I was sure that Father was senseless, drunk. Sanjeev Kumar entered our room without asking, pulled up the old chair and began to speak with Thakuma. I withdrew into the kitchen, my heart beating wildly. She opened her betel box and began her storytelling. He held the tail of the noose which was around my neck; he kept tugging at it now and then. Unable to resist, I kept going to the door. He took no notice of me. Disappointed, I shook my head and withdrew, only to be pulled there again. But this time I could not withdraw. For the sight I saw left me shocked and frozen: Sanjeev Kumar Mitra had his camera out and was clicking pictures of Ramu da. Because he had no hands to cover his face with, Ramu da was trying to shield himself by pulling down his brows and tightly squeezing his eyes shut. An intense rage flared up in my blood. I dashed into the room, snatched the camera and flung it on the ground. It hit the floor hard, bounced, turned upside down and lay still on its side. The dirt from our broken floor covered it. Everyone was stunned.

'How dare you!' I lashed out.

Sanjeev Kumar took off his glasses and stared grimly at me. I saw his eyes for the first time. He too was seeing me for the first time. A smile played on his lips; but his green-tinted eyes seemed to flash with hatred and resentment. He picked up the camera, brushed off the dust, put it back into his bag, and touched Thakuma's feet reverentially. Thakuma's betel box fell on the floor; the things it held scattered. He gathered them, put them back inside the betel box, closed it, handed it to Thakuma and went out, kissing her sweetly on the cheek. I came to my senses. And felt tied up in a sense of regret. I shrunk back into the darkness of the courtyard, towards the washing stone. Coming close to me, he paused. My heart beat so loudly, the whole world should have been able to hear it. I longed for a tender apology. But his eyes flashed vengefully; and this is what he whispered to me in a voice so low that only I could hear it: 'I want to fuck you hard, even if only once!'

Acid sourness sped through my body, piercing my bones. I fell from the sky to the earth. The last circular train passed by, making the earth tremble. The stench from some sinner's pyre spread all around. Hearses that had been waiting for the railway gate to open now crossed the tracks, jingling. Sanjeev Kumar Mitra disappeared into the dark. In the middle of all this, Thakuma's wail rose: 'Eesh! Ma Kali! My gold coin . . . where is my gold coin?'

The priceless gold coin, the only token we had of the memory of Grandfather Mosh Grddha Mullick, was nowhere to be seen. Sanjeev Kumar Mitra had stolen it even as we were all watching.

It is easy to steal the wealth of the poor. No one except me believed that he had stolen it. But he had got away, leaving around my neck an improperly placed noose. The vertebrae weren't the right ones. The neck didn't break. But my breath stopped. For the first time in my life, I hated my body. That night, I imagined making him stand on the hangman's plank, putting the death-hood on his face, placing the noose around his neck, and pulling hard—in seven hundred and twenty-seven different ways.

4

Thakuma, Bhuvaneswari Devi, would remind us time and again that the death penalty was not just the delivery of justice but also the imprint of power. The evidence of this was in the stories about Grandfather Bhishma Grddha Mullick. He lived during the reign of the eighth-century Pala kings. The first Pala king, Go Pala, was elected to kingship by his people. The land flourished and peace prevailed under these rulers who were Mahayana Buddhists. But the credit for this blissful state of affairs actually belonged to our forebearer's genius. More deft and precise than a master butcher, he despatched hundreds of people every day through beheadings and hangings.

Once, a Hindu sannyasi was condemned to death. His crime was that he spoke against the Buddhist faith. In those times the practice was to offer the hangman a bagful of money on the eve of the execution. That day, Grandfather Bhishma submitted that it was against the Buddhist faith to kill a sannyasi. But the ministers declared in one voice that Religion and State should remain separate. The sannyasi laughed and told the king, Maharaja, you cannot kill me. I am only forty now. According to the stars, I will die only after I turn a hundred.

The king now grew quite determined. Send this fellow to the City of the God of Death at the soonest, he snarled. Grandfather Bhishma tried to tell him that the sannyasi showed no signs of impending death. The king paid no heed. In the end, at the very last minute, the precise moment when the sannyasi stood in the gallows ready for the noose, news arrived that one of the queens had given birth. The hanging was postponed on the advice of the astrologers. It would be carried out ninety days later. Exactly ninety days later, the queen died. Mourning was declared for forty-one days. The king now became doubly obstinate. The hanging would be held at sunrise on the day after the mourning period ended. But the king's foster mother died the night before that dawn. In this way, for some reason or the other, the death by hanging was put off seven times. The eighth time, when our progenitor paid his ceremonial visit to the condemned man on the eve of the hanging, the headstrong king went along with him.

'Bhishma, will it happen tomorrow?' the king asked Grandfather Bhishma, a threat echoing in his voice.

My ancestor looked carefully at the sannyasi's face. 'There are no signs of death, O King!' he said regretfully.

The sannyasi burst out laughing. Furious, the king glared at Grandfather and roared: 'If this does not happen tomorrow, that will be the end of you, Bhishma!'

'No, Your Majesty,' Grandfather Bhishma answered him calmly, 'I too bear no signs which say that I will die tomorrow.'

That day when he came back home, our ancestor caught a fever and a chill. He was bedridden for months with smallpox. The king could not execute either of them. Lurching between pain and unconsciousness, Grandfather Bhishma thought impassively about life's strange twists and turns. He composed a kavya about his forefather who had begun as a healer and ended up as an executioner. The day it was completed, the Utkalas attacked the Pala kingdom. They broke open the prisons and freed the prisoners. The sannyasi made his escape. King Dharma Pala admitted defeat. Before long, he set off for the City of the God of Death.

Deva Pala ascended the throne after Dharma Pala. When he attacked Utkala and began to butcher its inhabitants, Grandfather Bhishma was ninety years old. King Deva Pala herded together large numbers of people and thrust them before him. With trembling hands, he placed the noose around the neck of each. As he moved forward, he came to a man as advanced in years as himself, and the latter asked: 'So, Bhishma, the time has finally come, has it not?'

My ancestor started violently. It was the sannyasi. Please, can't he be spared? Grandfather Bhishma pleaded with the king and the crowd. But the crowd was adamant. This man, who had evaded death so many times, must be despatched swiftly, they yelled. My ancestor felt the sannyasi's skin. His blood vessels were boiling. It is time, Grandfather Bhishma said. It is time, the sannyasi repeated. He pulled the rope. The sannyasi died without the slightest distress. My forefather returned home that night and had an oil bath. He prayed to Ma Kali, cutting his right thumb and letting the blood fall, then had a sumptuous meal and went to bed. He died peacefully in his sleep.

Whenever Father spoke of the day he had gone to hang Jabbar

Singh, Thakuma told this story. The execution did not take place on the appointed day; it was postponed. The stay order reached Alipore Central Jail only after Father—exhausted after a whole week of preparing the noose, doing a dummy test with a sandbag and performing Kali puja the whole night—got there. A pall of gloom fell on our family. Father had been struggling to put together money for my older sister Niharika's wedding. He had asked for a reward of two thousand five hundred rupees, and a job in the municipality for Ramu da, who was fourteen then. In the end, the government agreed to a thousand rupees. Drawing darkness down upon the family which awaited Father's return with the thousand-rupee reward, the President of India, Giani Zail Singh, granted Jabbar Singh's mercy petition at the very last minute.

'Did you not look for the signs of death?' Thakuma scolded Father.

Father vowed that he had. 'He had begun to breathe through his mouth. The doctor told me that his pulse was pounding.' Father paused and then said, 'He ought to be dead in fifteen days.'

I recalled this with great astonishment after I grew up—it had indeed come true. Father could never hang Jabbar Singh. But neither did Jabbar Singh live beyond fifteen days. One morning, he was found dead with his body against the cell wall, half standing, half sitting. Father part jested and part lamented that the man had upset his thousand-rupee reward. Niharika's wedding had to be postponed. After many years, Niharika was married off with a loan raised on plunderer's interest rates. Constant want and wrangle filled the house. Later, she came back home because her dowry was not enough. I was just five years old. One morning, she was found hanging in Father's room, from the beam on which he hung his gamchha and vest to dry. Hers was the first death by hanging I ever witnessed.

Father woke very late the day after Sanjeev Kumar Mitra made off with Thakuma's gold coin. All of us waited for him with dour faces. As usual, Ma took him some tea and poured out harsh words. He called her father the choicest names. She then turned her tongue on his secret affairs. Thakuma kept searching for her gold coin. When I poured Ramu da his tea, I could not chit-chat with him like every day. 'I want to fuck you hard, even if only once!' rang in my ears. The day Maruti Prasad had tried to grab me from behind came back to my mind. It was easy to ignore it as an act of violation; it was easy to overcome. But the insult from the words, with the body left untouched—that burned. But I was not clear what had wounded me more. Was it the words 'only once' or 'fuck'? Was it the way he uttered them? What happened to you, Ramu da kept asking me. His face was pale and sallow from not having seen the sun or the wind in a long time. Whenever I looked at it, I remembered Amartya Ghosh.

It was in the pages of the newspapers framed and displayed in Father's room that I saw Amartya Ghosh. He had been convicted for the murder of four—the south Calcutta industrialist Chandrasen Ghosh and his three children, aged ten, six and three. The good-looking Amartya had been a servant in Chandrasen Ghosh's house. He and Chandrasen's wife, Devapriya, fell in love. When their relationship became intense, he demanded that she leave with him. She refused. He was furious. The mad frenzy of love possessed him. One night, when Chandrasen went into Devapriya's room and shut the door, Amartya lost all control. He took a gun from Chandrasen's room, went upstairs, opened the door to the children's room and turned on the lights. Standing at the door, he shot all three children dead, one by one. Only the oldest child managed to scream; the youngest did not get a chance. Chandrasen, who rushed up on hearing the commotion, fell next. Devapriya fainted in shock. By the time the other servants and the security guards hurried in, Amartya had escaped. He stayed in hiding for many months. Finally, he was arrested, all skin and bones from starving. On the strength of all the evidence, the court sentenced him to death. The high court and the Supreme Court upheld the sentence. President R. Venkataraman rejected his mercy petition. On 4 July 1990, his death sentence was confirmed.

Up to this point in the story, none of us featured in it. But after this, Amartya's story became our story. One day after the sentence was confirmed, an old man came to see Father. They sat talking for a long time behind closed doors. Father's voice rose.

'Ami ki korbo? How can I give up my work just because your wife didn't give birth again? Dada, I didn't start in this profession today or yesterday. Our family has been doing this even before Bharat itself—

don't forget that! Our history is the history of Bengal, of India itself, do you know? You should have raised your son well. This Phanibhushan Grddha Mullick is simply not willing to sign away the history of his family for your measly coins, Dada!'

'Grddha, he is a simple fellow. She got the devil into his head . . . she's done black magic on him!'

Tears flowed down the old man's wrinkled cheeks.

'Not one, not two, but four . . . three tender little children . . . is he even human? Or is he a beast? Chi-chi! Even beasts would have compassion for little children!' Father's anger grew more shrill.

'Grddha da, she drugged him with something. He won't do anything wrong from now . . . isn't he in prison? Please, let him stay there, at least he will be alive. We won't live after we light his pyre, Grddha da!' the old man begged.

Father opened the door, fanned off the sweat with his gamchha and went out. It was very hot then. Ma was cleaning fish on the washing stone. Ramu da, who was an East Bengal fan, was reading the papers over and over again, sweltering in football fever. Those were the days of the fourteenth World Cup. I was trying to learn how to calculate the LCM. But my mind was not on my maths textbook. The misery etched on the old man's face was deep enough to shake the heart of an eight-year-old girl. He stood weeping in the front yard of our house for a very, very long time. He left eventually, but returned, pleading, begging. Father refused to listen. When he came the third time, he had with him a woman so thin and frail that the wind could sweep her off the ground. She fell at Ma's and Thakuma's feet and begged for mercy. Father should feign illness on the eve of the execution—that was what she pleaded. He is our only son, Dada, please don't kill him, the woman cried, her heart writhing in pain. Thakuma tried to offer counsel. Ma wiped her eyes and went inside. Father, however, did not budge. On the eve of the execution, the old man returned, drunk senseless. Instead of the familiar piteous expression, his face and words blazed with furious rage.

'Mark my words! If anything happens to my son, you will regret it!'

His threat rang so loud that it echoed in the Ganga, in the marble palace that stood beyond the Thakurbari. Though the policemen posted to guard Father took him away, his trembling, fatigued voice lingered in my ears. Finally, it was night. At two o'clock, the jeep arrived to pick up Father. Father and Kaku left. Father was very uneasy. Before he left, he patted me and Ramu da on our heads; Ramu da was busy trying to catch the commentary of the World Cup match between Italy and Argentina on the radio. Father climbed into the back seat of the vehicle. Till he disappeared from sight, Father kept looking at us, and we, who had stepped on to the road, kept looking at him. Those who have not known our sorrows can hardly fathom the pain of people who make a living from the deaths of others.

This was the newspaper report that Father had framed and hung up:

My Life is for the Nation: Grddha

Calcutta: Hangman Phanibhushan Grddha Mullick declares that he is not afraid of death, and that if he loses his life while doing his duty, it would be self-sacrifice for the sake of the nation. He is merely the instrument of the government, he says. His duty is to carry out whatever the government asks him to do. Personal likes and dislikes and decisions have no place in it. Grddha Mullick was speaking to reporters hours before the execution of Amartya Ghosh. He was responding to reports about death threats to him by members of Ghosh's family. Since time immemorial, members of his family have worked as hangmen in this country. This is our cultural and historical legacy; only the law and the judiciary can dissuade us from it, he claimed. He announced that the Mullicks would not flinch before the threats issued by the family of the condemned man. The word Grddha means vulture in Bengali. Because of their rounded, bulging eyes and thick eyelids, the Mullicks are generally known as Grddha Mullicks. Seventy-five-year-old Phanibhushan Grddha Mullick claims to have executed 445 people. He began performing such duties at the age of nineteen, assisting his father, Purushottam Mullick.

In the meantime, there are unconfirmed reports from the jail that the impending execution has affected Amartya Ghosh's mental state. The jailers had to struggle hard to return Amartya to his cell after he broke down completely during a meeting with his aged parents, embracing them and crying aloud piteously. His last wish, apparently, is to have a glimpse of Devapriya, the wife of his victim, Chandrasen Gupta. But Devapriya, who is now with her parents in Delhi, has ignored this request. She has made it clear that the person who murdered her loving husband and her innocent, beloved little children can be nothing but demonic and that even his memory is utterly distasteful to her.

There was also a photograph with this report. The clever photographer had captured Ramu da leaning against a wall, face wan and deep in thought. His face filled the loop made by the noose that Father held up. A young man of twenty-two, in a white jubba and lungi. Six feet tall. Lean, fair body. A splendid head of hair, high nose, wide eyes. At first glance, it looked as though he had been hanged by his father. The caption of the photo was: 'Hangman Phanibhushan Grddha Mullick displaying the noose that he has readied for Amartya Ghosh; in the background, his only son, second-year MA student of literature at New Providence College, Ramdev Grddha Mullick.'

Amartya's body was cremated at Nimtala Ghat. His parents carried his body past our house with tearless eyes. When his pyre was lit, his aged mother tried to end her life by throwing herself on it. Badly burned, she died in the hospital. Two days later, his father lay in wait for Ramu da and attacked him. Ramu da was returning from college after a game of football and chattering excitedly about the World Cup matches. The old man hacked off his limbs with an enormous chopper.

All the money Father had earned from the execution was spent on hospital bills. It was after this that Father insisted that photographs of his family members not be published. He went to the office of the newspaper which had published Ramu da's photo and created a big fuss. They gave him a bottle and a hundred rupees. Thereafter Father began to set fees for reports. By the time it was Jatindranath Banerjee's turn, he was taking five hundred rupees from newspapers and a thousand from television channels. Bottles began to line the space under his cot, and behind the images of Ma Kali and Grandfather Purushottam Grddha Mullick on the stand.

34

I had sat down to prepare the potatoes, thinking how strangers like Amartya and Jatindranath could change our lives. Ma was beginning to make dough for the luchis. Suddenly, Kakima rushed in, looking sick with worry: 'They are looking for someone else!' she announced, wiping her sweaty brow. For some time now, her youthful face wore a look of want and worry.

Angered that Father had raised his demands, the government was trying to find a hangman from other states, she said. Ma stopped mixing the dough. The potato fell from my hand. Me, a one-day-hangwoman, I thought, amused. Ma Kali, Ma called, letting out a heavy sigh. She went back to kneading the dough. I, too, after a moment of silence, the sort you see on TV, went back to the potatoes. They weren't that good—hard, and not sweet enough.

'Dada was too mulish. Now even others can't get what they could've,' Kakima muttered.

'Then go to your husband and tell him to hang the fellow!' Father, who had come in unexpectedly, bellowed. 'Would've been great if that sissy could even kill a hen . . . I deserve this—for lugging him along, thinking, here is a sibling, let him get a few coins!'

He filled the water bowl with some water, went inside, and came out soon after, wiping his mouth. 'Just watch, all of you . . . Jatindranath is going to die by this Phanibhushan Grddha Mullick's hands. I am sure of that . . . his name is in my account book.'

I washed the potatoes in silence. Mother rolled out the luchis wordlessly. Kakima collected the dirty dishes and went out her face an unpleasant grey. I put the washed potatoes in a bowl and went for a bath. When I came back from my bath, the air was filled with smoke and the stench of funeral pyres. More corpses were being cremated at Nimtala Ghat than usual. As I walked in drying my hair, my gaze fell on the framed photos hanging in Father's room. Where is Devapriya now, I wondered. What does she look like? Right then, Sanjeev Kumar Mitra appeared on the TV that Father had switched on, giving me a shock.

'It was the innocent young Ramdev Grddha Mullick who paid the price for Amartya's life. Devapriya, who moved in with another industrialist after the death of Chandrasen Ghosh, left him three years later and married her present husband, a London-based industrialist. It was to possess her that Amartya murdered four, including three little children. He had to give his own life for this act. Amartya's family took their revenge on the son of Phanibhushan Grddha Mullick, the man appointed to carry out his execution. In short, the person who paid the greatest price for Amartya's desire for Devapriya was this young man, Ramdev, who had never seen her. And now the government is trying to get rid of the hapless Grddha Mullick who is asking for a government job for at least one of his children. The state government has already approached four well-known hangmen in the country to carry out Jatindranath's execution. But all four of them demand flight tickets and five-star accommodation. Compared to such wasteful expenditure, the fairness of Grddha Mullick's demand that his daughter be given a government job is only too clear. Also, if Chetna Grddha Mullick is appointed to the hangman's post, the government will earn credit for having appointed a woman to this post for the very first time in the whole world. Sanjeev Kumar Mitra, along with cameraman Atul Kishore Chandra, CNC . . .'

Ramu da squinted hard and turned his face to the wall. The only part of his body he could still move was his head. I turned off the TV, completely flustered. Without much delay, Father's black telephone began to ring. The fear that I always felt when I heard it ring, that someone was dying somewhere, filled my heart. Finishing his call, Father came running with a big smile on his face. 'Chetu, Ramu, we have won! IG babu just called to tell me to accept the court order!'

I stood still, not knowing what to say. Ramu da gave Father a look of pity and shut his eyes. Under his eyelids, his eyeballs rolled like two tiny footballs. Father looked respectfully at the blank screen of the TV. He shook his head and grinned, all his teeth showing. 'Looks like a crook, no doubt, but the fellow knows how to make news.'

If he was called upon to accept the court order, it meant that the government had accepted Father's demands. It meant that I would have to work as a hangwoman. Another hearse passed by our yard, bells tinkling. Even though the TV was switched off, Sanjeev Kumar Mitra's green eyes constricted in rage on the black screen. Everybody is in need of the death of somebody or the other to leave behind the imprint of power.

<h1 style="text-align:center">5</h1>

The first step in carrying out a death sentence is fixing the date. The court fixes the date of the execution. A copy of the order is given to the condemned. At the same time, the hangman receives the announcement. He has to go to the jail three or four times after that. A contract is signed with the IG. The condemned man's physical and mental condition is ascertained. Arrangements are reviewed. These are things even our neighbours know by heart.

'Will Chetna have to go to the jail too?' Ma asked, worried.

'Must go if she has to. She's not going alone, is she? Baba and Kaku will be with her, right?' Kakima said that as if it were nothing. She seemed completely changed. These days, her eyes brimmed over with harsh, hateful looks. She often went off to her mother's house in Budge Budge and stayed there for long spells. Before, she used to be very loving. All of us would sit on the floor near Ramu da's cot and chat. Ma and Kakima and I would let Champa and Rari lie on our laps and sometimes Kaku and Thakuma would join us in sharing the local news and cinema stories. Kakima's father had been a millworker. He got a cancer which corroded his cheeks, and eventually died at the SSKM Hospital. His last rites were at Nimtala Ghat. The Kakima who had wept aloud, hugging me hard, had been a completely different woman.

From the kitchen, I went straight up to the TV and switched it on. The images took time to firm up. Give it one on the head, joked Ramu da. With a couple of firm knocks on the TV's sides and back, CNC jolted into view. My heart struggled. Just after the report about the CPM's rejection of the Congress' invitation to join the central ministry, Sanjeev Kumar Mitra came into my home again with the story of the suicide of a seventeen-year-old housemaid in Bhavanipur. In the images on the TV, some five hundred people had gathered in front of an apartment and were creating a ruckus. The camera tilted up towards the window of Flat 4A and a circle appeared around it. The girl's body had apparently been found there. Sanjeev Kumar Mitra also presented a special programme on young girls from Egra in east Midnapore who come to the city looking for jobs. Not long after he faded from the screen, his big vehicle stopped in front of our house just behind a funeral procession; my bones began to turn into steam. I writhed uneasily. Ramu da lay looking at the ceiling. When I went near him and sat down on the bare floor after pacing about restlessly, he threw me a questioning look. I pulled the sheet up and hid the empty space of his lost arms. 'What happened?' he asked with an effort. I noticed only then that his beard was beginning to turn grey. That it had begun so soon made me feel very sad.

Father had taken Sanjeev Kumar Mitra into his room and shut the door. The scent of liquor and cigarette smoke seeped out unremittingly. Father, who had boasted that Sanjeev Kumar's death would be at his hands, was swiftly and skilfully tamed by him. He was an exceptionally gifted pilferer—not only of Thakuma's gold coin, but also of people's hearts.

Ma took him a glass of water. Unable to contain myself, I walked by the room and peeped inside. Father had already opened for him the wooden box which held our family's ancient, invaluable historical records.

'See this? This is the handle of the knife that was used to sacrifice a cock on the grave of the wife of Job Charnock, known to be the founder of Kolkata. By Shivraja Grddha Mullick, our seventeenth-century ancestor. The knife is gone, rusted away, now only this teakwood handle remains . . .'

Father passed on to him a piece of carved wood, worn and chipped. In my memory, Job Charnock was the sahib who had saved the beautiful widow who had been pushed into her husband's pyre to burn as a sati. The story is that he turned to Indian ways after he married her. The other sahibs were contemptuous of the Indian sahib who wore a kurta and pyjama, and smoked his hookah in the shade of a tree. He did not ask his wife to convert, but he did change her name to Maria. And gave her a Christian funeral when she died after nineteen years. But even then, sacrificed a cock on her grave.

'There's one thing, Mitra babu . . . to be born, the city of Kolkata did not need a sahib. This Chitpur existed one hundred and fifty years before Charnock was born. Today the gurudwara stands on the spot where Guru Nanak preached Sikhism when he came here to spread the faith. This Chitpur, Mitra babu, is like the Mahabharata . . . Things here you may see elsewhere, but that which is not here will not be anywhere!' Father pulled eagerly at his cigarette, thinking.

'Chetu, come here,' Father called aloud.

I stepped inside the room, feeling sheepish. Sanjeev Kumar Mitra was rummaging inside the wooden box; Father held a large liquor bottle in his hand and was examining it. I felt infinitely insulted. It troubled me that he was taking away the priceless traditions and history of our family from Father in return for a few bottles of liquor and a little cash.

'Chetu, this babu wants an interview with you. He not only shoots for TV but also writes in the papers . . . *boro manush!*'

Father cuddled the liquor bottle and tucked it under the cot.

'Ask, Mitra babu, I'll give you the answers . . . let her learn. Won't she have to give many interviews from now? I won't be around for all time to teach her, will I? I am eighty-eight now . . .'

A smile bloomed on Sanjeev Kumar Mitra's face and he lapped me up with his eyes, head to foot. When I pressed myself against the wall somewhat agitated, his greenish gaze shot out of his eyes and pierced my breasts. Irritated, I pulled down my faded and threadbare dupatta and fixed my eyes on the framed photograph of my father's father, Purushottam Mullick. He looked like Chhabi Biswas. A very gentle face. The hangman's job simply didn't suit his form—it belonged to a filmstar or a primary school teacher.

'All right, this is my first question. Chetna, you are heir to the great traditions of this family. What do you have to say of it?' he asked me.

Before I could respond, Father began to speak.

'What is to be said of it? What a question, Babu. The story of my family is older than this country. Have you heard of William Marwood? It was he who discovered the long-drop hanging method that is now used all over the world to execute human beings. Do ask whom he learned it

39

from. From Jnananatha Grddha Mullick, father of Kalicharan Grddha Mullick, who was the father of Purushottam Grddha Mullick, who was the father of my father, Phanibhushan Grddha Mullick. That patriarch was a great expert in mathematics, would you believe it? He turned away from our line of work and became a teacher of mathematics in his village. A sahib he met in the village took him to London, and he met Marwood there. Once, during Christmas time, the sahib struggled to kill a pig for the feast. Grandfather Jnananatha was very amused. He made a small noose and hung the pig. It died instantly, the bones behind its neck snapping in a second. Marwood was amazed. Ah! An Indian, and so skilful? My ancestor then revealed to the sahib that we Grddha Mullicks have been executioners for many centuries and that we had a special science of noose making. Marwood was deeply interested. Grandfather Jnananatha taught him the fundamentals of execution by hanging. To hang someone, the length of the rope has to be ascertained keeping his weight in mind. That was discovered by the very first hangman in our family, Radharaman Mullick. If the length is correct, only the bones of the neck will break and the person will be dead in a couple of seconds. If the length is wrong, the condemned person will struggle, bite his tongue. Even the gallows will shake as the person struggles in desperation . . . sometimes, the head might come off . . .'

Father paused, lit a cigarette and blew out the smoke. Sanjeev Kumar Mitra listened in rapt attention. But even so, he threw troubling glances at me.

'The very next day, Marwood approached the jail authorities with his discovery. He was not an executioner. But he insisted that he be allowed to try this method. The authorities agreed. Thus Marwood executed a criminal using this new method. It was my grandfather who calculated his weight. One hundred and twenty-seven pounds, he said at a single glance. It was Grandfather who measured out the rope and prepared the noose. All over in just one minute! The British were very happy. They appointed Marwood executioner. He then carried out some two hundred or more hangings . . .'

'And what about Jnananatha Grddha Mullick?'

'Grandfather got close with a white woman; they had a relationship. But she didn't love him. She went after Marwood. My ancestor returned,

40

his heart broken. His father and older brother were working as hangmen. But soon his older brother got tuberculosis. They took him to Varanasi and left him there to die. It was expected that my forefather would take up the family profession when they returned. But he had changed totally. The feeling that Marwood had usurped something that rightfully belonged to him was damaging. He tried to find refuge in opium. Too much opium turned him mad. But no matter how mad he was, in front of the gallows, he was totally professional, Babu, totally professional!'

'He was mad? What do you mean?'

'He believed that he was trying to solve a very difficult mathematical problem. He filled all the walls with charcoal jottings. Some of those jottings were there . . . until very recently . . . on the wall behind the gallows at Alipore, did you know? My father Phanibhusan Grddha Mullick could recognize his hand . . .'

Father smiled and drew smoke from his cigarette.

'I hope you got what I meant when I said "my father Phanibhushan Grddha Mullick"? This should be printed as not my words, but Chetna's.'

'Ha! You are impossible, Grddha babu!' Sanjeev Kumar Mitra laughed out aloud.

With faux ruefulness that asked oh-did-you-notice-it-only-now, Father filled his cheeks with cigarette smoke and looked at him. Letting it out after a moment, he smiled slowly.

'So, Chetna, what do you think of your father, Phanibhushan Grddha Mullick?'

I leaned against the wall uneasily. In truth, I had enough sense of humour to like that question and the playfulness with which he put it to me. But all I could feel was a terrible tension. Somehow I felt that he had been attacking my body all that while in some horrible manner. I found it hard to forgive him for defiling the secrets of my body with filthy looks and dirty words, secrets which I had kept safe for someone who would desire and respect me deeply. But I was intensely attracted to him as well. The reason for that was clear. There was something in him that was vibrantly alive. In his smile, his conversation, even in that green-tinted glance. The hangman's blood that flowed in my veins yearned for the vitality of his soul.

'My father Phanibhushan Grddha Mullick . . .' Father began to recite dramatically the words I was to speak. 'I adore my father Phanibhushan Grddha Mullick. My father is my God.'

Father looked at me and smiled half mischievously, half in doubt. 'Why, Chetu, isn't it true?'

I had to smile, involuntarily, at that moment. I felt a sudden rush of affection for him, as if towards a child. I saw it then, these are the things he secretly desired! God, indeed! Poor Father!

'Ah . . . Mitra babu, keep recording. That is, I have no word beyond my baba's. Because he is now eighty-eight years old. He became the official hangman of the province of Bengal at the age of twenty. From then, he chanced to work in many parts of the country. We cannot imagine anyone more skilled than him at this work. It is important to sustain law and justice in this world. There can be no nation if law and justice do not prevail. No government. None of us will exist. The hangman is the last link in the chain of duty performed by the police and the army. The hangman is not a hired killer. He is a responsible officer of the government. The tahsildar may take away a farmer's land for the sake of the nation—to build a road or a school. The hangman's job is similar. He takes away a person's life for the sake of the nation. He delivers justice . . .'

Father puffed hard at his cigarette and asked Sanjeev Kumar with his eyes: how did that sound?

'But then, Chetna, you are young. If you continue in this job, who will marry you?'

Suddenly, I spoke. 'I need someone who loves me, not someone who loves my job.'

Sanjeev Kumar Mitra sent me a piercing look. 'Can someone's personality be separated from the work he does?'

I had no answer. He then switched his handycam off, got up and held his hand out to Father. Father took his hand, not knowing why it had been extended. Keeping his eyes on me, Sanjeev Kumar said, 'Grddha babu, when this bustle is over, if you have no objections, give Chetna to me . . . as my wife . . .'

Father was stunned. I stood still, inert. Very slowly, my heart began to smoulder. Tears followed soon. My heart had expected him to make that demand someday. But I was so inexperienced, so immature those

42

days; I could not see that he asked for me only because he had sworn to fuck me at least once.

Father's eyes filled with tears. Like all men swamped by unexpected joy, he had turned completely weak. He leapt up, came close and looked again and again at Sanjeev Kumar Mitra and me. His eyes moved towards the images of Ma Kali and Grandfather fixed on the wall; his hands were folded in prayer. Then, like a father in a TV serial, he turned his palms up towards me. 'Here she is, Mitra babu, take your woman . . .'

Wiping his eyes on the ragged gamchha that lay on his shoulder, Father suddenly went out of the room. Later, Ma told me that he wept aloud in the kitchen. Sanjeev Kumar Mitra and I were left alone in the room. Someone twisted a silken rope tightly around my body. The delicate, soft threads suffocated and tickled me at the same time. He came up and stood right in front of me, fixing me with a stare. His head turned from side to side, making an assessment. Then, with complete ease, he grabbed my left breast and squeezed it hard. Before I knew what was happening, he hissed, 'That camera was worth many lakh rupees!'

The sourness pierced my bones and whizzed through my body again. When I thrust off his hand and fled into Ramu da's room, I was panting hard. The sight of his legless armless body covered with a torn sheet gave me some relief. After all, this man could not, even if he wished to, hurt a woman who loved him.

The first heavy shower of the year came down that night. A stench more intense than that of the funeral pyre pierced the nostrils. The sounds outside were drowned by the rain's steady drone. The garbage heaps in the narrow by-lanes began to rot and stink. My heart hung heavy like a soggy, torn sack. I remembered, for no reason, the young girl who had come from the village to the city to work in a house, and had hanged herself. When I rolled out my mat by the window and lay down on Ma's torn sari, drops of rain kept falling on my sweaty forehead. I was twenty-two; I knew little of the world except that the touch of an unloving male was rough and that his stink was unbearable. Maruti Prasad's touch was ravenous. Sanjeev Kumar Mitra's was pervaded by the arrogance of a ravishing 'I'. I can forgive greed. But not that 'I' bent on conquest. Maybe it was such an experience which drove away that seventeen-year-old girl from life. I flung aside my blanket. Raindrops, hard as stones, hit my face. I could find no man about whom I could say: This is my God. Everyone demanded worship. Not one could prove he deserved it. Though I tightened the noose around my heart, hot tears mingled with the raindrops and trickled down my face. My left breast throbbed painfully as if it were filled with pus; I burned—and resolved to myself: I will measure out his rope accurately. Not an inch more. Not an inch less. I too want to have him. At least once.

6

Father came out of his room the next morning singing a song sung by Bibek, played by Abhi Bhushan Bhattacharya, in the jatra *Surat Udhaar*. It went

> March ahead looking into your own heart
> This is the ripe moment.

Bibek represented the conscience of the characters in the story. It entered and exited at will, into and out of heaven and hell, the royal court and cremation ground, the bedroom and temple, as a wild force—with wild tresses and tangled beard, naked feet and a long robe in white, black or ochre, eyes touched with madness. Thakuma boasted that it had been Grandfather Kalicharan who conceived of such a figure in jatra performances. He was the greatest of the artistes born in our family.

That day Father guzzled liquor till and even after Sanjeev Kumar left our place. He grabbed the coins Ma had collected selling tea since morning. They had a scuffle over that, followed by lots of screaming. Father slapped Ma hard. Though I tried to get in the way, his hand fell heavily on the bridge of her nose; blood spurted out of it. I ran to get some ice from the Ghat. Pushing past the crowd and making my way through the row of petty shops lined up opposite the ghat, I found the ice seller, Nabanit da. He was selling ice to children who had come for a funeral. Running back with two sticks of coloured ice, I slammed against a rusted iron cart. It tilted to one side. Suddenly, Sircar mama's memory sprang up. The corpse which lay in the cart, its face uncovered, began to slide off. As I stood frozen and stunned, the cart driver, clad in a torn lungi, pulled it back in, scolding me. I apologized and ran home. The puja had begun in Hemant Mullick's Kali temple. It was right on the road, just half a metre wide. Apart from Ma Kali and Hemu da, it could barely accommodate a cock or a goat. There was an ancient guillotine in front of the idol. A wooden one, carved in the shape of a pot. Once the head of the animal is shoved into the small circle, it stands still, ready for slaughter. Hemu da would sever the head with a single blow. People yelling at the sight of the sacrifice blocked my way again. Ma was up again by the time I got back home. She had begun to clean fish for dinner. I was exhausted. I wiped the sweat off my face and sat down cross-legged on the floor next to Champa who was studying. We heard Kakima scolding Champa's sister Rari somewhere outside. Champa asked me something; I snapped at her, irritated. She went off in a huff.

Ramu da gave me a kindly look. 'Where is he from?' he asked.

I realized only then that Sanjeev Kumar Mitra had already arrived. The expression on my face changed a little. Father called me to his room just then. My hair stood on end. I felt thorns piercing my flesh at the very thought of being in the same space as him.

'Chotdi, come, let me tell you . . .' Father clapped his hands in high spirits, summoning me.

Sanjeev Kumar Mitra watched me with a serious expression. The blood rushed into my face. His light-green shirt was reflected in his darkish glasses. Strands of hair kept falling onto his forehead every now and then. It was clear, from the way he sat and his very scent, that this poor, musty room filled with the damp of wet clothes did not suit him.

'He's complaining that you haven't said anything firm about the marriage proposal,' Father said, overcome with joy.

'If you don't like me, Chetna, please say so.'

Sanjeev Kumar shot a glance through the gap made by his glasses when they slipped down his nose; it was a glance whose meaning only I could decipher. I pretended not to notice.

'Don't worry, Sanju babu, she likes you. My daughter doesn't talk much. She's been like that since she was a child.'

Father was now slurring and swaying.

'Chetu, when we go to see the IG babu, they may interview you . . . that is, ask you questions about the job . . . for example, whether you know how to make a noose . . .'

Father fished out a piece of rope from under his cot and held it out to me. I took it without raising my head. Not looking at Sanjeev Kumar Mitra, I fashioned a single-loop noose in a trice.

Father was triumphant; he displayed it before Sanjeev Kumar Mitra. 'Look, look, Sanju babu! How well she makes it . . . didn't I tell you? Our lineage is as old as this land of Bharat . . . this courage, this strength, this sense of justice, all of it is in our blood . . .'

Father taught me to prepare the rope while Sanjeev Kumar watched. He showed me how to make the noose and smoothen its circle with the flesh of a banana, ghee and soap. I picked it up instantly. Like Father said, such things were in our blood. Sanjeev Kumar Mitra wore the noose I had prepared around his neck and looked at me. 'Want to try?' he asked me sarcastically.

Maruti Prasad Yadav's face rose before me. My hands tingled.

'You are six feet tall . . . You'll need a rope that is eight feet and two inches long . . . that rope is for someone who is five feet and ten inches tall.'

My voice was calm. Sanjeev Kumar Mitra looked at me as if he couldn't believe his ears. 'What's the problem if you use this rope to hang me?'

'It'll be a waste of time.'

'Okay, how much rope would you need, Chetna?'

I fell silent for a moment. I was the same height as Jatindranath Banerjee. So this rope would have suited me as well.

'Sanju babu, in the olden days, preparing the noose was itself a big ceremony. The very day the rope arrived, the Sakti puja would begin. Once smoothened with banana, ghee and soap, it would be safely locked away in a big wooden box. Otherwise, it might be nibbled upon by a rat! This happened in Aurangzeb's time, I've heard Father say. The rat took the rope. After the British came, an iron box was procured to keep

46

it safe. Nowadays, the rope is kept in the custody of the government. We go to the prison the day before and examine it. Then we come back home, perform the puja and return there . . .'

Respect for the prospective son-in-law was already showing in Father's voice. A victorious expression shone in Sanjeev Kumar's eyes. All the smiles he bestowed on me were contemptuous smirks. I wished dearly to return such a smirk. But couldn't, however much I tried. My heart struggled without breath like a condemned man hung on a rope too short. The agony was prolonged: I wished I would die soon, but continued to stay conscious.

'The murders in the old days were of many sorts. But Sanju babu, this is the most decent form of penalty in the world. It is the hangman's skill that makes it decent. Chetu, I am saying this so that you'll listen too. After the condemned has been brought out of the cell, don't waste a single moment until everything's over. Always remember, we are not about to hang a cock or a snake . . . it is a human being. He knows he has just moments to live. He'll think, I'll be alive for another ten minutes. But our ability lies in killing him in five seconds. Five seconds . . . one, two, three, four, five . . . it must be over by then. My dadu Kalicharan Mullick did not need half a second to finish the job. His noose was that accurate!'

'What about you, Grddha babu?'

Father laughed.

'From half to one minute. Only once did I need more time. But that was under the British . . .'

Father was silent for a moment. Then he ordered me: 'Chetu, go inside . . . come out only when I call.'

I left. His voice drifted from inside the room. 'I don't like to remember that incident, Sanju babu. Because, before I became a hangman, I was a singer and actor. I had a beloved those days. I sent Chetna away because I don't want her to hear about that.'

The bottle scraped the floor. Father had begun to drink again.

'Her name was Ashapurna. In the jatra in which we were performing, *Shashti ki Shanti*, she was the singer and I the villain. The hero was the actor Satyapal Chakrabarti. Very handsome! When he came on stage the entire audience would be thrilled and an *isshhh* . . . of pleasure could be heard. He was a show all by himself!'

Father had already begun to shine in villainous roles at the age of sixteen, with his bulging eyes and protruding cheeks. The pinkish white hero and the dark-skinned villain filled the stage. Father fell in love with Ashapurna. Ashapurna fell in love with Satyapal. Whenever he could, Satyapal put Father down; in those days Father dreamt constantly of becoming a celebrated artist. Satyapal persuaded Ashapurna to live with him. Heartbroken, Father left the drama company and went off to Bombay for some time. After two years, another troupe in Kolkata invited him to play the hero. And then, when he was returning from a performance, he met Ashapurna again. She had become a prostitute.

I could distinctly hear Father break into sobs as he ended the story.

'I loved her endlessly, Mitra babu. When we met again, she broke into tears and begged me to forgive her. I was ready to accept her even then. But she would not let me. Even as I watched, she went off with a cart driver for her daily bread. Mitra babu, how could a young man of eighteen have borne this agony?'

Father laughed and wept. I was dumbstruck.

'When did you become a hangman, Grddha babu?'

'When I was with the drama troupe, my father was assisted by one of my brothers. He died of jaundice. Another brother, Nagbhushan Mullick, had been dismissed from service by the British government. That's another story . . . I'll tell you some other time. Baba called me when he had no assistant. Those days, children weren't bold enough to disobey their parents. I went with him, for the first time, to execute a death sentence. I cursed my father and God when I set out. Those days, there would be four or five hangings the same day. Remember, this was the year 1934–35. I cursed myself as I accompanied Father to the prison. He ordered, Phani, do this, do that. I obeyed him. By then, the condemned man was brought. "Tie his hands, Phani," said Father. I caught hold of the man's hands and tied them up. When Father went up to him to put the hood on his face, he suddenly turned his head, looked at me and called, Phanibhushan! I was shocked. Sanju babu, do you know who that was? None other than Satyapal Chakrabarti!'

There was another interval to draw in a cheekful of smoke or for a gulp of liquor.

'Oh, to think of my condition at that moment! Even now, my hair

48

stands on end when I remember it. Phani, I want to live, he told me, tears in his eyes. I was petrified. But Baba quickly put the hood on his head and the noose around his neck. He was lightning fast. It wasn't for naught that the jailers used to call him Lightning Mullick. After putting the noose around his neck, Baba told me to pull the lever. But a demon got into me at that moment. Those days there used to be a small fastener on the gallows tree with which one could increase or decrease the length of the rope. I suddenly pulled the rope a little bit through the fastener. I still don't know why I did that. Because the truth is, I was too stunned to think or do anything. Dear Sanju babu, Baba told me, Phani, hey Phani, pull the lever . . . I pulled the lever. The plank slid off. The condemned man fell. But because the rope was shorter, his head was above the mouth of the well. Usually, it goes under. We don't see the head and the struggle. We see only the rope shudder and tremble. If you touch the rope, you'll know whether it is all over yet. His head quavered and shook in agony at the floor level in front of my eyes. It was a terrible sight. Baba was shocked. It took the man exactly half an hour to die. But I stood there, still as a rock, watching him struggle in the throes of death. I can do at least this little for my Asha—that was all I could think of!'

Father blew his nose and wiped it.

'You won't understand me when I say this, Sanju babu . . . she was like a goddess. I have never seen another woman with such beautiful lips. Her walk, how she carried herself . . . her laugh. What a perfectly beautiful face. Her ways, so lovely . . . no one could help falling in love with her. It was such a girl that this villain, this scoundrel, turned into a prostitute. How could I bear it?'

Father's voice now rose higher.

'My father, Purushottam Grddha Mullick, swung his arm and hit me hard on my face. But I was rooted to the spot. The rope shuddered and quivered in front of my eyes and then slowly, slowly, it became still. I touched it. It was all over. Baba called aloud to the doctor babu. The demon broke loose in me again. I loosened the rope in an instant. The body fell and hit the floor of the well with a thud. Baba's arm rose again to slap me. I was brimming with happiness, I was satisfied, no number of blows would have had any effect. But when I came out,

Sanju babu, all my happiness evaporated. When the body was brought out and I saw the person who waited to receive it, I was shattered. It was Asha. She and her little child, poor lame thing. She fell upon the body, wailing and beating her breast. I simply wanted to die, Sanju babu. I have never been able to understand this creature called woman. I have seen so many women till now. But why this animal will love one man and hate another . . . even in this eighty-eighth year, I haven't been able to fathom.'

Father blew his nose again.

'Were there no women in your life after that, Grddha babu?'

'Oh well, of course! But I have loved no one like I loved Asha . . .'

'What happened to her?'

'I don't know . . . never saw her after that day.'

'What kind of women did you say were in your life? Prostitutes?'

'No, I don't like buying women for cash . . . must take a liking . . . I must feel, ah, she is nice. Only then can I take her . . .'

If this were a jatra, Bibek would have made its entrance now. The whole of Bengal knew that the place Father set off to on better days in the tea shop, clad in his white jubba, his belt around his waist, hair and moustache combed and in place, was none other than Sonagachi.

'How did you meet Chetna's mother?'

'Hey, she's the girl Baba found me. The thing is that her mother was the woman Baba wanted to marry. But that didn't happen . . . and she died after many years. Baba saw this girl go through hell under her stepmother and so decided to pile her on my head. The truth is that this daughter of a dog doesn't know my value and will never care to find out either.'

'Ah, so there is someone else who knows your value?'

'Ha, there are four!' Father laughed.

'Eh? Goodness! Not bad at all! Quite something, eh!'

'What to do? Wasn't I born a man? I am eighty-eight. My wife is twenty-one years younger than me . . . by the time she was twenty-five she had back pains and nose pains and all. Then I met Malti. She was thirty-five then. That went on for about ten years. And then she too started getting back pains, and her children had also grown up. I was past fifty-five then. But, Mitra babu, is it not true that a man's life starts

50

only at fifty-five? Around that time, I met Savitri. She was a widow at thirty. Poor thing! She had to struggle to raise her children . . . I was a big help to her. Fifteen years passed like that. One day she said that her eldest son had got a job in Bombay and she was leaving with him. I was alone, again. And, of course, older now. So what, is not a man's age a matter of the mind? My great good luck, I met Sudakshina. She is fifty now, but that's okay . . .'

'Does Chetna's mother know all this?'

'Oh, she's a woman, right? Mark my words: this creature called wife, she will sniff out another woman even if she's just barely grazed you.'

The intermixed scents of booze, the burning ghat and the fish cooking in the kitchen pierced my nostrils. I wanted to throw up. All this while, Mother, bleeding from her nose, had been cooking fish for Father in the kitchen.

'So, Grddha babu, don't we have to go to meet the IG at the jail tomorrow? I'll bring a car . . .' Sanjeev Kumar Mitra got up and stretched his limbs. He was terribly bored; his voice said so.

'Not necessary, Sanju babu. We will take a rickshaw or an auto rickshaw.'

Father had turned modest.

'Uh-ha . . . I came to tell you this . . . that is, about getting Chetna this job. I—my TV channel, that is—will make sure she gets it.'

'Eh, is it true, Sanju babu? Chetu! O Chetu, come here quick . . .'

Father was very excited. I stepped into the room only after a moment.

'Did you hear this? Sanju babu's TV channel will make sure you get the job. We are saved, my daughter. Listen to your baba—don't ever forget this man. He is our God . . . our saviour . . .'

Father took Sanjeev Kumar's hands in his, squeezed them, and began to weep and sob.

'Chi, what is this, Grddha babu? Let me finish.'

He made Father sit on the cot, sat next to him and looked at me indifferently.

'We'll get Chetna the job. Though there is plenty of protest against the death penalty, most judges in this country wish to retain it . . . so no reason to fear that she will lose her job. And in any case, I am around. I know how to support my wife.'

'Sanju babu, ask me, if you want my soul in return for these favours, I will give even that to you . . .'

Father became more emotional.

'Not your soul, we want your life—'

'Life?'

'Your life stories, that is.'

Father suddenly fell silent. Though completely drunk by now, a calculating glimmer sprang up in his eyes.

'Do you see it? Stories of the hangings you have overseen in your life. I don't know if you are aware that the company that owns our channel has one hundred and twenty-seven publications. The new publication they are about to launch wants to publish your autobiography.'

Father stroked his beard once.

'I can give it to you, if it is for one issue . . .'

'No, they want it serialized.'

'I don't remember so much, Sanju babu,' Father got up as if to quietly pull himself out of this.

'If that is so, it will be hard to get Chetna that job.' Sanjeev Kumar Mitra's face hardened.

'I'll tell you my experiences, Sanju babu. But I don't want to see them in print . . . many of those are very personal,' Father announced, playing a sad part now.

Sanjeev Kumar Mitra stayed on for some more time, trying to put pressure on him. But Father stood his ground.

'I'll do something else instead. After the hanging, I'll appear first on your channel—exclusive interview. I have been receiving offers of lakhs of rupees from channels in London and America . . . but no, you don't have to pay me a paisa. Because, Mitra babu, you are going to become my son-in-law, right?'

Sanjeev Kumar Mitra gave it a thought.

'In that case, Chetna will do . . . not you.'

The painful throb in my left breast became worse.

'Chetna's time, henceforth, must be exclusively for our channel. She must not speak to other newspapers or TV channels. Wherever she goes, we will go with her . . . till the eve of the hanging.'

Father's mouth fell open.

'For example, she'll have to meet the IG and the DGP. She'll have to go to Alipore Jail. We will be everywhere. Every move she makes from now, we are taking it . . . for a decent price.'

He pulled out a folded piece of paper from his pocket. That's how I saw, and signed on, stamp paper for the first time in my life.

I, Chetna Mullick, daughter of Phanibhushan Grddha Mullick, hereby agree that all rights towards transmitting and publishing interviews with me for twenty-four days from today, until 24 June, on which date the death sentence of Jatindranath Banerjee is to be executed as announced by the Government of India, will be solely owned by CNC Channel, a subsidiary of CNC Publishing House. During this time, I agree not to speak with anyone other than the authorized representatives of CNC Channel. A sum of Rs 5000 has been fixed as remuneration, of which I have received Rs 1001 as advance.

Yours faithfully
Signature

First witness: Phanibhushan Grddha Mullick
Second witness: Sanjeev Kumar Mitra

Father did not ask me what I thought of it. He ordered me to sign. I signed. Sanjeev Kumar Mitra counted out a thousand and one rupees. When he handed over a thousand rupees to Father and one rupee to me, he deliberately brushed his fingers against mine. My age was such—that of a lotus bud yearning to bloom. A gentle caress would have made it blossom. But his touch was not gentle. I pulled away my fingers. The one rupee coin scorched my palm. I turned abruptly, seeking to get out of the room. But I could not walk as fast as I wished. My feet ached as if my toes were ready to fall off. Everything had been bought for a price—my movements, words, experiences. I felt as though a worm had burrowed into my flesh and was squirming inside. Right inside that left breast which he had touched, not with love but contempt.

7

'Really? Did he agree to be the Speaker? Great news! Just watch—this is a historic moment!' Sanjeev Kumar Mitra exclaimed excitedly into his cell phone from the front seat of the channel's vehicle.

'Hey Atul, Grddha da, Somu da has agreed to be the Lok Sabha Speaker. The discussion went on all day yesterday, right? But they'll announce it only today evening, by six.'

Since the day before, one discussion had followed another on TV about whether the CPM should accept the Speaker's position in the new Parliament or not. Till two days ago, it had been about whether the CPM should join the government or not. Our eyes had been glued to the TV screen, waiting to see if anything was being announced about Jatindranath Chatterjee or my appointment; and so even Thakuma had memorized all the arguments for and against. Debates maddened me; life slipping through my fingers saddened me. Thakuma kept reminding me that we are members of a family older than even the king, we are but instruments of power. Clad in a worn salwar kameez, my hair in two braids, I sat hunched up in the backseat of the car, plagued with unease at being slighted. The difference between Sonia Gandhi's prime ministership and Jyoti Basu's prime ministership did not make any sense to me.

Seeing the city after a very long while, I looked at the sun and the bustle, buildings old and new, with a sense of disbelief. I had travelled outside of Chitpur only rarely. Except for a few free trips from school and a visit to the Durga Puja at Kalighat, I had not been anywhere. Whenever the circular trains passed screeching harshly, louder than the sound of the rain falling on them and scattering like smoke, I always imagined trains that ran in lines and not circles, and the faraway places they could reach.

It was rather cold inside Sanjeev Kumar Mitra's vehicle. I was all sweaty by the time I touched Thakuma's feet, bid goodbye to Ramu da and Ma, and got into it; the cold was a relief. Father and I sat where the cameraman pointed. He began shooting even before the car started moving. I saw the camera and felt nothing. I had seen on TV how I appeared to other people. That very moment, all sense of anxiety about how I looked had left me. I saw the sights through the windows, their dark-tinted glass resembling Sanjeev Kumar's spectacles. The city I had never seen split its jaws wide. All the walls we passed were covered with hammer-and-sickle signs and exhortations to vote for someone or the other. Crumbling walls. Broken roads. Human forms, thin, gaunt, pulling rickshaws. Women seeking alms with babies in their ragged bundles. A madwoman with wild eyes and flying hair ran behind the car, screaming something. I turned around to look at her, feeling troubled. In the jatra, the character of Bibek, the Conscience, had been created to get rid of the singing chorus but retain the songs. Conscience thus set the cash registers jingling through its singing. This madwoman is the Bibek of the jatra of my life, I thought. She did not sing, she screamed. I began to have second thoughts.

'Jyoti babu was not wise to have decided like that then, but . . .' Father murmured, stroking his moustache and looking out. Then he turned towards Sanjeev Kumar with a broad smile. 'Listen, Sanju babu . . . take note of this . . . after my death, me and Jyoti babu—our names and lives will become deathless in India and the world over.'

'Grddha da, you are witty, really.' Sanjeev Kumar laughed aloud.

I was not amused. This is how a person being led to the gallows must feel, I thought. What next, what next—the fear, what next. I had no clue, what next. I wished I could hide my hands somewhere. The day I realized that my hands had the strength to kill someone, I started fearing them. I was now frozen with fear, deep in distress. When we got out of the car, I called out to Father.

'Baba. . .'

'Uh-uh?'

I stood there looking at him. My mouth was totally dry.

'Don't have to do this, Baba,' I murmured somehow.

'What? What happened? Is Chetna beginning to get scared?' Brushing back his locks with a round red comb he had pulled out of his pocket, Sanjeev Kumar came up close to ask me. 'Don't be afraid, Chetna. There's nothing to worry about.' His face was full of sympathy and his voice overflowed with kindness. I stood there, completely miserable.

Father stroked his moustache, looking daggers at me.

'It'll be shameful to withdraw now after coming so far. Look, Chetna, don't be foolish. You are getting a government job by a fluke. Don't let it go. It is a contract job for now—but I assure you—we'll do the needful and make it permanent. That'll make sure that your family has a steady income.'

'Aren't there other kinds of work in this land?'

Sanjeev Kumar Mitra laughed aloud. 'Don't be idiotic, Chetna! What kind of work are you going to find with just a Plus Two education? Be thankful for what you have in hand now.'

'You have nothing to fear. Am I not going to be there? Sudev as well? You just have to be there when it happens, that's all. Look, this is our family's tradition. Nothing in it to feel ashamed of or guilty about. You better come along. Otherwise I'll change my tone, mind you!' Father was clearly irked.

As he stomped ahead of us, Sanjeev Kumar looked at me. 'You can do it, Chetna. You are strong. You have courage. And strength. Be bold. I'll always be with you, always. Come along.' His voice grew tender.

I felt the tears coming. The love which had strangled me earlier and which I had tried to kill—it raised its hood again inside me. Caught, helpless, confused, my heart grew weak. I looked again into his eyes, hopefully. They were masked by those dark glasses. I wished to believe that he loved me. In the strength of that faith, I followed Father.

The cameraman followed us right up to the office on the fourth floor of E Block in Writers' Buildings. There was a signboard that read 'ADGP and AGCS' in front. The cameraman had no entry beyond this point. In my imagination, the IG's office was a beautiful building, like the ones in the TV serials that we watched regularly. I was astonished to see the front yard littered with empty water bottles and broken tea cups. The ancient building hadn't received a fresh coat of paint in ages. From a room on the floor above, stains of chewed betel trickled down, as red as flowing blood. We had to wait for about an hour. Everyone was agitated over the mass transfer of fifty-seven IPS officers, Sanjeev Kumar Mitra told Father. It was only after eleven-thirty that Ajoy Chakrabarti came to his office, chewing betel and dragging his feet, as listless as a half-hearted student dragging himself to school. His eyes fell on me as he entered. Father jumped up and folded his hands respectfully. The IG stood before us, sizing me up from head to toe.

'Why, Phani, is this your girl?' he asked, chewing his betel peculiarly.

Sanjeev Kumar Mitra stepped forward and shook hands with the IG. They exchanged pleasantries. We were asked in.

Inside, Sanjeev Kumar Mitra was offered a chair. Father stood stooping like a slave. I cowered behind him, half hidden, abandoned.

'What is your name?' the IG asked, craning his neck so that he could see me at the back.

'Chetna,' Father answered.

'She is very beautiful. Why send her for this work?' The IG leaned back in his chair, rocked his legs, and kept looking at me.

'Chetna passed the Plus Two exams with distinction,' Sanjeev Kumar Mitra intervened.

When he looked at me with pride and satisfaction, the ache in my left breast got worse.

'I couldn't educate her after that, Babu . . . how could I? Don't you know how badly off we are at home?'

'Shut your trap, Phani . . . ah, whatever, you're big-mouthed . . . too much . . .' the IG who was just half Father's age, raised his voice. Father lowered his head meekly. Fear rushed into my blood. It was clear that I had ventured into a strange world. It was not a world I could enter counting on my father.

The IG picked up a file, put it on the table and looked at Sanjeev Kumar Mitra.

'You've pushed me into an awful dilemma, Sanjeev babu.'

'Please consider it somehow . . . with sympathy, Ajoy babu. Shouldn't the government be able to do at least this much for Grddha da? He's been a party supporter too.'

'That's all right. But look, read the rules regarding the hangman's post.'

He then read it out.

'Qualification: Applicant should be an adult, over five feet four inches tall. Only males need apply.'

He then looked at us one by one, again and again.

'Do you understand? For this job there's just one qualification. It has to be a man, over five feet four inches tall . . . that's all . . .'

He looked at the three of us in turn again.

'But we have obtained a special order from the government to consider women also. What's the problem then?' Sanjeev Kumar wiped his glasses and put them back on his nose.

'This isn't an ordinary job. The hangman must possess a resolute mind. If the hangman stands before the gallows and then cries, oh no, I can't do this, he will go to jail. You know that, don't you?'

'You don't know Chetna, Babu. She is a girl with a mind stronger than us men.'

Sanjeev Kumar threw me another pleased glance. I tried to control myself but went red in the face.

'These women . . . by their very nature they are second-thoughters. This isn't a job for them.'

'Don't let the feminists hear you.' Sanjeev Kumar Mitra smiled at the IG.

'If IG babu permits, may this humble Phani ask a question?' Father asked, stooping all the more. 'I'll make her do all of this and show you. Will that do?'

The IG looked at the two of us in turn again and again.

'Is your father right, girl?'

He looked at me again, chewing betel. I did not raise my head but held my body as if to say yes.

'This is not a permanent job, Sanjeev babu.' The IG shot Sanjeev Kumar Mitra a discouraging look.

'I know that, Ajoy babu. It's only a contractual appointment. Just a seventy-five-rupee-per-month allowance . . . have to report for work whenever summoned. Chetna's agreed to all of this.'

'So what about Sukhdev Mullick?'

'Is he good for anything at all, IG babu? He faints when it's time to pull the lever. He's good for some odd jobs, that's all . . .' Father complained.

'Then why give him the seventy-five-rupee allowance? I'll have it stopped.' The IG was angry.

'IG babu, it is very saddening to hear you say this. Does he not have a family that depends on him? I need him for odd jobs. A hangman needs two assistants, Babu, haven't I said that many times? There's another thing, IG babu—in our Mullick family, only one person becomes a star at a time. That's been our history.'

Father looked at Sanjeev Kumar, feeling high as he began to tell a story.

'Listen, Sanju babu. This was in 1923, the time of the Bangla Pact. I was but a kid, just six or seven. I used to go to court with Dadu. Desbandhu Chittaranjan Das babu was a famous lawyer then. He used to give me an anna whenever he saw me. Have you heard of him, Babu? What a great man! But what to do, the Hindus did not recognize his greatness. He signed a pact that said Hindu processions would stop playing music when they passed by mosques. And that cow slaughter would be allowed when necessary. My goodness . . . what a storm that kicked up! There was lots of bickering over it and during one such row, Brijendra Singh beat a Muslim to death, and, as a result, was sentenced to death himself. Those days, my father used to be accompanied by my dada Nagbhushan Mullick. But on the day he received the order for Brijendra Singh's hanging, Baba was down with fever. And so Nagu da went instead. He started on the booze early in the day. Drank late into the night, and by daybreak his feet weren't on the floor. The policemen woke him up somehow at three-thirty. He stood by the gallows, reeling, unable to even open his eyes. The condemned man was brought to the gallows at four. Dada was so drunk, he couldn't even make out where the head was, and where the feet. Somehow, they put the hood on the condemned man. It didn't fit properly. Paying no attention, Nagu da put the noose around his neck. That wasn't properly done, either. Brijendra Singh, you know, was nicknamed "Owl"—so narrow was his neck and so broad was his nose . . . there was no neck to speak of. Nagu da's noose ended up being hitched on his nose. Swaying and tottering, Nagu da pulled the lever . . .'

Father paused dramatically for a moment and looked at us.

'Normally, the noose would have come loose. But the plank slid off when the lever was pulled. The man hung by his nose. His legs thrashed about for a moment. And then became still. The British officers and the doctor who were watching were dazed; there was no way that the man could have died with a noose like that! When the doctor went into the cellar below, he was amazed . . . Bhagawan! The bones in the neck were broken perfectly! The British crossed themselves. Nagu da was given a reward of a hundred pounds, as was the practice then. Babu—this one thing, please note it down—we Grddha Mullicks, even if we have to come straight out of bed and hang someone . . . A mishap? No, that just can't happen! Uh-uh.'

Father looked at each of us, beaming proudly. I was elated. No one can tell a story like my father. He revealed only the part about the hundred-pound reward. He didn't disclose the part about how Uncle Nagbhushan was dismissed from service with immediate effect. Don't ever be found anywhere near the gallows, the jail superintendent had bellowed at him, apparently. That's why Father, who had been an actor and singer, had to rub the greasepaint off his face and pick up the hangman's rope.

'Okay, okay, go and see Sibdev. Not many days left . . . don't you know?'

The IG tore off a sheet of paper, signed on it and gave it to Sanjeev Kumar. He shooed us out with his other hand as if we were flies to be swatted. Father and I exited quickly. Sanjeev Kumar stayed back to say something to the IG.

'I . . . I am someone who's seen people like Chittaranjan babu with my own eyes, do you know? When he died, three lakh people waited at the railway station in the pouring rain for his body to be brought down from Darjeeling. I, too, all of nine then, waited. In that crowd, the whole day. These fellows will never make sense of such things. Here, look, Writers' Buildings. How many great men have sat here! You must remember that whenever you pass this way. You must honour this soil, salute it . . .'

Father stayed immersed in memories for some time. He then looked at me seriously. 'He's a bright chap. If you get him, consider that your great good fortune.'

I did not reply. My heart trembled like the piece of paper that the IG had signed, and I felt short of breath, as if a man's corpse had been tied to my ribcage. By the time we got out of the office through the ground floor where two policemen with guns were chatting away by the elevator, I was soaked in sweat.

'This too is a historic moment . . .' As he ran up to the vehicle and stepped inside smartly, Sanjeev Kumar Mitra waved the piece of paper at me as if I were his best friend of many years. 'If you had let this opportunity go, that would've been a historic blunder.'

I could not bring myself to raise my eyes and look at him. Walking with my eyes fixed on the ground, like a donkey carrying an unbearably heavy load, I desired deeply to forget the expression on his face and his voice when he had crushed my flesh.

'She will make my name and my life eternal to Bharat and the world after my demise, Sanju babu. I am indebted to you for that.'

When he got into the vehicle, Father turned towards Sanjeev Kumar Mitra and folded his hands theatrically. Then, like an actor back in the green room after having delivered his lines, he wiped his neck and face with his gamchha and fanned himself with it. 'Oh, this heat! Where is the damned rain?'

'What is the difference between rain and no rain? You sweat if it rains, and you sweat if it doesn't. The rain should be like the rain back in my town—just one shower, and the earth cools,' Sanjeev Kumar said to me, pulling out a blue kerchief from his pocket and wiping his face.

Something moved in my heart. That moment, he was not someone who had hurt and humiliated me with his words and touch.

'So you are not from Bengal, Sanju babu?' Father asked, astonished.

'We journalists are all alike, wherever we are born, Grddha da.'

'But everyone has some birthplace or the other?'

'Another place like Bengal . . . but not this bad. Not this good, either.' He said that as if he were mired in another thought.

'Bhagawan! But who can make that out from your Bangla?'

'My mother gave birth to me in Bengal.'

Sanjeev Kumar Mitra tried to smile. But I saw it turn into a grimace. Though his eyes were hidden behind his dark glasses, I felt that something he did not wish to reveal lay in their depths, collected in a pool.

'Where is your mother now?' Father inquired again.

'She is no more.'

He was cryptic. Then, after a short silence, he turned towards me, smiling. 'I saw her off to the cremation ground in a red kasi silk sari, in the most expensive hearse available . . .'

His voice broke. The toes of my feet tingled. Unease swept over me; I withdrew my leg feeling that my big toes were bound together. I was assailed by fear—the unreasonable fear that the woman who had lain inside the first hearse that had rolled over the hailstones of the hail shower many years ago had been Sanjeev Kumar Mitra's mother. It was in these ways that he tightened the noose around my heart. Whenever I struggled and writhed, he increased the length of the rope. And so the noose never became tight enough. He took off his glasses, revealing those dreamy eyes, and smiled at me. For a moment, I was deluded, thinking that this was how a man looked at the woman he loved. Conscience never made its appearance. It also did not warn me that if my name too were to become eternal in Bharat and outside after my death, it would be through this wretched love which could be made real only by the shedding of my heart's blood.

8

Like the world outside, the jail too was a man's world. And its colour was red. Crossing the gate which looked like the entrance to a fortress, and getting inside the walls which were as tall as two men, I found that the building inside was also red. To reach the gallows one has to cross three gates, reminded Father. Each of these is well guarded.

'Is Sibdev babu inside? Babu, please tell him that hangman Grddha is here to see him,' Father requested the guards on duty at the first gate.

The gate opened after some time and we went in with Sanjeev Kumar. Once inside, Father became excited. 'The jail is behind the third gate.'

A police jeep drove up to the superintendent's office. A handcuffed man emerged from the jeep in front. He walked past us nonchalantly. Sanjeev Kumar Mitra cast his eyes on me and smiled: 'That could be one of Chetna's victims . . .'

'Hey, hardly!' It was Father who replied. 'Looks like death by the rope won't survive much longer. Sanju babu, mark my words . . . maybe Jatindranath's will be the last. Isn't the whole world against the death sentence?' Father let out a sigh of regret, his eyes wandering.

'In my father's time, there used to be twenty . . . thirty jobs, sometimes fifty, every month. Those days, the death sentence wasn't just for murderers. It was the same in my youth too . . . But now? It's been twelve or thirteen years since I had a job. Is that because people are committing fewer crimes? No. In the old days, murders occurred once a year or so. But now, how many murders happen each day! Don't tell anyone that I told you, Sanju babu, even the Puranas say that evil men should be killed so that the earth's burden is eased. Were Vyasa and Valmiki senseless people? Was Bhagawan Krishna ignorant?'

'Chetna, I must say, your father is remarkable. Even at his age he's in touch with everything that happens in this world.'

'Ha, and why is that? Because I gobble every word of the *Anandabazar Patrika* every day. I watch the news on TV. Does the difference between the poor unlettered and the rest matter when it comes to watching television, Sanju babu?'

Father walked briskly, wiping his face with his gamchha. We saw the superintendent's office when we got past the second gate. Father walked in like someone who knew his way around well. I tarried on the path, still doubtful. A jeep appeared through the gate of the jailer's office on our left. Beyond the third gate of the prison, which was right before us, I could see a two-storeyed building. The prisoner we had seen earlier was going there. On its top storey, white-clad prisoners hung around lazily. Fear bloomed in my heart. Heavy, cold darkness hung everywhere. Till then, the biggest house I had seen was Thakurbari. The moment I stepped into it, the music of the jal tarang rang in my heart. The moment I stepped into the Alipore Correctional Home, my heart froze. It had happened before once, at the gate of Nimtala Ghat. The jail is a cremation ground too of the thing that makes human beings human, like soul-force.

'Grddha da, what news? Are you well?' Sibdev Ghosh greeted us, holding his hands out in a friendly gesture.

Sibdev babu was a bright-faced fifty-year-old man. He did not look like someone who handled criminals every day. His face was warm and smiling, like Narayan da's—Narayan da who made litters for corpses out of raw bamboo. I liked Sibdev babu on sight. Sanjeev Kumar was given a front seat here too. We stood leaning against the wall. This room was smaller and narrower than the IG's. Except for four iron almirahs of half-height, there was nothing in there.

'Everything is well with your blessings, Babu.' Father turned meek.

Sibdev babu studied me, scratching the left side of his greying head.

'Uh-uh . . . the allowance is seventy-five rupees . . . understand?'

I smiled foolishly.

'The hanging's been fixed for the twenty-fourth. Exactly twenty-nine days from now . . .'

He opened a file bound with a red string, took out a sheet of paper, signed on it and handed it to me. 'This is your appointment order, understand?'

I held out my hand like an idiot and took it.

'Chetna, my daughter, your father advises you, listen, for the rest of your life, you must give this man the respect that you give the gods.'

Father suddenly turned into the stage actor of old and began to deliver his lines.

'This gentleman, this Sibdev babu, as far as your father is concerned, he is a divine messenger. It is he who increased our allowance from fifty to seventy-five.'

'Isn't seventy-five disgracefully low, Sibdev babu?' Sanjeev Kumar Mitra interrupted.

'That's all the law permits . . . the intellectuals will make a fuss if we raise it. And of course, the job's irregular too. Whenever there is one, Grddha makes sure to bargain and get the best deal. Look, right now, he's asked for twenty thousand.'

'I'm not willing to reduce it by one anna or one paisa,' Father cooed.

Sibdev babu got up with his bunch of keys, a slight smile on his face. Father rubbed his face hard with his gamchha and gestured that I should follow him. Sanjeev Kumar started to accompany us. Sibdev turned to him, retaining his gentle manner.

'By rule, outsiders are not allowed here.'

'Our job is to break the rules, isn't it so, Sibdev babu? I have got the DGP to speak for me. No risk to you.' Sanjeev Kumar smiled.

Sibdev babu did not object further. He walked ahead towards the third gate. When it opened, a policeman hurried up, saluted him and came along with us. Crossing the printing press, the school and the kitchen on the right, we went towards the godown.

'This jail dates from British times. Look, how it was built . . .' Sanjeev Kumar spoke to me as if he were speaking to a friend.

My heart quavered. Whenever he spoke like a different person, wiping away his words and deeds of the past few days, I was filled with anger. And anxiety. It seemed to me that I was in some other world as I walked with him on the veranda. The two-storeyed building was now very close. Red verandas, walls painted red. Massive granite pillars. We had stepped out of the office block and on to the jail veranda. The barred doors of the cells were open, but the prisoners were nowhere to be seen in the vast jail yard. The echo of someone's racking cough rang out. It was a terrible, tormenting cough, strong enough to wrench out the lungs. Reaching the door of the next cell, I saw that it came from a very old man stretched out on the cot inside and covered with a black blanket. I saw clearly his shaven head and sunken eyes. I began to be afraid again.

The key to the godown was a fat black one. The policeman who stepped in ahead of us sneezed four or five times. He switched on the light. A big room came into sight in the yellow gleam. I took one look and saw four iron boxes piled one upon the other. I knew what they held. My body trembled.

'This is it . . . this box will do . . .' Father announced merrily as if he had found a long-lost toy.

The policeman fumbled with the keys, found another one and opened the topmost box.

'Chotdi, take a look,' Father ordered me lovingly.

I stepped into the room on trembling feet. The awful scent of the air trapped in the room assailed me. I too sneezed four or five times. Father paid no attention; he opened the lid of the box. My hair stood on end. Inside the box, ropes that were a century old lay coiled like enormous black cobras preparing to lay eggs.

'This will do, Sibdev babu . . . do you know what this is? It is the one with which we hung two fellows together . . . the best stuff . . .'

Father picked up a coil of rope proudly and pulled it straight. It had five knots. I looked on, finding it hard to breathe.

'Isn't this Manila rope, Grddha da? We have Buxar rope too.' Sibdev turned towards Sanjeev Kumar and smiled. 'They make this rope in the Buxar jail in Bihar . . . very durable stuff. But Grddha da isn't too happy with it.'

'This rope is from the Ganga Ropes Company, Sanju babu. They aren't in business any more, but I haven't seen better quality rope in my life. Look, forty kilos heavy . . . sixty feet long . . . Sanju babu, to be hung by this . . . you need to be really lucky.' Father kissed the rope affectionately.

'Do you reuse a rope that's already been used to hang a person?' Sanjeev Kumar asked.

'The belief is that the rope belongs to the hangman. In many places the hangman takes it home and sells it piece by piece. People believe that if you burn that bit of rope and drink its ashes, you'll be cured of diseases that have no cure.'

Hearing Sibdev babu's words, Father raised his hand as if to stop him.

'All that is nonsense. Superstition! A hundred more can be hung with this rope . . . why cut it up and burn it?'

Father rummaged in the box again and brought up another coil of rope.

'This has been here since my father's time. See this knot at the end? Only Baba could have tied this knot so perfectly . . .'

Father looked at the rope with deep reverence.

'Oh, I remember . . . yes . . . Dinesh Chandra Gupta was hanged with this rope,' Father sighed. 'That was the first time I saw Baba weep. That was the only job he did against his will. Dinesh Chandra Gupta was just nineteen . . . poor man . . . how great he would have become had he lived, this young man . . . it was young people like him who made us want to lay down our lives for the freedom struggle. Sanju babu, that's a long story. I'll tell you later, when it's convenient . . . with it you can sell a hundred copies of your corporation's magazine like hot cakes.'

Father coiled the rope again and put it back into the box with a sigh. He picked up the first coil again.

'So, Sibdev babu, this will do for Jatindranath. Let's fix this.'

'As you wish, Grddha da.' Sibdev babu smiled.

Father looked at me after he took the rope out. 'We'll have to come here two more times. A week before the hanging and the day before, to inspect the gallows, the cellar below and the lever. We must try a mock hanging with a sack of sand. Babu, what did you say his weight was?'

'Just about fifty kilos. Five feet ten inches tall. He is a reedy fellow,' Sibdev babu said.

'So, Chetu, with what weight must we try our mock hanging?' Father asked, to test and display my knowledge.

'One and a half times his body weight—seventy-five kilos,' I said.

'Right, what about the length of the rope?' Father asked, triumphant.

'Seven feet, two inches.'

'Make a noose and show Babu.'

I had no way out now. I touched the big rope slowly. The tiny strands poking out of the rope pierced my palms like sharp thorns. Nervousness was making me feel weak. The rope was very heavy. I lifted it slowly. Sibdev babu and the policeman were looking at me, anxious. Father wiped his sweat with the gamchha. I coiled the rope into a noose slowly and then handed it over to Father.

'Ha, perfect.' Father took it happily and held it up for everyone to see. 'See, see, Sibdev babu, see, Sanju babu! Did I not tell you, this is in the blood of my line. Don't rule her out because she is a woman. She is my daughter, she has all the strength and genius of the Grddha Mullicks.'

When Sibdev, Sanjeev Kumar and the policeman agreed, nodding vigorously, I experienced a sinking feeling. The thought that fate had handed me a noose instead of all the appreciation and recognition that I richly deserved in this life distressed me. I wiped my sweat-soaked neck and forehead with the fringes of my dupatta.

'All right, let's look at the other things on 18 June,' Father announced as if he'd remembered something just then.

'Shouldn't we take a look at the gallows?' Sanjeev Kumar Mitra wanted to know.

'Sanju babu, this isn't the time for that.'

Sanjeev Kumar's face fell, but Father ignored that completely. I guessed he had a reason, but only the next day did I learn what it was.

We stepped right into the camera's eye. Sanjeev Kumar's cameraman had been waiting to shoot Father and me coming out. Sanjeev Kumar fished out a tin of face powder from his pocket, touched up his face and combed his hair, and, taking the microphone from the cameraman, spoke into it: 'And so, for the first time in the world, a woman has been officially appointed to the post of hangman. Accepting all the demands made by the state's famous hangman Phanibhushan Grddha Mullick, the government of Bengal has appointed his daughter Chetna Grddha Mullick to the office of the hangman. Chetna Grddha Mullick has received the order, visited the IG of police and the superintendent of the Alipore Correctional Home, and completed the first phase of arrangements. You are watching Chetna and her father leaving the jail. Chetna Grddha Mullick passed her Plus Two exams with very high marks. Chetna, welcome to CNC. What do you have to say about your new job? Do you feel scared working as an executioner?' Sanjeev Kumar asked me that question without warning.

'We Grddha Mullicks don't know what fear is,' I spat that out unthinkingly. Father's face broke into a broad smile.

'Are you happy to get this job?'

'All the women in the world can be proud of this moment.'

'Is there any basis to say so—that all the women in the world can be proud because you have become an executioner?'

'This will prove that there is no job that women can't do.'

'Are you a feminist?'

'I don't know. What do you think?'

He didn't expect my response; that was clear from his face.

'Chetna Grddha Mullick prepares to take up the job of the hangman, raising before us the question of whether or not she is a feminist. With this, Jatindranath Banerjee gains the good fortune of securing passage to the other world through a noose fashioned by bangle-clad wrists for the very first time in history. CNC is proud to announce to our viewers that till the date of the execution, we will have exclusive access to Chetna Grddha Mullick. Watch out for the special programme on Jatindranath Banerjee tomorrow in the seven-thirty news bulletin! From 1 June, every day, we will feature exclusive updates on the execution from Chetna Grddha Mullick who has been appointed as assistant to the chief executioner. *Hangwoman's Diary* only on CNC! From the gates of the Alipore Correctional Home, with cameraman Atul Kishore Chandra, this is Sanjeev Kumar Mitra for CNC.'

He waited a minute for the camera to be turned off, handed the microphone to the cameraman and turned to us.

'Chetna, you are marvellous! Grddha da, your daughter is an extraordinary woman. She should continue her education. I will help in whatever way I can.'

'Sanju babu, we have no words to thank you . . .' Father wiped tears of joy.

'We must have Chetna's interview on the seven-thirty bulletin on Wednesday. You must be at the studio by seven at least. I will send the car at six. Chetna should be ready.'

'Sure, Sanju babu. May I say something from my life's experience?'

Father became modest. Sanjeev Kumar looked up with interest.

'The truth is that it is TV channels like yours that give freedom and equality to poor folk like us. No one listened to our stories before. Not any more. Take my daughter's experience, for example. Would she have got such a high position so easily before? No, and even if she had, would she have been recognized this way? Never.'

It was a scornful grimace that bloomed on Sanjeev Kumar Mitra's lips. 'You are very right, Grddha da. I need to get this CD to the studio as soon as possible. Do you mind going home by yourselves?'

'By all means, we will, Sanju babu. I will coach Chetna about what she has to say in the interview on 1 June.'

Father wiped his forehead with the gamchha and raised his hand as if to bid goodbye.

'Not necessary, I'd think . . . no need to teach the baby squirrel tree-climbing.'

Sanjeev Kumar Mitra said that in a serious tone, all the while hurrying to get into the vehicle. Father laughed aloud. I stood there, eyes fixed on the red walls. When I was outside, those red walls looked like the best escape route available to me. But inside, they appeared to be my biggest obstacle. The throb in my breast had eased. But I still felt the worm writhing inside. When we took our leave, I did not look at him. That was the only revenge that a weak woman like me could take on a powerful man like him. Total disregard. But let me admit ruefully—this may be impossible for you to imagine—that even then, my heart, like a rain-drenched lotus bud, yearned to bloom in the warmth of a patient caress. A totally undesirable longing, like the yearning to build a hearth at the head of a burning pyre.

9

I was rudely jolted awake that night by a weird nightmare in which a huge banyan tree—the one that grew in the moss-covered warehouse on Rabindra Sarani—had taken root on my head. Instead of the long locks of hair, long brown roots flowed down to my waist. Dismayed, I touched the smooth, shiny red root-tips. My fingers moved up and stopped at the tangles. Those were not roots; those were hangman's nooses, softened and readied with soap and banana flesh and wax. I sprang up from my mat.

It was barely past five. But daylight had begun to spread outside. I told Thakuma about the nightmare when I went to serve her tea. She was terrified. A death sign, she said. Taking a fifty-paisa coin in her fist, she made a circle around my head with it and tottered down to the cremation ground. She came back with a piece of red string which had been blessed and some ash from a pyre; she marked my forehead with the ash and tied the string around my neck.

It was a tense day at home. After Father and I had returned the previous evening, the house had grown noisier than Strand Road. So, ultimately, one's own blood counts more, Kakima had shouted. No point sending a girl to do such work, said Kaku. Thakuma lay on the coir cot in Ramu da's room, buried in her blanket, chanting Ram-naam. Ma ran about the house, wiping her eyes and blowing her nose, busy with her chores. Contradictory feelings racked my mind; I was exhausted. Soon after I had given Ramu da his dinner, I spread my mat and lay down. When Champa and Rari came to me for English and maths lessons, I said, tomorrow; that too triggered loud complaints. Kakima started off all over again. Ramu da lay silent and still, eyes fixed on the asbestos sheet above. I wanted to simply slip into sleep, sealing my eyes and ears. But a sacrificial animal's seemingly never-ending cries rose from Hemu da's Kali temple. When Kakima woke up in the morning and opened the door, she found droplets of blood splattered all over the doorstep. An evil omen, she screamed. Father, who came out hearing the commotion, laughed away her fears. No better omen for the hangman than blood, he asserted. He turned scornfully towards Kaku who recoiled with fear at the sight of blood.

'Dumb sucker who can't kill even a fowl by himself! Hey, you have to see, I've just sacrificed my daughter for your sake . . .' Father dug up the previous day's quarrel.

'Oh, you needn't have bothered so much about me, Dada. Chetna is a woman, she must get married and settle down to family life . . . don't forget,' reminded Kaku in a dejected tone.

'Just wait and see, she'll be swept off her feet by suitors.' Father laughed.

'Heard that the fellow who came here has proposed. Is that true?' asked Kakima, coming out.

'Uh-uh . . . he did . . . but we haven't decided anything. Is she an ordinary woman now? It's the first time in the whole world that a woman's been appointed an executioner. She is a symbol of strength and self-respect to the whole world now . . . don't forget that. Chetu, get ready quickly, we have to go out.'

I had no idea where we had to go; there was no way of guessing either. All I knew was that we had to go to the TV channel from 1 June onwards. Doesn't Sanjeev Kumar Mitra own all my mobility until the date of the execution, I wanted to ask Father. When he combed his hair, smoothed his moustache and began to hurry me up at eleven o'clock, I braided my hair and wore my only good pair of clothes—a violet salwar kameez. It was rush hour in bus no. 62. A tongue of flame rose and singed my insides as the red walls of Alipore came into view. Not daring to ask Father why we were there again, I glanced at him. Shouldn't we tell Sanjeev Kumar Mitra? Shouldn't we?

As if he had read my mind, Father mused: 'He is smart, and has been helpful to us too . . . but sometimes you can't take journalists into confidence.'

I stared, unable to grasp what he was getting at.

'You have been appointed to a job by the government. The

government is now your master. You shouldn't feel greater gratitude towards anyone else.'

Father didn't say anything more until we walked through the gate of the jail. As I waited outside Sibdev babu's office, Father came out with a policeman. I followed them blindly. This time, they turned left after we crossed the second gate. I couldn't even guess where they were headed.

'Look there . . . those are the cells of the condemned,' said Father.

My eyes opened wide as I looked where he was pointing. Three little barred cells in a row. Inside each, the yellow glow of a bulb. The light blinded me, so I could hardly see who was inside. Later, whenever I thought of those barred doors, all I could remember was that blinding yellow light. We had reached a place that looked like a martyrs' pavilion. A piece of wood rose to the sky like a flagstaff mounted upon a raised platform. Father whispered, 'Phansi kaath . . .'

The gallows! I looked up, feeling something tug hard inside me. The ancient black rosewood caught my eye first. It looked like a headless man lost in the rigours of some penance, long right leg rooted firmly on the ground, short left leg bent and planted on the right. Here, this is the hook on which you tie the rope . . . this is the pulley for the rope . . . the noose should be here—Father was giving me lessons. I stood below the hook and looked up. At that moment, an invisible bird flew in through my left breast and began to beat its wings inside my body. The sound of beating wings rang clear and loud in my breast. Its sharp beak and talons bruised me from inside and I began to bleed from within.

'Here, this is the lever . . .' Father said. I went close slowly and touched it. I stared at it through hazy eyes. The iron rod which had borne the touch of my ancestors for many, many centuries. They had made sure that their mission continued through centuries—whenever one retired and proceeded towards death, he would dedicate to the world another soul who would continue to carry out justice. And here I was, finally, deputed to continue that mission. And what a mission, I sorrowed. A completely meaningless one. I caressed the lever. Then tried to raise it with a single pull. But it didn't budge; it was so rusty. Father too tried but it didn't move. We need oil, Babu, it is all rusty, Father complained to the policeman. I'll get it now, said the policeman. He and Father came down from the platform and made their way back to the veranda.

I was left alone with the gallows tree. Under the grey sky in the dim light, it looked like an incomplete sculpture. The lime plaster on the veranda behind it had begun to peel. When it struck me that some part of me had reached here after travelling through the ages, I felt strangely tranquil. This, maybe, is our lineage's ocean. It is this ocean that we seek, rushing towards it like the drops of water that flow in the Ganga. The hangman's job can't be a mechanical, bureaucratic government assignment, I felt. No female-born human can pull this lever without waging a war against herself and winning it. I sensed that someone was standing behind me and turned sharply to see Father there. A smile dawned slowly on his face.

'I was scared to bring you here along with the others yesterday,' he said. 'If you had taken fright in front of all the others, it would have been a blow for us. I am relieved now. Chetu, you are a brave girl, really.'

I lowered my head and remained silent. I alone knew that it was not a matter of courage; it was more of helplessness. This was my last refuge, this gallows tree.

'So many years have passed since I came here last . . . but each time I come, it feels as though I was here just the other day . . .'

Father looked around, wiping the sweat with his gamchha.

'Here, see this? This floor is so many years old. Look, there used to be a wall here . . . Dadu's calculations were still on it. In the old days, there used to be another door here. The sahibs used to watch the execution from there . . . Look, it is here that the DGP, the superintendent and the magistrate stand. Once the condemned man is brought in, and we make him wear a hood that covers his whole head and tie his hands, the magistrate will drop a red kerchief . . . that's the sign . . . the lever must be pulled then . . .'

I stared at Father, unable to utter a word.

'Presence of mind is the quality that a hangman cannot do without . . . don't think of anything else. Forget everything. See only the lever and the red kerchief. Dedicate your intelligence and your intellect to it.'

Father let out a sigh.

'All we do is carry out justice. Take, for example, Jatindranath whom we will soon punish. Remember the little girl he murdered. She was on her way to the medical shop, to get medicines for her mother. She must have cried and pleaded with him . . . but he did not listen to her. In that moment, he was terribly evil. It is the job of the government to find a way to heal that. We are sent to confiscate the life of the doer of injustice. It is our duty, our karma, the fruit of our deeds . . .'

Father raised an ardent gaze towards the ancient gallows tree and was quiet for a few moments.

'A clicking sound will be all that you hear when the noose tightens. That's the sound of the bones in the neck breaking. With this, the nerves that connect the body to the brain are cut, and the hanged man loses consciousness. If there is even a tiny flaw, for that single moment, his nails will grow longer. They will tear at the flesh. He will pass urine and stools and the rest . . .'

My soul-force turned to vapour! The mission that I had to take up sent its roots around my neck and strangled me like the banyan tree that had sprouted and spread upon my head. During the reign of the Sena kings, our ancestor Chitswarup Mullick had been the hangman. The Sena kings had defeated the last of the Pala kings, Madana Pala. Grandfather Chitswarup was deputed to execute the defeated king. While he was in power, Madana Pala had been like a lion. In fetters, he was but a lowly fox. In the end, coming face to face with death, the maharaja had whined like a mangy cur. Thakuma recounted this story from time to time so that we would remember that the majesty of emperors was merely a game of illusions played by power. Only Maharaja Nandakumar was an exception. But he was not a king, really. As I recalled that monarchs and mendicants figured alike among those who pissed and shat in sheer agony because of the hangman's unsure hand, my heart pounded desperately.

Father began to say something standing in front of the gallows, but fell silent at the sight of the policeman approaching with the oil. They began to grease the lever's screw. I looked up, moving towards the foot of the gallows tree again. Cobwebs covered the triangular space at the top. A speckled female spider slept peacefully in them. Its excessively bloated white belly looked like a big egg. Just then I heard heavy footsteps on the veranda and spun around. It was indeed he. Sanjeev Kumar Mitra. I was stunned. The bird which had flown inside me earlier began to beat its wings and wound me again.

74

'So, you sign a contract one day and violate it on the next! Grddha babu, you shouldn't have done this to me!' His voice resonated as if from within an upturned vessel.

I looked at Father, anxious.

'Sanju babu, why, what's wrong?' Father laughed loudly and went on oiling the screw.

'Nothing's wrong? Really? Did I not tell you clearly that Chetna's days belong to the channel from now?' His voice was filled with irritation.

'But you did not ask for today, did you?' Father was not yielding an inch. 'When we parted last evening, all that you asked was that she should participate in the programme on 1 June. Other than that, did we discuss anything at all about today? Don't get angry without reason, Sanju babu, we are government servants and this is our job. Shooting for the channel is yours. I haven't given my word that we will report to you each time we turn and toss, sneeze and shit. There's nothing to that effect in the contract. Even if there is, it is simply not practical.'

I saw clearly the anger rise in waves and lash about on Sanjeev Kumar Mitra's face; he was struggling to control it.

'I handed you five thousand rupees. Have you forgotten, Grddha da?'

'Sanju babu, you counted out just one thousand rupees. Hand me the rest, then we can talk.'

'But aren't there things more valued than money, Grddha da? Your word, for instance?'

'I have always kept my word, Sanju babu. But you are demanding that I keep a word that I never gave.'

For a minute, Sanjeev Kumar Mitra looked at Father and me. The veins in his temples throbbed hard. He smiled with an effort. 'If it were someone else, I'd have reacted quite differently. But you are not a stranger to me, Grddha da. You are the father of the girl whom I wish to marry. I cannot forget the respect due to my future father-in-law . . .'

'That's not in the contract!'

My retort was so swift that it surprised even me. Father lifted his head, gave me a look and went back to oiling the lever. Sanjeev Kumar Mitra was shocked. He trained a stern gaze on me. My left breast began to ache again. The old worm began to gnaw at my flesh again with its delicate but sharp teeth.

'Isn't she right? I will marry her, you said. But are there any documents? Is there any guarantee? Is it in our agreement? Or, are you two in love? My daughter has never said that she will marry only you. You said that, Sanju babu . . . and we didn't see you making any arrangements.' Father pointed out sharply.

'That's not in the contract,' I repeated.

A terrible turbulence seized me. The ache in my left breast became unbearable—as though it was being ripped out. I felt a demon crouching in his gaze, appearance and voice. I wanted to hate him.

'This is okay now,' Father said suddenly.

Sanjeev Kumar slowly shifted his gaze towards him.

'You'll have to pull it to really know,' said the policeman who was assisting Father. Father turned to say something when, without warning, Sanjeev Kumar Mitra stepped up.

'Oh, so this is the lever? Let me take a look?'

He touched it once. Face brimming over with curiosity, he winked at Father and the policeman and pulled the lever hard. A sound like a burp from a full tummy rose from the lever. Suddenly, the ground dropped away beneath my right foot. A thunderous crash, terrifying enough to make the ends of the earth shudder and shake, rent the air. I tried to hang on, but failed. With a terrified scream, without a noose around my neck, I descended into the netherworld, into which many thousands of human lives had fallen. Sanjeev Kumar Mitra jumped in after me. In that dark hole which reeked of the stench of vile creatures that fed on the shit and piss of the thousands of human beings who had died at the gallows, his hands crushed and mutilated my body. I knew then how painful the piercing roots of the banyan could be. The meaning of Thakuma's words about death signs also became clear to me.

'So that's not in the contract, eh?' He bit my lips hard and snarled.

The words echoed in the cellar like the furious growling of ghosts. He kicked my body, crushing it. More than sorrow, insult and rage shattered me. I realized that if the noose was in the wrong place because the length of the rope was wrong, men dying in agony passed not just urine and faeces but also semen. No one had told me. But a woman does not need special lessons to know that. That was the turning point in my story. After that, I did not have the heart to let him off.

10

For a long time, it was Avinash Sircar, who worked by the wayside on Strand Road, who gave Father his regular shave. We called him Sircar mama. I used to see him on the street on my way to the primary school on the other side of the cremation ground. He sat right next to Narayan da's shop, which came after the railway tracks and before the cremation ground, the one that sold bamboo litters for corpses. He would be shaving people's faces or cutting their hair, his body bent like a piece of wire, his dirty, ragged vest rolled right up to his chest like a woman's blouse. The light that reflected off his mirror which he hung from a nail hammered into a political party's flagstaff—a crack ran right through the mirror in the middle like a streak of lightning— could be seen even before one reached the railway tracks. We got to see in the mirror Sircar mama at work as his back was turned to us. Without turning around, he would shout, say hello to Sircar mama, Chetu ma! And gift me a grin showing all his scarred teeth with those sunken cheeks pulled back. Whenever he came to our house, he brought me tamarind sweets. Sircar mama would come straight to our tea shop to meet Father once his day's work was done. They read the newspapers to each other, listened to the news on radio and discussed politics. One day, I woke up to the news that a woman had been found dead near the railway tunnel. All of us ran there to look at the corpse. People milled around the body. I couldn't see anything and walked back disappointed; Sircar mama, who was shaving a stranger's face on the other side of the gate, comforted me through the mirror—never mind, Chetu, next time I'll lift you on my shoulders. He fished out two tamarind sweets from the waistband of his dhoti and held them out to me. In the days that followed, Thakuma, Ma and I, barely six or seven then, crowded at the door for news about the woman's dead body.

'The body of the woman found near the railway tunnel still unidentified—the police'

'The body found near the railway tunnel is that of Vijayamallika, missing from Sonagachi—the police'

'The killer of the woman found dead near the railway tunnel will be nabbed soon—the police.'

Each day, he read to us news of this sort. He even teased Father on the day the news 'Husband of the dead woman found' appeared.

'Hey, Grddha, work ahead for you!'

Father and everyone else who heard him laughed. Two months later, another woman died. This time, on the roadside, in Bhawanipore. The next morning, when Ma was plaiting my hair on our doorstep, we heard the din of a crowd in the distance. A large dog came running, pulling behind it someone in a white vest and khaki trousers. Four or five policemen chased after them, followed by a crowd. Police, police! Scared, Ma pulled the pallu of her sari over her head and stepped back into the house. The dog ran past me towards the railway tracks. I followed them, just one plait done. The train passed by just then. The dog stood beside the tracks, barking at it impatiently. The commuters stuck their heads out, enjoying the show. As soon as the train was gone, even before the tracks ceased to vibrate, the dog leapt across. It jumped on Sircar mama who sat with his back turned to us, getting the soap ready to shave someone's face. He fell and rolled on the ground with a scream; the dog bit him and dragged him on to the road. By then the policemen had surrounded him. What happened before my eyes was simply beyond a child's belief. The police took him right before us, hitting and shoving him. As he struggled to free himself from the policemen's grip, Sircar mama saw me. Chetu . . . Chotdi . . . Daughter, tell them to set Mama free, he screamed. I felt terribly helpless, really, really wanting, to run after the policemen and scratch their hands bloody or bite them and free Sircar mama. But after some time, the din of the crowd returned.

It was Ramu da who brought home the news he had heard from one of the men who had gathered and were talking: 'It was he who murdered those women. He's confessed everything!'

I felt as if I'd exploded from inside, shaken to my core. In the days that followed, the newspapers carried stories of how Sircar mama had killed four women who had disappeared from Sonagachi and dumped their bodies in different locations. There was a reason why I remembered him again when I opened my eyes after I had been brought out of the cellar beneath the gallows. When I gained consciousness, Father was

78

sitting beside me, looking totally worn out. An elderly doctor examined my pulse and said there was nothing to worry about. The back of my only pair of good clothes was torn. The glass bangles on both wrists had shattered and pierced my thighs and my back. No one took very seriously the wounds on my lips, breasts and stomach. Nor did they see the fatal wounds in my soul. Just then, the jail superintendent Sibdev Ghosh stormed in.

'What's happening? There is a limit to breaking the law! I know that you can tip my policeman's cap if you decide to do so, but my patience does have a limit.'

'My apologies, Sibdev babu.' Sanjeev Kumar Mitra sat up and folded his palms.

I saw only then that there was a big reddish blue mark on his forehead.

'Chetna was to spend all her time with our channel from now on. She's signed a contract. When I heard that these two had made such an important visit without letting me know, I simply forgot everything else.'

'Sibdev babu, this is our duty. We work for the government, not for the channel.'

'Sanjeev Mitra, Grddha da has a point there.'

Sanjeev Kumar got up and pointed to me. 'I wish to marry this young woman, Sibdev babu. Ever since I first saw her, I have only her on my mind.'

He acted it out even better than Father. I tried to control my face, but it turned bloodless.

'Ha! Good news indeed! What do you say, Grddha?'

Father shot me a sideways glance and smiled. 'I've no objection. He's been saying this for some time. But there should be some guarantee, some papers, for it?'

Sanjeev Kumar pulled out a little box from his pocket, took a gold ring from it and held it up. A small diamond glinted on it. Without any warning, he came close, took my right ring finger which was still throbbing with the pain he had inflicted on it earlier, and slipped on the ring.

'I have submitted evidence of my love in front of responsible police officers, the doctor and the girl's father.'

I felt as if my breath had stopped. If he had placed an ornament around my neck or arm, I would not have been so shocked. Sibdev Ghosh, the policemen and the doctor applauded. Father smiled slowly.

I got up with an effort. 'No . . . I don't need this . . .' My voice trembled as I said this.

Before I could complete my sentence, Sanjeev Kumar laughed aloud. 'How dark it was in there! Do you know, I have been scared of the dark since I was a child? But all I could think of was that I had to rescue Chetna somehow. Otherwise, am I crazy to jump from such a height?'

No one had an answer to that. I turned my eyes towards Father for support. But he rolled his eyes in anger. His look frightened me. In school and at home, I was taught never to utter a word against Father. And so all I could do was grit my teeth and bear the searing pain that racked my body. Father did not look at me even once until we reached home. Get inside the house only after you've had a bath—that was all he said.

I bathed. My whole body was bruised and hurting. For the rest of my life, the memory of falling into those depths from high above would be a recurring nightmare. And I have not been able to imagine a man more terrifying than the one who attacked my body with a smile. Kaku, Kakima and the children had left for Budge Budge before we got home. Father started drinking as soon as we reached. The fact that the bottle was Sanjeev Kumar Mitra's gift doubly infuriated me. When I came out of the bathroom Thakuma brought out a piece of string that had been blessed at the Kali temple and tied it on my wrist. I pulled the gold ring off my crushed finger and gave it to Ma.

'I don't want it. Give it back to him when he comes.'

'Bhagawan! Is this a diamond?' she asked, stunned.

'Let me see, let me see!' Thakuma came running.

'He's a good boy . . . loving fellow . . . but not for our Chetu . . .' said she. And became angry when Ma disagreed, saying that this was the greatest luck that would come by me.

'Girl, this is a family of hangmen, two thousand years old. There should be a boy to take it forward after Phani's days. Else, our family's profession dies.'

'You aren't going to say anything different. Very educated, he is . . . I want my daughter to escape this damned cellar.' Ma's response was firm.

'I am afraid of him . . .' I whispered slowly to Ramu da who was straining his ears to catch the conversation.

'He will not love you . . .' he whispered back. 'But will keep hunting you. And calling it love . . .'

'Do you remember old Sircar mama, Ramu da?' I asked him while untangling my hair. My waist-length hair lay on my back in wet tangled locks that looked like the roots of a banyan tree.

Ramu da sighed. 'How can one know what human beings are like deep inside? How can one peer deep?'

He spoke as if human beings were some alien species. I thought again about Sircar mama. Six months after he was arrested, one day, Sircar mama had appeared at the tea shop. Father saw him and rained abuses on him instantly.

'Grddha Mullick's house is not the place where robbers and murderers can gallivant. Get out! Out!'

'Grddha, don't give me up . . . I have no one else but you . . . I don't know anything about it, Grddha . . . they beat me so hard, I confessed . . .'

He folded his palms, weeping. Thakuma and Ma, who had been standing at the doorstep, bubbling angrily, now began to relent.

'Maybe it is true. He is a mild fellow . . . the police must have hit him bad . . .' Kaku, who was watching, said.

'Yes, yes, can human beings act so well? Could he walk around as if nothing has happened if he'd really murdered so many?' Ma chipped in innocently.

'Go away, woman, don't speak rubbish. It could be, and more besides. But this fellow's a meek sort. Maybe he lost his mind when he did it.' Thakuma too offered support.

But Father was adamant. Criminals cannot appear before a government servant like him, he insisted. I liked to believe that Sircar mama was innocent. For many months after, he continued to work in front of the cremation ground and fight the case. One day, when I went up close to him and asked if he had really done it, he smeared some shaving cream on my nose and laughed loudly. 'Chetu ma, you wait and see. Mama will win. And will then teach all these policemen a lesson!'

After that, each time he went to court for the hearings and returned, he would tell me with much happy hope, 'All the truth has come out

81

today. Didn't Mama tell you Mama has done no wrong? Those policemen laid a trap for me.'

The day before the judgment was pronounced on his case, Mama was waiting for me in the street when I came back from school.

'Tomorrow Mama's judgment will be out, Chetu ma,' lovingly, he told me. 'The court will set me free. After that, I want to teach them the lesson of their lives. Mama will bring Chetu a whole packet of chocolates, okay?'

I looked at him with hope. He took out a small bundle from the waistband of his dhoti and held it out to me. 'This is Mama's gift to Chetu. Keep it safe, it is your dowry when you get married!'

Hide it somewhere in the house where no one else will find it, he told me. Tomorrow when I return after winning the case, Mama will bring you a bigger gift, he promised. When we parted, he turned his cheek for a kiss. Very reluctantly, I kissed the sunken cheek covered with grey stubble. He caressed my head and grinned, showing his black teeth, and walked with me till we reached the other side of the railway tracks. I hid the bundle among my books and went home and, later, stowed it away in the big wooden box in which Ramu da kept his old books. When I came home from school the next day, a crowd had gathered around Father in the tea shop. They were talking of the death sentence that Avinash Sircar had received. Shattered, I wept in sheer disbelief, sobbing loudly. I will hang with my own hands the policeman who did this to an innocent man like him—I announced to Ramu da in between sobs.

'What wrong did the policeman do? He owned up to everything in court. Even pointed out the places where he had buried two women he'd killed earlier,' Ramu da told me angrily, raising his head from the book he was reading. I felt all the more ruined. A noose had tightened inside, stifling me. Why had he lied to me repeatedly if he had admitted to the crimes in court? I could make no sense of it. I tried to hate Sircar mama. I feared to tell anyone about the bundle he had given me. Within months, he was sentenced to death. He did not appeal to a higher court or submit a mercy petition. So the date of his execution was decided quickly. As the date neared, I became very uneasy. When Father began the puja to Kali, I began to quibble with Ma over trivial things.

After the Kali puja, after reverentially touching the box which held our ancient relics, after offering liquor to Grandfather Purushottam, after touching Thakuma's feet and pouring liquor into her mouth, after casting a look at us, Father set out. Kaku followed him obediently. When the jeep carrying Father vanished from view, I could not hold back my tears any more. That night, I screamed seeing in my sleep a ghoul shave his face in the cracked mirror that hung from the political party's flagstaff. The demon's got into the child, Thakuma screamed; she circled my head with a coin in her fist and set it apart for Kali. I pressed my face on Ma's breast and slipped into sleep, sobbing. The next day, I burned with fever. I did not go to school. Lying on Ramu da's cot, all bundled up, I wept away all the sorrows I could not speak of, with the fever as an excuse. Father walked in at high noon, drenched in sweat as if he had had a dip in the Ganga. That was the only time I ever saw him sober after a hanging.

'Oh, terrible day today,' he told Thakuma, who had just come in. 'My friend since childhood . . . him too, with this hand of mine . . .'

'Karma . . .' Thakuma tried to console him.

'When I went up to put the hood over his face, he smiled. Grddha, in the end, I made trouble for you, didn't I, he asked. I had nothing to say. But somehow I managed, this is my food, Avinash da, forgive me. He shut his eyes still smiling, and raised his head to me.'

Father's voice was broken with terrible agitation. He then came to me—I was straining to hear his words, my heart was pounding—and felt my forehead, bidding me, 'Come, get up soon. Let's go and see Sircar mama off.'

Taken by surprise, I pulled open my eyelids and looked at Father.

'The poor fellow . . . there was no one to receive him . . . how could I dump him there?'

'But! Wicked man! Murdered four!' Ma protested.

'Even if he killed not four but forty, a guilty man can die but once. And there is no greater reparation than death,' Father proclaimed, his voice glum.

'The child is ill, let her be.' Ma tried to oppose him again.

'No, she must come. Grddha, make our Chetu offer me a ball of rice—that was his last request.'

83

Father's voice fell again. Everyone fell silent. I alone shuddered in fright. Father went out to arrange the funeral. Thakuma followed him with her stooped walk. Those days, the Nimtala Ghat had only wooden pyres. Father bought the wood for Sircar mama's pyre with the remuneration he had received as the hangman. That was my first journey to the cremation ground to see anyone off.

When Ma left me to go shut the tea shop, I took out the little bundle Sircar mama had given me and opened it. Held within a piece of red-bordered cloth, four finger rings bared their teeth at me. I hid them in the pocket of my frock. The dead body which had arrived in a jerking, juddering cart was lifted into a bamboo litter bought from Narayan da's. I burst into tears again. I wept as I circled the pyre. When the pyre began to burn, we immersed ourselves three times in the Ganga. The third time, I dropped the bundle quietly into the water. A miraculous peace descended on me. By the time we came back home, my fever had abated completely.

When it hit the tangles in my hair, my right ring finger, which Sanjeev Kumar Mitra had cruelly crushed, ached. I yearned to wash away the dirt from the bruises that my body and soul had suffered in that cellar where the semen of countless men hanged at the gallows, including Sircar mama, must have fallen. Sircar mama's rings left me when I had thrown them into the Ganga. But Sanjeev Kumar's ring stayed stuck on my finger even though I had pulled it off. I had loved Sircar mama. But the keepsake that he had offered a child was a share of spoils. Some sixteen years later, Sanjeev Kumar Mitra had done the same. He too had forced on me a share of his crime.

11

On 1 June, Father got up late and began his day with booze. When the channel's vehicle arrived at six in the evening, he was dead to the world. The driver was impatient, so I set out alone. It was not natural courage but sheer helplessness that goaded me on. Bruised, my body and soul still seethed. The Bibek of my life's jatra ran behind the car, screaming. The CNC studio was on Ashutosh Mukherjee Road in a compound full of gulmohar trees. Like the jail, I was seeing it too for the first time. Many rooms, bright shiny floors, smartly dressed busy men and women everywhere. A pretty usher led us in amid the constant stream of chatter that flowed from the many TV screens on the walls. And so, I wore make-up for the first time in my life. The chairs and mirrors in the make-up room reminded me of Kaku's salon. There was a TV in the salon too, just the size of a notebook, which played love songs. On the TV in the make-up room, the chief minister was making a statement, that the prime minister's office is not a shopping mall. Many problems that go back to 1999 still continue to plague Bengal, he grumbled; the soil erosion in the Ganga, the closure of the cotton mills, poverty and the reduction of interest rates on small savings are all making the lives of people miserable. I baulked at the prospect of the Ganga all filled up. If all the water dried up and the riverbed was exposed, along with the skeletons of animals, men and women, Sircar mama's cloth bundle would also become visible. I saw my painted face in the mirror and felt tears in my eyes.

A slight, fair young man, his curly hair caught in a ponytail, took me to the studio. Sanjeev Kumar Mitra sat in front of a white-topped table. He greeted me enthusiastically. The bluish mark of dead blood was no longer to be seen on his forehead. Blindingly bright lights were set up around me. My eyes burned. A gigantic tree, too heavy for me to carry, grew on top of my head. Its roots penetrated my throat and heart. In between the roots, a bird beat its wings, desperate, fearing for its life. I sat in my faded salwar kameez and the tattered dupatta Ma had hastily darned, waiting for questions, wary that he would pull the lever unexpectedly and throw me down into the damned depths.

'All around the world, there is a call to end the death penalty. But the government of Bengal has decided to go ahead with Jatindranath Banerjee's death sentence. The chief minister's statement that the government values the human rights of the victim more than those of the perpetrator has also become controversial. On top of this, the government has appointed a woman to the post of hangman for the first time in India. Many women's organizations around the world have welcomed the appointment of Phanibhushan Grddha Mullick's daughter Chetna Grddha Mullick as his assistant. Chetna will speak to us about the latest developments every day until the date of execution. Let us talk to her now. Namaskar, Chetna, this is the second week since you received the government order. What have your experiences been in these two weeks as a hangwoman?'

'The question about these two weeks is irrelevant. My experiences stretch back over two thousand years,' I said, struggling to control my heart. I was feeling just what Father must have felt on the stage singing and acting. People don't want simple truths. They want sweet, blatant lies. I loved the trepidation that appeared on Sanjeev Kumar's face. Surely, the *dhak-dhak-dhak* sound that I heard was his heart beating. He gave me a searching look.

'From my earliest childhood, I have grown up listening to tales about my forefathers. Their experiences are the wealth that belongs to all of us in the family. One of them—the most notorious man in our family—was Kala Grddha Mullick. Once, a condemned man whom he was leading to the gallows kicked him hard and he fell on the ground. The hanging was carried out at the appointed hour, but my forefather's hip was sorely injured. Back then there were hangings every day, so he could not find the time to take care of it. His posture became twisted, permanently. From then on, he carried an iron staff to dispatch the condemned man instantly, hitting him hard on the head if he did not die soon enough on the noose.'

Sanjeev Kumar's face lit up with interest. I suddenly gained confidence, realizing intuitively that the words of whoever speaks of death, however slight she may be, carry inflated value. It was not at all likely that the famous writers or artists who had sat in this chair before me had had anything more weighty to say than my Thakuma, Bhuvaneswari Devi.

'Chetna, have you ever tried putting a noose around a person's neck?'

'The midwives of then and the doctors of now are of the view that infants born in our family learn to make a noose when they are still in their mother's womb.'

Sanjeev Kumar Mitra was taken aback again.

'What preparations have you made in the past two weeks?'

'There was nothing I could do until the formal order of the government arrived. After I got it, I went with my father to meet the IG. Then we went to the Alipore Correctional Home and examined the gallows and the rope. The rest we need to do a week before the event.'

'This is work that can throw even men off balance. Do you think that a woman like you, Chetna, is capable of it?'

'There is nothing a woman can't do.'

Sanjeev Kumar shot me a penetrating look again.

'Doesn't the sense of sin at having to kill another human being bother you?'

'I don't kill, I merely pull the lever.'

It sounded like a joke to him. He laughed. 'Everyone knows that is just an excuse.'

'Who registers the case against the accused? Who investigates it, and makes the arrests? The government's police. Who pronounces the sentence? The government's court of law. Who gives it assent? The head of the state, the President of India. Who decides the date of execution? The government's court of law, again. Who keeps the accused confined? The jails run by the government. After all this, one day, at dawn, at four-thirty, who drops the red handkerchief? Even that is a magistrate appointed by the government. So how is the hangman responsible?'

Words just flowed, surprising me. Sanjeev Kumar looked rather flustered. Maybe because a mere Plus Two-educated female like me seemed fairly unshaken even after her experience in the cellar beneath the gallows.

'But, Chetna, the condemned man does not actually die until the lever is pulled. That is the difference . . .' He let out a long sigh.

'The hangman merely hangs. It is the court that orders that the condemned man be hanged by the neck till he dies.'

'So you mean to say that there is nothing wrong in what you do?'

'How are we to know what is right and what is wrong in our doings? If that were really possible, wouldn't we all have become gods? Maybe what I do is wrong. But the court of law and the state say that it is not wrong under the existent system. All that a poorly educated woman like me can do is trust them.'

'Chetna, you speak very well.'

'I listen carefully to the discussions on your channel every day, Sanjeev babu.'

The ponytailed young man gestured from behind the camera that it was time to end the show with my words. Sanjeev Kumar turned towards the camera, whipping out the broad smile meant for the viewers.

'Thought-provoking ideas from Chetna Grddha Mullick in *Hangwoman's Diary* every day exclusively on CNC. Call us this time tomorrow to speak directly with Chetna. Cell phone subscribers, please call the numbers appearing at the bottom of the TV screen . . . See you again, same channel, same time, tomorrow!'

When I came out of the make-up room after wiping my face clean, Sanjeev Kumar Mitra invited me into a room which was marked 'Director, Programmes'. Inside, a very fair, middle-aged man with an impatient expression was speaking on the phone to someone. He gestured towards a chair. Sanjeev Kumar pulled up one and sat down. Neither he nor his superior asked me to sit. And so I stood by the door.

'Harish babu, this is the Chetna Mullick I've been talking about. I'm hoping the wedding will be in September . . .'

The man grunted, putting down the phone, but still impatient.

'The programme's been appreciated till now. Chetna is cooperating really well,' said Sanjeev Kumar. He looked as if he was acting out a well-prepared part in a play.

'Okay, all the best for the programme. And all the best for a happy married life.'

'Thank you, Babu,' Sanjeev Kumar replied.

When we came out, he turned to me with a keen look. 'A taxi's been arranged to take you home, Chetna.'

'I'll take the bus.' My words were full of distaste.

'No, all this is included in our contract,' he said, looking straight into my eyes. I, however, pulled my eyes away. When I got into the taxi, he also got into the back seat with me. His nearness and scent set my heart beating wildly. Desire and disappointment tormented me in equal measure. My hands tingled. I began, involuntarily, to fashion a noose with my worn dupatta. If he hurts me again, no matter what happens, I will teach him a lesson—I was sure about that.

The taxi moved forward. The city flowed past like a river of darkness upon which mud lamps, glowing and dead, floated. Shops, big and small; apartment blocks, new and old. Bustling wayside markets. Waiting sheds in bus stops where washing lay drying. Cloth cradles swinging on roadside handrails. My head was reeling. A cry of sorrow rose up within me, hankering to be released.

Sanjeev Kumar Mitra stopped the vehicle and paid the fare. He then got out and held the door open for me.

'What place is this?' I asked, bewildered.

'Lal Bazar, don't you know?' he asked.

Through my mind passed Thakuma's evocative descriptions of the four villages of Kalighat, Suttanutti, Govindpur and Chitpur which had survived on weaving and agriculture and selling fish before the Englishman Job Charnock disembarked on the banks of the Hooghly. She sounded as if she had indeed seen them with her own eyes, so haunting was her storytelling. When the enterprising Seths reached the banks of the Hooghly, they cleared the forests and set up the village of Govindpur. There they built and dedicated a temple to their deity, Govindji. One branch of the Seth family migrated north from Govindpur to Kalighat which belonged to our family those days. The path from Chitpur to Kalighat was through a dense forest. On the way was the Shiva temple built by an abandoned prince named Chowringeenath. The Ganga, in those days, had a wider bed and extended past Strand Road. The Seths and Basaks built their houses to the west of Lal Digi. The villages that poor folk like us built after clearing the jungle for the Seths they sold later to the British at hefty prices. Our fields and weaving sheds became their Maidan, a vast open ground. Because the stories of our forefathers were also stories of Kolkata, they spoke of not just death and love, but also of the land, loving and losing it to traders. I remember, when I was in class eight, Jyoti Basu initiated shilpayan, inviting industrialists, and Thakuma knew what it would bring. Traders arrive by water—they are not of the land, she declared in anger. To seize the land, they need, power.

Amidst the city's sounds, the scent of mustard oil and masala enveloped me. As if reading my mind, Sanjeev Kumar bought two packets of jhalmuri from a vendor nearby and held out one to me. Rice crisps, peanuts and cashewnuts blended together had the most mouthwatering aroma and a wonderful spicy edge. As we ate standing right in the middle of the swirling city crowds, I felt teary again. I did want to be carefree, to laugh and share jhalmuri with the man I loved, but we did not acknowledge each other's hearts. Sanjeev Kumar dusted the last of the jhalmuri off his palms and walked briskly towards a large textile shop with a prominent white signboard on which its name was written in bold purple letters.

'You will have to come every day to the studio till the twenty-fourth, Chetna. You aren't allowed to wear the same clothes each day.'

'I don't need clothes you've paid for.' I was livid.

He did not like the firmness of my tone. 'These days people are what they wear. Don't forget, Chetna, the whole world is watching you.'

I was somewhat taken aback.

'Don't say, "but that isn't in the contract". That need not be in the contract. And, do remember, this is the first time I am buying a girl clothes.'

When he took off his glasses, the city lights fell on his eyes and made them brighter. I felt tiny nooses tightening within me.

'When my mother was alive I didn't get the chance to buy her clothes . . .'

He looked deeply into my eyes again and smiled. Terrified for my life, I abruptly walked ahead. I had begun to fear this man deeply. His threat to fuck me at least once, the ache in my breast, the innumerable injuries he had inflicted on me in the cellar below the gallows—all these raised their hoods together menacingly. Had Sircar mama approached those four women similarly?

The darkness of the city and its neon lights made me terribly cowardly. I who had never felt any fear even in the milling crowds of Nimtala Ghat. But standing there on a broad street in the centre of the city, I feared the huge buildings might collapse on my head and the large vehicles would smash me to the ground. The city looked like a cellar with many lights. I did not know the way back home.

As I stood there not knowing where to go next, an aged bangle seller clad in a shirt with a tattered collar and trousers too short for him came up to me and begged, 'Madam, come, take a look at these!'

I had no money in my purse, but my eyes fell briefly on the bangles.

'Take these bangles, Madam. Three hundred a pair. Excellent hand work, Madam. Look at these beads, they will never fall.'

Because he hadn't noticed my torn dupatta, he pressed a few bangles into my hand. I enjoyed the weight and the coolness of the blood-red bangles set with white and green stones.

'Which bangle do you want, Chetna?'

Sanjeev Kumar Mitra's voice at my back ruffled me.

'I don't want any,' I snapped as I put the bangles back on the heap.

'Babu, Madam liked these. Excellent work, Babu . . . just three hundred rupees.'

'Why! Are these gold bangles?' he exclaimed rudely as he examined the bangles.

'Babu, I will give them to you for two hundred and seventy-five rupees.'

'Fifty, that's it,' he said.

I felt quite bad. To value those bangles so low was to insult both the bangle seller and the bangles.

'I don't want them, let's go,' I began to hurry him.

But Sanjeev Kumar hung on, rummaging for some more time in the bangle heap, cracking jokes with the bangle seller. 'Okay, okay, if you don't want them, Chetna, let us go.'

He walked ahead in a greater hurry than me, hailed a taxi, and got into the front seat. We rode in silence. He only opened his mouth to tell the driver to park the taxi at the turning from Rabindra Sarani to Strand Road. When I opened the door and got out, he too stepped out and accompanied me to the house. There was a line of waiting vehicles on the road which nearly formed a whole wall, because the railway gate was closed. I sought a small opening in between the many different kinds of hearses to cross the road.

'One minute . . .'

He came up in the shadow of a vehicle and caught me by my arm. When his fingers pressed on my wrist where the wounds from the broken bangles were beginning to fester, it hurt. I yelped in pain

'Let me make amends . . .'

Before I could stop him, he had pushed a few bangles on to my wrists. Then, opening my palms, he kissed them, the fine bristles of his moustache gently brushing my skin. And then he went away. My palms felt scalded, then frozen. Suddenly, the circular train to the south passed, leaving the ground quivering. The vehicles waiting to go to the Ghat began to move. In the light of an ambulance, I saw my wrists. The juices in my mouth dried up. All my wounds filled with pus and ached. Blood-red bangles with green and white stones. Stolen, without a trace of conscience, in full view of the city, before our very eyes—mine and the bangle seller's.

I have never been able to make sense of Sanjeev Kumar Mitra. He washed away all his dirt on my body as if it were the Ganga in which he immersed himself. He made sure first that his spiritual merit was assured—and then lamented the perils that the erosion posed. What I had done to deserve such scorn, I could not fathom. Rankling insult and seething anger drove me crazy. Much later, after I had given him his rightful due, whenever I remembered this day, I felt like yelling: *Tomar amaar shathe oirokom kora uchit chhilo na!* You shouldn't have done that to me!

12

'We're old-fashioned folk, Grddha da.'

While Manavendra Bose spoke to Father in that majestic voice that sounded like the mighty roar of a lion, I sat huddled in corner of the kitchen, listless as a bundle of rags, my body sore and aching. What's happened to you, Thakuma and Ma asked me many times. Can't, can't, I told Ma. Did something get into the child in the cellar, Ma asked in a controlled whisper. Worried, Thakuma got kumkum and sacred ash from the Kali temple and the Shiva temple next to the cremation ground and smeared them on me. But something still hung heavy on my heart. It was not a heaviness which could be eased by three dips in the Ganga. And besides, I had begun to fear the Ganga that was more mud than water. It lay prone, glinting black and only too ready to let anyone dip themselves any number of times and immerse in it any kind of dirt.

'Buying someone off . . . getting a contract signed . . . I'm surprised. Such bonded labour in this Bengal where the Left Front rules?' Bose babu's voice rose again.

'Ha! Bose babu, not just now . . . haven't you people ruled us always? The government and the party are just toys. Is there anything that won't happen in this great country if the media decides to make it happen?'

'I have never thought of the work I do in those terms,' Bose babu's voice was full of dejection. 'Where is Chetna? She spoke really well on TV yesterday! What a talented child she is, Grddha da! If only you would educate her properly instead of sending her to this nonsensical—'

'Bhagawan! What are you saying, Bose babu? Who'd know her if all she did was get a degree somehow, scrape through to a government job and get lucky enough to marry someone? Look who she has become today! Has she not become a symbol of strength and self-respect for the whole world?'

'It will be so only if it was her own decision.'

Father thought for a moment. 'But you shouldn't feel bad, Bose babu. I am still the chief hangman, of course. I won't speak to any other channel or newspaper till Jatindranath's hanging. Instead, just pay me ten thousand rupees, what do you say?'

Because I couldn't hear his reply, I got up and peeped into the tea shop through the window of the kitchen. Bose babu was staring at Father. He then began laughing, but glumly.

'No, Grddha da, I am happy if this brings you some money. But our generation simply can't stomach the idea of buying news.'

'What's wrong with that? I provide you with what you need to make your paper sell, and you give me enough for my livelihood. That way don't we both survive?'

'I do this work for the passion of it. Buying happiness or recognition brings me no passion. It's like going to Sonagachi. I am not queasy about sleeping with a girl from there. But if I go to her room, I must love her. She too must be ready to sleep with me without payment.'

'Oh Bose babu, then you are done for!' Father guffawed. 'You are more educated than me. You are more familiar with the world. But there's one thing—I know that the end justifies the means. No matter where she is—inside Sonagachi or inside the house—a woman serves

93

the same purpose, right? It is just that one is called a wife. Otherwise what is the difference? This is like that. You want news. I'll give it to you. You can run behind an ambulance or a hearse on Strand Road, take pictures in secret and make news. Or, you can simply drink the tea I serve you, record my story and publish it. Both are the same. The second is a bit easier.'

When he got up to leave, Father got up too.

'Bose babu, you must meet that boy, Sanjeev Kumar Mitra. What a bright chap! He knows how to turn something into news. It's he who got Chetna her job, and the moment she got it, he pulled out the stamp paper! To tell you the truth, I bowed to him!'

Bose babu smiled at Father. 'This is their time, isn't it? Anyway, I heard that four infants have died in Nashipur from the influenza . . . I have to go there.'

'Influenza? But they said yesterday on TV that it was some new kind of fever?'

Bose babu laughed. 'Aren't those infants the offspring of the poor? They are so malnourished, even a strong wind could kill them. And your Mitra babus are not interested in signing contracts with them. Their faces aren't good enough for TV.'

I saw him walk ahead without waiting for Father's reply, dragging his bad leg into the street crowded with hearses. Soon two vehicles with press stickers on them swept in. Before those who had come in the first vehicle could get out, two young men who had arrived in the second one leapt out and ran into the tea shop. The occupants of the first vehicle stood at a distance, quarrelling among themselves. Ma came up behind me at the window and asked who it was.

'They haven't come for tea, for sure . . .' I murmured. My guess was right. Father was shaking hands with them. They spoke to Father in hushed whispers.

'Oh no, that can't be . . . it isn't a matter of ten or twenty thousand . . . I have given my word, and I must honour it . . . he who can't keep his word is as good as dead. He's then no longer good enough to be hanged, leave alone be a hangman.'

Father fanned himself with his gamchha and kept resisting them, hard-faced as a merchant. In between he also threw a glance at those who had come in the first vehicle and were still standing outside. They waved at him. Father excused himself for a minute, went to the end of the veranda past the window of the kitchen, and spoke with them. I heard him.

'Babu, this is not about Chetna. We've reached an agreement about that.'

They pleaded with Father in hushed tones. He looked at his watch and asked them to return after some time. He returned to his chair, looked at the men from the second vehicle, and said in laughing tones: 'They say that I will do, because after all, I am the chief hangman. Chetna is only my assistant, isn't she? And she has no experience, anyway.'

I turned away from the kitchen window and went to Ramu da's room. Ma had helped him lie face down. I saw the reddish welts on the fair, beautiful skin on his back. When I went closer and sat down on the bare floor, he turned his neck towards me and looked at me with interest.

'Yesterday you looked really pretty on TV.'

A smile bloomed by itself on my face.

'You have become a big star!'

He sighed deeply. 'It's possible that all this will die down after the twenty-fourth . . . always remember that.'.

As I struggled to smile, he fixed his eyes on my face and began to say something. Just then, I heard Kaku's voice. My ears became sharp. He was speaking with two young men.

'I'll get all that done . . . but just one thing, make sure I get my commission.'

Ramu da and I looked at each other.

'What's the use of getting Chetna? Isn't Phani da the world-famous hangman still? He's famous all over India! Not because of anything else—his hand hasn't erred even once.' Kaku was about to say something more, but saw me and withdrew hurriedly.

Ramu da smiled.

'So it's selling and buying everywhere. Those who buy, they then sell . . . those who sell, they go on to buy . . .'

That day, it was the vehicle which came to pick up Father that arrived first, at six o'clock. Another vehicle followed, asking for Kaku. Then, CNC's vehicle came to pick me up. And soon we will see vehicles arriving to swoop up Thakuma, Kakima and Ma, joked Ramu da. After I reached the studio and they had done my make-up, the make-up man handed me a new outfit.

'Chetna, Mitra sir said you must wear this.'

As I was wondering what to do, Sanjeev Kumar walked in looking very impatient. Why isn't she ready yet, he scolded the make-up man. I was reminded of the day Kaku had bought a rusty chair for the salon. He had applied a coat of red paint over its flaking blue to make it look new. All objects are obliged to submit to such a process, I thought, in bitter self-contempt. I went into the changing room with the dress. It was tea-brown with gold trimmings on the neck and sleeves. It hurt my bruised body but I felt like a new person.

When I came out, Sanjeev Kumar cast an assessing gaze on me. 'You look good,' he said. 'And you must speak a bit seriously from now on. We need something to hold the viewers' attention till the twenty-fourth. It is impossible to shoot inside the jail. That's why we are focusing on the hangman.'

I did not respond.

Someone came up and handed him a slip of paper. He looked up at me incredulously. 'Grddha Mullick is on AVA? Is that true?'

I remained silent.

'If that's true, then it's Chetna's job to make sure that their TRP isn't higher than ours.'

He sounded annoyed. We saw Father on a TV screen on the other side of the glass wall, speaking animatedly.

'Your father has a way with words, Chetna. He can sense what the viewers want and keep them glued to the screen. I expect the same from you. You must deliver something that he can't.'

That was an order. Clearly, Sanjeev Kumar was uneasy. He was not bubbling with his usual confidence when he began the show.

'The distance to the gallows has become even shorter, Chetna. What preparations have you made in these last few days?'

'We went to the jail and examined the ropes. We found one that will suit Jatindranath. It has already been used to hang two prisoners. But it is in good condition, so we have decided to reuse it.'

I added as much seriousness as I could to my words.

'Though I did feel a bit afraid when I held it, the fact that it was handled by my father, grandfather, and his father and grandfather before him, made me feel proud too. The hangman's job is not an easy one. There are people who get frightened at the mention of a hangman. But they forget this is also a kind of work.'

'One second, Chetna—there is a viewer on the line. Let us hear what he has to say . . . Hello, may I know who is calling?'

'Hello . . . this is Biswas Chakrabarti . . . I would like to ask Chetna . . . Madam, it is really sad that a young woman like you should sit on TV and make such speeches. Is it right for all the criminals in the world to be murdered? No! They must be turned into good human beings. We need to change them, Madam, change them . . .'

Sanjeev Kumar Mitra turned to me. I said blank-facedly, 'If someone can be reformed and not put to death, I welcome that. But it doesn't work out that way many a time. If the death of a criminal can reform or even deter many others, what is wrong in that?'

I then turned towards Sanjeev Kumar.

'My dadu was fond of the rope from the Yamuna Company in Uttar Pradesh. The company is closed now. The only son of the owner fell in love with a young woman. When his father opposed their love, they tried to elope. His father brought him back home by force, locked him up, and set a bunch of strong men to keep watch on him. That evening when the father opened the door, he found his son hanging from the ceiling by a rope made by his own company!'

I tried once again to smile and look straight into Sanjeev Kumar's eyes as if nothing out of the ordinary had happened.

'This completely shattered the father. The company was closed for a long time. Finally, a seth from Bombay bought it. The father happened to see the seth's wife when he went to the Grand Hotel, where the seth was staying, to sign the sale deed. It was the same girl his son had been in love with. He saw with his own eyes the agony she was suffering on account of that old love affair; he was devastated. He left immediately, not waiting even to receive the payment from the seth. Two days later, he hanged himself.'

Because people love drama, I paused for a moment, keeping Father's image in my mind. Sanjeev Kumar's eyes were fixed on my face in rapt attention. Then I let out a long sigh, and in a chilly voice, said, '. . . and he too had hanged himself with his own company's rope.'

'Oh! Is there any proof of this?' Sanjeev Kumar asked.

'All stories do not need proof,' I continued, after I had gazed steadily at him in silence. 'The company owner only knew how to make the rope; he did not know how to make a noose. After he had decided to kill himself, he came to our house to see Dadu.'

Sanjeev Kumar's face brightened with interest.

'But Dadu and my father were not at home that day. Only Kaku was home, playing about. He is the son my thakuma had in her old age—Sukhdev Grddha Mullick. Younger than my father by twenty-three years. The company owner came in his car. His servant deposited a heavy coil of rope in our front yard. He told Thakuma that he wanted to make sure of its quality, to see whether it would make a good noose. Kaku climbed on to the coil playfully while they talked. When Thakuma turned after telling the company owner that my father had gone off to act in a play and would be late, she saw that Kaku, who was just five or six then, had already made a noose with the rope.'

'And then?'

'The owner was very pleased. He left after showering us with many gifts. Soon we heard news of his death. Only much later did we realize that he had hanged himself with the noose that Kaku had made unwittingly.'

'Did this really happen?'

I smiled, forgetting that the man sitting in front of me was someone I desired with one corner of my heart and despised with the rest of it. The company owner really did commit suicide. That Kaku had made a fatal noose while still a child was also true. Only, it wasn't the company owner who had died of that noose. It was also true that a merchant who suffered terribly from an incurable illness had once called Kaku into his shop, plied him with fresh jalebis and made him tie a noose in return.

The crowd that gathered to see his corpse dangling from the ceiling of his shop had reached our doorstep. That was the first time the police came in search of Kaku. Thakuma always grieved that he could never tie a noose properly after that terrible ordeal.

After the programme, when I changed back into my faded old garments and came out, Harish Nath was speaking with Sanjeev Kumar Mitra. Seeing me, his lips twisted into a smile. 'When the ratings come there's going to be stiff competition between daughter, father and uncle. Let's see who wins!'

'Baba has a lot of experience,' I said, my head bowed.

'It's not experience that counts on television; it's how you present it.' His voice was disdainful.

I did not respond.

That day too Sanjeev Kumar Mitra had arranged for a taxi to take me home. When he came up as if to see me off, I gathered all my mental strength and, sounding as warm as I could, asked, 'Aren't you coming?'

Because he wasn't expecting that question, he looked at me quizzically. I smiled at him again. His face, on which a dark shadow had fallen because of the yellowish light outside, changed in expression slightly. Trying to control my fingers, which had already begun to twist my dupatta, I got into the back seat of the vehicle, throwing him an inviting look. After a moment's hesitation, Sanjeev Kumar Mitra accepted it. When the purple-on-white signboard of the textile shop where he had taken me the previous evening came into view, I asked the driver to stop. The bangle seller was in the same place as the day before, selling his wares. Come, I invited Sanjeev Kumar Mitra again. My body ached from top to toe.

A few young women were crowding around the bangle seller. The alluring scent that wafted around them announced these women were rich and glamorous. I slunk in through that crowd towards the bangle seller, and told him, 'Dada, weren't some bangles stolen from your shop the other day? I have come to return them.'

The man grabbed the bangles I held out to him. When he was sure that these were indeed the missing bangles, he became very angry. He threw a sharp look at Sanjeev Kumar Mitra, who was standing behind me petrified, and jumped up and caught hold of his collar.

'Thief! No one will catch you if you wear white trousers and shirt, eh? Do you really need to grab from the rice bowls of poor folk like us?'

The young women now looked at us.

'Oh God! Sanjeev Kumar Mitra!'

Recognizing him, they raised their shrill voices. I saw with my own eyes Sanjeev Kumar Mitra crumble like the Pala king in Thakuma's tale. I will never forget the sight of him shrugging off the bangle seller's arm and running away to safety. In the melee and the darkness, I too escaped into the taxi.

'Where is . . .?' asked the driver.

'He's not coming. Let's go to Strand Road.'

The scent of fish doused with mustard and green chillies cooking in the shorse bata khal greeted me when I reached home. I went straight to the tap and had a long bath. Then I shared the news of the city with Ramu da and Ma; consoled Thakuma who was murmuring to herself about the lost gold coin, her hand-held fan moving mechanically; and heartily ate my dinner of parathas and fish curry. I went to bed that night with the same sense of relief I had felt when I dipped myself three times in the Ganga and got rid of Sircar mama's stolen wealth. In the heady heights of victory I wanted to hum a song. The same Tagore song which I had proofread in Maruti Prasad's press: *Jodi tor dak shune keu na ashe tobe ekla chalo re* . . . Suddenly I remembered, during the Emergency, they had broken Manavendra Bose's leg for singing this song aloud. Twenty-six of Rabindranath's songs were banned in those days. *If no one answers your call, then set out alone* . . .

13

'What place is this, Dada?'

We were trapped in the middle of an unbroken chain of traffic. The lustreless sun of six o'clock looked like a burned-out cow dung kiln. Bored, I turned to the driver.

Surprised at my ignorance, he said, 'Lal Bazar.'

My eyes widened in enthusiasm as I looked out. I spotted an old two-storeyed building with banyan saplings growing in its windowsills and pipes, and a new one with five floors rising up next to it with fancy glass panels and all. Sweat-soaked people hurried up and down the street. They crowded in front of the shops selling bags and belts. A thin boy was selling cotton candy, which I had craved when I was a schoolgirl. Sadness and pity overcame me when I saw in my mind that little girl who had skipped down the Ghat road whenever she managed to get a few coins from her mother, ecstatic at the taste of the hair-like strands of that whitish-coloured sweet in her mouth. I leaned back against the comfortable seat of the air-conditioned vehicle like a rich woman and tried to see if the bangle seller from the day before was around. The Coolie Bazar was probably somewhere near. That was the place where the Indian named Nandakumar, who had borne the title of maharaja, was put to death. The day he ascended the gallows, everyone in our family fasted and prayed. The hangman of those times, my ancestor Manohar Dev Grddha Mullick, fasted continuously and observed a vow of silence for seven whole days. The sun of justice has set, he lamented, and the hangman is but a hired assassin now. He gave up the executioner's job and took up farming for the rest of his life. He had been a hangman for forty-four years. He was just sixty when he left the job. He lived another forty-four years as a farmer.

Maharaja Nandakumar's was a story which always left Thakuma choked with passion. He was a faithful courtier of Nawab Mir Jafar and was respected all over Bengal. It was the nawab who had bestowed upon him the title of maharaja. When Warren Hastings demanded bribes from the nawab's widow Munni Begum, an infuriated Nandakumar complained to the governor-general and the Bengal Council of the East India Company. There was evidence that proved that Warren Hastings had amassed forty lakh rupees illegally, he contended in his complaint. But Hastings sent him to prison, claiming the evidence was forged. A jury consisting of the chief justice of the Supreme Court, Sir Elijah Impey, ten Englishmen and two men from elsewhere, heard the case. They ruled that the three witnesses Nandakumar had produced were not trustworthy. They were punished for bearing false witness. On 5 August, Nandakumar was hanged on a special platform erected near Coolie Bazar.

That was a day when the pride of the Indian flew high in British Kolkata, Thakuma would say, completely overcome. When he walked from the jail to the gallows, Nandakumar was serene and calm. His walk was as dignified as a maharaja's. Thousands of people had gathered there to witness the hanging early that morning. When he went up to put the mask on him, Grandfather Manohar held the maharaja's hands and sobbed uncontrollably. 'Do your work,' commanded the maharaja with a smile. Grandfather Manohar made him wear the mask, still tearful. He then slipped the noose around Nandakumar's neck. It was all over in a few seconds. My precursor did not claim his customary remuneration; he ran straight to the Ganga. Immersing himself in the river a thousand and eight times did not give him back his breath. As she described this event, Thakuma would cull out its lessons for me: 'Never accept favours from the high and mighty. If you do, you will have to put up with all their evil deeds.'

Thakuma's story always raised questions in my mind.

'Did Lal Mohan Seth really dig Lal Digi?'

'Of course! That's why it has his name.'

'The British built the red-walled Fort William near Lal Digi and because its red shadow fell on the water, it got the name Lal Digi,' Ramu da, who had been listening, intervened.

'Did Lal Mohan Seth dig it all on his own?'

'No, no, he hired thousands of labourers. Some poor members of our family were there too.'

'Then how can it be in just the seth's name?'

'My dear girl, people remember only the names of those who spend the money. There are many who labour, but very few provide the cash . . . it's easier to remember them,' said Thakuma.

This never convinced me, neither then nor now. I had already found out for myself while learning to calculate profit in class seven that if labourers were given fair wages then no one could possibly become rich. All the stories told me that throughout history the life of the poor was the same. In the 1700s when Manohar Dev Mullick and Dharmaraja

Mullick lived, every white man's bungalow in Kolkata was served by hundreds of servants. They carried water in leather bags from Lal Digi for their masters and washed their dirty dishes. The sahibs received huge sums from London ostensibly to pay the servants' wages. All the sahibs who set foot in Kolkata amassed tens of thousands of pounds. Beware of traders, Thakuma reminded me again. If the poor could not be bought, there would be no rich people at all, added Ramu da.

When I reached the studio, Manna Dey and Indrani Sen were singing Rabindra Sangeet on TV in a programme meant to raise funds for the poor children in Tollygunje Cheshire Home and Shishuteertha at Santhiniketan. I sat to get my make-up done listening to the line *Aloker eyi jharna dhare . . .* I wore a new blue dress this time for the camera. But when I saw that someone else was in the anchor's seat, things looked dim all of a sudden. My wish to sit in the chair opposite Sanjeev Kumar Mitra and bestow upon him in return precisely the smiles he had showered upon me remained unfulfilled. The new anchor, a gentle person, started that day's talk by telling me that Sanju da was busy and couldn't make it.

'In no country has the death penalty reduced the number of crimes or criminals. Given this, is the state not committing a major transgression against humanity by denying a human being the right to stay alive? By expressing your willingness to take up such a line of work, Chetna, aren't you too participating in this transgression?'

A streak of lightning flashed through my body. The memory of four rings rolled up in a bundle, and the bead-studded bangles on my wrists, surfaced suddenly, making me uneasy.

'Are we not party every single day, in many ways, to the crimes of others? If one must run away from all that, the only way left is renunciation, taking refuge in the Himalayas.' I smiled softly.

'What crimes do you mean, Chetna?'

'All of it . . . from dawn to dusk . . . how many are the injustices we bear . . . how many we let past ourselves, not uttering a word . . . that is the biggest crime.'

'All right, tell us about your father, Chetna.'

'Baba is someone who loves this job. You should have seen his excitement when he first took me to visit the prison. When we went down the long veranda to the locked strongroom where we saw the ropes that had been kept safely in boxes he was like a child who had found a lost storybook!'

'Do you talk of death at home?'

'Death lingers in our home like the scent of fish curry or luchis fried in ghee. We cannot remember our forefathers without speaking of death. And neither can we speak of death without speaking of our forefathers.'

I sighed heavily.

'From the time I grew up and became old enough to think, I have been hearing of death. And also, we live right opposite Nimtala Ghat. We wake up and sleep to the juddering and humming of hearses and the sound of their horns. On some days almost a hundred and fifty bodies are cremated there. That is about six bodies every hour. There are no clear intervals for this like there are for the circular trains that run on the railway track nearby. Deaths—they happen anytime. Completely unpredictable. I will never forget a particular death I witnessed in my childhood—that of Alok Nath dadu, the father of Narayan da, who makes bamboo litters in which people carry corpses to the cremation ground. He was a very hardworking man. Each morning, he would make several litters and stack them against the tin wall of the shed. One day, he came to our tea shop at eleven in the morning and had a cup of tea. Raising the cup after he had finished, he said, this is all there is to man—from the soil and back there again. In between, this cup is good for some people to drink tea, to take their medicines, and maybe to poison themselves too. Then he returned to his shop and lay down on a litter. Everyone thought he was asleep. But when somebody who came to buy a litter tried to shake him awake, they found that he had died.'

The anchor looked at me, amazed.

'What really shook me up was this: when he came into the tea shop for tea, my thakuma, Bhuvaneswari Devi, said, "It is time, it seems, for Alok Nath to leave. Can't you see the flies are already devouring him?"'

I paused. The anchor was completely tongue-tied.

'I was just six or seven years old then. I ran into the shop and found that she was right. There were flies scouring his back and thighs. And many more flying around him, biding their time.'

We shared a moment of silence, looking at each other.

'Flies can sense the impending death of a human being. And not just flies, ants too. They will keep reminding the human concerned in many ways—it is time you became our food. My thakuma can guess a person's approaching death from their face even when it is a year away.'

The anchor now looked at me, fear flashing in his eyes. The scent of death now spreads in the studio like the fragrance of luchis, I thought. The half hour just flew. As we got up, a stylishly made-up young woman with shoulder-length hair went over to the desk at the far end of the studio to read the news. I heard it in the make-up room.

'Namaskar . . . the main news today . . . The chief minister announced that the CPM will drop two ministers from the Cabinet to conform to the rule that the number of ministers should not exceed fifteen per cent of the strength of the Assembly . . . Italy promises support to conserve historic buildings in Kolkata . . . The young woman who was found dead in the Maidan has still not been identified, say police sources . . .'

I wiped off my make-up and changed into my clothes. Yesterday's triumph had lost its gleam. Some lack—like that of salt in one's food—continued to plague me. The news was still on when I stepped out into the corridor with a sigh.

'In the middle of all this, complaints about theft in the roadside shops in Lal Bazar are growing. The police have spread the net for young women who pilfer from the shops. Yesterday, local people nabbed a young woman named Chetna who has been stealing bangles from a bangle seller in Lal Bazar. The seller said that he could not see Chetna's face properly in the dim light and she managed to escape into the dark . . .'

I froze. My mouth went dry; the darkness rushed into my eyes.

The old bangle seller appeared on the screen with a stupid grin on his face. 'Uh-uh . . . Really, she tried to get away with the bangles. I caught hold of her, Babu. And so many people were watching too! I can make out her face . . . Our life is very difficult, Babu . . . who do we have to speak for us?'

And then Sanjeev Kumar Mitra appeared with the microphone.

'The biggest threat faced by these poor folk who slog day and night, in rain and shine, for each meal is such theft. The experience of this poor man in Lal Bazar is not an isolated one . . .'

Darkness clouded my eyes. I was alone in the taxi that evening. Seeing Lal Bazar again on the way back, I was seized with fright. I longed to escape from the White Town to our Black Town. There, somewhere, is Coolie Bazar. There, a Bengali who tried to tell the truth was hanged to death once. The editor of the *Bengal Gazette*, which published an editorial affirming that truth, was sent to prison by the governor-general; the newspaper was shut down. During the same period, Ramjoy Ghosh, an Indian who was caught stealing ten pennies, was thrown into prison. He was whipped all the way from Lal Digi through Lal Bazar till Bowbazar up to Bara Bazar for four hours and then thrown into the river from Chitpur Bridge. I sat, utterly choked, in the middle of the traffic jam. A demonstration of CPM workers protesting against the Trinamool passed by parallel to the vehicles. A little later, a counter-jatha of Trinamool workers followed. I realized fearfully that the faces of the people in both groups looked the same. Those who were killed, they too had the same faces. I tried to call up in my mind the names of all the four hundred and fifty-one convicts whom Father had sent to their deaths in his lifetime. Most of them had been guilty of murder. They did not regret that their actions had deprived another of the right to be alive.

I sat in the car, soaked in sweat. Outside, the city's night scene hummed. Women and men with tired faces returning from work crossed the streets. I shut my eyes, exhausted. When I finally reached home and stepped inside, I could hear Father's tipsy laugh. *He* was in Father's room. They were talking about the arrest of two Trinamool leaders for immoral activities.

'In truth, Sanju babu, did they err?'

'I don't know . . . . maybe they were trapped . . . it is quite common in my father's place too.'

Seeing me standing outside, he smiled sarcastically, taking off his glasses. Our eyes met, and I looked into his dreamy eyes again. I knew then that the emptiness I had felt till that moment was because of his absence. When Father called, I went in, my body shuddering from the insult.

'Did you see what Sanju babu has brought you?'

Father opened a little plastic box. Two gold bangles glinted inside. Sanjeev Kumar took a piece of paper from his pocket and held it out to me.

'Here is the bill. I bought them . . .'

I dashed into my room without taking the bangles. I struggled for air. The darkness spread in front of my eyes. I couldn't see. There was now only the dark, everywhere. The sun of justice that had once shone for all beings had set long, long ago!

14

The rains fell upon us all of a sudden in jarring sounds. The sky flung translucent nooses on to the earth with demonic energy. In Burdwan, Rabia Khatun died, struck by lightning. She was just twelve. The nine girls who had been with her suffered burns. They were all children of the poor. All through the morning, I lay curled up under my sheet making an excuse of the rain. I had not slept at all the night before. Tears erupted in my eyes but froze before they could pour out. This had been my greatest challenge ever since I had grown up—breaking into tears. I could never do it. I lost my balance completely when Ramu da, still half asleep, hummed the lines *Aamare tumi ashesh korecho* at dawn. I have known since I was a child that Tagore's *Gitanjali* began with that line: *Thou hast made me endless* . . . On sad nights, Father would look at the pictures that hung on the walls of his room and sing the whole song loudly. When he reached *This frail vessel thou emptiest again and again, and fillest it ever with fresh life*, renewed vigour would surge through his voice. But when Ramu da sang it in a voice that would never rise from the sickbed, only deep sadness welled up within my heart. Thakuma, who was groping inside the pillowcase to see if the gold coin was lodged somewhere in the sewed-up border of the pillow, sang the rest of Ramu da's song in her quavering voice, *Amar shudhu ekti muthi bhori ditecho daan dibosho-bibhabori* . . . I somehow felt that everyone was making fun of me, knowingly or not. Before the last lines

Thy infinite gifts come to me only on these very small hands of mine
Ages pass, and still thou pourest . . .

I exploded.

'Can I have some peace around here?'

'Is it proper for girls to be sleeping till noon?' Thakuma stopped singing and scolded me.

'I can't . . . I am a human being . . . I need to rest for two days . . .'

The rage in my voice shocked me.

'Don't you have to go to the studio?' Ma sounded worried. 'What if they don't give us the money they agreed to if you don't go? We need it to change the cracked asbestos . . . see, the rain has soaked the kitchen floor . . .' Her voice faltered as she helped Ramu da turn over on his stomach.

'Let them pay up first, and I'll go. What if they don't pay up later?' I pulled the sheet over my head.

'Do you really have a fever, Chetu?' Ramu da asked later, lovingly. As was usual in the rainy season, his head was shaved. Lying on his stomach with his tonsured head, he reminded me of a frog. His large bulging eyes held a pathetic expression in them. The pang that I always felt whenever the thought—if only Ramu da had not lost his limbs—occurred to me shot through me again. I was sure that my life would have been different if Ramu da hadn't lost his limbs, and Niharika her life.

'You've been always reserved, even as a child,' Ramu da said tenderly.

True it was. I was taught at a tender age that women do not reveal their troubles. I always had to think a lot before speaking openly. And I would end up lowering myself in my own eyes, revealing things too late. One reason for that, surely, was Thakuma's advice: 'Do you understand, in this family, men have always suffered because of the women?' Her examples began from the very first hangman Radharaman Mullick. Chinmayi Devi, the woman he had fallen in love with, served him as if he were her living god. She never moped about her lost love or blamed her husband for the loss. But day after day, the very sight of her made his guilt grow. Even after she had given birth to ten of his children, Grandfather Radharaman never believed fully that her heart belonged to him. The moment she had stepped into his bedroom as a bride, she had forsaken words and laughter. He must have tried to ask her questions. Must have begged her forgiveness, must have tried to soothe her. But she never uttered a single word. She never offered her breast to her ten children; never cuddled them. She took refuge in her own silence, the biggest punishment that he could ever receive. When she moves in bed, her large eyes stay still as if they were dead, he wrote on a bhurjapatra leaf, so said Devavrata Mullick, his son by his first wife who later inherited the executioner's job. This was recorded by Kumarachandra Mullick who lived in the time of the Sunga kings.

Kumarachandra Mullick lived during the reign of King Pushyamitra Sunga. The king had come to power after overthrowing and executing King Brihadratha. Kumarachandra's ancestor Agnimitra Mullick had lived in the time of Emperor Asoka. He married six times. Five of his wives did not give him any heirs. The sixth wife became pregnant, but she died in childbirth. The five wives quarrelled over her infant, Udayamitra. Grandfather Agnimitra had to marry another young woman to raise him. This woman abandoned the baby and eloped with her lover. Later my ancestor converted to Buddhism along with the emperor.

Udayamitra Mullick lived through the reign of six kings. It was the time of Buddhism and Ahimsa, but the prison system and the death penalty remained unaffected. He had seven children, but only one by a wedded wife. The rest were born of an infamous prostitute of those times. After giving birth each time, she left the infant at his doorstep. Grandmother took each child into the house and raised it as her own. All seven became hangmen. Buddha Mullick became a hangman in the time of King Vikramaditya. His wife had a secret liaison, and she tried to murder her husband many times. Once, she tried to poison his food, but he survived even that. Thinking him dead, she too eloped with her lover, taking her child with her. The lover took her to the jungle, murdered her, and stole her ornaments and money. Buddha Mullick woke up from his stupor and went looking for his wife. He found his little son weeping beside his mother's body in the forest, and took him back home. This ancestor later became an ascetic.

'So you mean to say that women of those times had no troubles at all?' As a little girl, I asked that with genuine curiosity. Only rarely did the history of the women in our family get recorded.

'Good women are those who bury their woes within themselves, child.'

'But what if the trouble is too big to be buried inside?'

'Oh well, what big trouble could women have? They stay inside the house and do little else but eat and sleep. What troubles do women have except that of giving birth to babies and bringing them up?' Thakuma laughed loudly.

'Thakuma, you never had any troubles?'

'A trouble becomes a trouble only when you think of it that way. Whenever I feel bad, I tell myself, I am Grddha Mullick's daughter. We hangmen have been around since the earliest days of the world. Without the hangman, no power can survive, be it kings, emperors, the British, or the sarkar that came after all of them . . .'

Brushing off the raindrops, Thakuma came in, sat down and started chewing her paan. I lay gazing at her, thinking of all those old stories.

'What are you thinking so deeply about, Chetu?' she asked me, paan in mouth.

'Didn't Dadu love you, Thakuma?' I asked her softly.

Thakuma laughed. 'Man's love is different from woman's. A man can love only the woman who gives him pleasure. But a woman is capable of loving even those who hurt her.'

Ramu da burst out laughing. I didn't. The story that Dadu Purushottam Grddha Mullick had been in love with Ma's mother is one we'd heard since childhood. All his life, he ached in the memory of his lost love, the childhood sweetheart who was married off and sent to East Bengal. Father used to boast that his father's anguish inspired Saratchandra Chatterjee to write *Devdas*. Her name was the same as that of the heroine of *Devdas*—Parbati.

Dadu and Parbati were neighbours and playmates. When she was twelve and Dadu was seventeen, her father came to the Grddha Mullick family and proposed marriage. Their castes didn't match, so the family refused the proposal; Dadu's father Kalicharan was furious. Parbati pleaded with Dadu not to abandon her, but he could not defy his kin. He ran away to Burma, where he met Saratchandra. There he related to him the tale of his love. Saratchandra advised him to take heart and return to Kolkata. Gathering courage, he went back, only to learn that she was now married and settled in East Bengal. He fell upon the road she had taken and beat his head in the dust. Like the hero of *Devdas*, he lost himself in liquor and opium for a while. But soon his father married him to his niece—Thakuma's older sister. She died after giving birth to two male children. Then Grandfather Purushottam took Thakuma as his wife.

'That woman knew how to coo and coddle and shed tears at the right moment. Your grandfather was dumb enough to fall for the show. He just melted! But, my dear, if you make another woman weep, you will surely not thrive. Ma Kali saw my tears. Isn't that why she was hacked to death by Muslims?' Thakuma laughed, still chewing betel.

'Oh yes, yes! Didn't the country end up being cut to pieces by Ma Kali? Hey, be careful before you utter a word about my mother! I don't care that you are old. Good people die soon. God finds a way to take them back. But the likes of you . . . even after a hundred years, you'll be stewing in this hell.' Ma entered the fray.

As the quarrel reached a crescendo, Ramu da lifted his eyebrows at me. 'Now, does that satisfy you?'

I pulled my sheet over my head again. Thakuma's words rang in my ears—a man will love only the woman who gives him pleasure. How come Parbati alone could make Purushottam happy? The question racked my brains. If I could find the answer to it, perhaps I would also learn how to make Sanjeev Kumar Mitra happy. But the very thought of wanting to make him happy made me feel very ashamed. Bibek appeared again, asking why I would want to make a man who stole without an iota of conscience happy. I had no answer.

When Thakuma stepped out of the room, Father approached and, with unusual tenderness, asked, 'Chotdi, what's wrong with you?'

Father had never babied or cuddled me as a child. She's young enough to be my grandchild, he always said whenever he saw me. He never indulged even Niharika, who was born after four of Ma's babies died during childbirth. Ramu da was born after Ma had lost two more babies at birth. It was Niharika who had cared for me, who was born in my parents' old age. Didi had been mother to me—she had bathed me, helped me take my first steps.

'You talk well on TV . . . better than me . . .'

Throwing a sideways glance at Ramu da who was lying on his stomach, Father made space in a corner of the cot and sat down there. Even in that pose, he retained an actor's finesse in his movements. He is sitting on an invisible throne, I thought, seeing him sit straight with both palms pressed down on his knees.

'But take note of this—they want our experiences. Don't speak as if you are handing out all of it, as if it is being finally given away. If they feel that you have done that, they won't want you any more.'

A smile of contempt appeared on Ramu da's face.

'People will respect us only if they feel that we have something that is yet unsaid. And we must be able to convince them that there remains much to be said.'

Father rose. 'Do you think they crowd here because I am the hangman?'

This time I looked at him directly.

'No, it's because I can speak well. People will throng for any amount of time in front of a monkey who can dance. But you need to figure out correctly when to end the dancing.'

'She doesn't like him.'

Ramu da spoke with an effort. His voice came out rasping, like the sound of a rusty car door opening. Father turned to face him, bulging eyes rolling.

'He is no good, Baba. No . . . we will regret it if we give her to him. We've lost Didi . . . not her too . . . No, let's not . . .'

'Ramu, this is an alliance we can't even dream of.' Father's voice was charged. 'He has two MA degrees. He has studied journalism. He's smart. Knows his line of work well. Let at least this girl escape this hell. He has an air-conditioned flat and a car. Speaks four or five languages too, did you know?'

Ramu da shook his head in distaste.

'And Chetu likes him. Why don't you ask her?' Father fixed me with a stern look.

I went red in the face. Truly, I wanted to say that I did not like him. But my voice hung back. My heart desired him even when he hurt me more and more.

The hearses that passed by the house grew in number once the rain became heavy. Impossible to get out of the house, such a crowd, Kakima complained. Thakuma had not yet returned from the Kali temple. I fell asleep lying on the mat. By the time Ma woke me up for lunch, my head had begun to ache and I felt chilly. When the vehicle from the channel arrived in the evening, it had become a full-blown fever.

'She isn't well . . . bad fever . . .' Ma told the driver. When he refused to leave, she tried to wake me up. The driver was standing on our doorstep. I raised my feverish face and looked at him. He saw my puffy red face and tired eyes, and left without further questions.

The next morning, Sanjeev Kumar Mitra himself came. 'The management is very uneasy that the programme was cancelled yesterday,' Sanjeev Kumar complained, taking over Thakuma's cot as soon as he arrived.

I turned over on my mat away from him and looked at Ramu da.

'Yesterday Grddha babu's programme on AVA had the highest ratings. Chetna on our channel had been leading till yesterday. Yesterday we fell behind . . . they got a lead on us.'

I did not respond.

'You must come today, Chetna. Or we will fall further behind.'

'I am unwell. Can't you see?' I asked harshly, raising my head involuntarily and looking at him.

'Did you forget we have a contract?'

'Why don't you file a case of breach of contract? Yes, go ahead!' I became furious.

'If you don't come, Chetna, that will affect my job.'

'Oh really? Too good then!'

113

'It won't be ethical on your part if you don't come, Chetna. You have taken money,' he said again.

I pulled off the sheet, sat up and looked at him. 'Don't you lecture me about ethics. I am not interested in continuing if I don't receive the rest of the agreed remuneration. And by the way, it is really a paltry sum.'

'The rest is due only on the day of the hanging.'

'I don't trust you to pay up after that day.'

'But I gave you my word.'

'Word? Is your word worth anything?' I laughed in bitter derision.

Sanjeev Kumar Mitra sat on the cot looking at me, completely impassive.

'I have never met a more dishonest person than you. And have no desire to meet one either. I don't like seeing you at all.' Lying down again on the mat, I drew the torn sheet over myself.

'But your smile is lovely, Chetna . . . even if it makes fun of me . . .'

My heart pounded hard as I lay under the sheet. Amused by my own surprise at his presence of mind, a smile broke inside me. Sanjeev Kumar Mitra waited for a while and then left. He didn't bother to say goodbye.

'He's gone,' Ramu da whispered.

I pulled down the sheet to look at him.

'His eyes didn't see this piece of flesh lying here—me . . .' Ramu da sighed.

I felt not just pain but also guilt. Something told me deep inside that I was somehow to blame for his condition.

Two days went by quickly. The channel's vehicle came to pick me up each day; I sent it back each time, declaring indisposition. On the third day, Sanjeev Kumar Mitra brought four thousand rupees. I was cutting vegetables in the kitchen. When he strode straight into the kitchen, Ma and Kakima pulled their pallus over their heads and shrunk into a corner. He held out the cash to me.

'Here it is . . . you must come at least today, Chetna.'

'This is not enough,' I murmured, not meeting his eyes. 'Your channel spends so much on those who appear in your programmes . . . so much per episode. I want decent money.'

The muscles in Sanjeev Kumar Mitra's face twitched. But his tinted glasses hid the expression in his eyes.

'Look, Chetna, this is not child's play. It's our channel that sweated the most so you could get this job. Don't forget that.'

'So, how do I gain from that? Seventy-five rupees per month . . . and what money will you make in these two months?'

The kitchen smelled strongly of asafoetida.

'I have been polite till now. But there's a limit to my patience,' he rasped.

'And to mine as well!'

I leapt up, knife in hand, knocking over the dish of vegetables.

'What the hell do you think? That you can get away with anything? Is my body your plaything? I lack only money, not self-respect. I don't need to sell my body for money.'

Ma and Kakima froze, completely aghast. Ma put her hands around me and snatched the knife from my hand. 'Chi! Shut your mouth! Is it right to speak like this to men?' she scolded.

'Ma, this man has hurt me many times. I forgave him each time, but not again. I don't want to see him again.'

I stormed out of the kitchen and ran into the next room to Ramu da's cot, sinking to the floor beside it. I sat there panting aloud, leaning on the cot. Ma or Kakima would rush in to comfort me, I expected. But no. They were busy trying to comfort him—he was wiping his eyes in the kitchen. A man's tears are always worth much more!

Ramu da hummed slowly without opening his eyes to look at me. *Klanti amaar khoma koro, Prabhu* . . . He was teasing me. Otherwise there was no need to sing the line *I am totally spent. Forgive me, o lord* . . . Suddenly, our house shook and shuddered violently as a sudden streak of lightning flashed over it. In love's deepest intensity, I cursed— if only Sanjeev Kumar Mitra had been reduced to cinders instead of Rabia. More stubborn now than I ever was as a child, eyes brimming with tears and lips curved in a smile of sadness, I tied a noose with my dupatta, pulled it tight on my own neck, looked at Ramu da and hummed determinedly: *Aar amar ami nijer shire bayibo naa . . . I will no longer carry myself on my head* . . . Ramu da stopped singing and tried to jump up in distress. When he shook his head in desperation, I loosened it, and took it off my neck. I looked into his stunned eyes and tried to sing the rest: *Aar nijer dware kangal hoy rayibo naa . . . I will not wait at my own doorstep for alms any more . . .* But then the tears began to flow.

15

Thakuma had many interesting stories about Kala Grddha Mullick whose career as a hangman lasted just a year. He was the son of Manohar Dev Grddha Mullick and the brother of Jnananatha Grddha Mullick. Kala was the first in our family to give death by hanging a makeover: he turned it into a public spectacle. He lived in a time when people were hung in public places. He was Grandfather Manohar's eldest son, thought by everyone to be a naughty, lazy child. Grandfather Manohar worked under his father, Dharmaraja Mullick, a famous hangman whose career lasted eighty years. Kala saw the gallows for the first time when he went along to assist his father after Dharmaraja Mullick's death. Six convicts were on death row that day. The first—a robber who looted lonely travellers near the Sunderbans and assaulted women as well—was to be executed at the crack of dawn, at four o'clock. It was the month of June. When he climbed on to the platform, Grandfather Manohar slipped on a puddle from the previous day's rain and broke a leg.

'Please go home and rest, Baba. I will take care of this,' said Kala excitedly.

Under his father's watchful eyes, he sprang up eagerly to place the noose around the condemned man's neck and pulled the lever. The planks moved apart. The man fell and died—all in the blink of an eye. Seeing how skilled his son was, Grandfather Manohar felt relieved. He went home. Kala put all the others to death all by himself. By the time he dispatched his third victim, Kala began to feel somewhat self-important. So when the fourth man was brought to the gallows, he asked him with all the innocence of a sixteen-year-old youth: 'Do you regret your actions?'

'No,' the man said. He was on death row for murdering his wife and children. His arrogant tone provoked my ancestor. Okay, I will show you, he said in a low whisper. He shortened the length of the rope of the man's noose. Quite naturally, the neck vertebrae did not break. Instead, his breath was cut off. He struggled in terrible distress and an awful scream broke out from behind the mask. It resounded in the distant Lal Digi and the altar of the old cathedral.

'This is the way to finish off such scoundrels . . .' Kala exclaimed to the then police inspector of Kolkata, Dinesh Deb Choudhury.

He then asked if the inspector had any paan on him and, taking one, began to chew it. Other than the police, there were just four or five witnesses to the hanging. As they watched open-mouthed, the condemned man writhed in the throes of death. A huge lantern lit up the place. The contortions of the body with its hands tied behind and feet bound together, lit up by the yellow glow, were as engaging as rope gymnastics. The small crowd was struck dumb. Before them on the platform of the gallows sat Kala, a smile playing on his face, dangling his legs coolly, swinging them, chewing his paan in peace, waiting for the hanged man to die. It took a full ten minutes for him to go.

'He does not regret, indeed!' he shouted to the small crowd, and it responded with lusty cheers.

Some even flung coins at him. By the time the sixth man was brought to the gallows, it was broad daylight and the small crowd of fourteen or fifteen spectators had grown to some two hundred people. Men lapped up hungrily the last struggles, cries and the death of a fellow man. Look at him flail and toss, he deserves it, they shouted. After the sixth man was executed, the crowd dispersed. People went away lighthearted and happy, as if departing after a grand festival. When Kala stepped off the platform after the final hanging, soaked in sweat, the crowd swept him up. Many pressed coins into his palms. For Kala, this was the happiest day in his life; like a singer who had excelled in his first concert, he returned home a victor and conqueror.

That was the beginning. The next hanging was five days later. A large crowd had gathered at three in the morning to witness it. Two men were to die that day—a robber and a murderer. The second man screamed for mercy, begging to be spared. That made Kala giddy with power. He made the rope shorter and challenged him to cry with his body. A piteous cry rose from the throat of the man whose limbs were bound. Kala was pleased; he bobbed his head in delight. He then grabbed the man's legs and tried to swing on them. Cries of delight and loud laughter broke out from the crowd. Kala's antics became bolder as the man contorted in agony. The crowd and the policemen were in splits. That day, by the time the two men were dispatched, the crowd stretched right up to Lal Bazar. Many had found perches in trees. McKey sahib and Laren sahib, white members of the Calcutta Council, came on their horses to witness the hanging of the second convict. Their wives arrived in their palanquins and watched the execution, lifting up the delicate side curtains. McKey sahib summoned Kala and handed him a large bag of money. From then on, hanging became a sight to be seen and enjoyed. Kala brought home the hanging rope and even started selling it. By the time the news of these innovations reached Grandfather Manohar who was recovering from his injury, Kala Grddha Mullick had dispatched fifty convicts. When he was able to walk with a stick, Grandfather Manohar went to see his son's performance, quietly staying in the crowd. He found Kala's antics utterly horrifying. Seeing his son pull the hanged man's legs and swing on them to please the crowd, he flew into a rage. He went right up to the platform, caught hold of him and slapped him hard on both cheeks. The crowd did not recognize him; they were enraged that he had interrupted their fun. In the end, the police and the mounted cavalry had to intervene to remove the hangman and the convicts. The hangings scheduled for the day were postponed to a later date. Grandfather Manohar met the governor sahib and complained. The latter was reluctant to intervene, but he stopped the practice of hanging people in public places. It then became something staged inside the prison, to be witnessed only by specially designated representatives of the people.

I had been absent for four days when a senior manager from CNC came to meet Father along with Sanjeev Kumar Mitra. Thakuma's words rang in my mind: 'People are fascinated by the sight of death; they love to hear about it too.'

'They have brought the cash. You must go today at least,' Father said with a broad smile as he came into the house.

'Better that you go, Baba.'

The fact that I had indeed talked back to him seemed to rattle him somewhat.

'I am old. They want young people. And besides, you are the symbol of women's strength and self-respect, for India and the whole world.' He was flushed with emotion.

'I can't do it,' I said.

'I'll give you one tight slap, mind you! Talking back to me, eh? Just see what happens when we hear women talk back around here—' He raised his hand to hit me. Scared, I jumped out of the way.

'Hey girl, they've brought five thousand now. And they'll give another five thousand. We'll go to the studio on the night before the hanging only if they pay up fully. That young fellow's been smart . . . all this, thanks to him . . . really fortunate that he got attached to you . . .'

I looked at Father.

'Your caste mattered most in the old days. If you were born an aristocrat, you had nothing to fear. But not today—no matter to whom you're born, it's money that counts. If you don't have hard cash, you're a nobody. Look, God has given you a chance. I'm not going to let you throw it away.'

So I had to go. But I insisted that Father or Kaku accompany me. I was thus forced to continue as the symbol of women's strength and self-respect for India and the whole world.

In the studio, they changed my hairstyle and gave me prettier clothes. Sanjeev Kumar Mitra was bursting with confidence when he faced me. His behaviour and gestures did not betray the fear or shame or sense of inferiority one might expect in a thief. I felt that I might go mad at the sight of his face.

He asked me that day: 'The day draws nearer, Chetna. What are the thoughts that cross your mind these days?'

'I am very tense.'

That was true. Except that it was not caused by fears about the hanging.

'What kind of tension do you feel?'

'Many kinds. For example, sadness when I think of that wasted life. The tension one feels when you can't hit back at a man who has harmed you even as you become party to the death of someone who hasn't. You have to go through it to know what it feels like.'

I stared hard at him. A cold smile appeared on his lips as if he had caught the drift of my words.

'Have you ever thought of Jatindranath Banerjee's family?'

'I am thinking of them this very moment.'

'Have you seen Jatindranath Banerjee yet?'

I sighed deeply. Fixing Father's image in my mind, I fed Sanjeev Kumar's jatra with my energy.

'I will have to talk of the day when I went to see the gallows for the very first time. What I saw there was completely different from all that I had heard about it. It is in an open space within an enclosed area inside the jail premises. Inside the enclosure, all the rooms are single cells occupied by condemned convicts and dangerous prisoners. As I walked past, I noticed someone inside cell no. 3. Later I read in the papers that that was Jatindranath Banerjee's cell.'

'Chetna, as you prepare to make a noose for him, do you wonder what he might be thinking at this moment?'

Despite myself, I looked at him. These questions were his way of assaulting me by other means. I closed my eyes for a second, let out a heavy, melodramatic sigh so that the jatra would be all the more meaty, and turned towards him.

'Sanjeev babu, I thought of him even as I lay in bed last night. When I think that way, I feel sorry for the man. He committed this crime when I was ten years old. He's been waiting for punishment all this while. If he was to be hanged anyway, why was he kept alive so long? That is my question. My second question is this: if he was ignored for so long, why not allow him to continue in jail? I don't have answers to either of these.'

The show wore me out. It was harder to speak like this than act in a jatra. A terrible labour it was indeed—of mind, body and soul. He created unexpected turns in the script, changed the scenes without warning. I had to write the dialogues on my own, all the while warding off unexpected blows. This continued each day that followed. Once, they caught me tying a noose with the wire of the lapel mike I had been wearing and made a big fuss of it on the show.

'Chetna, teach me to tie a noose like that . . .'

He held out the wire of the mike to me. I fixed him with a serious stare and shook my head. 'This is no laughing matter, Sanjeev babu. It is about dispensing justice in the world's largest democracy.'

Sanjeev Kumar blushed. 'Yes, yes, Chetna, you are very right,' he said humbly, and ended that day's episode. But Father demonstrated the technique of tying the noose on AVA the next day and their TRP ratings shot up.

The next day Harish Nath summoned me before the show. 'If only you had cooperated a bit more we would have cut them down . . .'

I looked at Sanjeev Kumar and Harish Nath.

'Do you have children, Babu?'

'Yes, a five year old.'

'I was just five when Ripper Ghosh was given the death penalty. I saw Father showing journalists who had come to talk to him how to make a noose, and then tried to imitate him.'

A mild pallor spread on Harish babu's face. I wanted to laugh at that moment.

'I tested the noose on my three-year-old neighbour . . .'

'And then?' They both looked at me anxiously.

'That's another story.'

'All that is fine. But we are mainly bothered about TRP ratings!' Harish Nath tried to make a joke of it.

'If you start being so stubborn about such small things, Chetna, we will be forced to try something extreme,' Sanjeev Kumar threatened.

I learned what he really meant only when I reached the studio the next day. After I got dressed and had my make-up done, and was about to pin the mike on my lapel, I noticed that there was a third chair next to mine on the studio floor. Sanjeev Kumar brought in a rural-looking woman wearing a nose stud and clad in a white sari with a black border, and asked her to take the chair. She too had been made to wear make-up. On her forehead was a big sticker bindi; an unnecessarily heavy streak of red sindoor ran through the parting in her hair. In that face with dark circles deeply etched under the eyes, all the signs of grinding poverty were evident. As I sat staring in sheer surprise, Sanjeev Kumar Mitra took his throne-like revolving chair and began the show.

'Namaskar, welcome to CNC's *Hangwoman's Diary*. The whole country is agog after the release of *Girlfriend*—a movie which depicts a relationship between two women. Today on the show we bring together two women. Along with the country's first hangwoman who is making final preparations with just ten days to go for Jatindranath Banerjee's execution, we have another guest in our studio—the wife of the condemned man, Kokila.'

That felled me completely. I was shivering in the uncomfortable cold of the air-conditioned studio. Kokila Banerjee readjusted her sticker bindi and sat up straight. It was really difficult for me to look at her. The prospect of having to talk of the hanging while sitting in front of her made my tongue go dry. Her face was hard as stone. Were waves of hatred reaching out to me from her eyes—those eyes which were utterly impassive and unemotional, bereft of hope and horror? I was afraid.

Sanjeev Kumar cleared his throat, lifted his eyebrows to bring sorrow into his features, and looked at Kokila. 'Kokila di, just ten more days . . . for the sindoor mark . . . the sign of marriage . . . do you think about it?'

The response was a rasping sob, like bamboo splitting apart. I did not know what to do. I thought I saw a flash of delight in Sanjeev Kumar's eyes. He covered his face with his hand as if he were in deep anguish. Kokila wept copiously. I was thunderstruck. Twenty minutes of the half-hour programme that day were washed away in her tears.

Sanjeev Kumar asked me only one question, a continuation of what he had asked Kokila: 'When you see the woman whom the government has deputed to kill your husband, what do you feel, Kokila di?' Kokila folded her palms together and looked at me. She did not utter a word. He then turned towards me: 'When you see this woman called Kokila up close, what do you feel, Chetna?'

'Pain . . .' I replied. It required quite an effort.

'Do you feel like quitting the job?'

'No.'

'Here are two women before us. One of them symbolizes all feminine power and has embarked on an important task. But how amazing that the worst wound to be inflicted by the performance of this task must be borne by another woman! When Kokila and Chetna come face to face, the question we must ask is: Should Jatindranath Banerjee be killed or spared? Viewers can participate in the poll. Do SMS us on . . .'

After the programme I went off quickly to remove my make-up and change. When I came out I saw Sanjeev Kumar counting out four or five hundred-rupee notes and handing them to Kokila. She left without even bothering to wipe off her make-up. Harish Nath, who came out of his cabin, grabbed Sanjeev Kumar's hand and shook it. 'Well done, Sanju. All that weeping! We climbed at least five points in the TRP ratings.'

Sanjeev Kumar laughed gleefully. 'I told her well in advance—better to just weep than blather!'

A cry welled up inside me when I heard his words, but as usual, the tears did not flow. Even if men's tears weigh more inside the home, on TV, a woman's tears are worth much more. When I stepped out of the studio, I saw Kokila Banerjee say something to the man who accompanied her and count the cash. I saw distinctly the mended tear in the sari which draped her shoulder. The man, too, had sunken cheeks. His incredibly worn slippers looked as though hundreds of cobblers had left the marks of their handiwork on them. It was only later that I learned the man was Jatindranath Banerjee's brother. I stood there looking at them. It was he who saw me first. Fear and hate glinted in turn on his face. Then Kokila Banerjee turned and saw me. Her face filled with anger but seeing the expression in my eyes it softened. I went up to her and took in my hands her bony, thin palm. Please don't hate me, I wanted to say. But the words would not come out. Trying to hide her tears, Kokila di withdrew her hand, handed the money to her brother-in-law and smiled at me.

'Have to send a petition to the President tomorrow . . . this isn't enough . . . but still . . .' she said. 'Have to go now . . . if we are late we may miss the last bus . . .'

Not pausing to say anything more, she wiped her face with the edge of her sari, and hobbling on her callused feet with difficulty, hailed an auto rickshaw. A large poster of Isha Koppikar in *Girlfriend* loomed on the wall in front. I felt the tears again. But what value do the tears of women have, especially when shed alone, in the dark?

16

Ratnamalika, who was born in our family in the thirteenth century, had a long birthmark that ran down her face from forehead to chin. She was the cousin of Ranbir Mullick who was the first in our family to take the title of Grddha. Ratnamalika was the daughter of his father's sister. When her father died, her mother, not yet seventeen, was forced to commit sati. Ratnamalika was just a toddler then; she had a severe fit seeing her mother being dragged to the funeral pyre. When she turned seven, the family tried to get her married. She splattered cow dung water on the groom's family, snarling furiously that she was Chamundi, not Sati. And very soon the dark scar made a thick layer on the right side of her face, covering it entirely. It made her face ugly and terrifying to look at. Young children who were frightened by her face—which was strikingly fair on one side and scarily dark and bear-like on the other—shouted, 'Demon, demon,' as they threw stones to drive her away. Ratnamalika spat unspeakable execrations at the crowd that gathered to watch as she convulsed and frothed from the mouth. You will bring forth a dead infant, she cursed the pregnant mother of one of the children who had stoned her. Before dawn broke the next day, the woman's womb convulsed and its fruit was spoiled. Ratnamalika's family subjected her to beatings; she was made to drink the ashes of the hangman's rope; she was treated by exorcists. Finally, they tied her to a pillar. The fits worsened as she became older. Foaming at the mouth, eyes bulging out of their sockets, tongue sticking out, she would roll her head side to side and make frenzied predictions. After seven days, she predicted, eighteen mounted soldiers led by a foreigner with long arms that reached his knees will reach the land of Vanga. Our home will be shattered beneath the hoof beats of a black Arabian horse with a golden mane. On the seventh day after this, Muhammed Bin Bakhtyar Khilji attacked Bengal with a cavalry of just eighteen horsemen, defeated King Lakshman Sen and captured Gaur and Nabadwip. One of the eighteen horses was black. As it descended the hill at amazing speed and drew close, its mane shimmered like waves of gold.

That day too, on my way to the studio I sat in the car with firm resolve: I will not carry you on my head any more. It was an evening on which the city shone, freshly washed by rain. Even through the tinted windows of the vehicle I could see the fresh green of the leaves. The old yellow taxis and auto rickshaws gleamed as if they had received a new coat of paint. Even buildings covered with centuries of dust looked spruced and fresh. Schoolchildren squeezed their way in between the jammed traffic on the road, jumping in the puddles collected in the potholes, merrily splashing the water around. I wanted to laugh too. In the Maidan, football players covered with mud looked like live mud statues chasing a brown ball. The sight made me gloomy. To free my mind from thoughts that weighed it down, I imagined myself walking on Rabindra Setu on a rain-swept dusk. Without the cars, buses, rickshaws, lorries; without the beggars, roadside vendors, or the villagers who flowed into town seeking work. Just me on the deserted bridge and the Ganga bubbling in the rain—that was the dusk I yearned for. Then I remembered the black Arabian horse with the golden mane that had swept down the hill in the thick of the windstorm.

'We have a great programme today too . . .' Sanjeev Kumar Mitra, who already had make-up on, came up to me with a smile that filled his face. 'Today too we will outsmart your father, Chetna.'

I looked at him, worried. Though I hadn't studied beyond Plus Two, I could well predict that the nooses that he made would fit my neck perfectly. When I changed and went up to the chair before the camera, Sanjeev Kumar opened the glass door and led in a diminutive old woman. The faint scent of cow dung trailed behind her. She wore a worn green sari and a white blouse which had been tailored in better times for it now hung loose on her; her arms and neck were bare, as was her forehead.

Without a trace of nervousness or fear, she sat down in the seat which Sanjeev Kumar pointed out to her and clipped on the lapel mike. The fair shoulder that was exposed when the loose blouse slipped a bit gave away the fact that the burned-out face with its sunken cheeks had once been fair and plump. Another woman like my mother. Sanjeev Kumar did not bother to introduce her; he had begun the show.

'Welcome again to *Hangwoman's Diary*. As Jatindranath Banerjee's execution draws nearer, and debates about the ethics of the death penalty continue all over the world, we have with us in our studio today along with Chetna Grddha Mullick, who has been deputed to hang him, Protima Ghosh, mother of Rameshchandra Ghosh, the last convict who was hanged at the gallows . . .'

Like any daughter who had to come face-to-face with a mother whose son had been hanged by her father, I felt my breath falter. Ramesh Ghosh was one of the last two prisoners Father had executed. His father Jitendra Ghosh, too, had received the death sentence in a case involving the brutal murder of six members of a family including an infant. The victims had been hacked to death. But taking into account his age and ill-health, the court had commuted the sentence to life imprisonment.

'Welcome, Chetna! Welcome, Protima di!'

With a triumphant smile that I felt was meant to remind me of the look of fury hidden behind his tinted glasses, Sanjeev Kumar Mitra continued.

'Welcome to CNC. Protima di, as a mother whose son was sentenced to death, what is your opinion about Jatindranath's death sentence?'

Seventy-year-old Protima Ghosh tilted her head sharply towards Sanjeev Kumar and glared mutinously at him.

'Opinion? What opinion, Babu? Did anyone ask my opinion when this girl's father hanged to death my son and his friend? Forget that, did anyone ask my views when my son and his father were given the death sentence? Did anyone ask me what to do with the bodies of my son who died on the gallows and my husband who died in his prison cell? Asking for my opinion after so much has happened, after so many years? Bah! I may be seventy, but my hand is one that wields the hoe . . . . I'll slap you tight on the cheek, mind you!'

Her voice was at the same time impassive and deeply penetrating. With great delight, I watched Sanjeev Kumar shrink and fold into himself as if he had indeed been slapped. But he bounced back with a smile, agile as a cat that manages to land on four feet, always.

'That's precisely my question, Protima di. What is your opinion about the demand being made now that the death penalty be abolished? Now, after so many years, so late?'

'My view is that it should not be abolished. For people like us, it is better to be hanged to death rather than suffer for years together! I have always felt relieved that my son is no more . . . otherwise he would have suffered a living death today. I am even more grateful that his father too was jailed and killed. Now I have nothing to fear, no one to worry about . . . Oh, I am only too grateful to you all . . .'

'Protima di, surely it wasn't us? Wasn't it the police that filed the case? Wasn't it the court that found him guilty and handed out the death sentence?'

'Yes, it was the police and the courts, the other side was rich . . . so the police slapped a case on my son. We had no money to hire a good lawyer, and so the court found him guilty.'

'But six people . . . your son . . .'

'Yes, six people. But why—did you ever inquire? We had eight and a half acres of paddy fields. We toiled on them so hard that our bones were ground to dust. And then, thirteen years back, the harsh summer . . . there was no rain . . . the crop died. He had to take a loan on interest to start again . . .'

Her story was one that had been told and retold, read and seen over and over again in the papers and TV channels. Farming, drought, loss, debt, interest, penal interest . . .

'We sold all that we had to pay the moneylender back. But he made false accounts . . . grabbed our land . . . when he learned that he would lose all his land, my son went to the usurer, and begged and begged and wept . . . then he challenged the evil man. The usurer sent his goons to beat up my son and his father. That made my son lose his mind . . . he picked up the first thing he saw and marched to the usurer's house. His father and his friend Dipak ran after him to stop him. But in the pushing and pulling there . . .'

127

She shook her head without emotion. 'What has happened has happened.'

'But six people including a mere infant . . .'

Wanting very much to see her weep, Sanjeev Kumar Mitra thrust hard again. As if sensing his intentions, her face became even more impenetrable.

'Yes, a tender infant . . . just nine months old. But even when he came back, my son was roaring, Kill them all, kill! I had never seen him before like that. He was insane then. Otherwise he wouldn't even harm a fly. All of them made him insane. They made him awfully cruel . . . but in the end, he alone was punished . . .'

When she reached this point in the story, a teardrop, thick as blood, oozed out slowly from the socket of her sunken eye.

'My son would have been alive today if we had had money to pay bribes. If we had had enough to pay the party leaders, the police, the lawyer . . . to give them all that asked for. My son would have been out of jail and walking with his chest out and head high . . . but . . .'

She flicked off the tear and calmly looked at Sanjeev Kumar Mitra.

'There was no one to send a mercy petition on his behalf. No organizations were around to campaign for him. No one insisted that he should live. Yet now all of you raise your voices for Jatindranath Banerjee. Let me ask you—my son had gone to ask about a great wrong that had been done to him. He had planned nothing. But Banerjee? He planned for days together, snared a little girl, ruined her and killed her as well. Which is the worse crime?'

Because he had no answer, Sanjeev Kumar turned to me.

'Chetna, maybe this is a question you can answer better . . .'

'Sanjeev babu, the hangman can only carry out the sentence . . . he cannot pass judgment,' said I.

'You are delighted, I suppose, to have got the chance to hang someone who murdered a young girl?'

'There is no male or female before duty, Babu. That's what my father Phanibhushan Grddha Mullick has taught me. Fourteen years ago, the father of Amartya Ghosh—whom my father had executed—hacked off my brother's limbs. Ramu da was just twenty-two then. Within a few years, my father had to hang Ramesh Ghosh and Dipak Lal . . . Our duty is our God, Father said. That is our prayer. But Father was deeply disturbed when he returned home after carrying out Ramesh's sentence. So young, so much like Ramu da . . . For days, he would not speak . . .'

That was true. When the black hood was put on him, Ramesh stood with eyes lowered like a young chap about to be caned by his schoolmaster. Tears flowed freely from his eyes. Dipak Lal collapsed in a faint. Scared, Kaku felt giddy and the new assistant Father had hired fled and was seen no more. The magistrate, the collector and some other eminent people had come to witness the hanging. For a long time, whenever he was drunk, Father would describe the terrible deathlike struggle he felt that moment.

When we came out after the show, Harish Nath wrinkled his nose at us. 'The stink of cow dung . . .'

Flustered, I looked at Protima di. Her expression changed suddenly.

'Will a woman who makes a living out of gathering cow dung from the wayside and making dung cakes smell of sandalwood?' she exploded. 'We used to smell of the good earth of the country. We lived by hard labour—what you gulp down three times a day are the fruits of our labour. And you dare insult me?'

In a trice she had turned into someone else. As Harish Nath and Sanjeev Kumar Mitra drowned in embarrassment, many ran up from inside the studio upon hearing the commotion.

'Didn't you all kill my son? Didn't you all bury my husband's body without letting me have a glimpse of him? Didn't you steal all his savings?'

When she flung down her plastic bag and advanced towards Harish Nath, he leapt back in fright. Protima di placed her hands on her head, which was nearly bald, and wailed loudly. Her voice resounded in that air-conditioned room lit with several tube lights. The glass walls shook as her terrifying wail lashed out at them.

'May you all be ground to dust, may the dust fill up in your mouths! May your mothers die peeing blood!'

As we watched thunderstruck, her body shook violently and she fell on the ground. Foaming at the mouth, she gasped and flailed on the floor like a fish out of water writhing on the ground.

'You will all be decimated . . . burned to ashes . . . in the days of

reckoning you will have to settle accounts with Allah . . . beware . . .
Ya Allah!'

In a voice that seemed to have no connection at all with her body,
she let out a terrible cackling laugh. While people stood by, stunned and
unable to move, I ran to her and tried to help her up. She was lighter
than Ramu da. She folded in my arms like a wilted branch. Somebody
brought some water. I sprinkled it on her face. In a few moments, she
sat up, wiped her face and looked at us. Then, even more composed
than before, she stood up, smoothed her hair, pulled her sari right and
picked up the plastic bag, and the few coins and a nearly burned out
candle which had fallen out of it.

'Do you need to go to the hospital?' Harish Nath asked, thoroughly
ruffled.

'No.' Her voice betrayed no emotion.

'Where do you live?'

'Near Mallick Bazar.'

'Who lives with you?'

'Fifteen hundred people.'

Her voice rang with disdain.

'In that case, Sanju da, do take her home,' Harish Nath suggested,
his patience wearing out. He then gestured to Sanjeev Kumar to come
closer and whispered something to him.

Protima di was ushered into the same taxi which was to take me
home. Given what had happened, I did not worry too much when
Sanjeev Kumar got into the front seat. As she got in, Protima di told me
that this was her first car ride. There is always a first time for everything,
she added as she leaned against the seat, and murmured to herself, Ya
Allah . . . Then turning to me in the dark, as if reading my mind, she
said: 'I was a Muslim. My name was Rukhiya. I converted to marry my
husband.'

I stared at her with surprise that bordered on shock. In my mind,
someone else rolled her head side to side. I saw before me the long
arms of the Turkish adventurer Iqtyaruddin Muhammed Bin Bakhtyar
Khilji. Flushed by victory over Bihar, he turned towards Bengal but
only eighteen of his horsemen could match the swiftness of his Arabian
steed. That's why the war on King Lakshman Sen became a campaign

with just eighteen horsemen. Unable to imagine eighteen riders as a hostile army of invaders, the guards opened the gates of the fort to them, thinking that these were merchants' animals. King Lakshman Sen was eighty then, a renowned poet and scholar. He was sitting down to dinner when Khilji and his eighteen men surrounded him. The wise king admitted defeat and retreated to the southeast. Hearing the news that the invaders had overcome King Lakshman Sen and taken over his palace, Hindus ran helter-skelter in fear, trying to hide.

The youth mounted on the black steed with the golden mane was very handsome. He had set off to see the countryside when the terrible screams of a young woman bound to a pillar inside an abandoned house reached his ears. He saw just the dark side of her face and it jolted him. As Ratnamalika gaped at the exceedingly handsome horseman, her veil dropped and he saw the beauty of the fair side of her face. He cut down the pillar to which she had been bound and, lifting her up by the loose end of the thick rope, he set her on his horse and rode away. Many years later, a remarkably beautiful Muslim woman arrived at the doors of the same house in a sandalwood palanquin with a baby in her arms. It was Ratnamalika. The bear-like half of her face was totally altered; the dark mark had vanished.

When I asked her how this could happen, Thakuma laughed: 'Isn't that the miracle, Chetu di? A handful of love is worth more than a heartful of bread.'

'But how, Thakuma?'

'Some men can do it,' Thakuma said breezily.

I imagined the mole which looked like an ink drop on my left nostril dissolving in my tears and spreading all over my face. My tongue itched to predict the doom of all the people I saw around me through the dark half of my face. And I prayed for the hoof beats of the golden-maned black Arabian steed that would bring to me, swifter than the wind, the handsome warrior who would make me a princess in the end.

When we turned from AJC Road towards Mallick Bazar, a rath-mela group passed us. We waited inside the vehicle until the group of children shouting 'rath, rath,' had crossed us and their voices faded in the distance. A horde of beggar children surrounded us. But seeing Protima di alight from the vehicle, they dispersed quickly. It was my first visit to that slum. In the dark, it looked as though an unending row of dog kennels thatched with grass and plastic lay stretched out before me. The stench of cow dung, shit and piss rattled my head. Sanjeev Kumar Mitra walked behind Protima di. Men who gave out the sharp smell of bhang and women reeking of sweat drifted past. In some places, slivers of yellow from electric bulbs and the flickering light from black-and-white TV screens fell on us. Somewhere, children were crying. Elsewhere, women spoke in loud voices, men bellowed. The air was alive with the sound of animated talk and radio music. We turned four times on the path and then Protima di stopped. She groped in her bag for that piece of candle which had fallen on the floor in the studio and lit it. Hers was a little hut of twigs and palm-leaf fronds, so frail that it looked as though a strong wind would knock it down. I went in with a very heavy heart. She lit a bottle-lamp, and laid out two torn grass mats for us to sit. I saw in the dim light that the floor was neatly polished with cow dung. Dung cakes were tidily stacked in a corner. On the bamboo poles that were hammered into the ground in lieu of a wall hung a small cloth bundle, a faded black-and-white photo and a calendar with an image of Mecca.

Protima di had come to the city from her village in Purulia to fight the case. She had fought it for ten long years. She sold her house. They lost. Her son was hanged. Her husband was given a life sentence. When she saw him in jail two months before he was to be released, he told her that he had saved some money working in jail. A whole month passed after the date on which he was to be set free but he did not return. When she went to find out, they told her that he had died and his body had been thrown into the Ganga. She never got the money. Some two thousand rupees it would have been, she sighed, if only I could have it. Just then four or five mice ran between us. I jumped to my feet in fright.

'Never seen mice?'

When she sent me a wounding look through the dim light, I sat down again. She washed two glasses, filled them with water and brought them to us. Then she picked up the lantern, searched around for a few coins and found them. 'I'll go buy us some tea.'

'No, Didi . . . I don't want anything . . .'

'No, you must. If my being a Muslim is the problem, don't worry, the fellow who makes the tea is a high-caste Hindu.'

As she swept out of the hut, like a breeze, I was left alone with Sanjeev Kumar and the candle. The dim light threw wisps of gold on his face and hair. When the same mice returned I rose up quickly and went to the bamboo wall where the calendar with the image of Mecca hung.

'If she is really a Muslim, then her marrying a Hindu must have led to murderous violence in her village.' Sanjeev Kumar, who now stood very close behind me, said.

I felt uneasy, as though something soft had caressed the back of my neck. Repeating in my mind the line *I will not wait at my own doorstep for alms any more*, I moved away from him with an effort and said harshly: 'In the thirteenth century, a woman in my family married a Muslim and accepted the faith. Thakuma says that her progeny are to be found among the Muslims you see in Bengal.'

I was angry. It is said that Ratnamalika lived in the palace till the end of the Khilji dynasty. Those days too the hangman was summoned to the palace to carry out executions. As Grandfather Grddha—that is, Ranbir Mullick—waited for his remuneration after finishing his work, a soldier would emerge with gifts covered in silk from the secluded women's quarters. They were a great relief to him; he who struggled to support a large joint family. When Khilji returned to Devkot after having conquered all the places in which he had set foot, he was broken in body. His trusted retainer Ali Mardan killed him on his sickbed and seized power. Known to be cruelty incarnate, Ali Mardan was beheaded by his own ministers. Eight years later, when Naziruddin Mahmud took over and established the Mamluk dynasty, Ratna Begum's husband was killed. The pithy part of Thakuma's tale was how she died instantly of a broken heart when she heard the news of her husband's death.

When I saw Sanjeev Kumar Mitra poke at the cloth bundle on the bamboo poles, I felt sorely irritated.

'There's nothing here to steal . . .' I said to no one in particular.

Sanjeev Kumar Mitra whirled around and hurled a hard look at me— that old look of arrogance, the ravishing 'I' clearly visible even in the weak light. I turned to go back to the grass mat and sit down. Suddenly the candle died. Darkness and silence filled the hut. I became alert. My hands sought the ends of my dupatta. But I felt that it could not take a heavy load and was afraid. In that moment Ratnamalika yearning to be Chamundi, not Sati, revealed herself to me. I now wished that a big dark mole would grow on one half of my face and cover it completely. I wished it to be so dark that only my one bulging eye would be visible on that side. My body too was in a terrible paroxysm. When Sanjeev Kumar crept close to grab me in the dark I proved true Father's words that a hangman's genius lies in tightening the rope before the condemned realizes what is happening; in an instant I flung a noose around his neck. Taken by surprise, utterly shaken, he tried to lower his head and free himself. Then the strands of his hair brushed my neck and cheeks. I felt a thrill pass through me. In the dark, he leapt about and beat his limbs like a golden-maned, black-hued Arabian steed which I held by the reins in my left hand. Through the single eye on the dark side of my face, I espied the future. It was a bedroom shining with the light from innumerable lamps and decorated like a bridal chamber with coverlets and curtains of red silk. But on the bed of silk, running hither and thither, were hordes of mice.

17

For a hangman, the most difficult moment is that in which he steps up to cover the face of the condemned man. In that crucial moment, their eyes meet. The last memory that the condemned man gathers for the next world is of the hangman's face—an expression of guilt, impenetrable boredom, or one that begs forgiveness. Sometimes the condemned man's tears spread on the black cloth. It thickens the texture of the black. Tears and sweat—when they spread, they thicken the black in their own distinct ways. It was in Britain, two hundred and fifty years ago, that the practice of covering the condemned man's face was established by law. It was in response to the last wish made by a condemned man who had decided the manner of his death—with his eyes covered. The first of such hoods was the nightcap common in Britain then. The condemned man had to bear the cost and like the nightcaps of those days, these too were white in colour. Noting that covering the condemned man's face made it better for both sides, many countries adopted the practice later. As far as the Grddha Mullicks are concerned, in our history, the black hood was used at times but not always—both before the British and after their advent. But after Independence, it was always first on the list of items to be bought and readied in the prison before the hanging:

BLACK CLOTH TO COVER THE HEAD OF THE CONDEMNED PRISONER – 1

When we met again at the studio the day after we had gone to Protima di's house in Mallick Bazar, Sanjeev Kumar Mitra and I looked at each other as if we had black hoods on. As he was applying his make-up in front of the large mirror below the TV that constantly played CNC programmes, I noted with glee that he was trying to ignore me. His glasses were gone. They had broken when I knocked them to the floor in the darkness that filled Protima di's single room. In that moment, he had been strong; it was hard to control him with just my left hand. And so, after being thrown off guard initially, he struggled and, with considerable effort, tried to loop the other end of the dupatta around my neck and pull me close. When I fought him with both hands, his glasses were knocked off. He gripped my shoulders fiercely, and I pulled hard to tighten the noose around his neck. Our legs stamping on the ground raised a racket louder than horses' hooves. I did not even hear Protima di reach the door, mud cups balanced on a plate in one hand and a light in the other. Ratnamalika had taken over my mind then. I had a revelation about how the horseman who had swept her off on his horse managed to erase her bear-face. I was so envious of Ratna Begum.

'Stop!' Protima di roared, putting the plate down.

We jumped apart. But because the dupatta was too short, our heads collided. I quickly undid the loop around my neck. He, however, could only loosen it somewhat; he could not take it off. Protima di strode into the house, looked straight into his eyes, and aimed a half-slap on his cheek.

'Bloody fool!'

I recalled how his face had turned a deep red, and smiled, and Sanjeev Kumar, who sent a sidelong glance at me through the mirror, noticed it. He said to the make-up man sternly: 'Hurry up. The number of dead in Amlasole is five now.'

The night before, when Protima di ordered him to sit down and drink up his tea, he had sat down passively, looking quite exhausted. Next to where he sat lay the broken spectacles. Picking them up—the lenses were intact, but the frame was broken—he looked helpless. I too was weary. I did not feel like yielding to the fact that this was the man who had first sounded in my heart the hoof beats of love. I was more the warrior who had left the battlefield briefly for a sip of water. The frenzied rage of war danced in my blood and flesh, in my very marrow.

Sanjeev Kumar tried very hard to get the noose off, both before and after he had his tea.

'You can't undo the hangman's noose,' Protima di said, as though to herself, when she saw his discomfort.

I wanted to see Jitendra Ghosh, who had reached Rukhiyabi's village after having got lost on his way to a friend's wedding in a village near Kurseong, some 550 miles from Kolkata. At very first sight, he decided that she would be his bride. He refused to leave the village until she agreed to go with him. Caring not for the mist and the sun and the rain, he pursued her for two whole years. At night, he hid himself in the bushes behind her house, whistling and waiting for her. When heavy mists fell for the fourteenth day in winter, she went out to him. His fair-skinned feet had swollen and turned blue in the cold. Holding their very lives fast within clenched fists, they hid in the bushes during the day and travelled by night, finally reaching Purulia; to live in peace there she took the name Protima. The bouts of epilepsy that she had suffered from ever since her mother remarried never recurred . . . until the day she learned that her husband had died in jail. Tears welled in my eyes as I heard her voice falter when she said this. Sanjeev Kumar's cell phone rang just then.

'Just two people, Harish babu? Isn't it a bother to go all that way for just two? Have we followed up on that gangrape? And what about the visuals of the new shop in New Market? Are they done? Okay, okay . . .'

Trying once more fruitlessly to undo the noose, he switched off the phone and said to me: 'Damn it! Hunger deaths in Amlasole, I'll have to go right now.'

Hearing such words in a place like that, my tears sprang up again. Thinking of Jitendra Ghosh made me terribly envious of Protima di. Her face betrayed no emotion at all. If only my dupatta were of stronger material; if only Protima di's hut had a stronger beam, rod or pillar, I wished fervently. The passion of the hangwoman inside me was of exactly this sort—the quickening eagerness of the noose fixed precisely between the third and fourth vertebrae.

His make-up done, Sanjeev Kumar stood up. He looked all the more handsome now. But those eyes, now deprived of their dark-tinted shields, ran hither and thither like grey mice. Even the night before, when he had stood there helplessly, the dupatta with its pattern of red circles hanging down from the noose around his neck, his eyes had made a cowardly retreat. The only way to remove the noose was to cut it. The dupatta was part of the salwar kameez stitched from the cheap cloth that Ma had told Kakima to buy from New Bazar for me to wear to the TV studio. Protima di handed me an old, handleless knife. I cut the noose below his neck with difficulty and draped the rest of the dupatta on my shoulders. When he touched Protima di's hand while bidding goodbye, Sanjeev Kumar slipped out two hundred-rupee notes: 'Do take these, from the channel . . .'

She stared down at the money and shook her head impassively.

'Well, if you don't want them . . .'

Like a thief, he pocketed the notes again and hurried out. You could have taken them, Didi, I tried to tell her sadly.

She looked hard at me and said, 'This great city has tried to make me beg many times. It didn't succeed. Do you think this fellow's channel will?'

The embers of anger had glowed again on her face. I feared that she would convulse again. But do not fear, go in peace, she insisted. Told me to take care as I walked back in the dark. Putting her bony hand on my shoulder, with no emotion whatsoever, she had said, 'Ramesh should have brought home a girl like you. That wasn't to be . . .'

As I sat in front of the camera, the heaviness of heart that I'd suffered the night before rushed back into me. Sanjeev Kumar cast a serious eye on me; he looked as though he had not lived through the previous day at all.

'Everyone's after Amlasole today. If we want good ratings for our show, you'd better be more energetic.'

That was the order and challenge issued to the slave by the master. So when he began as usual with All right, Chetna, as the day approaches, what is the latest news about the execution, I responded with the same coin.

'Look here, Sanjeev Kumar Mitra, there are many things in a hangman's life that you cannot understand . . .'

I looked at him as though he were my equal or even my inferior.

'It's easy for you to simply say: a noose, the gallows. But only those who have felt the noose around their necks know what that experience is. I can easily loop this dupatta around someone's neck and kill him. But that's not what citizens expect a responsible government to do. When the government undertakes to do it, it must be done in a faultless, neat way. The government and the worker appointed by the government, the hangman, cannot simply hang and murder someone like some hired killer. No, simply not possible.'

I continued in a serious manner, 'Take, for example, the rope and the noose. Without the rope, there is no hanging. The rope is an instrument of justice. You can't use just any rope or make any noose. Strict instructions have to be followed in each case. One of my father's great-grandfathers, Jnananatha Grddha Mullick, used to make his noose by burning the end of the rope and inserting an iron ring. The ring would fall exactly on the vertebrae of the neck; such was his skill in making the noose. At the same time, my father, Phanibhushan Grddha Mullick, believes that the practice of looping around one end of the rope to form a noose symbolizes our life and work. An iron ring need not come between life and death, he thinks. He prefers the simple noose, what the British call the halter-style noose.'

I had picked up that word three years ago when an English novelist had come to interview Father. Father made him a noose with his gamchha and the man had exclaimed in surprise, hey this is just a halter-style noose. Sanjeev Kumar Mitra sat up, alert now.

'For a long time, rope made by John Eddington and Co. was imported especially for the hangings in Kolkata. But there was a shipping delay once after which local companies began to be preferred. The imported rope was very elegant—its edges neatly sewn up, not frayed. That rope, 3.8 metres long and three-quarters of an inch thick, was woven from four strands. When my father's elder brother, the late Sasibhushan Grddha Mullick, hanged a criminal for the first time, the rope he had to use was covered with leather.'

I paused and looked at Sanjeev Kumar Mitra's face.

'Uncle Sasibhushan did not want to become a hangman at all. His passion was football. On his first day as a hangman, a match was on, and Sailesh Bose, who was Jorabagan's star player, was to play that day. Dadu—Purushottam Grddha Mullick—had to give him a terrible beating to get him to do the job. Uncle, who was still a teenager then, was teary-eyed and morose when he put the noose around the neck of the first man brought to him. The position of the noose was correct, but this rope was of the new sort and so his calculations went wrong. The leather covering cut the poor man's vein and he bled and bled. The noose didn't stay in the right place; the head was torn off the neck; the body fell into the well with a loud thud; the head lingered in the noose for a moment and then it too fell, like a ball of cloth, and rolled on the floor. Uncle screamed in terror . . .'

Sanjeev Kumar was motionless. I paused dramatically and continued after a minute or two.

'After that, Grandfather informed the government that such a rope couldn't be used. Later, an order was passed that made smoothening the lower end of the rope with a kind of wax—called gutta perccha those days—a necessary practice. If the rope isn't softened before the hanging, it will be hard as stone. So if someone is to be hanged at four in the morning, the softening of the wax-coated part must begin at three o'clock at least. When the condemned persons were brought out of their cells, the scent of the softening wax would reach them. Just think, Sanju babu, how it would be if you were a condemned man. That situation—when the aroma of softening wax fills the jail yard, reminding you in those last moments of your life, in the breaking dawn, that it's time, almost, to go . . .'

Sanjeev Kumar's face was now redder than it had been when Protima di had called him a bloody fool. With a subdued smile, I took over the reins completely and continued: 'The British rope at that time was all made in Italy. The British decided to insert a leather washer to make sure that the noose would not move. They ordered that such a rope be used. My forefathers did not like that. Then when rubber became common, the leather was replaced by rubber. As far as my father is concerned, the rope is the symbol of Yamadharma, the God of Death. He won't let it be polluted with leather or metal.'

'And what about you, Chetna?' Sanjeev Kumar was clearly uneasy when he asked that.

'This is a democratic country, Sanju babu. It is the government elected by the people and of the people that must decide how we live and die.'

When that day's show ended, Harish Nath hurried up to me and congratulated me, Chetna, you were terrific. I saw the scenes of poverty deaths in Amlasole on TV only when I was wiping off my make-up. The terror that I had felt as I walked back to the car from Protima di's hut rose up in me again. Standing in that studio room flooded with white light, I saw the paddy and wheat fields go dry and black in the unrelenting summer; I saw, as if before my eyes, the cattle collapse and die from sheer exhaustion. Most of those who slept on both sides of the path—so narrow you could barely walk on it—that ran through the slum had come to the city because they had been betrayed either by the rain or by religion. They lived—sometimes ten or twelve together—in rooms so tiny that you couldn't stretch out your arm. When it rained, they sheltered under bits of tarpaulin or hurriedly torn pieces of advertisement hoardings. They collected water from taps where a hundred or hundred and fifty people waited; they learned how to shit and piss in the open after darkness fell and before the morning light came. They got used to eating, sleeping and making love among rats and cockroaches and worms and mosquitoes. The dogs and cows and cats and goats and fowl squeezed in between somehow.

Then, the pretty newsreader began to read her news on TV: 'Meanwhile, following the controversy around his initial statement that the deaths in Amlasole were not because of lack of food but due to some nutrients in the food, the chief minister has announced that he is withdrawing it. He has admitted that poverty still exists in some parts of the state and that such situations may arise again . . .'

I remembered the adivasi family that had come to Nimtala Ghat the summer before. One of the women huddled at our doorstep with two little children, begging for some food. Ma gave them a little rice and a few rotis; the children screamed with sheer want. When she told us that they had survived for a whole month on nothing but the flesh of mynahs, Thakuma pressed her hand to her breast and called out to Bhagawan Mahadev. The children who were small enough to be toddlers were actually six and eight. Their mother looked as old as Thakuma, but was really just my age. When she got up to leave after wolfing down the food and thanking us, I saw her breasts through her frayed, weather-beaten sari—two bits of leather that hung like gloves, somewhat dark at the tips.

The anchor's face came on again as I was walking out of the make-up room. 'Minister for the western region, Parameswar Burman, declared that the deaths in Amlasole were not caused by hunger but by disease . . .'

I was rooted to the spot as the minister's fat white face appeared: 'It is pure absurdity to say that these deaths are hunger deaths. Have any of you have visited the place? Well, I have—it's a place where it would be hard for hunger deaths to take place. Plenty of natural resources there, yes, natural resources! For example, you get babui grass throughout the year there. It can be woven into rope; the adivasis can get ten rupees a kilo for it, do you know? And besides, every house has cattle, plenty of them . . . every house I went to has eighteen to twenty-five goats.'

'So you mean to say that none among the dead are poor, sir?' someone asked.

'Yes, of course. All the young fellows I saw were smartly dressed . . . they even had watches. When I asked them, they said they play cricket and watch it on TV too. There's no starvation there. No poverty either.'

From my earliest childhood I had grown up hearing how mindful the state was—even of trifles like the deaths that their citizens deserved.

The newsreader had begun to read the next bit of news. 'A US bank survey conducted recently reveals that there is a twenty-two per cent increase in the number of millionaires in India this year. Observers point out that although of the seventy-seven lakh millionaires around the world only sixty-one thousand are from India, the increase in their numbers has been substantial, indicating India's robust economic growth in the recent years . . .'

I finally exited the studio without listening to the rest.

I was outside, looking for the vehicle to go back home, when Sanjeev Kumar came up to me, his make-up still intact.

'Chetna, I need to talk with you about something serious.'

I looked up but with no interest at all in what he had to say.

'Since we have come so far now, my life has no meaning at all if I don't marry you.'

'Marriage should only take place between equals.'

'It's true, I have been up to naughty things. But that's only because I adore you. Like Protima Ghosh's husband, I too have set my heart on you.'

The reference to Protima di's story made me feel weak-kneed. Like an immensely skilled hangman, he threw the noose around my neck and pulled hard, all in the flicker of a second. And it landed right in the middle of the third and fourth vertebrae.

18

Eight days before the hanging, Sanjeev Kumar Mitra tightened the noose around my neck once more. That was a terrible day. The cry *Maa ektu faan diyo* . . . rang from afar in the silences that fell between the steady sounds of vehicles on the road, arising from a throat that could not be classified as human or animal. Thakuma leapt up in fear.

'Bhagawan! The famine . . . famine!'

Ramu da and I were jolted from our sleep by her cries. In my sleep I had been all alone in the vast yard of the Alipore Correctional Home one relentless noon, hanging someone to death. In the blazing midday sun, darkness rushed into my eyes and the face of the condemned man became invisible. I felt something tightening around my throat when I jumped awake. Thakuma's scream made certain that I would not sleep again. At the word famine images of Amlasole rushed back into my mind. The adivasis there had had no food rations for many months. A local trader had taken away all their ration cards. And when news of the hunger deaths broke, he went promptly into hiding. The villagers did not even know how much food they were to receive as rations every month. Still half asleep, Ramu da tried to console Thakuma—don't worry, if there is famine, the government will provide food. That made her furious: 'Huh! I am not educated, but I do know it is the government that lets the famine come in the first place. Did I not see it with my own eyes in 1943? My mashima went mad hearing the cry for a drop of rice gruel, did you know? Every morning we woke up to see the crows and the dogs feed on the bodies of the dead in the streets . . .'

That cry continued to be heard from a distance. Thakuma, who was about to lie down in her bed, sat up instead, distressed, saying that it was indeed a cry of hunger. I then thought of the tale of Aloknath Grddha Mullick who was the brother of my own grandfather. He worked as a sweeper in Writers' Building which was then a structure used by the lower officials of the government. Hearing the talk of his masters all the time, the sweeper turned into a scholar. He would say, if only Gandhiji had not pitted Pattabhi Sitaramayya against Subhash Chandra Bose, who had been elected president of the Indian National Congress in the Haripura Congress of 1938, so many people would not have died in Kolkata. Subhash Bose was wounded by Gandhiji's groupism and he resigned to form the Forward Bloc. He was accused of fomenting subversion and put under house arrest; he, however, escaped and sought refuge in Germany. From there he went to Japan in a submarine. Once he had formed the Indian National Army, he declared war on the Allies. When Japan overran Burma, the Bengalis, who had depended on rice imported from Burma for seven years, faced massive want. And then a terrible rain wiped out the harvest. The crops in Midnapore and 24 Parganas rotted completely. Farmers who had some surplus hid it away. And on top of that, in the summer of 1943, even the entry of boats and bullock carts into the region was restricted. The people in those areas were completely isolated. After months of grinding starvation, they lost all hope and began to flow into Kolkata.

'Everywhere there were corpses, vultures, wolves . . . even to feed the hungry was a frightening experience. Once a woman who ate the rice my thakuma served her died right in front of our eyes—her stomach split open.'

At that memory, Thakuma wiped her eyes again. Something flared up inside my stomach too when I tried to imagine people who had lost their crops, sold their farmlands, even loosened the main pillar that held up the roof of their homes to sell it, and then stood dazed and helpless. They first asked orphaned relatives and then senior members to leave. Then left their children at the doors of the rich. Abandoned their villages and wandered in strange places. Ate even grass. Ate even cow dung and waste and struggled to keep living. Sold their children for just a few coins. Most of those who drifted into Kolkata were women. Most of the men had perished in the whirlwind. When they were served free food in the city, the bellies of those who had not eaten for months swelled like balloons; their skin became translucent, like egg whites. They died content, having finally eaten a decent meal.

Thakuma kept mumbling these stories till daybreak; the cry continued to sound. When dawn broke, she went in search of the sufferers. Much later, when I sat down to have my rotis in the kitchen, our neighbour Hari da came in to tell me that Thakuma wanted me. I put away my food and went out. Hari da pointed to the road that turned left from our house, away from that which went to the Ghat. Thakuma stood in between the row of houses to which our house belonged and the next, a lane so narrow there was barely space for a man's outstretched arm. A drain ran there. A family was beginning to settle on top of that.

'Chetu chotdi, come and look,' Thakuma called me with a look of sorrow.

Bowing my head as if I was entering a hencoop, I went in—and was stunned. There lay a young boy, ten or fourteen, naked. A body with a swollen head and belly, like a corpse that had rotted in water for many days. The candle beside him was dim; so I did not see him clearly at first. But when my eyes got used to the light I saw that what trickled out of the corners of the child's eyes was not pus—it was a row of termites. Seeing brown ants pour out of his nostrils and blue flies come out of his ears, I stood there dumbstruck with shock. He was completely exhausted and drawing his last breath; when the mouth opened, red gnats jumped out. And when he squirmed, out of his penis flew silver-winged moths, soaring towards the flame of the candle.

I could not believe my eyes. My stomach clenched and my mouth was filled with bitterness. A year ago, there had been reports in the papers and on TV about flies coming out of a child's body. His family too had come to Kolkata from Midnapore seeking work after the crops had failed. They had arrived in Howrah with all their worldly belongings gathered up in a meagre bundle. As they hung on, spending the nights at the bus stop or on the pavement, one day moths began to fly out of their older son Ratan's penis. People crowded to see the wonder. A beggars' agent took him around Kolkata for a while and collected money. When the news of this appeared in the papers, the government ordered that the child be treated. The newspapers lost interest a week or two after. The boy's family had no money; the doctors and hospital staff lost interest too. His illness was never diagnosed. And the newspapers did not seek him out again. By then termites had begun to come out of his eyes, and ants from his nose. Creatures crawling in his nose and ears caused him unbearable pain. Other families that lived on the pavements and in the bus stops drove them away and they had ended up in the drain. His mother Mrinmayi, who had arrived with the scavenged remains of vegetable waste, looked at the creatures flowing out of her son's wasted body and said, her voice laced with sympathy: 'Poor things! They can find nothing to eat inside!'

As I stood there unable to say a word, Thakuma pressed my hand and whispered: 'The signs are that he won't last the week . . . God is merciful!'

The death sign that Thakuma saw was in his eyes; when she fed him rice gruel, the sunken eyes in the emaciated face did not reflect her image. I looked at him again. Despite his weak effort to smile, I could not see even his eyeballs, let alone my image, in those sockets. As we watched, he burped and a vague smile crossed his lips. The creatures that had flowed out of him now rushed back inside.

That day when I went to the studio to record *Hangwoman's Diary*, Sanjeev Kumar Mitra, who was chatting with Harish Nath, tried to be friendly, asking me if something was wrong and why my face looked so wan. Looking at his made-up face and his tinted glasses, now set in their new gold frames, the memory of Ratan's eyes sunk in their sockets made me convulse.

'Someone died near our house . . . a young boy,' I said impassively.

'Oh!' Sanjeev Kumar's response was casual.

I continued. 'Many kinds of creatures were crawling out of his body. I heard the news when I was sitting down to breakfast. I left the food . . . couldn't eat after that.'

A small streak of recognition passed over their faces.

'Why?'

'The insects were crawling in my food . . .'

They were silent for a moment. Harish Nath tried to smile then. 'Oh yes, we'd done one such story last year. That was before you came, Sanju da.'

I paid no attention and kept talking: 'His skin was like fields bereft of moisture at the height of summer. His eyes overflowed with yellow termites, his ears with flies . . . white moths came out of his penis . . .'

I stopped and looked at them.

'But the worst was the gnats that flew out of his mouth . . . how they stank! Even though they tied his chin and jaw together, they kept coming out relentlessly.'

'Enough! Enough.' Sanjeev Kumar stopped me, very uneasy now.

But I did not stop. 'They did not cremate him. They have no money for that. They put him in a boat, took him to the middle of the river and threw him into it.'

The furore around the starvation deaths in Amlasole had abated, and a human rights activist had been drafted to make *Hangwoman's Diary* meatier that day. This was the well-heeled Sankar Prasad Majumdar, president of the Anti Death Penalty Organization. His air of supreme confidence, shining clean-shaven face and spruce, trim suit troubled me.

'The death penalty is a barbaric practice. No civilized nation favours it. In such circumstances, the fact that a young woman like Chetna Grddha Mullick, who does have some education, has agreed to do such work is regrettable indeed. If Chetna had been unwilling, perhaps this death sentence itself may have been averted. A human life would have lasted longer . . .'

When he paused thus in the discussion, Sanjeev Kumar Mitra turned towards me. 'What do you say to that, Chetna?'

'Starvation deaths abound in Amlasole. There, children die in pain; there are worms eating their bodies and creatures crawling in and out. I wonder, really, why human rights activists are not bothered about extending those lives. Tell me, Majumdar babu, why does the nation condemn the guiltless to worse agonies than the guilty? By what standards can that be permitted?'

'If you are referring to Amlasole, Miss Chetna, then there are facts you do not know . . . it's not that there was no help from the government. It was not distributed properly.'

His bhadralok self-confidence made me very impatient once again.

'These very same words were said by a British minister in the British Parliament in 1943, Majumdar babu. India has no dearth of food, he said. Just that the bread couldn't be buttered evenly, he was sure! In that year, till July, the British had taken away eighty thousand tons of food. The great famine that had broken out sixty years ago was also because the British had exported ten lakh tons of rice and one lakh tons of wheat . . .'

'We seem to be wandering off track now. Many such things might have happened under the British!' Sanjeev Kumar interrupted, impatiently.

I looked at him emotionlessly. 'All I mean to say is that all governments offer the same justifications, at all times. In July 1943 when a member of the Assembly demanded that Bengal be declared a famine-stricken area, he was not opposed by the British, but by the food minister, Suhrawady. Those were days in which people were forced to eat dogs and cats and even cotton swabs with blood and pus on them. But he declared in his speech that the shops in Calcutta were filled with plenty of food . . .'

Majumdar shook his head, expressing distaste. 'That is another matter, Let's go back to the death penalty. Just think—Jatin Banerjee has been in jail for more than a decade. Many whose crimes are worse than his have received clemency. It is not the mark of civilization that people convicted of the same crime should receive such different punishments.'

'In a country where crores of people suffer in dire poverty and just sixty thousand possess a sizeable share of wealth, how can the guilty alone hope for equal treatment? On what grounds, Babu?'

'Miss Chetna Mullick, you are mixing up two entirely different things! Poverty is one thing; the death penalty is another . . .'

'No, never. My father has hanged four hundred and fifty-one convicts. Of them, four hundred were miserably poor. With no money to hire good lawyers . . .'

'What about the others ?'

'They were pitted against people much stronger than them.'

Majumdar shook his head again to indicate that all this was wrong.

'If, as you said, all those who receive the death penalty are poor, surely they stand to gain from abolishing it?'

'I do believe that it is better to kill the poor through the death penalty than kill them slowly by abandoning them to starvation.'

'That is a very cruel statement . . . How can a woman like you say such things?' He pulled up his collar, his face filling with worry and pain.

'Because I grew up in the midst of poverty. The people we see on Strand Road by Nimtala Ghat are very poor. They have no one. They die on the roadside; their bodies are torn apart by street dogs . . . I believe they would be better off dying quickly and painlessly, in two minutes, on the gallows; it is much better than being killed slowly in hunger and want.'

My voice began to turn harsh. The very uselessness of this conversation made me uneasy. When the show ended, I sighed in relief.

'I don't agree with you, Chetna,' Sanjeev Kumar said when we were about to leave after the show. 'Most people in our country believe that poverty is their fate. That's not true—it is a choice. Poor people stay poor because they are not willing to work hard and spend wisely.'

I looked at him obliquely. His eyes were hidden behind the tinted lenses. Bitterly, I thought of Ratan. I too had gone to see him off at the Ghat. When his body was thrown into the still black waters that looked as if they were marked by ugly dark warts all over, a large cloud of insects had risen from it. His body floated for some time like a hollow log; the water drew him down only after a long time. Maybe those creatures had devoured all his inner organs. Poor things, like his mother said; they too were probably exhausted from starving inside.

'Come out now, the time of the great famine has passed!' Sanjeev Kumar Mitra got out and called to me, after stopping the taxi at Park Street.

His words made no ripples in my mind. All I could do was float above, like a hollow trunk upon water. He took me to a restaurant meant only for the rich. When we entered, the drinkers lifted their heads and looked at us. We could hear women talk from the small cabins around.

'The food here is good,' Sanjeev Kumar told me.

As my nostrils filled with many kinds of appetizing aromas, I became truly ravenous. While we waited for the food, Sanjeev Kumar folded his arms on the table, rested his head on them and looked at me. The tenderness in his look upset me. The words 'I want to fuck you at least once' rang in my ears.

'Years before, I had the urge for biryani one day . . . I was just ten or twelve then. But I didn't have money . . .'

His eyes were now warm. It stirred my heart.

'I was the son of a poor sick man . . .'

He removed his glasses. They reflected the pain of a wounded child.

'Do you like biryani? The yellow one with a white boiled egg on top?' He sighed and looked at me. 'In 1988, it cost forty rupees. When the waiter brought the bill, I didn't have enough cash. He slapped me hard. The manager hit me on the head. Shouted that I looked like a crook; scolded the waiter for having taken my order. All those who were there felt that I ought to be severely punished if I were not to grow up into a seasoned thief. They shoved me into the kitchen, pulled off my shirt and pants, and made me wash the dirty dishes . . .'

He extended his hand and touched mine slowly. I could not bring myself to pull mine away. His touch was gentle and loving at that moment, one that gave me pleasure.

'I washed dishes from eleven-thirty in the morning. My legs ached. So did my back. My palms were wrinkled from being soaked in water and the skin on my fingertips began to break. All those were biryani dishes. Full of leftovers—bones people had sucked, half-eaten eggs, long grains of rice mixed in curd and pickle and papad.'

He caressed my fingertips with his own ever so softly. I trembled like a vine in the wind.

'The boys who worked there made fun of me and grabbed me between my legs when they passed that way.'

He covered my palm with his and looked at me.

'The lunch break at the restaurant was between three and four. Everyone ate and made me wash their plates. Then they told me to go. I put on my shirt and pants. But when I passed the manager's desk, I deliberately knocked down the plate which held caraway sweets and toothpicks. As he picked them up, showering abuse all the while, I grabbed some money from the drawer that lay open—that was my very first act of revenge.'

He was now running his hands over both my palms. Blood cells crawled down my veins like worms. All the blood in my body collected around my fingertips; I felt as if a thousand moths had gathered there.

'I have never eaten biryani after that . . . its very scent fills me with a thirst for revenge.'

He then leaned over the table and drew my cheek close, pressing his lips on it. I wilted. My body shrank. Opening my palm, he placed on it Thakuma's old gold coin.

'This too was revenge? On poor old Thakuma?' I turned it over and examined it. Somehow, touching it made me feel afraid.

'No, on you. You reminded me of my weaknesses.'

The waiter came in with the food then. This was my first meal in such a restaurant. Naan, chicken, pulao.

'Just eight more days to Jatindranath Banerjee's hanging . . .' Sanjeev Kumar whispered, looking into my eyes.

Despite the tempting array of food, I felt revolted. It was not hunger that harried me. It was his eyes, which sent out termites. In those eyes, which reflected everything in that room, only my reflection was not visible.

19

I had gone to get dahi for the feast Ma had cooked for Sanjeev Kumar Mitra that noon. As I turned left from the salon and walked past Mriganka Dutt's charity eatery and Harihar Jha's shoe repair shop to reach Prasen Dutt's shop, I felt many eyes upon me. Even in the place where I was born and raised, I had turned into something to be gawked at.

'Ah-ha! Chetu di! Come, come . . . These days one has to turn on the TV to see you! They give you good money, no? Ah, good! I've known for a long time, you will go far!. But all of this is the fruit of your mother's prayers, remember! Never forget . . . the poor lady, Sachinmayi di! This will be a great relief to her. How she has suffered! . . . And her only boy—ailing so long!'

The moment he saw me, Prasen da bared his betel-stained teeth in a broad smile and broke into chit-chat. In between, he balanced a charcoal-stained brush on the stump of his right arm and drew me on a sheet of old newspaper. He sketched the figure in a rectangular frame with bulging eyes raised to the skies in prayer. Salim chacha, who repaired tablas in the next shop, suddenly called out: 'Suparna di, please rescue this girl before your husband chops her up with his tongue!'

Hearing that, Prasen da's wife Suparna di came out stooping, asking me how many bowls of dahi I needed. Prasen da held out the change— six rupees—after taking the price of two bowls, but did not give it to me. He kept grinning: 'Tell Sachinmayi di I asked about her, all right? Also ask Syamili di why we don't see her much these days.'

'Yes, Dada.'

As Suparna di carefully measured out two bowls and handed the dahi to me, Salim chacha, who was testing a tabla with a small hammer, ears pressed on it, smiled: 'Suparna di, your husband is so compassionate towards the wives of all other men in this world . . .'

She went inside, her face completely expressionless, and Prasen da turned his grin at Salim chacha. 'Salim bhai, where women are worshipped, there the gods are pleased.'

'Oh yeah, yeah!'

Salim chacha pressed his palms on the ground and moved his body to a corner of the room. Finding the box which held the small chisel, he crawled back to where he had sat earlier, and hummed in agreement.

I used to love their talk even when I was just a little child. Everyone on Strand Road thought it amusing that Prasen da, who had only one arm, and Salim chacha, who had lost both legs, had shops next to each other. Prasen da and Salim chacha had actually met in the hospital when they were both victims of what is known as the Great Calcutta Killing—a result of the call for Direct Action on the demand for Pakistan.

For as long as I can remember, I had seen Prasen da arrange mud pots of pristine white dahi in many amazingly artistic ways, like the pandals raised during puja. Whatever he touched with his one good hand, in that he revealed impeccable artistry. He would pull up the dirty tattered vest over his potbelly, smile and chat with even the crow flying by or the dog loitering around, and keep sketching.

Salim chacha was born in a rich Muslim family. His family was butchered by militant agitators who also set fire to his ancestral home. He was the only one to survive. He played the tabla so well that even the corpses who passed by on Strand Road couldn't help keeping rhythm.

'Sudev da's love for Syamili di hasn't faded, I hope?' Prasen da asked as he finally handed me the change.

I laughed. So did Salim chacha who struck the tabla a few times, chuckling, as did Prasen da himself, shaking his potbelly.

During the Great Famine, in Noakhali, those who begged for a little food all day long would reach the bazar exhausted by evening and lie down there to die. Most of them were Muslim farmers. Father once told me that the sight of people coming there early at dawn every day to examine each corpse and determine which faith it belonged to gave him a terrible fright. The Muslims took only Muslim corpses and the Hindus took only Hindu corpses, leaving the rest behind. The Muslims buried their corpses after the prayer; the Hindus threw them into the Ganga.

Father turned thirty in the year of the Direct Action Day. He never got over witnessing the riots on his way back after hanging two prisoners; he narrated the story of it again and again. The prisoners were sentenced to death in a case related to the famine of 1943. It was an effort to show that the famine was brought about not by the government, but by merchants who were black marketeers. When Raman Kumar Mukherjee, a trusted lieutenant of Ranada Prasad Saha, was arrested, someone remarked that there could be trouble if only a Hindu was arrested in such a case. So they decided—let's arrest a Muslim too, and caught hold of Ahmed Shah from Midnapore. Both were found guilty and hanged to death. The hanging was at Presidency Jail, at four o'clock, at dawn. Both Hindu and Muslim wilted alike at the sight of the hangman's noose. Both struggled and died with equal ease fifteen seconds after the lever was pulled. Father had rushed into an arrack shop run by someone called Gopal da after the deed was done. The riot began around then.

'I pushed open the door hurriedly, desperate for a drink of water. Gopal da was opening his shop in a leisurely manner. And then, in the a distance . . . a menacing buzz. Rath-mela, I thought. Then the sounds became clearer: Lad ke lenge Pakistan . . . When he heard that, Gopal da shut the shop again. If that happens, Grddha da, we Hindus are a gonecase, he exclaimed in fear. It happened all in a flash. He ran about and collected others. They pooled money, went to the American Camp, bought grenades and two pistols for two hundred and fifty rupees. A crowd collected very fast. Ten rupees per head chopped off, the reward was fixed. Five per limb. Those were times when the British government wouldn't give me even a full rupee to hang someone. They urged me to go along but I didn't . . .'

Father stroked his moustache in pride and revealed the reason for that decision: 'A true hangman cannot weigh death and sell it like that.'

When the Hindus and Muslims attacked each other in front of his eyes, Father fled the scene, consoling himself that he would be back after a sip of water. For many years after, the murderous howls and the piteous cries rang in my ears, he said. It was then that he learned that the smell of clotting blood was even more wretched and frightful than the stink of rotting flesh. As I walked back, I cast my eye fearfully on the dark soil under my feet. This soil, a poisonous black under the heavy footfall of all the centuries that had passed this way, was already drunk with the sweat, blood, phlegm and pus of so many human beings.

I could hear Sanjeev Kumar Mitra's voice from the road near the house. 'The attention around hunger deaths is over . . . Now's the time . . . We should leap to act, Phani da, you shouldn't continue your show. We want to do the exclusive telecast of the day before the hanging. Two days before the hanging we will begin a twenty-four-hour live telecast. I want both father and daughter. Not for free . . . one thousand rupees and a bottle . . .'

He shot a glance at me while devouring the sandesh Father had brought the other day.

'Uh-um! Did you know, Sanju babu, my channel pays me fifteen hundred rupees for each day's show?'

Sanjeev Kumar sniggered. 'There's one zero missing in the actual amount, right, Phani da? We know of every paisa that you get! Okay, if this is too low . . . then . . . We have already given you five thousand rupees for Chetna . . . Actually, according to our contract, I needn't pay a single paisa more, but I have decided to pay you five thousand more. I'm doing this because I am partial to you, Phani da. Think and decide,' he said, focusing on the sandesh now.

Father didn't respond. He sat there looking thoughtful, stroking his moustache and rubbing the part of his leg that peeped out between the bottom of his folded-up dhoti and knee.

'You weren't keen on the plan I told you about . . . it would have fetched a bigger profit,' Sanjeev Kumar said in an offended voice as he licked the remnants of the sandesh off his fingers.

Father lit a cigarette, held it between his fingers for a moment, then drew in the smoke contemplatively and slowly let it out. 'Memories are armour to a man. Better to go out naked into the street and beg than sell all my memories to you . . .'

'When I give you my daughter, Sanju Babu, I am not just giving you a woman but also all the memories we have cherished in our family. Memories in our family are not owned by individuals . . . they belong to us all of us.'

Having polished off the sandesh, Sanjeev Kumar was wiping his fingers with a black handkerchief. 'Your daughter is far shrewder than you,' I heard him say when I went back to the room after leaving the dishes with Ma in the kitchen.

'Phani da, what if we build a replica of the gallows by ourselves?'

Father reacted after a moment's thought.

'Where? At home, or in the studio?' He paused and then suggested an answer to his own question: 'Not at home . . . better in the studio.'

Puffing harder at his cigarette, he became animated.

'It will help your channel in the present mood. Isn't the interest and curiosity of the viewers evident? Many duffers may bark at the death penalty, but I tell you, Sanju babu, it is impossible to ban it in this country! Because our minds are too attuned to relishing the idea of death, of letting it slowly melt inside like this sandesh in your mouth!'

'Wonderful sandesh . . . where did you get this from?'

'Ganguram's, Elgin Street,' said Father happily. 'That used to be Satyajit Ray's favourite shop. He bought sandesh only from there till his very last days, did you know?'

'Sandesh is a great invention, Grddha da. Only Bengalis could make something like this out of milk fat and ghee and sugar.'

Picking up a piece encased in butter paper and decorated with edible yellow beads, Father gazed at it admiringly, then laughed. 'Sanju babu, have you ever wondered why all the things that harm the body taste so good? Whether it is ghee, sugar, booze, or women? If you find the answer to that then you've grasped the crux of life!'

Sanjeev Kumar guffawed, but the words he spoke were serious. 'I propose that we set up the gallows for real in the studio on the day of the hanging. Phani da, you and Chetna must be in our studio that day. If you show the viewers how it was actually done, that'll give them a truly unique experience,' he said as he wiped his face. 'It'll be great if we're able to show the real gallows instead of just a set. That is, show how the gallows are built, step by step . . .'

Ramu da, who had been staring at the wall and laughing heartily to himself, turned his eyes towards me with a broad smile and said, 'Chetu, I was thinking of Maradona's goal . . . the Hand of God . . .'

I tried but a smile would not appear on my face.

'I had a dream last night. That my legs sprouted back. You should've seen! Like a sprout from a seed. I thought it was a leaf's veins . . . but no, it was my foot. I realized only then, the design of a leaf and a man's feet are so similar . . .'

My heart trembled.

'What's the news about the Euro Cup? Will the cable operators' strike end by then?'

He had been uneasy ever since the TV channels and cable operators had fallen out with each other.

Another of Sanjeev Kumar's guffaws rose up from Father's room. Ramu da looked at me: 'What's the big joke? Your wedding?'

'He wants to build a gallows for his show . . .'

'Where?'

When I gestured my ignorance, his face clouded.

'I've been thinking about why people are this way these days. Everyone's changed so much, Chetu. Ever remember seeing anyone like Sanjeev Kumar in our childhood?'

The image of yellow biryani with a white egg hidden inside appeared in my mind then. Thakuma's gold coin was still inside my purse. My heart beat hard, wanting to give Sanjeev Kumar more time to turn over a new leaf. So I turned my back to Ramu da and fished it out secretly from my purse. Putting back stolen things discreetly was as hard as stealing them, I realized. Somehow I managed to slip it under Thakuma's pillow without Ramu da noticing. At night when I was at the studio, Ma would make the bed; when the coin fell on the ground with a jingle, Thakuma would jump up in delight!

I had to leave for the studio rather early after lunch with Sanjeev Kumar.

'Just seven more days . . .'

As we sped forward in the car, Sanjeev Kumar gave me a smile. But I continued to hold back, not sure whether to return the smile or not.

'Tomorrow is the day for the sandbag test, Phani da said.'

That made me glum.

'Seven days later, the experiment will be with a living man's body . . .'

'That will not be an experiment,' I reminded him, uneasy now.

Sanjeev Kumar laughed. 'I want to see it, Chetna . . . I have asked for permission.'

'Father says that many who come to witness a hanging pass out or throw up.'

'You don't have to fear that of me.' He sounded confident.

When we reached the studio, there was an unusual amount of chaos. Before I entered the make-up room, Sanjeev Kumar came looking for me.

'No, Chetna, no need. No *Hangwoman's Diary* today.'

When I turned around in surprise, he told me: 'An assassination attempt on the chief minister of Gujarat . . . three people killed by the police, including a college girl . . . We need to be careful . . . This could blow up into a communal riot.'

On the TV screen above, images of the college girl's flat were being shown. Seven people lived there, left helpless after the death of the father some time ago. Images of her mentally challenged sister laughing delightedly at the camera; of her mother waiting for her in the flat which had no electricity; of a police officer saying that it was not clear why she had gone to Gujarat, apparently packed for a two-day visit. I remembered Niharika again.

'There's time . . . why don't we go for a walk?' Sanjeev Kumar proposed, when I was getting ready to return home. It was one of the most charming evenings in the city that monsoon. Raindrops from a previous shower dripped slowly from the gulmohar that stood in front of the CNC building. Yellow mynahs chattered merrily from its low-hanging branches. Sanjeev Kumar took my right hand and held it in his, without seeking my permission. I looked at him, frightened. The mild drizzle and the retreating sun had painted the city a faint ochre. He helped me into a cycle rickshaw. A softly warm wet wind passed by, caressing my palm. Once we were seated, he took my hand again gently. Someone inside me screamed: This is only a dream; in reality, you are standing in the harsh white, eye-piercing light of the studio in front of Sanjeev Kumar Mitra, ready to pull a lever, beneath a three-legged gallows tree. The gallows was really a huge camera. The lever, a large mike. As I fell into the cellar, I tried to raise my eyes towards the camera and flutter my wings in delight, like a mentally challenged child. I, Chetna Grddha Mullick, the symbol of strength and self-respect of all women in India and the whole world.

20

In truth, my love was like the monsoon in Kolkata which did not cool the air, making us swelter all the more instead. Rather than giving me peace, it left me terrified. The cycle rickshaw Sanjeev Kumar Mitra and I were in had a weather-worn rubber tiger with steadily waning stripes fixed on its rusty handle. The seat cover was torn in the middle; the sponge underneath and the decaying skeleton showed. I sat trembling on the torn seat as Sanjeev Kumar stretched out his left arm and held me close. My heart felt as helpless as a bird trapped in the hollow of a burning tree, feathers stiff and throat parched, able neither to fly nor burst into flames. His body grew warmer still, as if a pit of fire burned furiously between the flesh and the bones under his blue shirt. That ride was indeed like a dream. The grey rain soon slanted off and ceased. The road grew clogged with vehicles and people. Through the dirty road—upon which plied dirty buses full of people with dirty clothes and faces; auto rickshaws; and fancy cars in which powdered and lipsticked people sat in ease, and on the sides of which pedestrians waited to cross, jostling for space—our cycle rickshaw glided ahead as if it were another planet in the solar system, as if it were not connected to this earth. The rickshaw wallah seemed to be dancing, standing instead of sitting upon the pedals, his grimy feet hardened with the scars of centuries. He led our rickshaw along some celestial path in outer space. Even the licence plate tied to his right wrist had a dream-like gleam. I was beginning to feel sleepy. A bird with its feathers on fire cannot feel worried about women's power and self-respect, I was convinced. That moment Sanjeev Kumar Mitra ceased to be the man who had menacingly muttered 'I want to fuck you hard, even if only once,' and I ceased to be the woman who had hanged him seven hundred and twenty-seven different ways. We became two nestling birds in a tree that swam in the air. I fought with myself to put out the fire in my wings.

The rickshaw turned south from the front of the General Post Office and reached the Royal Insurance Company buildings; it then turned left and coursed through Bankshall Street that connected Koilaghat and Hare Street. The building known earlier as the Company House came into sight. It stood on the spot where the Sabarna Roy Choudhury family had erected its court building before the British. We then passed the red-brick building that is now the railway manager's office. I imagined this building back in time when it used to be the governor's residence. I saw the red roses that bloomed in its spacious gardens which once stretched right up to Lal Digi shrivel and fall in the cannon fire when Siraj-ud-Daula's forces captured the fort in 1756. I saw the British take that land again and build on it what came to be called the Marine House. As the Cutchery building with its balconies all hung with washing and door as high as a coconut tree came into sight, I turned my head the other way, looking for a worn old building, which I had heard used to be just opposite. Sanjeev Kumar Mitra held me closer and threw me a questioning look. I sank into his shoulder almost involuntarily.

'That was the old Criterion Hotel. My dadu's big dream was to have a cup of tea there . . .'

When Sanjeev Kumar saw that seedy-looking structure, now hive-like with many tiny shops crowding in it, and laughed scornfully, the rickshaw driver turned towards us. He had a handlebar moustache longer than my father's. It hung on the sunken cheeks of his sunburned face as if it had been strung from the high nose that rose on it. He spoke with seriousness: 'Babu, that used to belong to my grandfather's grandfather.'

When Sanjeev Kumar burst into laughter again, I sat up, alert. 'Don't laugh . . . this is Kolkata,' I murmured.

When he looked at me, puzzled, the rickshaw driver turned towards us once again.

'My grandfather's grandfather was a sultan, Babu,' he continued, panting as he pedalled.

'A sultan?' Sanjeev Kumar laughed again.

'Yes, from Mysore . . .'

He got off the cycle and began walking, pulling the rickshaw along, looking at us and gasping heavily for breath. 'Have you heard of Tipu Sultan?' he asked.

I was struck with surprise. Sanjeev Kumar who had started to laugh, stopped and now looked keenly at him. He panted like a scrawny old horse, pulling the rickshaw with all his strength and speaking in a loud hollow tone as he took us forward. 'Tipu Sultan's son Shahzada Moinud-din Sultan Sahib was my grandfather's grandfather. My grandfather's father had a big palace here. It's where he grew up. What to say? Koro paushmas, koro shorbonash!'

I stayed quiet, looking at him. He heaved once more and then climbed back on to the cycle, his feet on the pedals, wiping his neck and face with one end of the torn gamchha wrapped around his forehead. His body kept rising and falling on the pedals as if he were dancing on them.

'This Kolkata of yours—it is a magical city. Sultans pull rickshaws, emperors polish shoes!' Disbelief echoed in Sanjeev Kumar Mitra's voice. When we got off near Bowbazar, he smiled at the rickshaw puller warmly: 'Sultan sahib, what about a cup of tea before you go?'

'Anwar Shah, that's my name, Babu.' He grinned, showing big stained teeth, and accompanied us into a tea shop. Sitting on one of the roadside benches he began to animatedly narrate his ancestors' stories. 'Tipu Sultan had four wives and sixteen children,' he began. 'The British who defeated Tipu sent his sons to Calcutta. They lived as sultans for a few more generations, then they slipped through the fingers of Time like the water of the Ganga and merged into this black soil.' I had heard Thakuma tell the story of one of Tipu Sultan's grandsons who killed himself. His greatest wealth had been music. Having lost all his worldly possessions in disputes with relatives, he moved into a rented house. One day, the grandson returned home to see the officials and the policemen seizing his musical instruments. He ran after their carriage for a long distance, begging them unsuccessfully to spare at least a tanpura. Shattered, he returned home, picked up the double-barrelled gun that hung on the wall, and shot himself in the head. The feathers from his turban floated around in the room. Bits of his brain stayed stuck to the ceiling and the walls of the house for many years after.

'After Tipu Sultan's death, we were given land in Tollygunje. There were about three hundred people in the group that arrived here from Mysore.'

I watched with interest as he drank his tea, sweeping aside the handlebar moustache. How would it look if Tipu Sultan himself were sitting with his turban and ceremonial sword on the wayside bench at a Bowbazar tea shop and drinking tea, I wondered. His palace used to be near our house. I had heard from Thakuma about the mosques that his sons built in his name.

'Grandfather Sultan was obsessed with tigers. He had a tiger's image etched or painted on his ceremonial sword, guns and cannons. He even had a mechanical toy—a tiger pouncing on a sahib. The sultan used to laugh when the tiger mauled the sahib, they say . . .'

'Anwar bhai, how long have you been pedalling this rickshaw?' asked Sanjeev Kumar.

'Oh, this one? This doesn't belong to me. It's owned by a Bihari. He owns a hundred and fifty such rickshaws. I used to be a farmer in Singur. All that is gone. I have four girls at home. My wife died two years ago. Maybe that's for the best. All I have from pedalling on and on are my swollen and painful balls.'

I stood staring into the retreating sunlight as though I could not make sense of his words.

'The descendants of Tipu Sultan who resisted the British live today as rickshaw wallahs and housemaids. The descendants of the nizam who submitted to them wholeheartedly roll about in luxury! What a contradiction, Babu!'

Flinging away the mud cup and wiping dry his moustache, Anwar Shah stood, erect, with the dignity of a sultan. The bones sticking out of his emaciated body pierced my eyes. His shoulders were hunched, they looked broken; his stomach caved inwards; his legs were little more than sticks. The rubber tiger bleached by the rain and sun reflected in his eyes, glinting in their cavernous depths.

Sanjeev Kumar sighed. 'Fate, what else, Bhai?'

Democracy, not fate, I wanted to say. I saw the heir of the sultan leave, standing up on the pedals and contorting his body. The ends of his moustache were being swept back by the wind. Maybe all he had of his royal legacy were the moustache and the rubber tiger.

Sanjeev Kumar took my hand lovingly. 'Chetu, what are you thinking?'

I was a little diffident now and wanted to move away from him. Memories of bygone generations had surged up in my veins after meeting the sultan's descendant.

'All these street corners where four roads met used to have gallows trees in the old days,' I murmured to Sanjeev Kumar Mitra.

I felt troubled. Anwar Shah's words had cut loose memories within me.

'The places where Lal Digi, Bowbazar, Chitpur Road and Bentick Street met . . . there used to be huge gallows trees towering over each . . .' I said.

He let go of my hand.

'So many have been hanged there by my forefathers . . .' Sanjeev Kumar sighed.

'In the past, the hangman needed but a sturdy tree. Then he began to fix two logs of wood on the ground and connect them with a pole. Baba says that the gallows have been shaped by scientific progress and revolutionary thought . . .'

Sanjeev Kumar looked at me, astonished. 'What a time to talk about the gallows!'

'Don't you want to build one for yourself?' I asked, sarcasm tinging my voice.

He smiled foolishly. 'That happens to be my trade. Your job is to carry out justice, mine is to make people sit transfixed before the TV.'

'Buying and selling.'

'Yes. Buying and selling.' He smiled, taking my hand again. 'It's a lovely evening . . . I wish to take a stroll with you, Chetna. Please don't talk to me now about gallows and hangman's knots and children with insects flying out of their noses and mouths . . .'

He walked leisurely, holding me close to his body. We walked into the rush in front of the bookshops in College Street. When we reached the ancient Coffee House building, little children, naked and covered with mud, mobbed us with begging bowls. This city is making needless noise, I felt. My head reeled from the sounds of vehicles, hawkers, beggars and students. I followed him, inhaling the scent of books, old and new. I was seeing this part of the city for the first time. From the main road, we turned into a small, obscure lane. It was a path from bygone times, lined with buildings from the British era. Most of the houses were shut; boards bearing the names of publishing houses and

162

various agencies hung in front of them. The setting sun was partially hidden beneath a raincloud, like a gold coin someone had stowed under it hastily.

Stopping in front of an old two-storeyed mansion which bore on its head a banyan tree as tall as a man, Sanjeev Kumar said: 'There will always be an old bungalow in the middle of any city, on the roof of which a banyan grows.' The gates of the building were rundown. A thick tree root split in two as it snaked out of a dilapidated awning; it reminded me of Anwar Shah's handlebar moustache. In the light of dusk that filtered through the banyan leaves, the sun looked like a blue spider dozing in the middle of a web of gold. Sanjeev Kumar stepped into the yard, holding my hand.

'This was built in the nineteenth century . . . was painted white then.'

'Have you been here before?' I asked, worried.

The silence of a forest hung within those gates. The nilmani latha creeper and the bansimar, lost in a tight embrace that broke down the walls of the ancient structure, were in full bloom. The intoxicating scent of a kanthali champa about to bloom wafted from one of the rooms inside. As he stepped into the mansion still holding my hand, Sanjeev Kumar Mitra whispered, 'This is my house . . .'

I turned my eyes to him in disbelief. The old house spread around us silently—its head from which the turban had been torn off, walls that were bereft of clothing, and cracked floors. This might have been a bungalow built by some white sahib for some pretty Bengali mistress, I concluded. It made me hallucinate about a woman with hennaed feet adorned with silver toe rings and anklets, her face covered with the pallu of her sari, walking softly in a room inside. Sanjeev Kumar Mitra took off his glasses and put them in his pocket. He lifted my chin and looked into my eyes. I began to feel very drowsy again, like a bird trapped in the burning tree. When I looked into his eyes, a thousand nilmani latha creepers sprouted beneath my feet and held out their tender vines towards him.

He pressed his lips on my forehead and was quiet for a few moments. Then in a deep low whisper, he asked, 'Shall I guess what you are thinking now?'

163

My eyes closed languidly; I leaned towards him and rested my head on his chest.

'About how to throw a noose around my neck if I hurt you . . . Right?'

I raised my head, opened my eyes, and smiled at him.

'Now I can see on your lips the kind of smile a woman bestows on a man. For the first time since we met. That means . . . I guessed correctly, didn't I?'

'No . . .' I said.

And felt extraordinarily light after. I discovered that a thousand varieties of creepers were thriving inside that house and was delighted. Ban kalami and ramsor and chehurlata and the angulilata, and the dusky blue-leaved, yellow-hearted miche—all hurried to spring up zestfully in every bit of space. When a breeze entered the house through a shattered window, my skin tingled in pleasure.

'My mother loved this flower . . .' Sanjeev Kumar said, taking in his hands a flower bud just bursting into bloom on a vine that peeped into the room. He came nearer, placed his hands on my shoulders, and turned me to face him. Looking into my eyes, he asked: 'Tell me, what are you thinking now?'

I leaned my forehead again on his chest and, in a tired voice, told him the truth. 'I want to fuck you hard, even if only once . . .'

Sanjeev Kumar's head jerked back as he looked at me. Tears brimmed in my eyes. We stood within the four walls of that jungle, silent for many moments. A small orange bird flew in and then flew away, twittering loudly. Sanjeev Kumar picked up my hand and slapped himself hard on his left cheek.

'I beg you, forgive me!'

A teardrop flowed down my cheek slowly.

'Look, Chetna, this is the first time I have ever begged forgiveness of anyone,' he said. I melted into his embrace. I had never ever loved anyone the way I loved him then. We stood there for a long while. Inviting me to love, he roused rapture in me. He kissed my wounds gently. He did not tell me how this ruined house had become his. When I came out with him, night had covered the city with a thick dark blanket. The force of love surged in my blood.

The next day, I successfully completed the first sandbag rehearsal of my very first hanging.

It was Kaku who got ready the sandbag weighing seventy-five kilos with which we were to test the strength of the rope to hang Jatindranath Banerjee. He weighed a mere fifty kilos but the weight of the sandbag for the test must be one and a half times that of the condemned man. Tying it up with a cord, I tried not to think. At the gallows tree, kneeling on the planks which had fallen away beneath my feet once before, I tied one end of the rope to the sandbag tightly. The lever's handle was cold. I imagined with trepidation the five-feet-ten-inches-tall body of Jatin Banerjee in place of the sandbag.

'Um, be brave. Pull the lever,' ordered Father, stroking his moustache and giving me a look of approval. My hand closed on the lever. The planks fell away, sounding like a war drum. The sandbag shook and fell into the cellar. I did not watch the rope shiver hard at first, slowing down gradually, and calmly swinging afterwards. Because of the unceasing rain in the past two days, the rainwater that had collected below the gallows platform had formed a pool. The many shrubs that the convicts had planted in front of the verandas now stood half submerged in the water, nevertheless holding themselves up, announcing their self-respect. The roads submerged in flood waters beneath Kolkata's new flyovers appeared in my mind's eye. I dreamt: leaning against Sanjeev Kumar Mitra's chest, I was going around a rain-soaked Kolkata in a cycle rickshaw under a silver-coloured sunshade.

The usual practice was to keep the sandbag hanging for at least an hour and a half to make sure that the rope would not break. Father, Kaku and I watched. As though a lever had been pulled in the sky, the rain fell headlong into the cellar. Like love, the downpour too left me terrified. Running to the veranda away from the rain, I saw the flower that Sanjeev Kumar Mitra's mother loved growing on a creeper below the gallows platform. It got tangled in the unending strands of the rain's tresses and fell off the vine. I loved it too. Aparajita—the unvanquished—was its name.

'My last major role in a jatra was in *Ma Mati Manush*. That was 1975. "Mother, Land, Man"—that's what it means. The land is like Mother, Sanju babu. The history of Bengal . . . why, of all of India . . . is about the struggle for land,' Father said to Sanjeev Kumar Mitra as he sat down on the cot, put the cigarette to his lips and puffed at it.

His lungi was folded above his knees. He rubbed his left knee in circles as he spoke. I stood leaning against the wall, listening to them. All three of us were in the room where Father's and our family's past was on display. When Sanjeev Kumar had come to our house before lunchtime, creepers of an unknown sort had begun to put out vines and shoots within my body. My left breast had forgotten the pain it had borne when he had crushed it in his hand; it now throbbed with desire for him. Whenever my eyes drew away from him, they turned to the beam from which Niharika's body had swung back and forth, lifeless. It struck me with an inward shudder that if his house bore the weight of a banyan tree with spreading roots, then in this house of ours, corpses of the past hung in each room.

'My hand shook when I picked up the hangman's rope for the first time. I felt as though the breath of a powerful, gigantic creature was falling on my body. It was the asura Jwara—the demon called Fever. After I came home from Satyapal Chakrabarty's hanging, I fell very ill. I could feel within me a thousand people breathing. I felt terribly uneasy. It dawned on me that I was not one man but many men in one body. They erupted from my body. Look, Sanju babu,' Father said running his fingers over his arm, 'they rose up on my skin like mustard seeds, piercing my flesh . . .'

The pox had broken out on his body then. He lay on the bare floor with neem paste smeared all over him. The goddess of the pox—Devi Sitala, who held a silver broom in one of her four hands, and in the other three a winnow, a pot of the sacred water of the Ganga, and a small bowl—had dragged him down. Her seed sprouted all over our house.

'But when I went up the stage, it was exactly the reverse. I would always feel a noose tighten around my neck. There would always be a struggle with death, a brief one, lasting just five or ten seconds. And I would dissolve. I always delivered my dialogues like gunfire, people say. But to tell you the truth, I can never remember what I said or did on stage. After the first piece of dialogue, I ceased to be Phanibhushan Grddha Mullick. Sanju babu, I think that I hang myself at that moment only to be reborn as the character I play. Don't know if all those who die by hanging feel that way . . .' Father let out a long sigh.

'All through my life, I've been beset by this confusion. Azar, the stage on which a jatra is performed, is open on three sides. Standing on it with make-up thick enough to look like a coat of white cement on my face, I've often felt that I am a condemned man wearing the death-hood. But standing before the gallows, lever in hand, I've felt that I am on stage, acting a part,' Father said with emotion, as if he was speaking lines on the stage.

I listened, silent. During the sandbag test, I was convinced that the hangman who stood facing the gallows needed an island of light to escape to. The sandbag fell into the cellar with a thud; instead of watching the rope twist, shiver and then become still before swinging mildly in the sudden burst of rain, my mind escaped to the ruined house in which roots flowed through the balconies, and leaves and branches peeped out of the doors and windows. I felt upon my neck and toes the gentle touch of vines on which the dark blue nilmani flowers bloomed. On the walls from which the plaster had fallen off flashed the many greens of the ferns and single-leaved plants that reminded one of single-cell creatures. Anwar Shah of the silver handlebar moustache glided in on his flaming rickshaw fitted with a yellow tiger amid a heavenly shower of blue-tinted aparajita flowers. Sanjeev Kumar held out his hand, inviting me to sit beside him on the rickshaw's burning seat. I imagined his heart throb for me, making the same sound which rose from around the stage when the audience stood up to applaud Father's performance.

Father drew another mouthful of smoke from the cigarette, took out the liquor bottle from behind Grandfather's picture, and poured himself a drink.

'I have never hanged anybody. Nor have I been in the jatra. But I do know the terrible struggle of the moment when the noose tightens . . .'

Sanjeev Kumar rubbed his neck ruefully, took off his glasses, and winked at me.

I could not tear my eyes off his face. My reflection glinted bluish in his green eyes, I felt. Each time he looked at me, the derelict mansion that held a whole jungle within came to my mind. I craved to hear once more the gentle murmur of leaves and the twitter of the little orange bird that had flown in through the window. My heart, strong enough to kill a man, became impatient again to hearken to the beating of his heart.

'*Ma Mati Manush* was a gigantic hit at the time. During S.S. Ray's glory days. It had Bhairab Gangopadhyay's mind-blowing dialogues. Six hundred shows were performed that year. Within two years, the communists were in power. Jyoti babu became chief minister. Get the point?'

Father emptied his glass, drew in another whiff of smoke and let it out slowly. Then he stood up and delivered a line to an imaginary audience: 'We are people who stood watching them build forts and mansions on land that was leased out to them for trade. In the end, when their cannons spat fire at our breasts, we had lost everything. My land, Mother, is like you. Like you, Mother, who bore me in your womb for ten months and brought me into this world in searing pain!'

'Is this a line from that play?'

'No, it is my own. When an actor has played many roles and appeared on stage many times, he doesn't need another person's lines, Sanju babu.'

Sanjeev Kumar Mitra smiled and applauded. I had seen Father act in the jatra only once or twice. The drama companies are on both sides of the zigzag road that runs from Strand Road, where our house stands, to the Chitpur tram road. On my way to school, I used to look up curiously at posters of *Tumi Badhu Tumi Mata*, or *Bhange Khare Chhador Alo* with pictures of lipstick-wearing women with thick layers of make-up, clad in sleeveless blouses and silk saris. I have trembled with fear seeing Father act on the azar. Ramu da had taken me to the play *Tumi Desh* that was performed one Durga Puja at Kumortuli, in which Father played the role of the zamindar.

The musicians took their places on the two-and-a-half-feet high stage with their tabla and cymbals on one side, and with the flute, violin and harmonium on the other side. The stage was awash with the bright light falling on it from the four pillars mounted on the sides. I could see someone walk and sit in the green room behind the stage through the gap in the curtain. When Father came on stage in his shiny boots, I saw his legs first under the curtain. I did not recognize him. Ramu da whispered into my ear, 'Baba, Baba,' and I sat up, wide-eyed, bursting with awe. His new form was majestic. When Father stepped into the spotlight in a shiny red kurta, stroking his abundant moustache, the lone chair in the room became his throne. The same chair became a window to some characters, a door to some others, and to a third set it became the shade of a tree. Why, to my amazement, it even turned into the gallows!

'In our time there used to be jatras that crossed a thousand performances. But then the numbers began to fall with every passing year. Even some ten or twenty years back, we could expect a hundred and fifty or two hundred performances, but now it's rare for them to cross even seventy-five.'

Father threw the cigarette stub out of the open door and lit another one.

'What is there to be surprised about it—isn't there a television playing in everyone's house twenty-four hours a day?'

'Don't blame the TV people, Phani da! Let us live too,' Sanjeev Kumar Mitra laughed out loud. 'But I can't help saying this—if you were a big performer in the jatra, your daughter is a big star on TV. Each day her performance leaves our editors and viewers speechless! No one believes that she's studied only up to Plus Two. It's all your cleverness, Phani da!'

'But didn't she slip up yesterday?' Father emoted scepticism, knitting his brows. 'When you asked about the sandbag she ought to have looked more serious. Instead, she was smiling, and her talk sounded too playful. Chetu, haven't you heard me correct Sudev so many times? We hangmen speak about death. We should always be careful, wary, when we do so. It is the most serious thing in life. Never speak of death smilingly. When we speak of it, our faces and voices must be marked by heavy seriousness. We shouldn't speak of death to entertain people, but to remind them of their own inevitable end.'

My face blanched. The swish of the orange bird's wings had reverberated in my ears as I sat in front of Sanjeev Kumar for

169

Hangwoman's Diary after the sandbag test. I had felt unnecessarily happy, energized—I forgot the camera's presence. When Sanjeev Kumar asked me how it felt to know that there would be a real human body hanging there in seven days, I had given him an unnecessarily broad smile.

'But have you forgotten your ancestor Kala Grddha Mullick?' Sanjeev Kumar intervened as though to help me.

'You haven't really understood my ancestor Kala. He viewed the act of hanging differently. The crowd those days knew only so much; its discernment was poor. Our days are not those, are they, Sanju babu? Aren't publicly spoken words more important today? We need to be politically correct, Sanju babu, that's my point.'

But I completely forgot Father's reminder the next day when I set out for the studio again with Sanjeev Kumar Mitra. My heart pounded. It yearned to go with him once again to the ruined bungalow that hid a forest within. It hankered for the moment when I could listen to the rustle of leaves in the midst of alluring verdure and be silent, my head resting on his chest. Between Strand Road and Bowbazar, he flagged down a rickshaw again. Just as the rickshaw-wallah stopped next to us he broke into a coughing fit at the end of which he spat a blob of phlegm on the road. Sanjeev Kumar looked at him keenly. 'Bhai, to which royal family do you belong?' he asked, leaning against the seat.

The man controlled his cough and looked irritated. 'Why, Babu, making fun of others?'

'No, no, never . . . I was just joking.'

The rickshaw-wallah looked again at both of us; the light of recognition appeared in his eyes. He returned to his pedalling. 'I am no king or emperor. We have been poor for generations.' His voice softened. 'Have you heard of the cholera that followed the famine in Nabgaon in 1943? A thousand people perished in it, including all of my mother's family. She lived on the streets and gave birth to four children, all fatherless. I am the youngest. That's the only the lineage I have . . .'

At the age of ten, he had gone to Jaipalguri and become a farm labourer. Soon he had risen to being a tenant farmer, and then bought some land with his hard-earned money. By then he was married with three children.

'The government acquired thirty-nine acres of land in Torol Pada village for medicinal plant farming, Babu. I lost my land. A factory was built on one acre; the rest is still fallow. They promised compensation and jobs for the children of those who had lost land. But it was like a line drawn on water.'

He had had to watch, helpless, as the waste from the pesticide plant ruined the land which had once yielded gold. His eldest son had died as a child. The second, a daughter, grew up, got married and went away to Kolkata. Sailendra and his wife watched their crops die and when life became unbearable, he and his wife came to Kolkata with their third daughter. He had drawn a hand-pulled rickshaw for four years after that, and had now moved on to the cycle rickshaw.

'I watch your programme, Babu,' he told us, when we got down at Chitpur Road.

'How is it, Dada? Are you for hanging or against it?'

He coughed again and spat out another blob of red-streaked phlegm. A smile of pain appeared on his face.

'Babu, years ago, when we were sleeping on the pavement with our child—a polio-stricken girl—four men beat me to the ground, made off with her, and raped her. It's been nine years since. We pointed the men out to the police but they didn't even register a case. When just one person is punished for that very same crime, the others walk free and fearless? It is folks like us who should die on the gallows! We'd escape our misery, and the government would save money . . .'

Sanjeev Kumar Mitra stood there stunned. We continued to stand there after the rickshaw-wallah had peddled away.

'Chetu, this place is driving me mad.'

'Really, why are you here then?' I asked, irritated.

'My mother is from here, that's why.'

'Is it true that the ruined mansion belongs to you?'

'Yes . . . that was the house my father bought forty years ago. He met my mother when he was staying there. He married her and took her to his native place. I was born there. When my father's business went bust and we lost all our wealth, my mother came back here . . .'

'Where is your mother's house?' I asked him without thinking.

He sighed. Then, pressing my palm, said, 'You must have heard of it . . . . it's very famous.' As dramatic as Father in his jatra role, he announced: 'Sonagachi.'

Where in Sonagachi, where brothels and homes line opposite sides of the street, I did not ask. He had stopped a taxi by then.

He did not look at me or speak again in the taxi. Maybe pain glinted in the green eyes behind the dark glasses At least at that moment, he did not resemble the painted, made-up person I knew in front of the camera. He too was an excellent actor. But facing the camera with my face made up, I felt like an actor as well. I imagined myself playing the role of Sanjeev Kumar's mother in *Ma Mati Manush*. I saw the son, abandoned by his mother, lie weeping in the darkness of his father's house. My left breast swelled with milk.

22

There was but one woman in our family who ever laid claim to the hangman's job. Her name was Pingalakeshini; she lived in the time of Tughral Tughan Khan, in the thirteenth century. Thakuma called him Glutton Sultan, because she found it simply impossible to pronounce his name. He had been in love with Raziya Sultan and so surrendered Bengal to her, she alleged. I was in front of the mirror, fixing my bindi after a bath. Seeing me laugh she thought that I should be reminded of Pingalakeshini's fate. Ramu da had been taken away for his bath and so there were just the two of us in that small room where the old yellowing mirror hung on the dirty wall. Thakuma, who lay curled up on her cot with her left arm under her head, looked up at me with distaste and asked, 'Chetu, why are you laughing for no reason?'

Her question made me feel awkward, so I laughed again to hide it. 'Ah, Thakuma, don't I have the freedom even to laugh—me, the symbol of woman power?'

'Women should not laugh. That's a bad omen. The house where a woman's laughter rings—it won't be long before it collapses. Haven't I told you Pingalakeshini's story?'

172

'If a house falls because of laughter, let it fall, Thakuma!'

'When Pingalakeshini laughed, not just the house, but the very land fell.' Her voice resounded with a threat.

'I dreamt last night that we found your gold coin, Thakuma,' I tried, eager to change the topic. 'I dreamt that it rolled out when we were making your bed.'

She let out a sigh of pain. 'That's gone. Will anyone who's stolen such a thing return it?'

That threw me off balance. I realized only then that she hadn't got her coin back. I helped her off the cot, and shook her bedding and sheets; no, it was not to be found. Someone else had taken it for sure. And I couldn't even try to find out who it was without letting slip the truth about my own involvement. Ma who made Thakuma's bed had her grouses but surely was not bold enough to filch the coin. Other than her and Ramu da, the only people in the house were Kaku and Kakima. Champa and Rari had still not returned from their uncle's house.

'That disappeared quite some time back, Chetu, don't you worry about it now,' Thakuma tried to console me as I went out of the room in a sad stoop.

I did want to open up to her—tell her that Sanjeev Kumar had given it back to me and that I had put it under her pillow to protect his reputation—but did not have the courage to do so. His reputation had become my liability. Sadly, it dawned on me that I was now obliged to protect it at any cost. Even after Ramu da came back from his bath and Thakuma from her walk, my laugh did not return. I was leaning against Ramu da's cot—he was waiting impatiently to know if the cable operators' strike was over—eating the bhelpuri Thakuma had bought from Hari da's shop when Sanjeev Kumar Mitra appeared on the eleven o'clock news bulletin. It was an investigative report about the young woman who had been killed in a police encounter in Gujarat. The young woman's mother did not have an answer to his question as to why she had hurriedly left for Ahmedabad. After the mother demanded a CBI inquiry through her tears, the father of one of the alleged terrorists spoke by telephone—and something happened that threw me off balance again.

'Sri Nair, can you tell us about your son who was killed? Was he in love with this young woman?'

I was stunned by the question—he spoke in a language I could not make out at all. I only knew what he meant because it appeared in Bangla translation at the bottom of the screen.

'Your Sanjeev Kumar—where is he from?' Ramu da did not hide his annoyance. 'Native place? Don't know! Language? Don't know! Who are his relatives? Don't know! Does he have a wife and child somewhere? Please try to make sure that he doesn't, before the marriage at least!'

I had no reply. My eyes were fixed on the little bit of bhelpuri masala left on my palm; my mind was empty. Sanjeev Kumar continued to speak on-screen. Not interested in what he had to say, I went out of the room. There was more mystery in the life of the man I loved than in the death of the young woman who had been shot. A bout of anger and frustration engulfed me. It was galling that I was now obliged to establish the honesty of a person who was not honest with me. By the time I reached the studio that day for *Hangwoman's Diary*, no trace of laughter remained on my face or in my mind.

During the short gap before the show began, Sanjeev Kumar asked me why my face looked so wan; I could not even manage a smile in response.

'When you take charge as the first hangwoman, Chetna—'

'I have talked about it many times before,' I snubbed him even before he began. 'I am not the first woman in my family to take up this work. There was Pingalakeshini in the thirteenth century. Her real name was Tripurasundari. She changed her name when she took up this profession.'

Sanjeev Kumar stared at me incredulously. I ignored him for my own peace of mind and launched into speech. Tripurasundari was a peerless beauty. Her laugh was like bells pealing, and it had the power to seduce any man. She was married off at the age of seven, according to the prevailing custom. Her husband was a rich nobleman. Once, when she was travelling with her husband in a palanquin on her way back from worshipping at a Kali shrine, Tughral Tughan Khan heard her talking and laughing with her husband in her alluring way. He stopped the palanquin and pulled them out, and was smitten by her glowing beauty. Her husband surrendered her to the Khan, hoping to save his own life. When Tughan Khan, old enough to be her father, lifted her up and threw her face down upon his horse, her veil came undone; through the gap, she shot a furious glance at the husband who had abandoned her thus. He had taken the bag of money the Khan had thrown at him and was trying to flee with his life. She was six months pregnant then. But Tughan Khan showed her no mercy. Whenever she was summoned to his rooms, the guards would have to carry out her torn and ravaged body afterwards. In the meantime he also made her convert; it enraged Tughan Khan to have the vermillion she wore smudge on his face.

Tripurasundari gave birth before term; fashioning a noose from the umbilical cord for the neck of her beautiful, golden-skinned baby, she satisfied the hangman's craving in her veins. For ten years, Tughan Khan was the ruler of Bengal. In those ten years, she gave birth nine times; all nine infants were dispatched with their own umbilical cords. It was then that Narasimha Dev, the king of Odisha, attacked Bengal. Though Tughan Khan captured one of Narasimha Dev's fortresses, the Odisha army hit back when the Khan's forces were celebrating their victory. The Khan had to retreat. The Odisha army pursued him right up to Lakhnavati, the capital of Bengal in those days. They laid siege to the city and soon captured it. The city's Muslims were massacred. Tripurasundari fell into the hands of the Odisha army. They made her wear a sari, marked her forehead once more with vermillion, and shut her up in Narasimha Dev's tent. Her lacerated body had to be carried out the next day. Tughan Khan sought help from the Delhi Sultan. The Odisha army withdrew in the face of the forces from Delhi, but Tughan Khan had lost his eminence. He had to return to Delhi. Seizing her chance, Tripurasundari, who had escaped from Narasimha Dev's tent, sought refuge in a Buddha vihara. She shaved her head and became a female mendicant. Meanwhile, many governors ruled Bengal. In 1272, when the governor Amin Khan destroyed the vihara were she lived, Tripurasundari was fifty. But her youth was undiminished; she was once again captured by the soldiers and turned into a kept woman. When Tughan Khan attacked Bengal again, defeated Amin Khan and retook his position as governor, his soldiers found Tripurasundari in the enemies' tents. Despite her shaved head and ochre robes, Tughan Khan recognized her. She had to change her faith again.

Tughan Khan ruled Bengal for the next nine years, and during this time, Tripurasundari continued to be his concubine. Then, steadily growing uneasy with Tughan's rise, Balban, the ruler of Delhi, led a campaign against him. Tughan Khan won in the first two encounters. During the third assault, Tripurasundari escaped from the royal quarters and sought refuge in a gypsy tent. As his soldiers dragged her out of the tent, Balban happened to see her. Tripurasundari promised to help him defeat Tughan Khan; in return, she asked for Khan's body. When Tughan Khan was finally defeated, he was thrown at her feet, bound hand and foot. What more do you want, asked Balban. A ten-foot long stake of teakwood, she replied; another piece of teak half as long, an iron hook, some rope and a carpenter. When all these things were brought to her, she asked the carpenter to fix the narrow edge of the shorter piece of wood on the longer piece. The iron hook was fixed on the shorter piece, closer to its free edge. She then secured the rope on it. A pit was dug in the ground and the ten-foot wooden stake was planted in it firmly. Thus, right before the eyes of the watching crowd, a gallows tree rose up inside the tent.

'What next?' asked Balban, amazed.

'Now I need only the body,' she said, lifting up Tughan Khan, an old man by then, and propping him on a small platform below the gallows. As the crowd watched, she untied her sari, made a noose out of it and placed it around the Khan's neck. She then kicked the stand down. When Tughan Khan died of a broken neck, she let out once again, after fifty years, that seductive laugh that sounded like the pealing of bells.

My laugh did not return even when I noticed how engrossed Sanjeev Kumar was in the story, so much so that he seemed to have even forgotten his questions.

'And then?' he asked, still dumbstruck.

'When Balban asked her what more she wanted, she demanded the hangman's job. The sultan appointed her hangwoman. Thereafter Tripurasundari took the name Pingalakeshini. She lived till ninety. According to Thakuma, Pingalakeshini dispatched a thousand people.'

The expression on Sanjeev Kumar's face changed. 'One can understand Pingalakeshini's murder of Tughan Khan. That was her revenge. But why did she want a hangman's job?'

'All I can say,' I told him, 'is that some women's anger is such that it cannot be satiated with the death of just one man.'

I looked straight at him. He looked back uncomprehendingly.

'It's very hard to understand the people in your family, Chetna,' he said.

The day's show ended there. He took me to Park Street that evening. I got out of the taxi and looked around in wonder. Reminding everyone that it never slept and was completely unafraid of the rain, Park Street continued to froth. A paan-wallah sold paan from a box that hung from a cord around his neck, his uneven teeth dark red in the neon lights. Everywhere there were shops and big cars and people walking enthusiastically on the clean, wide road. He pulled me on to the footpath and hugged me to his side as we began to walk. I was hot and cold at the same time. Park Street throbbed with sounds and lights and many kinds of scents. We passed a few obese men on the road, and he said, 'Should we eat something? We can go to Trincas. These are the loveliest nights of the year in Kolkata. We can celebrate this lovely night in Park Street. Blue Fox, Barbeque, Olympia . . .'

When he laughed, I was still looking around; my own laugh had not yet returned. Park Street was born out of the park Sir Elijah Impey had laid to raise spotted deer. In the row of lights from the Maidan to Park Circus, instead of deer and peacocks, people and vehicles flitted up and down. In between the dirty buses and the cars big and small, an ambulance was trying to squeeze its way ahead; next to it was a rickshaw, pulled by a twig-like creature, in which a fat woman sat. Even as efforts were on to ban hand-pulled rickshaws, Sanjeev Kumar reminded me, thousands of men in the city continued to pull them, always running short of breath and dying, spitting blood. When the rickshaw and the puller disappeared in the stream of traffic I closed my eyes and tried to imagine how Park Street must have looked when my grandfather's grandfather was my age. It must have been filled with palanquins and horse-drawn carriages instead of cars and buses. I knew Thakuma remembered building number eight on the corner of Radha Bazar Street and Old Court Road. The carriages used by the British aristocracy were crafted by Stuart and Co. which functioned in the yard of that building. Those plush vehicles began to acquire a special touch after James Stuart came to Kolkata in the eighteenth century. Satchidananda Grddha Mullick, the brother of Grandfather Kalicharan Grddha Mullick, was a servant in the house of a Dutch artist who was visiting Kolkata at that time. Grandfather Satchidananda was a true artist, adept at building coaches embellished with silver carvings and embroidering the edges of the red satin seats with gold thread. It was he who fashioned the two palanquins that were ordered by Lord Cornwallis for the princes of Mysore with gold and silver carvings. For each palanquin, the Dutchman Solvines received seven thousand rupees, and his servant Satchidananda a gift of one British rupee. The white man and his wife went back after this, and my forefather died of too much drinking.

Sanjeev Kumar led me towards Chowringhee. The scent of jhalmuri filled the air. He bought us some jhalmuri and we continued to walk, munching the spicy and tangy beads of puffed rice. We spotted the rickshaw-wallah we'd seen in the road earlier; he sat leaning against the handle of the rickshaw, smoking a bidi. His greying beard, yellowing eyes and sunburned, blackened face with its stony impassiveness reminded me of Jatindranath Banerjee. Not love but death pervaded my heart as I walked on Park Street with the man I desired. I felt very uneasy.

'What are you thinking, Chetna?' Sanjeev Kumar ran his finger lazily on my wrist.

'What language did you speak today on TV at noon, Sanju babu?' I asked.

'Oh that . . . that's my father's language,' he said rather casually. It didn't sound so simple to me. But I could not see if his expression had changed. The dark and his glasses hid him well.

'Hey, we are planning the eve-of-the-hanging show in a big way. We need your help and somehow must steal Grddha da too. Look, Chetu, this is a prestige issue for me. No one has ever even thought of something like this. Understand? This is the wedding gift you should give me.'

'What?' I asked, flustered.

'The success of that day's show.'

My heart wilted again.

'Thakuma's gold coin got lost again,' I said, not addressing him in particular.

'Eh? How? You should have been careful,' he said.

The thief accuses the owner, I thought, and it made me want to laugh. We were silent then for some time.

'This is the first time I am seeing Park Street at night. There are many shops, aren't there?' I looked around. We were in front of the Zaveri Sari Emporium.

'Do you want to buy something, Chetna? Saris?' he asked me in a tempting tone.

I looked deep into his eyes and shook my head, laughing enigmatically. Pingalakeshini had retained her strength and health to the very end. The sultan built her a mansion close to the prison. Till she died she invited a different man to her bed each night, announcing a reward for the man who could conquer her in bed. Her death came at the age of ninety— after dispatching yet another at the gallows, she had a bath followed by a full meal and was sleeping with the man of the night when death claimed her.

'I have a wish . . .' I murmured in a seductive voice.

Remembering Father's advice that no story should be fully told, I had not revealed the vital parts of Pingalakeshini's story on *Hangwoman's Diary* that day. When Pingalakeshini untied her sari to make a noose for Tughan Khan, she was completely naked. Tughan Khan's eyes fell on her body, but instead of desire, fear glinted in them. She did not kill him at one go. She stood him on the platform, kicked it down, enjoyed his struggle for breath and then restored the platform beneath his feet. Relieved, Tughan Khan tried to loosen the knot around his neck. Then she kicked away the stand again. He hung once more, flailing desperately. This went on all night long.

'What is it that you want, Chetu? Let me buy it for you,' Sanjeev Kumar ran his finger lovingly on the curve of my neck.

'Don't buy it . . .' I closed my eyes and whispered amorously.

'Then?' His voice became tenderer.

'Steal it!' I whispered, stroking his palm with my left hand.

Sanjeev Kumar stopped, unable to believe his ears. Then he laughed, embarrassed. I wanted to know how he accomplished his thefts. I gave him half-an-hour's time, but he returned in five minutes.

'You have to come with me, Chetna, otherwise it is difficult to steal a sari.'

I laughed out loud. 'Some things you have to do by yourself,' I challenged him.

He looked at me, helpless, and said, 'In that case, let's go to another shop. One where men's clothes are also sold.' He scratched his head, ruffled. 'This sari is a complicated garment . . .'

I remembered all of Thakuma's complaints about the sari; her grandmother had apparently cursed Keshab Chandra Sen till the end of her life for having popularized such a tight-fitting, stifling garment in the name of the Bengal Renaissance. How comfortable the old style was, she grumbled—just wrap one end around the waist, throw the other over the shoulder!

'I can filch anything in this world except a sari. Or a woman should come with me . . .'

I enjoyed the joke and laughed.

He looked at me, puzzled. 'But truly, why did you ask me to steal?'

'Just to check if you'd do as I ask . . . and I also wanted to see how you do it.'

'No one can see. That's the artistic knack to stealing. Like magic. You need a hand that's quick. And a tongue that will keep people's attention.'

'Even if you did steal it, I'd have asked you to return it to the same shop.'

His face grew heavy. 'No, I have never returned anything except your gold coin. And I won't do it, ever.' His tone was filled with resentment.

We were silent for a while as we walked on the footpath where light mingled with dark. As the brilliant lights of the Park Plaza Hotel appeared in the distance, he stopped. 'What if we go to my place tonight?' He asked in a casual tone.

'No.'

'Don't you want to see the house where you'll live?'

That was offered seductively. And my mind was not left untouched by the memory of the house where the nilmani latha and the aparajita bloomed.

'That's my father's house. We will live in my mother's house . . .'

I looked at him, a little suspicious.

' . . . in Sonagachi . . .'

He sounded calm. Before I could ask why, he laughed and grabbed my hand tightly. 'That's a long story, not to be told while we walk down Park Street. My bride-to-be should hear it in my house, in the bedroom, lying on my lap.'

'Another day,' I said.

'When? The days are going by so fast. Today is the twentieth . . . just four days to go, and after that . . . I insist that you know everything about me before we are married, Chetna.'

I looked at him, helpless, not knowing what thoughts gathered in the green eyes behind those dark glasses. When he caressed my palms with his fingertips I was assailed by a sudden sense of frustration. His fingertips throbbed not with tenderness for the woman he loved, I felt, but with the wile and agility of a thief. In my heart, a hundred serpents raised their hoods in apprehension, thrusting out their forked tongues, alert for sounds and scents.

As we walked back down the street which was now a beehive of many kinds of lights, he turned his gaze uneasily towards the sari shop. I found the laugh which I had lost. When he accepted my challenge and went in, I waited outside in the ancient youthfulness of Park Street, feeling hot and cold at the same time. To recover her lost laugh, Pingalakeshini made Tughan Khan ascend the gallows again and again. Seven hundred and twenty-seven times to be exact.

23

A straight line. That was what Gautam Deb drew first on my broken slate. Above it he drew something that looked like an eyeball with small straight lines, like eyelashes, around it. When he finished he smiled, showing all his small white teeth, saying, here Chetu di, look, the sun. A couple of hours later, when he was hanging from a branch of the guava tree behind his hut, his eyes bulged out like brown solar orbs rising in the white sky. His body was suspended in a straight line, dark and thin. There was no fear or pain on his face; it was lit up with curiosity. His mother, Aruna, was returning with pots of water on her head and hip. She flung them to the ground, clasped his legs to her breast and broke down. Seeing me in the crowd that had gathered, she cursed: May the lightning fall upon your head. Even then, I did not know what I had done wrong. We were playing the hangman's game. Only when I grew older did I realize that it was a game that cancelled out one of the players.

That was one morning in 1987. A greying journalist had brought a clean-shaven young man with a large leather bag on his shoulder to meet Father. Father had already announced loudly enough for all the corpses on Strand Road to hear that the journalist would be coming to our house by taxi, having flown down all the way from Delhi. I can still see him throw away his smouldering cigarette, receive the men with great respect, and lead them to his room. No sooner had he got out of the car than the young man took a camera out of the leather bag and started taking our pictures. Gautam, Champa, Aparna, Amalendu and I—all of us laughed loudly and tried to run away, feeling very shy. As we ran we looked back, hoping that he would take more pictures of us.

'Let's peep into Grddha da's room,' Amalendu began to make a fuss. He would die of a fever in SSKM Hospital later. All of us peeped into Father's room through the tiny window, brimming over with excitement and sheer happiness. All I remember of that is the image of the senior reporter filling the round chair, the plastic weave of which was frayed and broken, his bulging tummy and a recorder in front of him. Father's moustache and hair were not so grey then. We saw him draw himself up, summoning the kind of dignity that he called up while playing the zamindar in the jatra, and make a noose from a piece of old rope as he talked.

'This is no ordinary job, Babu. It is a duty, a vital duty. It is believed that our earliest ancestor, the first hangman, Radharaman Mullick, received a boon from Bhagawan Mahadev: whoever died by Radharaman's hands would enter heaven. That has continued through generations to this day—anyone who dies by our hands will indeed reach heaven. And so, to tell you the truth, the old jail IG, Basu babu, he would pat the condemned men and tell them, your great luck, you are to be dispatched by Grddha Mullick . . . you will go straight to heaven. See, Babu, this is the noose we make . . . it is special because only Grddha Mullicks can tie it. Many people have tried to learn this art from us. But none of them could make such a perfect, beautiful knot . . . oh, no!'

Father held it up.

'Grddhaji, your victim is an infamous murderer. Are you afraid?'

'No, Babu. God has chosen me to kill this cruel murderer. It is my mission, my fate. Why should I be afraid?'

He was to hang the infamous killer Vinod Gaurav, a refugee from Bangladesh who had strangled to death nearly a hundred children with his handkerchief. His pleasure was to travel all over Bengal, lure children with sweets, and then murder them. When he had slain his hundredth victim, he went to a police station and confessed that he had killed a hundred children and destroyed their bodies with acid.

'Children are the incarnations of God, Babu. The reprobate who kills them should be hanged not once but a hundred times. That is what I wish.'

But outside, there was a scuffle going on near the small window, with both Champa and Aparna trying to peep in at the same time and shoving each other out of the way. Aparna scratched Champa and Champa tried to hit her. But her hand fell on Amalendu instead. He leapt on her and pulled her hair. She screamed. Father was really mad—he stood up and shouted, get lost, be quiet, you kids. We ran away past the kitchen yard, past Champa's, Aparna's and Amalendu's mud huts which stood behind my house, and reached the backyard of Gautam's house. That too was a mud hut. We leapt over the urinal drain running out from Amalendu's house and reached the shade of the guava tree, panting heavily. Gautam picked up a length of rope from the ground, tied it to a branch, knotted the loose end into a noose, and put it around Amalendu's neck, saying, 'I am the hangman Grddha Mullick. I am going to hang Amal da now . . .'

'Oh no, Grddha da, don't kill me!' Amalendu acted as if he were trembling with fear and bowed down to Gautam.

All of us laughed. That's how the game began. Gautam's noose came undone in the middle of the game. Then Amalendu tied one; he didn't make a good one. The others tried, they couldn't manage either. Then the rope came to me. Somebody rolled a rock under the tree to make a platform. Amalendu climbed on it. When we removed it he held the

183

branch with his hands, swung his legs and pretended to die. My hair stands on end whenever I think of that day. It was only much later that I realized my fingers had knotted the noose as though someone was guiding me, like the way someone holds your hand when you learn to write. Amalendu put it around Gautam's neck; I fixed it there. Amalendu tied the other end to the branch of the tree. Each of us took turns at playing the hangman. Then there was a fight between Champa and Amalendu about who would be the hangman next. He hit her and she ran away crying. Everything that happened afterwards surfaces in my memory as sound. The sound of Amalendu's mother calling him. The patter of his soiled black feet. Champa calling Aparna loudly; of her thin legs running away. The sound of the gravel grating beneath my feet as I turned back towards home, suddenly feeling bored when everyone had left. The sound of Gautam calling to me from behind. When I turned I saw Gautam standing on the platform looking angry and hurt; the noose was still around his neck, its other end tied to the branch. It made me laugh. Then his legs slid off the stone and he began to struggle. It was fun to watch. I returned there much later, only after I heard loud and desperate wails. Weeks after his death, our picture—the picture of Gautam, Champa, Aparna, Amalendu and me running away, laughing—appeared in the English magazine *Sunday*. Because I looked at that photo for so long, the image of Gautam that filled my memory was that of him running away, his face turned towards the photographer. Jatindranath Banerjee's photo, which appeared earlier in the *Statesman*, was of a man turning to look back as he got into the jeep. Only there was no smile on his face.

I could not sleep that night. Outside the hearses waited in a row. The queue for free food distributed after someone's last rites snaked on. The sight of men and women squatting impassively on the ground that was moist with the rain that had fallen sometime that evening made me uneasy. The smoke from the pyres on the banks of the Ganga filled the sky above like fog. It announced: four days from now, Jatindranath Banerjee's body too will turn into dust and smoke in this very same cremation ground.

'The wedding's not even been fixed. We have only his word for it . . . It's not proper, this, you going around with him . . .' Ma's voice was unnecessarily loud; she had started her harangue when she saw me come in.

'Your father does not have the slightest sense. Give him a bottle and some cash and he'd swing from a tree like a monkey. Aren't you an educated girl? Shouldn't you have some concern about your future?'

'What was to be my future, Ma?' I asked her vacantly.

Ma was like Devi Sitala, with the broom and the winnow, the pot of sacred water and the basin to fetch more of it. Sweeping and cleaning and sprinkling the ground with water, and bursting in hot oil like a mustard seed—that was all there was to Ma's life. Even her food was like Sitala's sacred food: leftover rice gruel. Cold and stale, the previous day's food. Both of them had seats of dignity—the donkey was their mount. That night when Father quarrelled with her, how I wished her mustard seeds would turn into the pustules of smallpox.

'You are useless, you ill-omened female! Women ought to love their husbands if they are women at all! A woman who's of no use to her husband shouldn't be alive!'

Knowing that what followed next would be the sound of a hard slap falling on Ma's face, I turned over. Anger smouldered on Ramu da's face.

'Try questioning me and I'll hang you by the neck!'

'Oh ho, indeed! Hang me? Hang me! Really, try doing that!'

'Ma . . .' Ramu da called, as if at the end of his patience.

Ma came out of Father's room hurriedly and stroked Ramu da's forehead gently, glancing at Thakuma and me.

'Do you want a sip of water?'

'No, I want some peace . . .' He closed his eyes, irritated.

'Okay, I won't say anything.'

She admitted defeat and went into the kitchen. The next day, I was helping Ma when Kakima came running in. 'Didi, look, what a pretty child!'

I left the half-kneaded dough in the kitchen and went out of the house. A procession had crossed over, twisting its way in between the rows of vehicles waiting for the railway gate to open. A lean man of forty or forty-five held a child's body in his arms. The child was not even five. He lay in his father's arms—they had decked his hair with a peacock feather and dabbed a spot of black on his cheek. His mother

185

kept swooning as she tried to walk. As the eight o'clock Prinsep Ghat Circular juddered past, the waiting vehicles began to move, spitting black smoke. The child's father, drained of life, made his way through the bustle, carrying his son's body. When we came face-to-face and his eyes fell on me, he started heavily and fixed me with a terrible stare. Fear overtook me. Though moving ahead in the push of the traffic and the crowd, his eyes stayed on me. The child too had played the hangman's game, I realized.

I ran back into the house where I collapsed on the floor, panting wildly. Ramu da looked up, very concerned. 'Just yesterday, three children . . .' There was deep sadness in his voice. Father just laughed when he got to know that the child had played hanging.

'Chetu, don't you worry. None of us—neither you, nor I, nor our family—has done anything wrong. Hanging is our duty. When we speak of it to a thousand people, if even six of them mend their ways, that's big.'

Father filled his jug with water and went back to his room. Just as I had induced Sanjeev Kumar to steal, the world was urging me to steal Jatindranath's life, I felt. As with theft, when meting out death too one needs a quick hand and a quicker tongue to distract other people's attention. There is but one difference. In this case, the stolen goods would be lost to the thief too. I sat leaning against Ramu da's cot, a void opening deep in my mind. Niharika's feet had been adorned with a pair of anklets with delicately carved silver leaves. When she walked, they tinkled gently. Even when her body had swayed slowly from the beam in Father's room, they had tinkled softly. When he was hanging from the branch of the guava tree, Gautam Deb was smiling. He must have died of a broken neck in a split second; by the time we ran there hearing his mother's scream, he was motionless. He was sent to heaven by me, with the first-ever noose I had fashioned.

That day, the Ghat was unusually crowded. Whenever I peeped out, I saw children with eyes like risen brown suns calling me to play the hangman's game. I stared at my own hands in terror.

24

THREE DAYS TO THE HANGING—HANGMAN STARTS BARGAINING screamed the *Telegraph*'s headline. There was a picture of Father sitting on the dirt-covered wooden chair in the tea shop, his six-foot-two frame drawn up with all the dignity it could amass, an expression of determination tinged with sadness on his face. Even the tiny curl of smoke from the half-smoked cigarette in his right hand and the small tear in the gamchha on his shoulder could be seen. I was reading out this news to Ramu da when the irritating buzz of the crowd outside distracted me. I went up to the doorstep and instantly realized that the ambulance on the road was carrying the body of the Bengali football player who had been shot dead, Pranoy Chatterjee. The crowd was following it. Garlanded portraits of Chatterjee were propped up on the front and the back of the vehicle which was decked with white orchids. In the picture on the back of the ambulance of Pranoy Chatterjee, clad in a white t-shirt and shorts, chasing the ball, the ball could not be seen. Two days ago, in Jamshedpur, Pranoy Chatterjee had barely stepped out of his house on his way to work when a stranger approached him with a piece of paper with someone's address on it. When Chatterjee looked down to read it, the stranger pulled out a gun from his pocket and shot him. Hearing the gunshot, Pranoy's wife Premlata Chatterjee came running. She hugged him, screaming. Ran after passing vehicles, crying for help. Finally, jumped in front of a taxi and took him to the hospital. Waited outside tearfully as the doctors fought to save him. Kept vigil at his bedside without a drop of water. TV channels and newspapers went into a tizzy extolling Premalata's extraordinarily passionate wifely love. And when Pranoy finally succumbed to his injuries, her wails were so loud that the whole hospital shook. But just when the wailing and weeping reached a crescendo, the police entered to arrest her. Now the channels and the newspapers went into yet another whirl: Pranoy Chatterjee had been murdered by a hitman hired by his wife's lover, their neighbour, and she had paid the money! Thakuma, who had just returned from the Shiva temple at the Ghat in her tattered white sari, cursed Premalata loudly: 'Women like her ought to be hanged! Pray to Mahadev that it happens by your hand!'

I heard that and smiled involuntarily. I was sure that no woman had ever received the death sentence in independent India. In this, the nation and the courts have conceded special status to women. As we watched, the ambulance and the other vehicles crossed the railway tracks and turned towards the cremation ground. The T-junction in front of our house became completely empty, something that happened very rarely. After a very long time I could see clearly the two shops right opposite our house: Suraj Das's photo studio, Photo Divine, and Gyan Nath da's sweetmeat shop. Two huge bulls that had been foraging in a pile of rubbish near the Port Trust workers' basti past Hemant da's Kali temple shook their jowls as they walked leisurely in the middle of the road. A young boy—a new face—with a swastika on his forehead and a trident in a greenish yellow plastic jug walked along the street, begging in the shops. The plastic water pot that Gautam Deb's mother Aruna had flung away on seeing her three-year-old son dangling from the tree branch had been the same greenish yellow colour. Plastic pots to store water had made their appearance in our lives a little before Gautam took leave of us. Champa's and Aparna's father Subrato used to sell mud pots. Once these light and unbreakable plastic pots became popular, he and his family went away. I never saw them again. My last memory of little Champa is of her in a brown petticoat, touching me as I stood in front of Hemant da's Kali temple sucking at a sweet Ramu da had given me. She was begging for a piece of the sweet, looking rather silly. The orange-coloured sea of sweetness in my mouth, I gave her an irked look. I then bit into the sweet, broke it, and swallowed it straightaway. This memory makes me feel more guilty than the one in which I put the noose around Gautam Deb's neck. It is a human being's past that makes him weak.

Because the water supply revived only at eleven-thirty, I was late to bathe. As I was getting ready to go to the tiny bathroom behind the house, where one person could just about squeeze in, Father called from the tea shop. I went up to the door of the kitchen. Sitting under the photo frame which held the article 'Hanging is no child's play: Grddha Mullick', Father looked at me with a serious expression as he took a cigarette from the table, lit it, and put it between his lips. 'Don't forget to tell the channel chaps that we will be busy from tomorrow and that you can't go to the show after today.'

That was a bit surprising. I could sense he had something in his mind. 'The contract with the channel . . .' I tried to say in a low voice.

But Father just rolled his eyes at me. 'Contract? What contract? Chetu, this is our chance . . . after the twenty-fifth, we will be completely useless, do you understand?' A large puff of smoke wafted from his mouth.

As I got ready to leave for the studio that day, I wondered what role had been assigned to me in this new drama of his. Earlier, there used to be just a small can of Cuticura powder next to our spotty old mirror; but now, there was not only face powder and talcum powder, but even Pond's cream. As I was doing my face, I heard him speaking in the tea shop.

'No! No interview, no nonsense. Is some mad thing rushing around in my head that I must keep on chattering? It is a busy day today. It would be better if you left without wasting my time . . .' Father was playing hard to get with some correspondent of a newspaper or channel.

I stuck a large red bindi on my forehead. My face looked like a watercolour on which an ink bottle had been splashed. I felt like measuring up my good looks all over again in the mirror. But perhaps Ramu da was not asleep; perhaps he was watching me?

And indeed, Big Brother was watching me. He half-opened his eyes and smiled sarcastically. 'It's going to be hard to kill time from now.'

'Huh?' I asked in the common Bengali sing-song tone.

'Yes . . . Baba's on the azar already.'

As I searched for my purse and umbrella, Ramu da let out a heavy sigh. 'Every day, the papers have some news or the other about you. The first woman in Indian history to occupy the hangman's post! The only one anywhere in the world . . . you've become history, Chetu!'

'I fear history.'

'All women do . . .' He smiled again.

I looked at him and felt what he said was wrong. It is not women who fear history; it is history that fears women. That's why there are so few of them in it. My place in it was assured only if I managed to put the noose around Jatindranath Banerjee's neck and he died in a flawlessly executed hanging. I went out into the road expecting the channel's

189

vehicle to be there any minute; a few handcarts passed by carrying dead bodies accompanied by weeping women in tattered, soiled saris, and a group of villagers. Cutting straight through that dreary line, paying no attention to anyone, Sanjeev Kumar Mitra came over from the other side of the street and strode into the tea shop. He was flushed with anger. I hesitated for a moment, but moved to the side of the shop past the saloon and waited on the road.

'Phani da, tumi amaar shaathe erokom korte parona!'

That was the first time I heard him burst out so loud in Bangla.

'What did I do, Sanju babu?'

Clad in a white jubba and dhoti, Father sat up in his chair, drawing himself up as if he were on stage. He pretended to be looking for a matchstick to light his cigarette.

'Didn't you promise that you'd set apart the last three days before the hanging exclusively for our channel? But I just heard that you've signed a contract with someone else for the twenty-fourth and twenty-fifth?' Sanjeev Kumar said with barely controlled agitation.

Father took a long time to light the matchstick.

'I was completely humiliated in front of my boss, Phani da. At the very least you should not have forgotten that I am to be your future son-in-law.'

'Son-in-law!' Father laughed out loudly. 'Have you heard of Mir Jafar Ali Khan, Sanju babu? He was the nawab of Bengal? Do you know who betrayed him? His own son-in-law. You should study history, Babu, history.'

Sanjeev Kumar's response to that was to fling a searing glance at me. I doubted if he knew that Mir Jafar Ali Khan had ruled Bengal in the time of Grandfather Manohar Dev Mullick. Mir Jafar, who had conspired with Jagat Seth, the richest merchant of those times, and the British to defeat Siraj-ud Daula, had an insatiable appetite for power. When Mir Kasim, his son-in-law, plotted against him and assumed power himself, Mir Jafar allied with the British and, after four years, returned to the throne, defeating Mir Kasim. In return, however, he had to surrender the land completely to the British.

When Father went inside to change, Sanjeev Kumar turned towards me.

'The old man's started haggling, hasn't he?' The muscles in his face had become taut, tight, I felt that it was his real expression; a cruel one. A smile seemed to cross Kakima's face as she made the tea. Sanjeev Kumar paid her no attention: 'Your father knows that this is the time he can quibble, Chetu. You have to stand by me now. I launched this programme to help *you*. You got this job because I pushed. You must realize that all the good things you're enjoying now are because of that . . .'

As I stared back at him, I remembered the story of Raja Nandakumar, and Thakuma's warning that one should never receive favours from the high and mighty—for one may have to bear the burden of their evil deeds. No one can ever amass riches and power without cheating someone in some way, she said. All the mighty mansions of wealth and power are built that way. Russomar Dutt, who began as a clerk in Hack and Davis Co. earned a monthly salary of sixteen rupees. When the company's fortunes plummeted, the bosses promised him ten thousand rupees to forge the accounts. Overnight, he became one of the city's richest men. A member of the Tagore family let out his building near Esplanade to the employees of the East India Company for eight hundred rupees a month. The Kerr-Tagore Company ventured into shipping, banking and coal mining; Shyam Sunder Sen joined hands with Richard Oakland to start cotton mills. Many Indians who waited worshipfully at the port to receive the Englishmen who came to grow fat on the riches of the Indian people became owners of lakhs and crores of rupees through the benevolence of their masters. And much later, the servants got together to get rid of their masters.

Inside the car, Sanjeev Kumar Mitra scolded me again and again in fits of agitation.

'Yeah, yeah, I richly deserve this . . . all the journalists in this land had warned me, don't trust them. But I didn't believe them. I could not, whenever I saw your face . . .'

'I can't say what decision Baba will take, and when.'

He glared at me.

'Can't you wriggle out of the other contract? You are not some ordinary female, remember. You are the symbol of the power and self-respect of Indian womanhood!'

I couldn't help laughing. He stopped talking and turned his head away sharply. When we reached the studio, the six o'clock news bulletin had begun.

'Namaskar . . . Narendra Modi will not be removed from chief ministership, says BJP President Atal Bihari Vajpayee . . . Paris gets ready for the world's costliest wedding . . . With just three days left for the first death by hanging in India in nine years, the hangman Phanibhushan Grddha Mullick has started bargaining . . .'

My eyes stayed on the TV screen as they applied make-up on me. The BJP president's statement breezed by quickly. The next news item, about the preparations for the Parisian wedding in the family of the Kolkata-born billionaire Lakshmi Mittal, took more time than expected. The reporter claimed that Indians had much reason to take pride in this event, which would cost over one hundred and fifty crore dollars. My patience was wearing thin. There was a short break. Then Father's face appeared on the screen. As the reporter announced that the chief hangman Phanibhushan Grddha Mullick had raised his demands three days before the hanging, asking for ten thousand rupees as remuneration for himself, a regular job in some government department for his daughter, and a thousand-rupee monthly pension for his son who has lost all his limbs, Father's ancient room with the news reports on the walls, the images of Ma Kali and Mahadev—all appeared on the screen.

Father began delivering his dialogues with a steadily glum expression shaded by cigarette smoke. 'Arre, what are you saying? Is this a trivial matter? Human rights organizations all over the world are agitating against the death penalty. If hanging were so simple, would they take so much trouble? This is a serious affair, Babu. It is something we do with complete dedication—of mind, body, intellect. My daughter, the girl whom all of you today venerate as the symbol of the power and self-respect of Indian womanhood, Chetna Grddha Mullick . . . just think of her . . . shouldn't she have a life after this event? Does this country have no commitment at all to our lineage which has dedicated itself to carrying out its justice and upholding its laws?'

His words were as flawless and penetrating as those long dialogues he delivered on the jatra's azar, but my unease continued to deepen. Soon, the reporter reappeared on the screen. 'At the same time, Minister Padmeshwar Choudhury has made it clear that while the government had agreed to all the demands that Grddha Mullick made initially, it is not prepared to yield any more. Talks will be held in the coming days, the minister's office announced. Our correspondent reports that this development has left the event in deep uncertainty. A demand has also been raised that Phanibhushan Grddha Mullick and Chetna Grddha Mullick be punished in case the execution keenly anticipated by the entire nation is postponed further.'

All the faces I encountered when I came out of the make-up room, it seemed, were casting suspicious looks at me. A gallows tree was being erected on the studio floor. The background was painted in black and grey, ostensibly to remind the viewer of impending death. I suddenly felt unusually tired. It was not easy to sit in front of the gallows and speak into the camera. It reminded me of Jatindranath Banerjee. He had spent more than twelve years in prison; his skin must be terribly pale. I saw clearly, as if he were standing before my eyes, his body with its shrivelled-up flesh and protruding veins and bones. Maybe Father will take over the task of putting the noose around his neck . . . . I may be spared the sight of the veins in his neck tightening, but I will have to pull the lever for sure. My right hand felt numb and frozen.

'With just a few days left, there is news that your Baba has started haggling with the government. Chetna, are you sure that he will not withdraw at the last moment?'

That's how Sanjeev Kumar Mitra opened that day's *Hangwoman's Diary*. Instead of the usual loving and friendly expression, his face bore an aloof, suspicious look. More than anyone else, I knew that Father could not withdraw. In this matter, he was more dangerous than Mir Jafar Ali Khan. Mir Jafar was the one who had rallied back, allying with Shuja-ud Daula of Oudh and Alam Shah II of Delhi to defeat Mir Kasim and send him into exile.

'Only Baba can explain his decision . . .'

'But what if he withdraws? You are the assistant hangman. What would be your stand if you had to undertake the task by yourself?'

That was a dangerous question. I kept my eyes on him while groping for an answer. 'Isn't it wiser to wait—till what's to happen happens—and then take a decision?' I tried to smile.

'Does that mean that your Baba is trying to haggle?'

'He does not speak nonsense.'

'So you admit that it is haggling.'

'Is this haggling, Sanju babu? Isn't it linked to our livelihood?'

'Chetna, this is Bharat. We have a tradition. Truth, duty, justice—all these blend together in the history of our nation. Don't the citizens of this country have a duty to uphold it?'

That moment I felt that Sanjeev Kumar's anger was actually towards himself. I sighed deeply. 'Sanju babu, in 1760, Mir Kasim would have become the emperor of India. He had stood his ground in battles against the British, but his father-in-law Mir Jafar Ali Khan allied with the British and defeated him. The vanquished Kasim was tied to a lame elephant and exiled. The elephant soon grew tired; it threw him off its back and ran away. He had no place to go. He sought refuge in Allahabad, Jodhpur, Kotwal, many other places, but was refused everywhere.'

'What's the connection here?' His eyes narrowed.

'The only person who stayed with him till the very end was my forefather Manohar Mullick's brother Atmaram Mullick.'

Sanjeev Kumar paused to listen.

'Mir Kasim did not have even a speck of gold or a single coin left. His war wounds were infected and filled with pus. And on top of it, he suffered from dropsy. He who had lived in luxury, covered in silks and jewels in the nawab's palace, wandered, homeless, with a swollen, blackened body, for thirteen years in the merciless summer and terrible winter . . .'

'Okay, okay, but what if Grddha da decides to withdraw?'

I tried to look steadily into his eyes. Thakuma's angry remonstrance that everyone shamelessly stretched out their hands for whatever the buyer offered, just to stay alive for one more day, rang in my ears.

'Sanju babu, there was even a song about Mir Jafar of Bengal and Mir Sadiq of Deccan who connived with the British to defeat Mir Kasim and Shuja-ud Daula. *Jaffaraz Bengal Sadiqaz Dakkan, nang-e-din, nang-e-adam, nang-e-millat, nang-e-watan*—Mir Jafar of Bengal and Mir Sadiq of Deccan are a disgrace to the faith, to humanity, and to the homeland.'

Though Sanjeev Kumar tried to cut in, clearly exasperated, my words continued to flow.

'Two centuries later, the British cut up this land in two before they left, and the great-grandson of Mir Jafar became the president of one of those pieces.'

'Chetna . . .'

'In Kotwal, one October, as the afternoon prayer rang from the mosque, Mir Kasim uttered the name of Allah and breathed his last. The last objects left with him—two worn Kashmiri shawls—had to be sold to pay for his burial . . . Do you now understand why Baba has to bargain?'

Sanjeev Kumar Mitra fell silent instantly and stared at me vacantly. I realized with a deep breath that all this while, we had been playing with an invisible ball. I had scored a goal. As Father would have put it, time now to make a politically correct statement. I gave him a kind look and said, 'Yes, this may be the truth, Sanju babu, but still . . . justice should be done, the law should be upheld!'

Sanjeev Kumar recoiled for a second. He was then neither the intruder who tried to break open my body, nor the lover who tried to fondle it. Just a peddler, a hawker. He lunged forward with eyes grown tiny, nostrils flaring, at the scent of a killing.

'Does that mean that if the chief hangman withdraws you will carry out the death sentence as the assistant hangman?'

I sighed again deeply. Then, as the symbol of Indian womanhood and self-respect, I proclaimed: 'Surely!'

My tongue tingled to say, 'One thumping line, right?' But I did not. The gallows that was coming up behind me lacked only a hook. When I sat in the make-up room removing the rouge, in the mirror I saw him coming into the room and taking off his spectacles. Our eyes met in the mirror. It looked as though the greenish yellow tinge had crept into my eyes as well. So easy a task these days, becoming the symbol of the power and self-respect of Indian womanhood.

25

The ilish fish swims twelve hundred kilometres from the sea into the Padma river to lay its eggs. It then returns to the sea. Niharika, my sister, had a life somewhat like that. She was married and sent off to Bardhaman but returned, only to commit suicide. Didi carried in her large eyes the silvery sparkle of the ilish. Ma's slim, fair body and Father's jet-black, straight hair made her more beautiful than the Durga idols made for puja. When she was fourteen, a young man who had come to Nimtala Ghat to perform his father's last rites fell in love with her. That had been a busy day at the Ghat. The queue formed by those who waited to register for cremation snaked past the railway track, the T-junction in front of our house, and further down. He let those who were behind him in the queue move up simply so he could keep Niharika, who was in the tea shop pouring tea into mud cups, in sight. Only when she disappeared into the house, hiding a smile, did he remember the shrouded body of his father lying in a pushcart in front of the Ghat. Days later, when she was sweeping Thakuma's little shrine, he stood in B.K. Patel and Co., across the road from our house, looking at her and feeding the doves that were all over the roadside. He had brought a paper packet to give her. Niharika, who opened it with all the carefree ardour of her fourteen years, saw in it a little statue of Durga seated on a lion, one leg folded with its foot resting on the other knee. His Durga had Niharika's black, winged brows, her large eyes, the same dimple which appeared on her left cheek when she smiled, and the innocent mischief of youth. Sitting in Bhojohori Manna restaurant near Star Theatre with Sanjeev Kumar Mitra and eating shorshe ilish, I could not take my eyes off the picture of Binodini Dasi that hung on the wall. She posed sitting on a chair, the left ankle over the right knee; her face radiated masculine energy and confidence, but, to me, her body seemed suffused with a feminine frustration.

Sanjeev Kumar Mitra was feeling victorious; I had, after all, declared on *Hangwoman's Diary* that I would carry out justice no matter what. When we got out of the studio, he didn't let the taxi go to Strand Road; he wanted to walk about in the city.

'Chetna, ask for anything you want and I'll get it for you. You saved my honour today!' he said, stroking my wrists.

'Father will never forgive me,' I whispered, my eyes on the lights which flowed past us. It was the hour when the evening markets closed down and the hawkers returned home with empty baskets. The truth was that none of us had the courage to speak against Father even inside the house. One day, after Didi and her lover had started meeting near Mayer Ghat and enjoying the breeze together, Father went into the room which she shared with Thakuma. Niharika stood leaning against the wall, smiling and eyes shining while Father went up to the little ledge in the wall, took in his hands the little statuette of Durga, and examined it.

'Very pretty, uh?'

A shy smile was about to bloom on her face at his comment. But he flung it down on the floor, hard. She straightened in shock. Like the body of Siva's consort, Sati, which was chopped into a thousand pieces by Mahavishnu's Sudarsana Chakra, it shattered on the floor. It was a sad sight to see the prettily painted exterior lie smashed on the ground with the stuffing of hay spilling out like exposed entrails.

'See—there's nothing but hay and black mud inside.' Father let out an angry laugh.

Niharika's ever-smiling eyes rained tears.

'What have you done! Sacrilege! Breaking Ma Durga's statue, Bhagawan!' Hearing the commotion Ma came in and started scolding Father.

She was eight months pregnant then. Those days I was busy killing time inside Ma's womb tying the umbilical cord into a noose.

'Why, is this statue made of gold? At most, it'll last six months—it'll get filthy with soot and smoke and grime, and start falling apart,' Father said with deep sarcasm.

Niharika was still weeping.

'The rope is born of the tree. The mud pot from the soil. The mud pot can't be fashioned out of a cord; nor can a rope be woven out of mud. Aren't you her mother? Give her some advice!' he roared.

Father's ire was against the potters of Kumortuli who were first brought there from Krishnanagore by Raja Nabokrishna Deb to perform pujas for the victory of the British at Plassey. One of these potters never

197

returned to Krishnanagore; the idol makers of Kumortuli were his offspring. Father could never think of them as his equals.

'It will never work. Our traditions and theirs simply don't mix.'

'Ah, my children have such a wicked man for their father! She is just a little child! Must you weave the rope of your wretched tradition and reduce her to misery?' Ma flew at Father.

'Don't utter another word!' Father rolled his eyes and jumped at her. 'Reduce the length of the rope a little, and the doctors won't be able to tell whether it was murder or suicide!'

He went over to Niharika who stood looking tearfully at the broken statue of Durga on the floor and stared hard into her eyes. 'Your baba's hand has dispatched four hundred and forty-six people. Don't ever forget that.'

Because she knew what that meant, Niharika sobbed soundlessly and picked up the broken pieces. Suddenly, Ma's birthing pangs began. Unable to sit or stand, Ma wailed, squirming, hand pressed to her left hip. Her wails resounded in Strand Road all night. In the end Kaku and the neighbours took her to the hospital. The doctors had a hard time pulling me out—I was busy tying the umbilical cord around my own neck. Father came to see me at the Calcutta Medical College only at noon the next day; I was lying next to Ma on the broken iron cot which Kaku had managed to secure through a bribe. I opened my big eyes and looked at him unwaveringly. Father swelled with pride at that look.

'Bhagawan! You have given me another son! Mark my words, he will carry forward our family tradition!'

'Shameless fellow! Spent the night crawling all over whorehouses and has now come to write the horoscope! Hey you, see, this is not a boy, it's a girl . . . another luckless creature, you evil man! You put her into me!' Ma blurted out her pain, bristling with anger, not even bothering to wipe her tears.

'Eh, what? Not a boy?' Father was still unconvinced. 'Can a girl look so unblinkingly?'

Okay, he said, even if it's a girl, I won't take back the blessing I've given; but he was quite disappointed, really, at my birth. Mother shed bitter tears seeing my little face, regretting that she had brought into this world yet another unfortunate creature. Only Niharika was delighted by

198

my arrival. It was I who helped her forget her shattered love with my cries and laughter and meaningless babble. It was she who bathed me, carried me, rocked me in my cradle and sang me lullabies. Till she left us when I was five, all the love and dependence I ought to have felt towards Ma, I felt towards her. The memory of her breasts, as delicate as doves, still lingers in my body. It was on one of those days soon after my birth that her young man came to call her out, and she silently carried the broken pieces of the Durga statue to the heap of rubbish near the main door, left them there, and walked back in. He never came after that. While crawling on my knees I found the single cheek with the dimple lying between the storage box and the unplastered wall, and made it my toy.

'How tasty this fish is!' Sanjeev Kumar Mitra exclaimed, separating the flesh carefully from the many delicate bones.

I was visiting this restaurant for the first time. The tables around me were overflowing with large shrimp as broad as my palm and big pieces of fish almost as long as my forearm.

'Didn't you hear the news? The fisheries minister said there's going to be a bumper catch of ilish this time?'

The minister had been responding to queries about why the price of ilish was still escalating rapidly even though its season had arrived. He explained that the delayed rainfall had resulted in the increased price of the fish. Thakuma too had seen the signs and concluded that there would be more fish this time at Diamond Harbour, Bakali and Frazergunj. We were people who could afford to get ilish just about once a year or so. I remember, right from my earliest days, Thakuma complaining loudly that eating tasty fish had become nearly impossible since the damned Farakka Bund had been built.

'Ten tons of ilish come every day from Bangladesh. That'll go up to a hundred tons by the end of the month, they say. We can make our wedding an ilish festival—what do you think, Chetna?'

Relishing the fish curry, Sanjeev Kumar looked at me lovingly. 'Why aren't you eating the fish?' He put a piece into his mouth, savoured it and continued to smile at me. 'Can't you farm this? Like shrimp?'

It was I who laughed this time.

'Ilish becomes ilish through its journeys. The journey from the sea to the river to spawn. And then back to the sea again.'

199

'Ah, I know, after the eggs hatch, the little fish also begin to travel to the sea.'

'If you destroy its urge to travel, there will be no ilish, and it won't taste so good either . . .'

He laughed aloud.

'You can laugh at this only because you are a man.' I was angry.

He stopped laughing and raised his brows at me. 'So there are no men among the ilish?'

He laughed again. I did not. For me, all ilish fish were female. Like women with smooth cheeks and big breasts, as if before my very own eyes I saw them swim in search of fresh water, driven by their bodies. Thakuma grieved that Niharika's smile too had broken to pieces along with the statue of Durga that Father had smashed, and that her dimple had disappeared. Marriage proposals began to arrive very soon. The dowry negotiations stretched endlessly; her head bowed down more and more each time. In the end, a young man from a farming family in Bardhaman, Suryaprakash Dharman, agreed to reduce the dowry somewhat. Whenever I thought of it later, I always felt that on the day of the holud koda, when she sat down to be smeared with turmeric, her face was like that of Radha abandoned by Krishna. We were to pay a dowry of five thousand rupees and five sovereigns of gold. Father had to struggle to get it together. Niharika sat expressionless, head bowed, in the silver horse-drawn carriage hired with borrowed money, the light from the petromax falling on her golden-hued face. Inside the bundle—which she carried in her flight back home from her husband's house within a year of the wedding—I found, after her death, the shining single cheek with the dimple on it.

When we continued our journey in another taxi after dinner, I thought about Father's hands which had sent four hundred and fifty-one people to their deaths.

As the taxi crawled through the stifling traffic, a signboard that said Banmali Sarkar Road made me wake up all of a sudden.

'Why don't we get off here and walk?' I asked. Despite the questioning look on his face, Sanjeev Kumar did not probe. Turning left from the main road, I walked onwards as if I came here regularly. Only the yellow spots of light from paan shops and tea and biscuit kiosks remained. In one or two places, children were playing carom in the light from lanterns. The lane looked mostly deserted.

'Where is this?' Sanjeev Kumar wanted to know.

'Banmali Sarkarer baari, Govindram Mitrer chodi, Omi Chander daadi, Jagat Sether kodi—ke na jaane?'

Banmali Sarkar's house, Govind Ram Mitra's stick, Omi Chand's beard, Jagat Seth's wealth—who hasn't heard of these? I was disheartened that he did not realize that we were walking on the dark paths of the past, of the egoism, the greed, the vengefulness, the labour of so many human beings!

'Stop joking . . . tell me where we are.' He looked around with astonishment.

Black mud was heaped there like cow dung and behind the bundles of long bamboos were the headless statues of Durga, fashioned out of hay, seated with one leg placed over the other knee. I pointed towards them in the failing light: 'Kumortuli.'

'Oh, the place where they make the Durga idols for puja.'

There was nothing around us except the pale yellow circles of light from inside the houses on both sides of the street which, four months from now, would be so completely packed with Durga idols that there would be no place to even stand. In the light and the shadows of the evening, many Durgas finished to different degrees stood around us. Structures built out of bamboo strips with headless forms made of hay tied on them stood as far as the eye could see. An old man walking by made way for us. 'How will you take pictures if you come at this hour?' he asked, mistaking us for press reporters.

'Dada, can you tell us where Himanshu Pal lives?' I asked.

He gave me a quick look. 'Go straight, turn left, fourth house.'

When he hobbled on, Sanjeev Kumar looked at me doubtfully. 'Who is Himanshu Pal?'

I didn't reply. As we walked carefully, watching our step in the dark, the scent of food being cooked in the kitchens behind the workshops wafted to us. The fourth house was buried in darkness—four or five weather-beaten Durgas with their stuffing sticking out were stacked against its walls. Inside the house, someone sat in the light of a forty-watt bulb, moulding black mud on a form fashioned out of hay. As I stood there, I felt that we should not have come.

'I want him! Only him!'

Waking up in the middle of the night, Niharika's voice rang harshly in my ears again. She had come back home a completely different person. Her face was now stiff as a statue, unable to smile even at me.

'Don't forget that this is a hand that's hanged four hundred and fifty-one people.'

Father's bellow. I could hear Ma and Thakuma beginning to say something.

'I will follow him no matter who stands in my way!'

Her voice too was an angry shout.

'Uh-hu-hu . . . so you will drag the family's name through the mud?'

'I will go, Ma, please tell him, I have no other way . . .'

'No, you won't. Not while this Phanibhushan Grddha Mullick is alive!'

'Baba, I came back in search of him!'

I heard Father utter an awful obscenity. But I was terribly sleepy and so I turned over and went back to sleep again. Early at dawn, I woke up hearing Ma's wail. I saw Niharika on Father's wall among the framed pictures, like yet another image. She hung there as if she were bending her head for someone to place a garland around her neck. Her eyes looked at me from the air, above. A stream of blood flowed down her fair and rounded toes.

'Who is it?'

The person who was working inside raised his head. He looked like an old man, grey, with a wrinkled forehead; but he was at least thirty years younger than Father.

I could not respond. He turned the table lamp towards the ceiling. The workshop flooded with light. Durgas filled the room as the yellow light bounced back down after hitting the ceiling. Durgas with large, wide-set eyes, rounded cheeks, with a dimple on the left one. All of them sat with one leg crossed over the other knee and smiled confidently.

'Chetna, at this hour? Why?' he asked as he came closer, the tone of his voice like that of a very near relative who had full freedom with me.

Trembling, I gripped Sanjeev Kumar Mitra's wrist.

'What happened?' he asked again, amazed. I was struck dumb. I tried my best not to imagine myself as a full-length idol hanging from the beam in Father's room between the gamchha and the vest. I felt a trickle of blood run down my calves. I cannot say with confidence any more that no women have been hanged to death by the Grddha Mullicks. Himanshu Pal took a small statue from a ledge on the unplastered wall and gave it to me. Durga again. Sitting with her left ankle on her right knee, showing the dimple in her left cheek, she smiled at me lovingly.

'Take.'

With great kindness, he packed it for me. We stepped out without goodbyes and walked along the train tracks lengthening towards Strand Road. The tracks gleamed from the ambient light as if they were coated with silver. Somewhere, lal champa trees were in bloom.

'Why, Chetna, what happened?'

Sanjeev Kumar walked beside me, holding me close. In the dark, he felt my eyes overflowing with tears. There was a cement bench next to an old building; he sat me down there. What if we go to your place, my heart wished to ask. Instead what I asked was: What if we go to Star Theatre?

'Why?'

'Binodini Dasi was the great love in the life of my ancestor Kalicharan Grddha Mullick.'

'And so?' he asked mildly.

I flew into a rage all of a sudden.

'She was the first stage actress in Bengal. But for her, Girish Chandra Ghosh's plays would have all ended up hollow and useless . . .'

Binodini, who had given life to eight characters in twelve years, had begun her career at the age of eleven. Grandfather Kalicharan and Girish Chandra Ghosh became her admirers after seeing her stellar performance in *Kapala Kundala*. As Chaitanya in Girish Ghosh's *Chaitanya Leela*, she created history. Ghosh and Binodini both dreamt of building a grand theatre. When they realized that the building could not be completed because there was no money, the great master of the theatre urged the actress, a devadasi, to prostitute herself. He promised to name the drama company after her once it was built. And so she became a prostitute so that she could be born again on stage as Sita, Draupadi, Radha and Savitri. But Ghosh betrayed his promise when the building

203

was complete. He named it Star Theatre. Binodini gave up acting at the height of her career.

When Sanjeev Kumar held me close, the scent of ilish, which lasts twenty-four hours, enveloped me. What journeys lie in wait for me, I worried, journeys through the sea, through the river? All that remains of Grandfather Kalicharan in our house is a copy of the same picture that hangs in Bhojohori Manna, now a moth-eaten, dog-eared piece of paper. The image of a woman in male attire, her left foot resting on her right knee. I looked at the statue of Durga in my hands. Seated upon a roaring lion, armed with weapons in all of her eight arms, her left leg crossed on her right knee. Images that crumble to dust; statues stuffed with hay and black mud.

26

'This world does not value a poor man's honesty. Even if you sell it by the kilo, it won't get you rice and fish,' Father announced, rising from his cot.

Such fine theatrics. On his face, challenge and threat staged a shadow play. As he neared, I leaned against the wall, afraid. I wanted to explain that I hadn't been able to find another answer to Sanjeev Kumar's question on *Hangwoman's Diary*, but I choked on my words.

'Chetna, only my word carries weight in this house,' Father said, trying very hard to control himself. 'I have made some demands of the government. If they don't agree, I will have to take hard decisions. And whatever they may be, you will have to obey.'

'But that won't be fair, Baba.' I found my words with great difficulty.

'It is I who know what's wrong and what's right. Better for everyone to accept that—do what I say and move on.'

'To ask for more money at the last minute will only sully the hangman's honour . . .'

'Chi! Shut your mouth now!'

Father raised his hand. I saw that big broad palm—the one that had taken the lives of four hundred and fifty-one human beings—come very close to my body. I wanted to burst out: Father, in the eyes of the world, I am the symbol of the power and self-respect of Indian womanhood. He pulled away his hand and, with an actor's finesse, walked back a few paces and turned towards me again.

'What about the thing I told you today? Did you tell them that you couldn't go to the studio any more? There are just three days to the hanging now. Remember, after these three days you will have no value at all. So we need to make the most of these three days.'

He fixed a stern look at me.

'Chotdi, your young blood will make you feel all sorts of things. But your baba has seen a lot of life. So take heed of this old man's words! The honesty of the poor man has such little value! You don't know the story of Grandfather Satyendranath, do you? Go and ask Thakuma . . .

'Uh! And what became of me in front of these people? Sibdev babu asked me, Grddha, so your daughter has pulled the rug from under your feet? I wanted the earth to open up so I could fall into it.'

'Baba, what else could I say?' I asked him sadly.

He returned a look of anger. 'You are not to serve up the secrets of your heart in front of the camera. You should just say what must be said, that is, things people like to hear. Chetu, you will not step out of this house from now without my permission. You will not speak to anyone without my knowledge.' His voice rose.

'But that is against our contract, Baba . . .'

A cracker exploded on my left cheek.

'Not a word more!' he bellowed.

Rubbing my cheek, I went to my room. Ma followed me there. The tears had dried up in her eyes.

'Just escape . . . convince that boy somehow, get married, and get away . . . or this man and his hag of a mother will dish out stale tales and traditions and ruin your life too . . .' Ma told me in a low voice.

But Thakuma heard it, and leapt up. 'So it's you! You're the one filling her little mind with poison!'

'She's not little! She's well past the age to marry.'

'That ought to be a mother's worry. Ah, what's the time now? Is this the hour when a girl of respectable birth comes home?'

'She was out for her work, wasn't she?'

'Her work was over at seven-thirty. I may be old, but I'm clever enough to know that!'

Thakuma pulled her frayed sari over her bald head.

'Chetu chotdi, I am telling you again, don't submit to a marriage that'll destroy our family traditions. That's simply not wise.'

I pulled out my mattress from under Thakuma's cot and got ready to go to bed, my head feeling like a smouldering pile of coals. I covered myself with the ragged sheet and tried to sleep but all I could do was toss and turn. A strange light filled my eyelids when I shut my eyes. My hands tingled to tear down the soot-covered, dirt-smeared walls and the cobwebbed asbestos ceiling, and rebuild everything. But my heart, like it always did when we were apart, remembered Sanjeev Kumar Mitra and swung between love and suspicion.

I had barely had a wink of sleep when Ramu da stirred, shouting, 'Pass it to the left, Dada!' Seeing his body curl like a ball and come dangerously close to falling off the narrow cot, I sprang up to hold him. What happened, I asked, but he just moved his head from side to side, and craned his neck towards the door.

'Where is Krishanu da?' he asked me, utterly astonished.

When I realized whom he was asking for, my words receded. It was a year ago that Ramu da had shut his eyes tight and sobbed at the news of Krishanu Dey's death in a Kolkata hospital; I too had wept with him. Krishanu Dey's hat-trick in Malaysia in 1986 had fetched me so many sweets from Ramu da! His face crumpled pathetically when he realized it was only a dream. But soon, he turned over and slept without a word. My sleep was completely shattered. In the dream he was on a rain-soaked football field chasing the ball between Krishanu Dey and Sailesh Bose, he told me the next morning, laughing with more excitement than he would have felt had he really been on the field with them. Unable to bear it, I went out and saw Father standing there, smoking his cigarette. He stared at me impassively.

'It looks like it is time for him to go . . .'

He pulled hard on the cigarette. Clearly, he was referring to the belief that dreaming of dead people is a sign of impending death. But the thought of Ramu da fading away like a dream from his narrow, asbestos-covered room that always rang with the cacophony of hearses and mourners' processions made me tremble violently.

Seeing my tremor, Father laughed. 'Even the grass and the worm have to die. At the moment of birth, the moment of death is also marked. You must fix that in your mind first if you want to do the hangman's job. That's the only way to make sure that your hand does not shake when you do it.'

He drew another puff of smoke forcefully and said, 'I've seen many, many deaths since my infancy. The first person I saw off after I knew the meaning of death was my older brother. Dada died vomiting blood. His condition was more pitiable than Ramu's. My baba, your dadu, told me bravely—he is dead now, do not love him any more! You must keep that in mind too. Do not love the dead. That'll suck the vigour from the living.'

Fear uncoiled in me as I kept looking at him. He was talking about the death of his older brother Sasibhushan, born to Dadu's first wife, Thakuma's didi. Like Ramu da, he too was mad about football. The story is that in 1911, when all of Calcutta was agog with the Mohun Bagan football club winning the IFA Shield at a time when Indians could play only for the Cooch Behar Cup and the Trades Cup, Uncle Sasibhushan, who rolled the ball in any empty space he found, had been invited to play with the Kumortuli Club team. He was then spotted by Suresh Chandra Choudhury, the vice-president of the Jora Bagan Club. Thus Sasibhushan Grddha Mullick became one of the players in the Jora Bagan line-up against Mohun Bagan in the Cooch Behar Cup to be played on 28 July 1920. However, some hubbub broke out on the day of the match. Jora Bagan took to the field without its best player, the half back Sailesh Bose. Suresh Chandra Choudhury had begged that he be included, but the captain would not agree. Furious, Choudhury stormed out of the field and decided, that very evening, to start a new football club. Exactly four days later, Raja Manmath Nath Choudhury, Sailesh Bose, Ramesh Chandra Sen and Arabindo Ghosh formed a new football club—the East Bengal Football Club. That month, they breezed through the Hercules Cup matches, becoming champions. Sasibhushan played in that team. Even Dadu who was very worried that his son was giving up the traditional profession was delighted by the news.

'I still remember the stories of how Sasi da and his friends went around searching for a field to practise in . . . only Mohun Bagan and another club from Behala were permitted to play in the Maidan. When that other club disbanded, Mohun Bagan took all of the Maidan for themselves. But would Choudhury da let that happen? They made a fuss for space in the Maidan. Mohun Bagan tried to oppose it, but failed. Two years later, East Bengal also obtained permission to play there. Those days, goalposts used to be set in the east and west. The space allotted to East Bengal faced the Red Road then . . . How glad Sasi da was! Oh, how he dreamt of glory! What heights he would have reached, my dada!'

Father threw away the cigarette stub and feigned a sigh. Not wanting to hear any more, I turned away, went into the kitchen, opened and closed the lids of various pots for no reason at all, and then returned to Ramu da's bedside. He lay there eyes shut, his face very pale. Because he had seen no sunlight for years, it was like a white man's face. His shrivelled thighs stuck out from under the sheet that covered him. In the beginning Ma had needed one of us to help take him out every morning. But now he had become so light, she could easily carry him out in her own two arms. His face used to be strikingly handsome, glowing with good health. But now all that remained were two large brown eyeballs that rolled about. Uncle Sasibhushan had caught a fever while training for some competition. He was treated for many years, but when it became clear that it was consumption, the family decided to take him to Benares and abandon him there. He was taken in a grass-covered bullock cart, accompanied by Dadu, his uncle Devi Charan and my father, who was only twelve at that time.

At noon, when I was getting ready in a hurry to go to the studio while Father took his nap, I felt Ramu da's eyes follow me suspiciously.

'Any idea when the sports channels' strike might end?' he asked in a tired voice.

'Talks are on, Ramu da,' I said impatiently as I did my hair.

'There is a sparkle on your face today.' His voice was low.

I tried to smile.

He smiled. 'Be careful. When friends become foes, and foes friends . . . be very careful.'

Thakuma hobbled in, eyeing me with suspicion. 'Be careful of what?' She sat on the cot with the rolled-up mattress on one end.

'Isn't her wedding near, Thakuma?'

'Oh, I thought you were talking about my gold coin.'

I shrank a bit but did not reply.

'I don't trust him. He will never love this girl. I have neither seen affection or love on his face nor heard it in his voice ever.' Ramu da's voice was cold as it accused Sanjeev Kumar Mitra.

'I too don't want this alliance.' Thakuma looked at us in turn, still sitting on the cot. 'Chetu, you are a hangman's daughter. His father and his grandfather, and all our forefathers, have been hangmen. Your bridegroom must be from a hangman's family, for sure. If not from our lineage then maybe from some other land. A man's strength is his courage. Better to sell your body than marry a man who lacks that . . .' Her voice grew very sharp.

'Oh, the murderers' job, Thakuma, right?' I tried to laugh in a flustered sort of way.

'Chi! Control your tongue! The hangman does not murder, he only carries out justice. Without justice there would be no king, no government, why . . . nothing at all on this earth.'

'There are many kinds of justice in the world, Thakuma. Whose justice are we carrying out?' I asked, setting right my braids and throwing the dupatta over my shoulders.

She looked at me wrathfully. 'The justice of the people! Chotdi, you must have respect for your own work, and your lineage—everyone, man or woman, needs to pay that respect. People who lack it will never have inner strength. Remember that!'

She sighed deeply and looked at both of us again. 'I have lived beyond a hundred years for some time now. I have seen it all—poverty, terror, sorrow, the death of children, siblings and spouse . . . But I feel perfectly comfortable about life even now. Because I remember that my family is as old as this land of Bharat. That the history of this land includes even me, this ripe old woman. You shouldn't forget the greatness of your family for a diamond ring or a couple of gold

209

bangles, Chetu!' she cried out shrilly.

Afraid that Father may have woken up, I glanced at the door. I too became a character in the long, long performance that generations of our family had been enacting for some two thousand years. The desire to become someone else cannot but grant some creatures the strength to swim many thousand miles against the tide.

27

Most of my forefathers preferred to have the hands of the condemned man tied behind his back. Not that they desisted from all innovation; some did try to experiment occasionally. Kala Grddha Mullick, for instance, occasionally hanged the condemned without tying their hands. Once a noose was firmly strung, the hanged man's death dance would be truly meaty entertainment only if his arms and legs were free—that was his opinion. It was Kalicharan Grddha Mullick, my grandfather, who convinced the British of the merits of the practice of tying the condemned prisoner's arms behind his back. Till then, even in Britain, the prisoner's hands were tied in front so that he could fold his hands and pray before death. But when the prisoners began converting that into the freedom to attack, the state had to think of another way. Thus the practice of securing both arms firmly to the body with a leather belt came to be adopted. But this had problems too. Sometimes prisoners in their death throes tried to pull their arms free and often ended up with their hands torn off their wrists. It was then that the British noticed the usefulness of my grandfather's practice of tying the condemned man's arms behind his back, and decided to adopt it. The British took from us not just cotton and indigo and opium; they also took our local knowledge about death, said Thakuma.

'Those days, when it came to legs being tied, it was only in the case of women condemned to death. That was because of Kadambari. She was hanged by Grandfather Mosh. Struggling for her last breath, she kicked hard and her garment flew up, revealing bare legs. The watching crowd pushed its way to the foot of the gallows . . .'

My attention wandered many times as I sat speaking to Sanjeev Kumar Mitra in *Hangwoman's Diary*. How had Father reacted when he found out that I had left the house against his orders? The thought nagged me. Kadambari was sentenced to death for killing her husband while he was having sex with another woman. She had hit him hard on the head. There were two charges against her. First, she murdered her husband, her living god. Second, she had interrupted the sexual act, which made a man's life as man meaningful. The pandits in the royal court debated for a long while about which of these was the more sinful transgression. Finally, they decided that both were equally venal and deserving of the cruellest punishment. That's how Grandfather Mosh was summoned to hang her. He visited her the night before to carry out the sandbag test, as was the usual practice then.

'Why did you do this, my daughter?' he asked her kindly.

'I loved him dearly,' she replied, not flinching.

'How did you have the heart to kill the man you loved?'

'I wasn't killing him,' she said, 'I was saving him from her.'

When kind-hearted Grandfather Mosh gazed at her with as much love as he would have had for his own daughter, she requested him happily: 'Please send me to him soonest?'

When Thakuma ended the tale remarking that such was the intensity of Kadambari's love for her husband, Father saw Ma who was passing that way with a tumbler of water and murmured, 'Won't let him be happy even in the other world . . .'

'Fellows like this one must have their balls chopped off,' she lashed back.

'The hanging is very close now, Chetna. Set aside today and tomorrow for the moment. On the day after that you will be putting the noose around the neck of a condemned man for the very first time. What are your thoughts now?'

Send me to him soonest, was what came to my tongue. My hands longed to be done with it soonest. A small noose. A red kerchief falling down. A lever being pulled. The sound of the war drum—of the planks moving apart. And then, the struggle on the rope hanging heavy.

'My heart is empty, Sanju babu. The biggest hurdle in the way of

211

delivering justice is making sure that it has indeed been delivered. All conversations are meaningless unless that is ensured.'

'While the hangwoman Chetna Grddha Mullick has decided to continue her mission, let us see what is happening in this faraway village where Jatindranath Banerjee's family lives . . .'

On the monitor before us, suddenly appeared images of fields and mud paths, and then of a narrow lane that led up to some grass-thatched huts. In front of one of those, a wizened old man lay on a coir cot covered with a ragged blanket. A girl of fifteen or so came from a distance with a pot of water. With an adolescent's self-consciousness about her growing body, she pulled her dupatta over her head, and disappeared into a house. A young boy with betel-stained black teeth, who might have been her brother, sat in the veranda of the house, arms stretched over his knees. The camera dwelled for some time on the tiger claw hanging from a once-black-now-bleached-nearly-white cord around his neck. Then it moved into the darkness of the kitchen where Kokila Banerjee showed how black the bottom of the rice pot was.

'No! Go away! We have nothing to tell you. Vultures! Ready to sell our lives for cold cash! Go . . . go!'

Twigs in hand, an old woman, more shrivelled up and shrunken than Thakuma, pulled the end of a much-washed, worn sari over her head, and tried to shoo away the camera.

'He would never do it . . . my son is not a criminal,' Banerjee's father said haltingly in his sinking voice.

'Then who is the criminal?' The reporter's face was not to be seen, but the voice definitely belonged to Sanjeev Kumar Mitra.

'How are we to know? Whoever it is, it isn't our son.'

'I don't know if it is he who did it . . . doesn't make a difference to me really either way. For the last ten or fifteen years, I have been struggling to feed this family. About half of the land we had is gone, sold to raise money to fight the case. These two children are growing . . . haven't saved a paisa for them.'

Kokila Banerjee's voice was flat and emotionless. Her voice, I remembered, was the same as when she had broken down in the studio. The man who had accompanied her was nowhere to be seen. For some reason, I felt like seeing him again.

'At the same time, jail authorities say that Jatin Banerjee has not given up hope.'

After the reporter's words, Sibdev babu's gentle and pleasant face came into view. 'Yes, he is fine. He has not yet given up hope. Even this morning when I met him, he told me, Babu, just watch, I will be free. Because his mercy petition has gone to the President. There will a response tomorrow, for sure. His hope is that the petition will be received favourably by the President.'

'Sibdev babu, how is he spending his time?'

'Oh, he is happy. He had a bath in the morning, ate well. Chatted with the jailers. Complained that there are too many mosquitoes in the cell at night! He is happy and very optimistic.'

'All right, Chetna, let us return to the conversation. What all will you be doing once you start your work at the gallows?' Sanjeev Kumar asked, drawing attention to the gallows tree behind us, from which a thick rope now hung through the fully finished hook.

I too turned to look at it. It was indeed made of wood. Sanjeev Kumar got up briskly, went towards it, and began to describe its parts.

'This—this is the most important part of the gallows tree. This stake has to be fixed one and a half or two feet below the ground and secured with concrete. The strength of this hook is also crucial. It is strong enough to hold a sandbag weighing one hundred and fifty kilos . . .' When he pulled the coiled rope down, the sandbag attached to one end became visible. He then pulled the lever slowly. There was a thunderous crash as the sandbag dropped into the cellar below.

'This is what really happens in the gallows. We now have a chance to see how Jatindranath Banerjee will be hanged by Chetna Grddha Mullick. The good news is that she will be with us in the studio the whole day tomorrow, morning onwards. Goodbye for now and stay tuned.'

When Sanjeev Kumar Mitra came up to me, brimming with enthusiasm from the day's show, I gave him a confused look.

'I can't do these things in front of the camera.'

His face fell.

'But, Chetna, it's very important for the TRP. Such things must be presented before the audience in a serious, utterly professional way. You must do it.'

'No, it's just not right,' I cut him short angrily. 'And besides, I have no idea whether I will be able to make it for the show tomorrow. I came today defying Baba. I can't predict what will happen tomorrow.'

He laughed, not taking that very seriously. 'Come, let's leave now; we can decide what to do later.'

When I came out after removing my make-up, I saw two men and a woman in the studio before the camera.

'Did you recognize her? The dacoit from Chambal, Seema Parihar,' said Sanjeev Kumar when we were out.

I looked at him questioningly.

'She's here to act in a movie—*Wounded*. This is the first time a female dacoit is playing herself in a movie.' He was very excited. 'She's been in Chambal since she was twenty. It's with great difficulty that the producers of the movie managed to get her parole for forty–forty-five days. Just watch . . . such courage, such confidence!'

On one of the TV screens I saw Seema Parihar smile broadly and declare: 'I didn't go away to Chambal because I wanted to go. I had no other way. My effort through this movie is to let the world know of the terrible travails of our womenfolk . . .'

I realized then that I'd left Kadambari's story incomplete. The fact that Kadambari's thighs and buttocks had been exposed when the lever was pulled caused a scandal in the royal court. A rule was passed soon after that condemned folk must be dressed such that they were covered fully, and their clothes and legs should be bound together. The pandits agreed unanimously that even a condemned woman's body must be protected from the eyes of men. And much later, the British government decided to extend that rule to men, too, just to make the hanging easier.

When we were sitting in the taxi, Sanjeev Kumar reached out his hand and took mine.

'Our *Hangwoman's Diary* is going to end. What did you think of that, Chetna?'

'I am not educated enough to give you an opinion.'

Much more frustration and sadness had been expressed by my voice than I wished to reveal. It did make me feel a bit foolish. But Sanjeev Kumar gazed at me with compassion.

'I am sure that is not true. Education is certainly not the measure of anyone's intelligence. Tell me, what did you think of it?'

'It opened a new world for me . . .'

I gazed at him, singing in a low voice:

Koto ajnaare jaana ele tumi,
Koto ghare dile tthayi—
Durke korile nikat, bandhu,
Porke karile bhai . . .

'Which means?'

I smiled.

'It's from the *Gitanjali*.'

How many are the strangers that you made me meet?
In how many homes did you make me space?
Those who were far, you made them near
Those who were strangers, you made them dear . . .

He laughed aloud. 'Very good song. And you sing well.'

I smiled to myself, looking out of the car's window. The next lines of the poem express worry: *What will I do when I leave the old home?* The taxi sped through Martin Luther Sarani that stretched from Park Street to Theatre Road. Earlier, it was called Wood Street. The Calcutta Corporation had renamed it when I was four. Allen Garden, which was on one side of the road, looked like a bushy forest. Once upon a time there used to be a triangular pond there. The corporation filled it up with rubbish, saying that it posed a danger to children. There was such a stench all around for miles that people started moving away from the locality. A woman who earned a living from taking in boarders lost her income when all of them moved out. She went to court, demanding compensation, and the corporation was ordered to pay her thirty thousand rupees. But for a very long time, no one would stay there. Whenever the awful stench of corpses filled our house, Thakuma would remember this woman. Sitting in the taxi, I wondered where her house might have been.

'Let's go home directly today,' I said. 'You must speak with Baba, Sanju babu. Otherwise, I may not be able to come tomorrow.'

'Chi! Chetna, you should take a stronger position in this. The whole world is looking at you! This is your big chance.'

'I want to keep my word, but Baba won't let me.'

Sanjeev Kumar was looking at me, but his glasses were so dark, I couldn't make out the expression in his eyes. I turned my gaze outward as the traffic light turned red and innumerable child beggars made their rounds between the vehicles waiting for the signal to turn green. Running between the red rear lights of vehicles in their wet clothes, they looked like huge moths. When we reached Ashutosh Mukherjee Road, Sanjeev Kumar stopped the car and got out. He walked straight into Binod Behari Jewellers; I followed. When the merchant and the staff recognized us and welcomed us warmly, Sanjeev Kumar pushed me forward with a broad smile.

'This pretty woman needs a pair of diamond ear studs.'

'No, I don't.' I recoiled, thoroughly flustered by his unexpected move.

'I'm to decide that. Lovers in this country have always had certain special rights.'

Before I could try to stop him, he had already begun dipping into boxes full of ear studs. There were only a few beautifully dressed men and women in the shop and they were choosing their jewellery with care. I stood there nonplussed, having entered such a shop for the very first time in my life.

'Look,' he picked a pair and gave it to the salesman, 'something smaller in the same design.'

When he turned towards the shelf, he whispered close to my ear: 'The whole place is full of cameras. See those dots? They are all watching us closely. But I will steal from this shop. Want to see?'

My blood froze.

'No.'

I looked at him, worried, wanting to run to safety. But he held me close. He too was bargaining with me, just like Father. In spite of that, my heart pounded when I thought that our days together would end soon and I would never be able to see him do it. When he picked up and put down stud after stud, my eyes were glued to his fingers. Each box had a fixed number of items and the salesman put back each after examining them carefully. Let him not be able to steal anything from this shop, I wished sincerely. Finally, we got out of the jewellers', and were back on the footpath; I, confident that he could not have stolen anything this time. But rough fingers emboldened by victory and domination fell on my shoulder. When we crossed the road and reached a safe place, he turned my right hand palm up. 'I kept my word!'

True, he had. Two ear studs with tiny diamonds glinting on them sat on my palm. My voice choked.

'Have no doubt, they are originals and they were stolen!'

'But how?' My throat grew parched. The two little diamonds scorched my palm when I looked at him. 'I don't want them . . .'

When I put them into his pocket and turned to go home, he grasped my hand firmly. 'Let's go to my house,' he whispered slowly.

'Which one?'

'The one I stay in.'

I fell silent. A bird gently opened its wings and shook its feathers.

'Let's go to your ancient house.'

'This time of the night? There will be cobras there . . .'

'I like it better . . .'

He pulled me gently towards his body and murmured, 'But this house you will remember forever.'

When I leaned against him thus, fear and a wild excitement overpowered me. The car buzzed through the darkness of the noisy street like a yellow bee. Traffic's thin today, I thought. The car turned towards Sonagachi through Chitpur Road. Leaning back against the seat, I closed my eyes and tried to predict the future, like Ratnamalika. In the dark, a red curtain emerged. I stood beneath a newly built gallows tree, ready to be killed. When the lever was pulled, I was pulled high up. My salwar came off from below and my kameez, from above. As I struggled, I saw a large crowd come nearer, shouting and screaming. When I opened my eyes in terror, we had entered a lane where people milled around as if at a festival fair. In the dark and the bustle, it was impossible to recognize anyone. I felt as if my feet were tied together. I felt that horrendous pain again—as if my toes were being torn off.

28

Grandfather Kalicharan met Binodini Dasi the first time at Jamuna Baiji's house, one monsoon. She was barely eight then, and already married. He was sitting in the veranda of Jamuna Baiji's house at Kalighat. Jamuna Baiji was a scholar and a very learned musician. Hers was a typical Bengali home with a central courtyard where kitchen utensils and clothes were washed, and the men bathed. There were rooms around it with balconies bound by delicately patterned iron grilles facing the courtyard. Grandfather saw a little girl, an angry pout on her face, clad in a single garment, the end of which was pulled over her head. She came in from the rain, shielding herself with a large leaf, a red kite with a broken string clutched to her chest. But it was when he saw her act on stage that she captured his heart. Grandfather was a strong man, of robust health, fond of the arts, and till then, free of the entanglements of love. But Binodini's acting left him shaken. Like the rope that extends into the cellar after the hanging is over, the veins in his heart trembled and shivered. She became a famous actor who shook all of Bengal.

When I set foot on the front yard of a bungalow that hid its face partially behind a decrepit old house on Avinash Kaviraj Street in Sonagachi, following Sanjeev Kumar Mitra, the image of Binodini Dasi sitting upright with her left leg resting on her right knee, dressed as Chaitanya in *Chaitanyaleela* flashed in my mind. For a moment I thought I was in her house. If it was indeed so, Grandfather too must have stood sighing at its doorstep, his heart heavy with love, head bowed with the weight of the inferiority of his old age. I was elated by the thought. There were four or five cars parked in front of the white-walled bungalow; I could see four or five men, some clad in a chauffeur's uniform. From the white porch, the pillars of which seemed to rise to the sky, there were nine flights of steps that circled the veranda leading to the interiors. The steps led to vast open doorways. My eyes were drawn to the innumerable windows in the building—the windowpanes were painted a strange red, and they glinted upon the white walls even in the darkness of night. Like a lamp gleaming from behind a curtain, the inside of the red-windowed bungalow glowed a deep yellow. The stories that Thakuma used to tell us of the two- and three-storeyed mansions in the turning from Chitpur Road to Cornwallis Street and towards Bowbazar and Maniktola, and the wealthy bazar women who owned them sprang to mind. I stared in fright at Sanjeev Kumar Mitra who was waiting for me at the door where the stairs ended.

'Are you afraid?' He took off his glasses and looked at me seductively.

I could hear vaguely some music being played inside; it sounded like raucous disco music. Father referred to my ancestor Kalicharan as 'bada artist'. Thakuma too insisted that he, who was a connoisseur of music and a lover of the arts, visited the house of a fallen woman, a Muslim at that, not for her body but for her peerless voice. He went seeking her at the age of sixteen, fired by rash youthfulness and egged on by friends, after selling the gold-encased tiger claw he wore on his neck. Jamuna Baiji was a unique woman. At the time, she was over forty years old. As she undressed, she hummed a little song. Like a cobra roused by the snake charmer's music, Grandfather was lulled and snared; he forgot his purpose. He fell at her feet in salutation.

In her time, Jamuna Baiji was greatly respected by the grandees of the city and by its artists and scholars. She taught Grandfather Kalicharan music for many years. Binodini's mother brought her daughter to her so that she could be taught not just music and dance, but also agreeable manners. Grandfather realized that such manners had to be learned only after he met Jamuna Baiji. He already had fathered six children by that time—all daughters. But seeing the twelve-year-old Binodini live on stage as a full-grown woman, he lost his heart to her. His irrepressible desire for her never left him. Finally, some seventeen years after he met her, did he beget a son—my father's father, Purushottam—through his ignorant and uncouth wife. When he died, at the age of eighty-five, he had twelve children. But when asked about his last wish, he muttered just two syllables, 'B . . . b . . .' Whatever that intense last wish that began with a 'B' was, it stayed unfulfilled when he died.

Sanjeev Kumar led me into a central courtyard that resembled the Jorasanko Thakurbari. Three women, well past their prime, who were washing dishes, stared hard at me, startled by my presence. Their heads were covered with their pallus and they wore large nose studs. Their faces were completely blank, devoid of all expression. The same sense of alienation that had assailed me in the jewellery shop once again overpowered me. From the cavernous interiors of that huge house sounds of music, dance, conversation and laughter floated out; the aromas of many kinds of food wafted in the air. I sent a sidelong glance at the many rooms that opened into the veranda. Expensive shoes that one sees in fancy advertisements had been left outside many of the doorways.

'I want to go back . . .' Worried, I looked at Sanjeev Kumar Mitra as we climbed those unending flights of steps. 'If Baba gets to know . . .'

'This is not a place where people like your baba can enter.'

There was a certain arrogance to his tone now. Because the memory of his rough palm woke up somewhere on the left side of my body, I stood unmoving on the steps.

'No, I need to go.'

'Who are you afraid of? Your baba or me?'

Sanjeev Kumar came down the steps he had climbed and put his hand on my shoulder kindly. 'Look, this house has more tales of history to tell than even you. There aren't many historical figures in the saga of Kolkata who haven't visited this place.'

His words were tender now.

'Sonagachi! The filmmakers from my father's place are very fond of it. Who doesn't like to hear tales about beshyas?' He pursed his lips sarcastically.

I climbed the steps slowly, thinking all the while about the word beshya. Binodini Dasi had hated her mother after she had shoved her into the bedchamber of a man older than her grandfather. She was eight years old then. He abandoned her after just one night. Binodini's mother dispatched her to Jamuna Baiji hoping to make her useless daughter's life secure by teaching her some music and dance so that she could become the concubine of some rich man. Jamuna Baiji discovered Binodini's genius. She turned her into an actor at the age of nine. Before eleven, she was a seasoned performer, one among the five pleasure women chosen by Girish Chandra Ghosh, who brought about a revolution by casting women in female roles, to be part of his theatre troupe. Grandfather Kalicharan urged his younger brothers and sons to replace him as the hangman; he preferred to hang around Girish Chandra's troupe.

Binodini Dasi performed her first lead role at the age of eleven to great success right before his eyes. She stole the limelight in the play *Shatusamhaar*, singing mellifluously and delivering her dialogues with great mastery. Grandfather, who could never gather the courage to go closer or reveal his ardour, lingered around her, burning inside all the while. All her love affairs unfolded in front of his eyes. When I heard that the zamindar had ordered Binodini to stop acting, my hands craved to fashion a noose for his neck, he wrote later. She was not ready to give up the stage. The young zamindar went away. Grandfather was also witness to the arrival of the Marwari millionaire Gurumukh Ray, who offered any amount of money if Binodini could be given over to him as his concubine. At that point Girish Chandra was in dire straits, unable to find enough money to complete Star Theatre. Can't you make this small sacrifice for the sake of art . . .for your own sake, pleaded Girish Chandra. A small sacrifice, she asked, grieved. She was rendered speechless when he told her, you are after all a beshya, what do you have to lose? My life is full of bedna gathas, heroic tales of sorrow, she wrote later in her autobiography. But they were more painful to my forefather who transformed the hangman's job into great art, flawless and dramatic in its execution.

Did I not mention that love that is not like the noose fixed between the third and fourth vertebrae is impossible in our family?

'Sanju babu, who is this lovely girl?' asked an old woman hobbling out of one of rooms, so bent that she touched the floor. Her beautiful face was touched with rose powder, and her brows and eyes were lined with kohl. She wore heavy gold jewellery; one of her arms full of gold bangles held up her waist as she walked. When the other arm waved in the air, the gold bangles on it jingled noisily. Even her wizened feet with all their veins showing were adorned with anklets.

'My client, Thakuma. She keeps me . . .' Sanjeev Kumar ran his hand over his moustache as he spoke.

The old woman laughed loudly. 'Is she in love with you?'

'I don't know.'

'Daughter, if you are a beshya, never fall in love; our mothers used to sing that when we were children. *Bhalo beshe mukhe aagun, shotru beri paayi . . .' Fire burns on the face of love; my feet are in chains,* went the song. She peered at me closely. 'Sanju, she reminds me of your mother at first look.'

'Yes, I thought so too, at first . . .' he murmured.

Parts of that bungalow reminded me of the Alipore Correction Home and the CNC office. Sanjeev Kumar Mitra opened a door on the second floor and invited me in. It was a room from which doors opened in several directions, like the aparajita vine.

'This is my home . . .'

He went in and sat on the large, satin-covered sofa. But there was more pain than pride in the way he said it. Maybe this bungalow had too many tales of sorrow to tell?

'You are very wealthy, aren't you?'

I sat down and looked around. The floors were red, polished so well that they reflected my face; the walls were white. The blood-red hue reflected everywhere in the room. Even the gilt-edged paintings on the wall were the same red, as were the sofas.

Hearing that Binodini had given in to Gurumukh Ray, the young zamindar was enraged and went in search of her. I will give you twenty thousand rupees to complete the construction of the theatre, he said. When he raged on, saying that he would give her all the money she wanted as long as she gave up acting, Binodini said, 'I have made money, yes, but money cannot make me.' He pulled out his sword and thrust it at her. Binodini, who was not even twenty then, faced him with more presence of mind than a fifty-year-old woman. She told him, 'Kill me if you wish. But what a terrible dishonour to your family it would be if you are hanged for killing a beshya! You will have to leave this world with a mark too shameful to be erased.' If it had happened, wrote Grandfather, I would have settled the score on the gallows. After his death, his children and grandchildren tore up his Book of Love. They knew well that his love for a beshya would bring them dishonour too.

I became all the more weary when I saw a young girl come in with tea, paan and sweetmeats, accompanied by the withered old woman. Outside, the darkness had thickened. I felt that we were in a place which could not be penetrated by even a tiny ripple of the swirling street sounds.

'Drink your tea,' the old woman ordered as she turned to leave. She hummed as she walked towards the door.

Kete diye premer khudi
Abar keno lotke dharo

When the door banged shut, Sanjeev Kumar looked at me.

'Do you know what those lines mean?'

'Isn't that the song of the kite flyers? *Why do you hang on like this, after breaking my kite string?*'

He took off his spectacles again, went over to bolt the door and bestowed on me a meaningful smile with those green eyes. And then, sliding behind my chair, he touched my shoulder with his hand, slowly extending his right hand to lift my chin, and sending a strange piercing look into my eyes.

'That's a song about physical love—between a man and a woman.'

I could not tear my eyes away from his.

'The woman sings: *You've cut too soon the kite which soared in the skies . . . and why now again . . .*'

His hand began to slither over my body.

'No, don't . . .' I stopped him, utterly discomposed.

He ignored my protest; pulling me close to his chest, he stroked my hair. The realization sank in that even the symbol of the self-respect of Indian womanhood could submit meekly if a man gently rubbed the unguent of love on her. It left me amazed.

The year after she started visiting Gurumukh Ray's bedchamber to raise the funds to complete Star Theatre, none other than Sri Ramakrishna Paramahamsa came to see her play Chaitanya in *Chaitanyaleela*. Completely carried away by her acting, he went and bowed to her. Mother, he said, you are indeed Chaitanyam! Grandfather recorded how the bhadralok ostracized him for showing goodwill towards the beshya and how he complained about that to Vivekananda. Soon after that, the zamindar made his way into Binodini's room, pulled her up by the hair and bellowed: 'Betrayer! Whore!' Binodini cast her eyes on him easily, as if she were on stage playing Sita or Draupadi, and smiled. Then she delivered the most powerful line she had ever uttered in her life: 'It is you men who have taught us to betray!' The rooms in Sanjeev Kumar Mitra's house opened out one behind the other. I knew that he was taking me very slowly over quite a distance through those rooms as he held me close. When Girish Chandra Ghosh died, none of the female actors he had introduced to the stage were allowed to pay their last respects. Binodini Dasi ended her acting career at the age of twenty. She became a rich man's concubine and soon bore a daughter, but the bhadralok would not let her educate the child. The little one died when she was eleven. Binodini returned to her old house in the beshyas' street like the ilish returning to the sea to die. Thank God, Grandfather Kalicharan did not survive to witness that part of her tale of sorrow. But the first blow I received when I heard the story was not from the bit about Binodini's death. After Grandfather Kalicharan's death, his wife, who was always dismissed as ignorant and uncultured, began to sing—that part really floored me. Her mellifluous kirtans filled the little Shiva temple near Nimtala Ghat every morning. The ripples of the Ganga echoed them joyfully.

When the strong rosewood door was opened, I spied the large cot and the mattress on it with my left eye. The bed and the red satin bedcover I had already seen in my dream. It made me afraid to think that rats may actually be romping on it. The lanes of Sonagachi were beginning to calm down. The pimps and beshyas now jostled there. The yellow lights glowed indifferently. On both sides of the lanes too narrow for even a single vehicle to ply, there milled around women, fat and thin, fair and dark and wheatish, all made up with layers of rose powder and heavy kohl, clad in tight blouses that revealed their breasts and midriff, with or without a bindi on their foreheads. They stood there waiting, hands on hips, chest wide open. I remembered the clay-smeared Durga statues left to dry in Kumortuli. The preparations for Navaratri must have begun. Thakuma used to say that the soil for the first puja in the houses of the rich has to be collected from the beshya's doorstep. When Sanjeev Kumar lowered his face towards mine on the red bedcover, I shut my eyes tightly. I felt a thousand rats with blood-red lips scamper all over my body. One half of my body desired his body. But the other half demanded his inner self too. I opened my eyes; my glance fell on a picture hanging above the bed. A woman. Below the forehead with the large red bindi, huge eyes that took up almost all the space between the nose and the forehead. The eyes gave a piercing look and the blood-red lips offered a strange smile. I pushed Sanjeev Kumar aside. His mobile phone started ringing that very moment. It irritated him, but he pulled it out of his pocket and jumped up.

'Uh-uh . . . tell me, Harish babu . . .'

Then, he turned sharply towards the little table beside the bed, picked up the remote control and switched on the television. As I got up, smoothed down my clothes and prepared to leave, the newsreader stared at me: 'Meanwhile, the government has decided that Jatindranath Banerjee, guilty of the rape and murder of a young girl, deserves no mercy. With this, the death sentence, which is to be carried out day after tomorrow, appears to be confirmed . . .'

I froze as if my feet had been tied together. Like the broken string of a kite that was flying high, my senses hung in the air, stunned and hapless. The newsreader continued: 'Banerjee has been in jail for the past fourteen years for a crime committed eighteen years ago. The chief minister arrived at this decision after having examined the petitions submitted to him by anti-death penalty groups in Bengal and all over India. According to the law, the state government can recommend the relaxation of the death penalty to the governor and the latter can repeal it. However, Home Secretary Amit Deb says that since the Supreme Court and the President of India have rejected Jatindranath Banerjee's mercy petition, the chief minister and his colleagues feel that he deserves the most severe punishment for his heinous crime. He also said that the district administration has been ordered to make all necessary arrangements . . .'

Sanjeev Kumar Mitra came closer, remote in hand. I did not know what to do; his face was lit up with joy.

'Fantastic! I was afraid that it would get put off at the last minute! Especially with your baba making things so difficult!'

I could only stare at him. As if I was seeing the radiance of that smile on his face for the first time. In truth, I had never seen him smile so heartily and openly before. I felt as if my body was rocking in the air.

'Let's go . . . must fix up things for tomorrow with your baba . . . I'll come too.'

He began to hurry, buttoning his shirt and combing his hair. I kept staring at him like a fool. My feet were still in chains. That moment I wanted to return to his arms and body. But he was busy getting ready and really didn't notice me. Opening his safe, he pulled out rupee notes and stuffed them in his wallet.

'Who knows what your Vulture Mullick is going to demand? This will fall out of my own pocket. The channel won't pay a paisa more. But I have no way out. It's a matter of my prestige, isn't it?'

I covered my face with both hands, and the line about fire on love's face sprang up in my mind. Not only pleasure women, even hangwomen should not fall in love. Come, come—Sanjeev Kumar was in a real hurry now. I shivered as I turned back and looked again and again at the picture on the wall. In the bustle of the street, the slurred voices of the poorer clients drunk on bungla could be heard. Sanjeev Kumar pushed me ahead through a marketplace where everyone declared their desires aloud. The scents of the gutter, of fish frying in sunflower oil and mutton curry simmering in large vessels whirled and eddied as Sanjeev Kumar walked ahead briskly, stepping upon crushed flower garlands and used condoms. Still trapped in that strange state of the soul flying high in the sky and the body hanging distraught and helpless like its broken string, seeking the earth below, I walked past women with stony faces whom no one had yet bought. They waited with paint and sweat running down their face and neck, legs tiring, spirits flagging, and perhaps feeling the pangs of hunger. The woman in the picture in Sanjeev Kumar Mitra's bedroom—what was her name? Durga? Or was it Chamundi?

29

When married women die and their bodies ascend the funeral pyre, their feet have to be a bright red, as if they had been walking in a pool of blood. No one, not even Thakuma, knew when this practice began.

But it is great good luck to ascend the pyre with the red of the sindoor on your forehead and the red of the alta on your feet, she insisted. It was when Niharika died that I first witnessed a woman's funeral. The locals filled our house and the yard hearing the news. Even those who had come to conduct funerals from distant villages left the corpses they were accompanying to catch a glimpse of her. The traffic stopped on Strand Road. The police arrived. Children were shooed away by older people. Slipping away from Amalendu and Champa, I peeped into Father's room through the window near the mirror in the room which Ramu da, Thakuma and I use now. I saw them cut down Niharika's body, pale and stiff like a wax doll. Ma fell on it and wailed, like in a jatra, and Father held her back with his left arm. The immersion of Durga idols decked and worshipped with glowing yellow garlands for nine whole days of puja, the sinking of those glorious deities seated regally upon lions into the muddy waters of the Ganga—has always troubled me. They remind me of Niharika's body, stiff and rigid as wood in death. When she was brought back after the post-mortem, Narayan da gave her his best bamboo litter, Gangadhar da his driest twigs for the pyre, and Hari da the freshest flowers. The women brought water from the Ganga. They bathed her under Thakuma's supervision and draped her in her wedding sari. Thakuma then marked her forehead with the blood-red sindoor that Hemant da had brought from his temple. As I watched, with my finger inside my nostril, she made a red paste of it with water and applied it carefully to Niharika's feet. They looked as though they had stepped in thick red blood.

When I reached Strand Road with Sanjeev Kumar Mitra, a silver hearse was blocking the traffic. My mind was empty. Death, like Sanjeev Kumar, hooked its fingers around mine sometimes. If I hanged Jatindranath, his body would dangle forever from my fingers, I feared. As I walked towards home, I peered at the woman who lay in the hearse, glowing like a golden statue. Among the dahlias, her face was like another beautiful flower. There was a bright red spot of sindoor on her forehead; her feet shone red with alta. The middle-aged man in funereal white clothes with a preoccupied look on his face must be her husband, I guessed. I imagined the way he would stand in the queue at the registration counter, away from the bustle of the vehicles, haggle with the priest, go down the black steps covered with ash from the pyres, and offer the oblations sitting on his haunches on the Ganga's wet mud, blackened with decaying hay and flowers.

'Look at the crowd, buzzing like flies!'

Sanjeev Kumar could see the young men with cameras in front of our tea shop even in the dark. He snapped angrily: 'Tell your baba there are some things more valuable in the world than money.'

I was impassive. 'I am nobody to teach him.'

When we neared the house a couple of reporters came towards us as if to greet him but really aiming for me.

'Go inside, Chetna, don't forget the contract . . .'

The words barely slipped through his lips, just loud enough for me to hear. He shook hands with the reporter who was closest to us.

'Hi, Jitin da, what news?'

'Sanjeev babu, long time since we met! What news?'

'Oh, I manage. When did you come? What's up? Did Grddha da say anything?'

'The old duffer! He's bargaining . . .'

'Who'll he bargain with after today?'

'He tried to wheedle some more cash out of the government . . . didn't succeed . . . the oldster was at Writers' Buildings and the police headquarters all day trying to make them cough up some more. The DGP finally agreed to another five hundred.'

'Uh! Stupid ass! We'd warned him . . . Get rid of the dad, make the girl do it.' Sanjeev Kumar gnashed his teeth.

I was petrified. My old aches were reborn at the pitiless rasp of his voice. He does not really love me, I was convinced. His concern and tenderness, the glimmer of love in his green eyes—they are all mere put-ons, I grieved. I went towards the house, feeling downcast, cutting through the line of poor folk waiting for the free food distributed after a funeral. But as I was about to enter by the side close to the salon, suddenly, I jumped in pain—it was as if my feet had been pierced with innumerable sharp needles. In the weak light of the bulb, I saw a large fish head covered with ants on the ground. Ferocious corpse-eater ants were crowding around it. I shook my feet hard and rushed in. Ramu da, who was watching the Euro Cup on TV, looked at me, slightly offended.

I changed, had a sip of water in the kitchen and was just stepping out when Sanjeev Kumar whirled in like a tornado: 'Chetna, this is cheating! Tomorrow some documentary guys are going to film your old man!'

I couldn't even look at his face. My heart was so heavy, so full of pain. He followed me around, making sure I didn't have a moment's peace. 'He's sold the entire slot tomorrow—from six o'clock in the morning till the hanging! Wasn't I the first to ask him for that time? And now . . .He shouldn't have done this to me now!'

Without asking anyone for permission, he sat down on Thakuma's coir cot and shouted.

'No . . . I won't allow this! This was *my* plan. Your baba has betrayed me. He didn't even consider the fact that I am going to marry you. My career, reputation . . . everything's gone! Tomorrow morning I too will be here with a camera. And if your old man gets too smart then—'

He jumped up when I threw a questioning look at him.

'I'll teach him the rules of the game!'

There was a threat in his voice. I tilted my head to look at Ramu da. He had been looking at each of us in turn. Sanjeev Kumar went out of the room and called me.

'I will go to that jewellery shop again. They must have discovered by now that a pair of diamond studs are missing.'

I stared, not comprehending.

'We were their last customers.'

His use of 'we' was worrying.

'In their view, between the two of us, I don't have any motive to steal.'

My blood boiled. Tears of fury welled inside my eyes.

'I knew that you played that role to trap me.' My voice broke with anger.

'Why did you come with me then?'

Having no answer to that, I stared hard at him. When he left, I wanted to throw and break everything around me. All the physical pain he had inflicted on me felt trivial. It was easier to bear such pain then. But now, the noose had tightened much more.

'So, are you scared of him?' asked Ramu da, with deep distaste.

'Didn't Baba break the contract?'

'If Baba broke the contract, then it is between them. Why should he bark at you? Who are you? His slave? And contract indeed, what contract? Couldn't you have opened your mouth and told him, "Get out, you corpse!"?'

My face fell.

'Chetu, he is an out-and-out cheat. I don't trust him at all. He's never going to marry you. I'm sure of that.'

His rage was shattered by an enormous cough. As I sat down next to him, rubbing his chest, he tried to stifle the cough and said, his eyes tearing up: 'You will end up in tears, Chetu.'

The pain in his voice shook me. It was a very unhappy night. I wandered about like a stringless kite. There was an air of celebration in the house around Father. Ramu da lay silent and still, eyes fixed on the ceiling, not even wanting to watch TV. Thakuma came back after roaming around the Ghat, complaining that her feet ached. Ma made tea non-stop, muttering under her breath that the curse of the condemned would destroy the family. Kaku hung around Father, making sure his face appeared in every photograph that was being taken. The truck drivers who brought goods to the transport company opposite our tea shop hung around to watch the big show at our house instead of setting off to Sonagachi. Father finally came in late at night, tottering, after the reporters went away.

'The movie people will be here at six. They will shoot from the morning, from our puja till we are ready to leave. There will be cameras—look—over there in my room and in the tea shop. No shooting inside the house, I've told them. So if anyone comes inside, drive them out.'

Ramu da, who was half-asleep, woke up with a start and gave me a piercing look. I was rubbing Thakuma's feet. Father didn't pay attention and continued: 'They will follow us in their van till we enter the jail. Make sure we all wear our best clothes . . . it will be embarrassing otherwise.'

'Will they also give us costumes?' Ramu da tried to convey his displeasure.

'This isn't a film of that sort.'

'Will I get to act too, Phani?' Thakuma asked, laughing.

'No. Just me, Chetna and Sudev. None of you must step out till they leave . . . Tell your old hag of a mother and Kakima.'

'No, I won't be there . . .' I got up suddenly and faced Father. 'I've had enough of this play-acting.'

My voice was sharper than I intended. Father's eyes turned red.

'You've become swollen-headed enough to challenge your father now! I've never questioned my father. "Father" means the father of the world—Bhagawan Mahadev. God does not forgive those who don't respect their father.'

'Baba, you yourself told us that God does not forgive those who do not keep their word.' I raised my voice again.

'Chetu, to denigrate your father is to denigrate your own self.'

'When my value increases, it is your honour that goes up, Baba.'

Father flinched. He stroked his moustache, fished out a cigarette from the fold pocket of his dhoti, lit it and he went inside. After some time, he came back.

'Uh-uh . . . you do have a point.' His eyes were more red than usual. 'Why should we piss off others? The movie fellows came in search of me. I'll give myself to them. That chap's channel wants you. I'll give you to them. It's better for us to make money as two than one.'

I wanted to laugh and cry at the same time. Thakuma dozed off but I stayed there wide awake. My blood pressure shot up. Life had been swinging above the earth all these days. But in a flash of a second, the rope had broken. In a month and six days, Chetna Grddha Mullick had been recast in a different mould. Like a statue built by daubing clay on delicate bamboo screens, then painted and decked with jewels, I too was put on display. I had acted as if I was omnipotent, full of dignity, seated with my ankle resting on the other knee, on a lion, with eight arms stretched out like wings. Now they will cast me out, in the same pose, into the Ganga, seeking atonement for their sins. Into waters stinking with the unbearable stench of the blood of sacrificed animals and floating funeral oblations, into the black mud in its depths, I will sink pitifully, all eight arms raised. The waves will slowly lick off my outer shell. The hay inside will rot and I will be consigned, once again, to the very dirt from which I came.

I woke up in the morning hearing the excitement about the policemen who had come to stand guard. Thakuma kept thanking Bhagawan Mahadev and Ma Kali for giving Father and Kaku a chance to practise their family profession again. Earlier, I too used to feel proud when the policemen came. It made me feel that we were more important than others. Only much later did the complexity of the practice strike me: the policemen stood guard, protecting one whom the government had hired to extinguish the life of another human being. Once I learned that the procedures of democracy included many such absurdities, I lost both the pride and the unease.

The film unit began work by shooting the remnants of Father's hunger for fame, framed and mounted on the wall. I sat quietly near Ramu da in our room. Father shone in his solo performance. He was about halfway through his dramatic rendering of the procedures of the hanging when Sanjeev Kumar arrived with his team.

'This is not right! We have the rights to shoot—granted much before!' he exploded.

The cinema group protested. A furious altercation broke out. Father tried to mediate. It almost came to fisticuffs; a couple of journalists also joined the fray. The policemen deputed to guard Father intervened. Father sided with the cinema people. Finally, an agreement was reached. We sat in the next room watching the cameras vie to capture Father sit, pace, scratch his head, sweat and wipe the sweat with his gamchha. The questions from the journalists crowding in the room buzzed in the air.

'How does the condemned react when he is hanged?'

'Ha, Babu, what a question! Can ordinary people watch it unblinkingly? What a struggle it is! That really is the struggle. As someone who's seen four hundred and fifty-one deaths, I can tell you that this thing called death . . . it never gets old or boring . . .'

'Among those you have executed, who has been the most unforgettable?'

'All are unforgettable, Babu . . . Death is a great leveller . . . We may have to do things we don't like. But karma must be fulfilled. The fruits of it, Bhagawan will give.'

Dadu had clung to Father's shoulders, unable to hold back tears—I completed the scene in my mind, sitting in the next room. They could not recognize Surya Sen. When he was about to place the noose around his neck, Dadu burst into tears. That was 1934. Father was just a teenager then, his mind full of dreams about the jatra and acting and music.

'That happens in all trades, Babu. We may have to do things we don't like. But karma has to be fulfilled. The fruits of it, Bhagawan will give.'

Father raised his right hand, which held a cigarette between the middle and index fingers, to the skies. His eyes rose dramatically to the ceiling. They lingered on the beam from which Niharika had dangled. In the midst of all this fuss, it began raining. Those who stood outside the house rushed in to escape the downpour. I bolted Ramu da's room securely from the inside. When Sanjeev Kumar knocked, I did not open the door. At four in the evening he came again, all sweaty and make-up undone from the heat in Father's chamber. He got me to come out of the room with Ma's help. My eyes fell first on the remnants of the previous night's fish head. Two holes instead of its eyes and a gaping mouth were all that remained of it. It was soaked in the rain; still a couple of ants rummaged in its mouth. Even the fragile skull of a fish, stripped of flesh and blood, was terrifying to see, I realized.

'What time do you start from here?' he asked, wiping his face and neck.

'Ten, Baba said.' My voice was cold.

'Okay. When you leave, I'll give you a mobile phone. Film the whole hanging as it happens.'

I looked at him, aghast. 'Film the hanging?' I asked him, not believing my ears.

He took off his glasses once more to wipe his eyes and face. When his eyes met mine, again I thought that he looked like a corpse-eater ant. 'Chetna, listen to me carefully. Take precise note in your mind of everything that happens there. And make sure you come to our studio soon after it is over. Not through the front gate of the jail complex. I have found another exit . . .'

He thrust his hand into his pocket, pulled out some cash, and pressed the notes into my palm. That moment, his lips turned an uncanny red, as if he wore lipstick. My vision blurred as I looked at the notes. Then his cell phone rang.

'Eh? When?'

It was as though the sky had fallen.

'My God!' He slammed his hand on his head and shrieked.

'Atul, Jaggu, Pranoy . . . all is lost! All is lost!'

He was hollering now. As I stood there, numb and perplexed, he rushed into Father's room. A great hubbub rose there. Reporters ran here and there like ants fleeing from a broken anthill. With three hearses crowding the road, the pushing and jostling mass of people in front of the house became completely unmanageable. In the midst of all this, a huge buffalo charged into the melee from across the railway tracks. The crowd scattered and ran.

'What? What happened?' someone asked, shouting.

Someone else replied: 'Hanging stayed!'

30

King Deva Pala's consort died in childbirth. He married another woman so that the newborn prince would be cared for. But this woman hated the prince. She wished to see her son on the throne and hence conspired to kill the prince and leave his body in the jungle. This mission she entrusted to Bhim, my ancestor Bhishma's evil brother. Bhim did not kill the infant; instead, he chopped off its arms and legs and abandoned it in the jungle. But as he was making his way out of the forest, wiping the blood off his sword, his legs froze. He found himself being pulled back by a magical force to the spot where he had abandoned the baby. There he found the sannyasi Gorakshanath with the infant, now little more than a piece of flesh, in his arms. Terrified, Bhim fled. But later, when he sat down for a meal, he began to see little fingers and toes instead of okra and cucumber. When he sipped water, it turned into blood. Utterly shaken, he returned to the forest where, overcome with contrition, he became the sannyasi's disciple and servant. Gorakshanath had taken the infant to his ashram and when the prince grew up, he trained him in yoga. Bhim witnessed the prince regain his limbs after twelve years of continuous and rigorous yogic exercise. To commemorate the sprouting of the four limbs, Gorakshanath named the prince Chowrangeenath. Padmavathy, the mother of Lakshmikant Roy Choudhury who was the head of the three villages from which Kolkata was formed, saw a ray of light rise from beneath the waters when she was bathing in the Adi Ganga. She received a swayambhu linga and a toe-shaped stone from the deep, and dedicated them to Chowrangeenath. She had a small hut built beside the Ganga and consecrated these. It was this hut that later became the Kalighat temple. Grandfather Bhim began to live in the hut. It was he who performed the very first animal sacrifice there, Thakuma would recollect proudly. He severed the animal's head in a single blow. That's how the custom of severing the head of the sacrificial beast in one blow so that it knew no pain in death began at Kalighat. Over time, in place of the hut, a concrete temple rose. And the surging Adi Ganga shrank to a little pond, the Kundu Pukur.

My mind was turbulent when we got off bus no. 33 at Shyama Prasad Mukherjee Road. Father was taking me to the temple where we would offer a sacrifice to Ma Kali to remove all the obstacles in our path. In the darkness the flagstaff of the temple resembled the gallows tree. People and vehicles rushed hither and thither. To the east went a wedding procession, to the west, a funeral cortège. The road was completely blocked. As we made our way through the milling crowd, the rows of innumerable shops on either side looked like golden-coloured trams. In all directions, like strange animals, people walked, sat, lay down and crawled. Those who were buying and selling haggled loudly. The stink of the drain, the scent of flowers and the aroma of sweets fried in ghee followed us. In the middle of the crowd, policemen sat relaxing on chairs, smoking and drinking tea. Like insects and cockroaches crawling out of the drain, innumerable women came out of the narrow dark by-lanes at night, with painted lips and heavily rouged cheeks. They hung around outside, surrounding lone men. Some went up to them to haggle. Others, they pulled in. I followed Father, quickening my step. 'Chetna Mullick, Chetna Mullick,' someone shouted. People tried to seek me out in the darkness. To avoid them, I fixed my mind on the red-and-white-and-yellow Durga statues in the shops. Like the fish head in the ilish curry, they were accurately cut. Durgas trapped inside plastic key chains and glass frames displayed themselves to the wayfarers. Those large wide-set eyes, the blood-red mark on the forehead, and the chiselled lips aroused memories of someone, again and again.

'Be careful of the pindaris,' Father reminded me, walking quickly in search of the queue for the darshan.

We took our place in the queue at Nijo Mandir. While we waited, Sanjeev Kumar's channel played on the fourteen-inch TV screen in the peda shop beside the entrance. The news bulletin began.

'In the evening, the FM radio sounded at cell no. 3 of the Alipore Correctional Home. There was just one person listening. And the news that was being broadcast made him blissfully happy . . .'

The pretty newsreader looked at me mockingly as she began to read the news.

'Jatindranath Banerjee has had a very narrow escape from the well-oiled rope that was being readied for him. It was decided earlier that Jatindranath Banerjee, who cruelly killed thirteen-year-old Mridula Chatterjee, would be hanged to death at four o'clock at dawn tomorrow. It would have been the very first execution by a woman—a hangwoman. However, the Supreme Court stayed the execution just when the chief hangman Phanibhushan Grddha Mullick, his daughter Chetna Grddha Mullick and his brother Sukhdev Grddha Mullick completed all preparations and were ready to set out for the prison. For what would have been his last meal, Jatin had asked for ilish, kachoris and jhalmuri, and the jail authorities had made necessary arrangements. He had also wished to be allowed to listen to Rabindra Sangeet the whole night. The home ministry had made a special allotment to purchase a music player for this purpose, but when it did not arrive on time the jail superintendent brought a music player and CDs of Rabindra Sangeet from his own residence. The Supreme Court decision has been widely commended by organizations which oppose the death penalty the world over. At the same time, the victim Mridula Chatterjee's family and many women's groups allege that these organizations are worried only about the human rights of criminals . . .'

In sheer ennui I had switched off the TV at home when this news was first read. Father had tried to invite in acquaintances and tell them what had happened, first sitting in the tea shop and then standing by the road. As soon as the news of the stay order spread, the policemen deputed to guard us stretched their arms and legs and walked away to the other side of the road, swinging their lathis casually. In just five or ten minutes, our house fell back into oblivion, like the fish head devoured by corpse-eater ants. After a while, the reporter of a small newspaper, who did not know of the stay order, rushed in. When he heard the news, he too put away his tape recorder and prepared to leave.

'Babu, please be seated. I have plenty of stories. I'll tell them only to you.' Father followed him, looking slightly pathetic.

'I'll come later, Dada,' the reporter said. 'I'm on my way back from Burdwan. I haven't had a drop of water today—why, I haven't even peed!'

'Why, what happened? Anyone at home unwell, Babu?' Father looked worried.

'No, nothing of that sort, thank God. This is a case in Burdwan. The death of a eighteen-month-old child . . . no nurses there . . . the mothers of sick children have been waiting with the injections since yesterday . . . no nurse turned up. In the end, one of those babies died. The mother was weeping, holding the medicines in her hand!'

'Ah, how terrible!The state of government hospitals even now . . . Really, Babu! But surely, since the hanging has been postponed, people will look for news about it in tomorrow's newspaper. What did the hangman Phanibhushan Grddha Mullick say? They'll want to know. What did his daughter Chetna Grddha Mullick say? Babu, don't you know, she is the world's only female hangman. If your paper carries a statement by her, that'll surely be something to be proud of. And she's never spoken to any newspaper till now. But she will, if I tell her. A statement by us and our photo will surely do your paper good. But that doesn't mean you have to dig deep in your pockets . . . just give me whatever you have. This is my statement, Babu: "The hanging has been postponed. Banerjee must be laughing now. But what about the family of his victim?"'

I stormed back in disgust into Ramu da's room, and so didn't hear the reporter's answer. But when I heard Father calling me in that tone of his, I could guess—he had taken the bait. Pretending not to hear, I sat down beside Ramu da's cot. Ramu da was watching the re-telecast of the Group D match between Germany and the Czech Republic in the Euro Cup when Father called me again. He gave me an anxious look.

'Who's going to win?' I asked him, not really interested.

Ramu da's eyes shone fondly. He sighed and turned them towards the TV screen again. 'The Czech Republic won yesterday's match by two goals. Germany lost.'

'Oh, that's sad, they are a good team.'

'That's why I'm glad. Let Portugal win . . . the match is on their home ground.'

My heart became warm again at his broad smile.

'Tonight, it's between England and Portugal. We'll know today . . . Chetu, mark my words, if Portugal wins tonight, the cup is going to be ours!' he declared with such passion that you'd think he was going to play the match.

I always shivered when I saw children making space on the wayside and in the middle of the street to play football because they reminded me of him. The feet that were hacked off his body at the age of twenty-two had smelled of ammonia because he had been running in the mud of the football ground. I remembered the blotchy old sheet that covered the mattress on the rickety old cot in SSKM Medical College that we'd managed to get into only because some policeman had put in a word for us. His blood too made dark patches on the sheet. Just three beds away, water from a leaky toilet nearby made a pool. The floor was so dirty, it looked as though it had never been washed. Everywhere we looked there were stains, marks, dirt, stench, pain and tears. When he regained consciousness, Ramu da tried to jump up, not realizing that he had lost his legs. My leg itches, he screamed. 'When can I go back to playing football?' he asked the doctor. Thakuma and Ma broke down, hearing him. All of us struggled to cope with his condition every day.

'Chetna, didn't you hear me call?'

Father's question was gently put.

I leapt up and stood before him, head bowed.

'Don't you know, there will be no respite for you in this world and the next if you defy your father?'

I didn't reply to that either.

'It's a big loss of face. I'd feared this . . . when Chakrabarty babu called, I asked him if this would happen, really. The court has no intelligence! If someone isn't hanged once in a while, will anyone have any fear at all? Hanging always fortifies society's inner strength, did you know?'

He paced the room uneasily. Fished out a cigarette from the pouch at his waist and lit it.

'Phani, listen to me,' said Thakuma from the doorstep. She had just come in with a heap of vegetables in her aanchal, probably scrounged from somewhere in the market. 'Go to Kalighat, appease Ma Kali with a sacrifice. She will bless you and your children.' That's how Father set off for the temple with me. The last time I had visited the temple was before Niharika's wedding. The temple and premises looked the same. Yet, things had changed. Noise filled the air; I longed for a little quiet. The queue moved at a snail's pace through the metal detectors. I waited, totally bored. The sellers of yellow garlands that looked like tennis balls strung together attacked us relentlessly.

'Come to the Jorbangala queue . . . Dada, come this way . . . your darshan can be completed in just five minutes . . . give what you like . . .' The brokers kept tempting the devotees.

'Don't pay attention to them. Their pockets swallow everything. The donations go to the Haldar family which ousted the Roy Choudhuris. It's now given out by auction . . . . all that devotees place before Ma Kali will be theirs in effect.' Father reminded me, irritated.

As I waited on the steps to Nijo Mandir, I saw a dark-skinned woman in a red sari give out the kumkum and prasad at Shoshtitala, believed to be the samadhi of Brahmanandagiri Swami. Jostled hard from behind, I stumbled into the temple, and was shoved right before the central shrine. There was such a crowd; I stayed in the space between the deity and the wall only for a few minutes. Kali, with her three red eyes like bael leaves upon her pitch-black face, smiled, her long golden tongue hanging almost to her breasts. A priest held out the sacred flame to me and snatched the change from my hand. He dug out a bit of sindoor from the idol and pressed it into my forehead. Before I could look one more time into Ma Kali's eyes, I had been pushed out by the pindaris. Father slipped as we came down the marble steps. As I stopped him from falling, my eyes became wet. Father went towards Harkat Tala past Nat Mandir, where a shirtless man was chopping meat. He paid for the sacrifice and came back; I walked out pretending not to see the heap of cow and goat heads. Two altars black with blood and red with silk drew my eyes towards them. On the large altar meant for cow and buffalo sacrifice, the remnants stuck like black mushrooms. On the smaller one, for goats, flies buzzed and seethed even in the dark. I felt sorry for Kali who drank more and more blood each day but still remained thirsty. And tried not to think of the animal which would be sacrificed for us.

'Ma Kali will not let us down—she was here before Kolkata. So were we,' Father said confidently as he put on the slippers he had left at the peda shop.

The image of Kali's three eyes was still impressed in my mind. In the beginning, the idol had only a face, Thakuma used to say. The four arms and the golden tongue were added later. The belief is that Sati's toe, the sati ango, is still somewhere in the temple. But it is kept in a secret place. During the snan yatra, the priests blindfold themselves and dip the toe in the Ganga from time to time.

'In the days that come, you should do exactly as I say,' Father told me as we walked through the haggling, the selling, the buying and the angry shrieks towards Shyama Prasad Mukherjee Road.

The TV news followed us everywhere.

'All preparations for the hanging at dawn tomorrow had been completed. The chief hangman Phanibhushan Grddha Mullick and his daughter Chetna Grddha Mullick had visited Alipore Jail and conducted the test hanging successfully. The Supreme Court has issued the stay order upon an appeal by Jatindranath Banerjee's wife Kokila Banerjee, which states that the sentence should not be carried out since the appeal to the President of India, filed after the Bengal governor rejected Jatindranath's mercy petition, is still pending.'

Father sighed deeply.

'Even the generator was set up in the jail . . . What to do! His time has not yet arrived.'

How Father had pontificated about death's vacillations yesterday as he was being filmed! My legs felt heavy as I walked, my head bent lower, my heart grew dim. I believed that this was because the crown of Indian womanhood and self-respect that I had been wearing for a month and six days had fallen off. The crown might have been heavy, but it had given me security.

The city flowed like a Ganga of hustle and bustle. Our bus got caught everywhere in the traffic. We reached home late. As I ate supper without any appetite, I knew that it was Sanjeev Kumar's absence that troubled me most. The memories of our strolls after *Hangwoman's Diary* rose up and gave me heartburn. How I wished to blend with him into the throngs of the rich and the poor in the city, in the excesses of sounds and sights and scents just one more time!

'I told you earlier, you shouldn't feel bad after this day—today,' Ramu da whispered.

I was sitting on the floor next to his cot, looking tired.

'Got used to it for a whole month, Ramu da . . .'

'Look, you have to get back to normal life slowly. You've got to undo it like you'd take off a noose. You must find work, make some money, attend an evening course and complete your education. No point hanging on to the rope of tradition, Chetu . . .'

His voice was moist with emotion.

'You have to slowly wipe off all the experiences and memories of this month. Like the past were just a recap you'd watch of a game on TV. From today, walk back little by little. Erase, throw out, one by one, each of the hopes and sights and memories you picked up on the way. You will not need them any more. He won't come in search of you. He doesn't need you any more.'

My face glowered. I visualized myself walking back and erasing each of the footprints on the path I'd walked a whole month. Images of the ant-eaten fish head, bodies with painted lips, aparajita vines that thrived and bloomed inside the ruined bungalow, diamond ear studs, cellar holes, the hand squeezing my left breast hard, the camera that focused on Ramu da which I had knocked to the floor, and Thakuma's gold coin zoomed past my eyes.

Thakuma came hobbling into the room and sat down on the bed then. 'Thakuma, did you find your gold coin?' I asked her without really thinking.

That was the deed of the hangman thirsting for the blood of others, I realized. My body was burning, trying to thrust away the tumult inside.

'Isn't it gone forever? What evidence does this old woman have of the great traditions of this family? Gone forever?' she asked haltingly.

'No,' I said, 'I had kept it under your pillow, Thakuma.'

Ramu da and Thakuma looked at me as though they couldn't believe their ears.

'So where is it, then?'

When I said that someone must have taken it, that led to a mighty commotion. Thakuma surged up. Her thin, reed-like body flew with remarkable vigour out of the room and into the kitchen. She grabbed the small cloth bag which Ma had hidden there and tore it to shreds. Sanjeev Kumar's ear studs and bangles fell on the ground but not the coin. Thakuma then stormed into Kaku's room. Hearing the upheaval, Father, who was having a drink in his room, rushed there.

'See, did you see what he's bought his wife? New gold earrings! Where did that money come from?'

A roar that shook the very foundations of the house rose from Thakuma's feeble body. Kaku and Kakima tried to shove her away. She slipped on the doorstep and fell on her back. Father picked her up with one hand, put her on the cot inside and dashed into their room. No, no, no, Ma screamed. Father's bellow, 'I'm going to crush this dog today,' and Kaku's cry, 'I'll stab you dead if you lay a finger on me,' filled the air. I sat, passive, holding on to the leg of Ramu da's cot. Father dragged Kaku out by one leg. His swarthy body bled everywhere. Father dropped him like an old sack at the foot of Thakuma's cot. At that moment, Kakima flew in, brandishing a huge fish chopper.

'Touch my man and I'll kill you!' she shrieked. Father snatched the chopper with his left hand and slapped her hard with his right. The chopper fell on the ground, making a huge racket. Kaku jumped up and tried to grab it. Blood splattered as he tried to hold on to the curved blade.

'I'll kill him today! He's out to destroy me!'

Kaku swung the chopper at Father. Though Father slipped away in the nick of time, Kaku jumped at him like a frenzied madman. Ma and Kakima tried to stop them, screaming. Thakuma alone stayed calm. She got up slowly, took out bits of betel from the box under the bed, and began to chew them. In the middle of the commotion, Ma collapsed. I moved quickly and caught her as she fell. The chopper grazed Father's hand and blood streamed out. Father was thrown back from the shock and hit the TV, which came on suddenly. The live telecast of the Euro Cup was on. Father caught hold of Kaku's arm and twisted it hard. He screamed and collapsed on the floor; Father stood over him, panting, holding the chopper. I was now convinced that Father was capable of killing someone without the magistrate's red kerchief. In the pushing and pulling afterwards, Kaku grabbed Ramu da's cot and lifted it. The legs of the cot almost hit the ceiling and fell back. Ramu da too was tossed up. The sight of a limbless man rising into the air was terrifying. The only part of Ramu da's body that Amartya Ghosh had not touched was his skull. That hit the ground now and shattered. Father fled, like Grandfather Bhim had after severing Chowrangeenath's limbs. Howling, Ma fell on Ramu da's body. Kakima dragged Kaku out of the room. Thakuma chewed betel unexcitedly. Entirely distanced from the event, I made and unmade fine nooses with my dupatta.

All of it looked like scenes on TV. All of us acted the best we could. The TV kept playing. Following the images of Portugal entering the semi-finals after beating England, Sanjeev Kumar appeared on the screen. In cell no. 3 of the Alipore prison, Jatindranath Banerjee laughed. When Father scooped up Ramu da, who had turned into a piece of flesh, and dashed out, I too tried to smile. But the smile that Sanjeev Kumar Mitra smiled on the channel was indeed worth seeing.

31

It was a nightmare: a man came running through the narrow alleys of Kalighat brandishing a large fish chopper. I jumped awake. In reality, I was like a grain of salt in an ocean, waiting with Ma outside SSKM Hospital, that accumulation of blood, pus and dirt. A huge crowd of people floated in and out of the hospital. In my dream I was in a blue sari. I feared that it was a sari Sanjeev Kumar Mitra had shoplifted. I was chased by someone in white clothes and with a large handlebar moustache. 'Elokeshi!' The call reverberated around me. I wished to respond that I was not she, but my voice would not emerge.

The group of men who had gone in with Ramu da came out. 'Nothing's sure yet. I had to pay them fifteen hundred rupees to get him into the ICU,' Father told us in a cold voice.

Ma sobbed hard.

'All the money we made yesterday is going to disappear. We hangmen don't take money to kill. But these fellows must be paid a bribe, even to kill,' he muttered.

I rubbed my eyes and expelled sleep. Red-and-white clouds lay scattered across the sky like severed limbs. I struggled to fix my eyeballs either on the sky or on the earth. The fear that everyone here wielded a chopper would not go away. I tried to calm myself by thinking of the vast stretch of the Maidan and the Victoria Hall beyond the wall. Then I saw Ramu da run, a ball at his feet, around the ancient wall of St Paul's Cathedral, in front of the utterly reddened Writers' Building. His soul must have left his body and ran out on to the Maidan. Among the players practising there in the morning, he headed the ball as the invisible twelfth player with a transparent body. His glass-like feet kicked hard at the ball that had turned brown from rolling about the mud. But from somewhere the man with the chopper reappeared behind me. I woke up again rudely. The dream had shaken me awake before I could see Ramu da's delicate feet smashed by the hard ball which looked as though it was made of fired clay; I was thankful.

Elokeshi was murdered in my forefather Kalicharan's time. She was hacked to death with a fish chopper by her husband Nabin Chandra Banerjee for having had illicit relations with the priest of the Tarakeswar temple, Madhav Chandra Giri Mahant. The murder occurred just after Nabin Chandra, who was an employee at the Military Press, returned home with his umbrella which had a curved handle. Elokeshi covered her head with the aanchal of her sari and bowed her head for the chopper.

The sun rose up above the Maidan in front of SSKM. It was a beautiful sight. But the entire yard was dirty and stinking. Patients clad in dirty white clothes lay on their cots or sat or strolled around glumly with heavy bandages, the pain visible on their faces. Near the gate there was a waste bin constantly rummaged by children, dogs and a seemingly mad man. That gate had opened to Indians only after Independence. Until then the hospital had been reserved exclusively for white people. There were two ponds and tennis and badminton courts on the premises in those days. The hospital building used to be the garden residence of Rev. Kirnander, the first Protestant vicar of Calcutta. The fact that the garden now was completely submerged under festering filth was itself one of the most important historical lessons of our times. The hospital was a dirt heap of used cotton swabs stained red or yellow, its walls and floors marked by betel stains and phlegm. I squirmed with unease, wanting to punish myself severely for many nameless crimes. The most serious of these crimes was the memory of the way in which I had stood inside his ruined mansion amidst vines that looked like serpents with risen hoods, locked in ardent embrace. As Ramu da fought death inside, outside, I fought the desire to live.

'Doesn't look like he'll survive the night. . . .' Father told Ma in an extraordinarily calm voice.

'Eesh, Bhagawan!' Ma cried.

Father's face grew dark. 'Don't waste your tears. What's meant to happen will happen. I've been seeing death signs on his face for quite some time now.'

'You're responsible for it all! Who reduced him to this state? You!'

Not paying attention to Ma's angry reproach, Father called to me to go with him. It wasn't clear what he had in mind. We went up to the waste bin where a competition was on between the kids, cats and dogs, and where a noxious smell overpowered one's senses. He turned to look at me. 'Do you have that boy's number with you? To call?'

I went red.

'There, those are the phone booths. I'll give you the money. Call him, let him know what happened to Ramu. This is a big news story, Chetu. The hangman's son on his deathbed the day the hanging was postponed—who wouldn't want to see that news on TV after hearing such a headline?'

Father looked enthusiastic.

'I don't have his number.'

He stared at me in disbelief. 'What? You don't have his number?'

'No.'

Anger and agony flashed on his face. 'Huh! You didn't have the sense to get his number after gadding about with him all this while?'

Father rubbed his face with his gamchha and returned it to his shoulder. Lighting a cigarette and puffing hard at it, he gave the matter some thought.

'Okay, okay, I'll get the number . . . we can call the channel office . . .'

Letting out smoke, he became pleasant again.

'If the event had happened, you'd have rolled in fame. But things didn't happen that way . . . For the time being, what you need is a government job. We'll hang on if you get it. Only he can help us with that.'

His voice carried the sheer load and fatigue of his eighty-eight years. I felt warm towards Father. The husband and paramour were both arrested after Elokeshi's murder. The court first ordered Nabin Chandra to be hanged to death. But the general public cried out, 'Punish the paramour, save the husband!' Nabin Chandra's sentence was converted to life imprisonment but thousands petitioned the court, and he was let off. At this news, Grandfather had reportedly said, 'Well, one less to hang.'

As I followed Father to the phone booth, the prospect of having to call Sanjeev Kumar made me sweat. I was troubled by the fact that he had discarded me like a used earthen cup and walked away as soon as the news of the postponement of the hanging had come. I was not the special person with whom he wanted to spend his life; rather, I was like a small rickshaw or some other vehicle, used only to get somewhere. Still my ears hankered to hear his voice again. While Father made several other calls from the booth, I stood quiet and tense. What an awful noose I wore around my neck! The thought made me feel weak.

'Hello . . . Sanju babu? This is me . . . Phanibhushan Grddha Mullick . . . Oh, were you asleep, Babu? Sorry for troubling you. My son Ramdev became very ill last night . . . fell off his cot . . . We brought him to the hospital immediately. Just think, Babu, the day the hanging got postponed, the hangman's son was taken grievously ill. Bhagawan! Will anyone believe this? His skull was shattered when it hit the floor . . . been bedridden for so long, his bones are all weak . . . that's what the doctors say. It's time for him to go, Babu . . . today or by tomorrow evening . . .'

I swallowed hard the humiliation that rose up in my throat. My only consolation was that few people recognized me in the hospital; the people who came there were mostly poor farmers from distant villages who didn't watch much TV. Many didn't even have electricity in their villages. I went back to Ma, who was sipping the tea Hari da had bought her. An old woman with a thin little child on her lap was complaining about something to her.

'Poor woman, she's from Midnapore. She's been here for two weeks,' Ma introduced her.

'Where do you stay?' I asked.

'By the road, where else? Somebody or the other from their village is usually here for treatment . . . they reserve some space by the road,' Ma said.

The woman left with the child, still complaining. Ma finished her tea and flung away the mud cup. 'That fellow, your old geezer, he'll give you all sorts of advice. Don't heed any of it,' she told me as if she were reading my mind.

'You say don't obey, but you never defy him, Ma.'

Running her finger on the long blood-red streak of sindoor on her head, Ma said, 'You are not like me, you are educated.'

I couldn't really take that in fully. The moments slipped by. School buses and other vehicles zoomed past.I could see the tops of those vehicles, big and small, the sleepy little faces inside. By noon, a vehicle bearing the logo of Sanjeev Kumar Mitra's channel entered the hospital yard. My blood froze. He might come—with a warm look and a loving smile—I hoped.

'Where is your baba?' he asked, not even bothering to smile. There was discontent and revulsion on his face.

'He was here . . .' My voice trailed away.

'Which room is your brother in? Quick! I've no time, I need to leave soon.'

'We heard that he was on the third floor, Babu.' Ma pulled her aanchal over her head and came up to us.

'Show me quickly, I've to shoot it and leave.'

I stared at him, not knowing what to do. He was giving instructions to the cameraman. Getting in through the emergency outpatient door, cutting through the queue of people waiting to see different doctors, we walked through the hall filled with a rotting stink towards the lift and waited after pressing the button. He did not look at me or speak to me.

'SSKM Hospital—what is this SSKM?' he asked the cameraman, who gestured his ignorance.

'This used to be called PG Hospital before, Presidency General Hospital. Later it became Seth Sukhlal Karnani Hospital,' I muttered to no one in particular.

'Who's that?'

'Someone who donated some money to the hospital.'

He acted as if he wasn't listening. Not even when we were walking briskly though the spit- and phlegm-stained corridor of the third floor towards the ICU did he acknowledge my presence. Ramu da lay on a rusty cot; there was an oxygen mask on his face, but his eyes were only half shut. The heavy bandage that covered his whole head down to the forehead was stained with blood. I broke down when I saw him. That moment, Atul Kishore Chandra's camera gaped at me.

'You can't shoot here,' a nurse who was passing by said, suppressing a yawn.

'Go and file a case!' snapped Sanjeev Kumar.

She turned around, but seeing that it was useless, went her way.

'Pull that sheet off,' he ordered me.

I shook my head in the negative. 'Better not see it.'

'Look, madam, I know what's worth seeing and what's not. If I tell you to pull off the sheet, you better do it!' He was relentless. 'You pull me out of bed before daybreak and now I have to listen to a lecture?'

It felt as if he had slapped me. He pulled the sheet off himself. Ramu da lay with a piece of green cloth covering his waist. His right side from which the arm had been fully severed and the stump of his left leg, severed above the knee, were in full view. The camera leapt greedily on the bed and, like Kali with her dreadful long tongue, licked him dry. I struggled to squash down the memory of Ramu da's tall, healthy, youthful form rising in my mind.

As I retreated with tearful eyes and a terrible pain throbbing within,

Sanjeev Kumar smiled derisively. 'Remember? That day when I tried to take a picture of him, you knocked down my camera? Now, you yourself have summoned me here to take pictures of him!'

I felt gutted. Even to look at him was revolting. My mind and body smouldered. Father entered then and, running up to Sanjeev Kumar Mitra and the cameraman, bowed to them and started explaining all sorts of things. My legs numb, I stumbled out slowly. Not in a state of mind to look for the lift, I climbed down the stairs, my eyes fixed on the ground. Tears fell. The salt of my tears joined with the many layers of dirt that had sedimented there. In my mind's eye I saw him, trying to photograph Ramu da that day. His words, I want to fuck you at least once, reverberated in my ears. I hated myself then. Who is this Sanjeev Kumar Mitra, I asked myself. A man. How is he related to you? He donated some love. Just a pittance. Mesmerized by it I sold myself, and ruined everything.

Father, Sanjeev Kumar Mitra and the cameraman had reached the ground floor before me.

'It won't work, Phani da. I know how smart you are at changing your tune. I learned my lesson from my last mistake.' His voice was hard.

I wiped off my sweat and observed them from behind.

'Oh, don't say that, Sanju babu. I have entrusted this girl to you . . .'

He was now begging. Sanjeev Kumar Mitra pretended not to hear.

'Okay, okay, I'll put in this news. It will start airing noon onwards.'

'Sanju babu, that won't be enough. Please exert some pressure on the government and get her a government job!'

'Let me think.' There was no warmth in those words.

'Okay, Atul, let's go. Phani da, we are leaving. One thing—if this news appears on any other channel before mine . . .'

That was a threat. He was in grey jeans and a white shirt, and his glasses were smokier than usual. He looked like an actor who had appeared without his costume, after the performance. The speed with which he changed expression left me dumbfounded.

'Never, Sanju babu, never! You can trust me. Phanibhushan is a man who does not go back on his word.'

'Oh yeah, yeah, I know that so well.'

'All right. Will you please drop her on the way? Let her go home and come back with some essential things. Looks like we'll have to be here for four or five days.'

'No, I'm busy.'

He walked away without another glance. Father's face fell; mine turned a deep red.

'He's in quite a fury!' Father said angrily.

'You brought it upon yourself,' Ma said, coming up. 'You made him play the merry fool, didn't you?'

'It's he who made us play the fool,' I said. 'He doesn't need us any more.'

'If that's the only reason why he did all this, then why did he give you those gold bangles and the ring? I don't agree. He was sincere. It's your nature that was the cause . . . .' Tears of rage filled her eyes. 'My fate! You killed the eldest one. The boy who should have lit my pyre . . . you made him this way. And this girl, the only one left, you're ruining her!'

'Chi! Shut your trap!' Father yelled, furious. He looked around as if he were at his wits' end and stomped off to Hari da who was chatting with someone beside the tea shop.

'Didn't the whole world get to know he was going to marry you? Bhagawan! What shame!' Ma turned to me.

'I have no shame at all!' I too snapped, furious.

'You don't know what trouble that is. My child, how will you live? Your father is eighty-eight. I am old too. Not to mention Thakuma. And Sudev and Syamili—will they let you live in peace? No, they'll sell you for what your flesh is worth.'

Ma looked at me in pain.

'Ma, don't worry about me. I've decided how I should live my life.'

'How?'

I didn't reply. We found some space on the granite half-wall near the Woodburn Block and sat there. Ma stretched out on it, exhausted. Just behind us, a young woman was sleeping with her infant. When the baby pulled at her sari, I saw her tattered blouse fastened with safety pins. I lifted Ma's head to my lap and caressed her hair. Ma half-opened her eyes and asked, 'Ramu is unconscious?'

I didn't reply.

'The poor lad . . . if only he'd go soon, without pain.'

My fingers froze.

'As long as I am alive, I can bathe and feed him. After my time?'

'I am still here, Ma.' My voice broke.

'You have a big future, Chetu. Don't ruin it.' She sat up and looked into my eyes. 'For women like us, marriage is an escape route. It was, for me. A place to sleep . . . some food, at least once a day . . . ' There were no tears in her eyes now. Her voice was calm. 'That boy is good. You shouldn't let him go now.'

'He doesn't love me, Ma.'

'Is that why he bought you gold?'

'It was because he could make money out of me.'

'Listen to me, men are like gods. If they have no one to fall at their feet or beg or worship them three times a day, they are mere stones. So don't let him go, hold on tight. You can escape only through him . . . '

'Where to?' I asked, astonished.

'There is a big world out there, Chetu, a very big world. A world where you can live as yourself. But to reach that place, you have to escape this broken little well. Just think of him as a ladder, nothing more.'

I was afraid to look at her. This is not my mother, I felt. Ma lay down with her head in my lap again. I ran my fingers through her hair once more and looked at the pond in front of us. There was a rusty speedboat half sunk in the water. A waterhen perched on it dived straight into the water, swift as lightning, coming up somewhere else much later.

'Ma, have you ever been in love?'

She smiled gently. 'Why? Why this doubt all of a sudden?'

I kept silent. She too kept quiet for a while, and then began to speak, 'Yes, I have. A boy in my village. When we crossed the border, they killed my ma . . . and his baba as well . . . '

My body grew chilled when I saw that the wounds inflicted on this country by Partition were to be found in my family as well.

'And then?' I asked, anxious to hear more.

'It was a time of terrible want. My baba married again. We didn't have food or a place to sleep. Your dadu came to see me when I'd turned thirteen. I thought then, it would be so wonderful to eat regularly at least once a day . . . ' she said, voice faltering.

'And what about him?'

'I just killed him . . . in my mind.'

My breath stopped. Her body was trembling, I thought.

'Didn't you love Baba, Ma?' I asked again.

'He's not one person but many.' Ma's words were rock hard. 'He knows that he doesn't deserve me. Isn't that why he goes to Sonagachi? Chetu, your father's heart is like a coconut shell with a hole in it. However much you pour, it just runs out. Never will it fill. So even if he had the Ganga all to himself, it would be of no use.'

'Does he know that you were once in love with someone else?'

'I haven't told him. But perhaps he knows. Maybe that's why he's run me down since the day he saw me. Your baba can't swim. So he wants to drain the river dry. I have never managed to forget that man. Perhaps I could have if only your baba had permitted me to forget.'

I felt a tremor in my very bones; I remembered Radharaman Mullick and Chinmayi Devi. Till now, in my mind, Father had been a zamindar, and Ma a soot-covered pot upon the hearth, full of boiling water. The waterhen perched again on the half-sunk boat and stretched out its wings to dry. This is not my mother lying in my lap, I thought again. I began to feel the exertion of running through those narrow lanes lined with shops hung with large-eyed, red-lipped Durgas, in a body like the one Ramu da had had in my dream: a body through which light could pass. 'Elokeshi!' I heard the cry again. Nabin Chandra was a fool. He shouldn't have killed Elokeshi. She has refused to die after many centuries only because she had been killed.

32

Whenever I visit Nimtala Ghat, I feel that the moment when the clock of life begins to tick backwards is what we call death. After that moment, those who were flesh and blood turn into reflections in the mirror of life. If death is the moment in which we walk away from relationships, then each person dies several times in a single lifetime!

I sat beside Ma, who was stretched out fast asleep on the little space we had managed to claim. I knew Sanjeev Kumar Mitra had begun to walk away from our relationship. In that sense, one of us was dying. As for Ramu da, who was hanging in the loops made by ventilator tubes, the clock of his life had begun to tick backwards quite sometime ago. The sky was ablaze as if it had totally forgotten the heavy showers that had fallen till yesterday.

Father appeared with someone in hospital uniform. He was stuffing into the pouch at his waist the currency notes Father had given him. He greeted me with a grin that revealed his betel-stained teeth. 'Ah, just like on TV, except for the tired face!' He turned to Father with an even broader grin. 'Dada, these notes you've given me will take care of everything. Have you forgotten how this hospital got this name? The Seth gifted some money to the hospital. Peanuts! But because of it, only because of it . . .'

Father sighed unexpectedly. 'That is my only male child. I don't say that you should heal him. But please don't make him die many living deaths . . .'

'Don't worry, Dada, I'll take care of it. I'll put in a special word for you with Doctor babu. This doctor doesn't usually attend to anyone but Party people. I'll convince him that you are much respected in the Party. And besides, you are Chetna Grddha Mullick's father! How lucky you are, Dada . . . to be on TV and everything . . .'

I wiped off the sweat and just sat there looking utterly blank. Ma was sleeping with her mouth wide open like someone who had finally got a chance to sleep in her life. Her dirty, cracked feet stuck out pathetically below her frayed sari. Elokeshi, I thought. If Elokeshi had lived, if she'd had children and grandchildren, she too would have had to hang around hospital premises with feet dirtier than these, keeping a vigil for her son's life. How saddening the thought was!

When the sweeper left, Father turned to me. 'Get ready soon, we have to go and see Sibdev babu. If he wishes to, he can help us get you a job.'

'What job?' Ma lumbered up. 'Enough job seeking for her. Try to get that marriage back on track. Got that boy worked up for no reason! If you hadn't done that, my daughter would have had a good future!'

253

Father looked at Ma with dislike. 'She'll have the future she's destined to have.'

Ma scratched her head roughly. She untied her hair and tied it up again. 'Oh indeed, she will, for sure, for sure!'

'Well, how could that not be? She's your daughter after all. Even after all these days, was she able to make him happy? No! But will he have any problem finding a woman? Of course not! To snare a man's mind, you need more than a full body . . . '

'Oh yes, of course, you have met many with such abilities in Sonagachi for sure! Why don't you go and live with one of them? I've no great wish to snare your mind. Really! What a priceless treasure it is for everyone to run after!' Ma spat in sheer contempt.

After a while she said, 'But think of it, it wasn't an alliance that suited our situation. Ramu didn't like it at all . . . '

But Father said, quite sure of himself, 'Situations need little time to change! Who was Rani Rashmani Debi? A starved wench from a godforsaken village! I've heard my thakuma talk about her. When she was brought to Kolkata at the age of thirteen, what a miserable sight she was. But then, didn't she control all the zamindari after her husband's death? Didn't she stand up even against the British? I bow to her whenever I see Nimtala Ghat. That's woman power, truly . . . '

Ma twisted her lips in contempt. They kept jabbering for some more time. In the end, I had to go again to Alipore with Father. On bus no. 228.

'Death is at once a fully determined and a completely random phenomenon,' Father muttered as if to himself, sitting in the bus.

The blazing sunlight blinded like white darkness. A certain numbness and melancholy, typical of bereavement, enveloped me.

'Death is inevitable. But one can't predict when it will happen. However, I can give you my word on one thing: If someone is meant to die by your hand, no one else can take him. And if he is not, then no matter how you try you can't kill him. My baba used to say that.'

Father sighed.

Thakuma repeated Dadu's words whenever she talked of Dinesh Chandra Gupta. It was July 1930, when it rained incessantly. Thakuma was pregnant then. The courtyard of the house, which was bigger then, had filled with rainwater. She had woken up early in the morning and was getting ready to light the hearth, when she slipped, fell into the water, and had a miscarriage. Sweeping up Thakuma who lay in a pool of blood, Dadu ran to fetch the vaidya. He got wet and that led to a fever which brought him down for a whole week. He had to inform the government that he couldn't be present for the hanging of Dinesh Chandra Gupta which had been fixed for 7 July. Instead, Dadu's older brother's son, Shivottam Grddha Mullick, was sent. He collapsed on his way and died. In the end, Dadu had to go despite the fever. In the *Canberra Times* that week, the news of Dinesh Chandra Gupta's death appeared in a small finger-length column along with news of the twister that devastated Sydney and of the sharp increase in the female population of Britain. Dadu always wept when he remembered that young man.

We waited at the prison gate for a while. When we were finally summoned, Father pulled out a comb and ran it through his hair enthusiastically.

'Sibdev babu will definitely help us. He is a good man.'

He was optimistic. I, worn out by now, tagged behind him, struggling to keep up. I was stinking, having sat up in the hospital yard for hours, unwashed and with no sleep. When the prisoners who were cleaning the yard saw us, they stopped their work to look. We could hear whistles and humming.

'Hey Dada, leave her here. We'll look after her.'

'Ooh . . .' someone said, 'that's Grddha Mullick. Go easy with your teasing . . .'

'Move quickly,' Father hurried me.

The gun-toting policeman in the corridor took us in. Cell no. 3 was on the left after the left turn past the next gate, I remembered. I was curious to know what Jatindranath Banerjee was doing that very moment in that cell where the electric bulb burned day and night.

'So, Grddha da, a slip between the cup and the lip, right?' Seeing us, Sibdev babu set aside the papers he had been writing on and gave us a broad smile.

'Bad luck, Babu. And now my son is in the hospital too.'

'Didn't I see it on TV? To know what is happening in your family, all one needs to do is check the TV.' He looked at me, smiling. 'I've watched you speak on TV. Till which class did you study?'

'Plus Two.'

'Oh, I really thought you'd studied much higher!'

'She was very bright as a student, Babu. But what to do? Shouldn't I have some money if I want to send her to college?' Father interjected, holding out a piece of paper to Sibdev babu. 'Please help her get a job somehow, Babu! Otherwise we will all have to commit suicide together.'

'As you said, terrible bad luck . . . if not, that hanging would have happened. She would have become a star! Why don't you perform a puja? Tie a piece of blessed string . . .'

'All that's useless, Babu. Tell us which temple to make the offering to, Babu . . .'

Father bent his back again and scratched it. Sibdev babu thought about it.

'Go and meet the DS. You may have to pay something, perhaps.' He leaned back in his chair, smiling. 'DS means district secretary. If the Party decides, she will definitely get a job.'

Father was about to say something when a policeman came in.

'Babu, the jeep and the staff are ready. It's time to take Jatin to the hospital.'

Sibdev babu got up, put his cap on, and went out. We followed him into the veranda. I saw a prisoner walk up between two policemen, his arms thrown around their shoulders for support. A thin man, he walked with a bit of a stoop. Father looked jolted. I did too when I recognized him. It was the person I was to have killed. His skin was terribly pale from having stayed indoors for so long. A thin, shrivelled body. The veins in his neck bulged a bit against his skin. I could clearly see the marks that the strands of the rope smoothened with banana flesh and soap would make on the white skin.

'Take care. The doctor's been informed, hasn't he?' I heard Sibdev babu say when I caught up.

'Yes, Babu.'

Jatindranath had a warm smile on his face when he turned to Sibdev babu.

'What happened, Jatin? Happy that your tummy got upset?'

'I was up early and shaved as usual. I had a nice bath and was humming a couple of tunes too! And then I became unwell . . . oh, isn't this the hangman, Grddha Mullick?'

His eyes opened wide. Father looked at him with a cast-iron expression on his face.

'Yes, and this is his daughter, Chetna Grddha Mullick. She was to have hanged you. You bugger, you have a very long life!'

'Yes, Babu, I do. No one can kill me!' He laughed merrily. 'Dada, don't you remember me? Didn't you come to meet me like this in 1994? Hey, don't ready the noose for me yet, all right? I am not going to go too soon! Sister, that was for you too!' He winked at me.

'May you not go too soon, son. May God bless you.' Father rose to the occasion, raised his hands and blessed him. I just watched. The prisoner's thick, small palms, ordinary looking legs and slightly snub nose reminded me of Sanjeev Kumar Mitra. But, in truth, there was no resemblance at all between the tall, well-formed, handsome Sanjeev Kumar and the thin, pale Jatindranath.

'What did you gobble up in the morning for your stomach to rebel?' Sibdev babu asked.

'Ate up all that they gave me. I got back my life today, didn't I?'

'Uh-hm! If you'd been good, you might have been at home eating your wife's cooking.'

At that he looked at Sibdev babu and me and beamed. That smile reminded me of soiled currency notes. After he left, Sibdev babu sighed. 'Will anyone who sees him smile believe that he cruelly murdered a young girl? I was in my fifth year of service when it happened. Poor thing! She was a good girl. She was still holding her mother's medicine tight as she lay dead.'

She was her parents' younger daughter. Her death drove her mother mad. Her father took refuge in drink and drugs. They went away from Kolkata.

'These kind of people have the best time these days. Look at him. Does he show the slightest hint of repentance?' Father was enraged. 'He will live here for another twenty years like this. He'll gobble food with the money that taxpayers pay. The government will take him to the hospital in a vehicle if he has an upset stomach. When I see this, I wonder, why not finish off a couple of people. I could spend the rest of my life in comfort inside the prison!'

Sibdev babu laughed loudly. 'Don't worry, Grddha da. The decision in the Writers' Buildings is that this chap should be finished off. It's possible that things will still work out the way you want them to.'

Father looked at him, puzzled.

'Today, just after the news of your son, the chief minister made a statement. The government's view is that cruel murderers indeed deserve the death penalty. That's the Party's stand too.'

'But what to say, Babu, shouldn't the President think so too?'

'Who's going to lose anything because one more chap lives, Grddha da? That's my position. Anyway, you can go now. We'll do all that we can.'

When we bid him goodbye and stepped out, Father laughed heartily. 'My mind says he won't escape!'

I looked at Father, bewildered.

'The signs of death are all on his face. Just a month more, not beyond. No, no!'

I said nothing. Sitting in the bus I felt distanced from the world and life. I saw Jatindranath Banerjee's form everywhere. The hollow cheeks on his freshly shaven face, the close-cropped hair, the sunken eyes, the prominent ear lobes—I saw them all clearly. There was a mismatch between his look and his laugh. The dregs of the memory of having grievously wounded a little girl, not yet thirteen, who was running to get her mother some medicine, lay in his eyes. The day grew hotter. My head ached. My ears itched terribly. I remembered Thakuma saying that this meant one would receive news of death. Someone who looked like Ramu da stood on the roadside. Ramu da was struggling to get away from the ventilator's nooses. I had barely stepped into the hospital when I heard Ma's loud wail. I got past the queue in front of the emergency outpatient ward, almost tripping over a man sitting there with both legs bandaged, biting into a guava leisurely, and ran up the steps. Ma lay on the third-floor veranda, rolling her head and wailing. Inside, Ramu da was in the last throes of his final struggle. It was the first time I saw someone die. It was like seeing a football match in slow motion on TV. His torso twisted and turned. His body heaved up and down. His eyeballs darted all around the room. Darkness rushed into my eyes; I grasped the iron cot tightly. Ma Kali, Bhagawan, Father was shouting. Seeing us there, people gathered around. And Father, seeing them, became energized. 'Goodbye, my son! Do not be afraid!' he said, kissing Ramu da's forehead.

I looked around. Will he now say, 'One thumping line, right?' I wondered. Suddenly, Ramu da gasped three times. His eyeballs rolled upwards. His body became motionless. The doctor came in and checked his pulse. He then removed the oxygen mask and the tubes, and left without a word. Ramu da's eyes made me feel afraid. My right hand extended involuntarily. My palm felt his eyelashes; they were so soft even then. His eyelids were like flower petals. Death crawled inside my palm. His eyelids closed like flower petals falling. Liberated from the ventilator, Ramu da lay, eyes shut, an innocent smile on his face. Ma ran in and threw herself on his body, weeping.

Father looked around again at the crowd that had gathered and raised his arm. 'Bhagawan! You've taken him back, now keep his soul safe!'

I held Ma close. Everything—laughter, tears, rage, sorrow—had left me. Inside my brain, the hand of a clock moved backwards. Tick-tock, tick-tock. Two helpers brought out the body swathed in a stained sheet and left it on the veranda. Ma hugged his body again and wept. I stood there motionless, without a clue as to what to do. After some time, two other helpers carried someone in on a stretcher—I recognized Jatindranath when I saw the policemen accompanying him. His gaze mocked the world around him. Our eyes met; his grew warm.

At home, Ramu da was laid in the same place as Niharika. Thakuma entered with water from the Ganga. While they bathed him and rubbed sandalwood paste on his forehead, I sat there motionless and tearless. He of course had no toes to be tied together. We offered water and puffed rice to his closed mouth. At Nimtala Ghat, Father circumambulated the pyre carrying a pot of water with a hole in it, following the clock that ran backwards. For a time Ramu da's head escaped the flames leaping on the wood. Gradually, the fire spread to his cropped hair. The smell of burning hair made me queasy. The flames burned higher. I waited on the banks of the Ganga until the blaze had consumed all of the body. The Ganga stank like a rotting corpse, choked with rotten flowers, silk cloth, bamboo litters. My head reeled. Wherever I looked, it was as

259

though everything was moving backwards. The ripples on the Ganga, the flames on the pyre, the smoke that reached the sky, everything, moved backwards with the tikc-tock, tick-tock sound. Back, and further back, to the soil, the air, the water, the past.

33

'There's a story Jyoti babu used to tell us. Once, an Englishwoman fell in love with an unlettered Indian man and married him. After a while, she decided to divorce him. This man knows no English and can't find even a small job, so he is totally useless to the children and me, she said. But how did you fall in love with someone who can't speak your language, asked the court. Know what her reply was? Milord, if two people fall in love, they don't need another language in common!'

Pushing back the unruly strands of silver hair which fell on his thick glasses, Manavendra Bose smiled at me. 'Did you understand? Love—love is a language in which we speak with ourselves.'

I could smile with ease looking at that face, so full of radiance even though it was well past eighty. I read once again with great care those lines written in a beautiful hand on the sheets of paper on the desk. The two hours I had spent waiting for Manavendra Bose, after the man with the slight build and betel-stained teeth who sat doing accounts in front of the *Bhavishyath*'s curved doorway told me he had gone to borrow some money, were not tiresome. Because sitting there was like sitting on history's doorstep watching the flow of the present. Three days had passed since Ramu da's death. I simply could not stay home. There, someone played football with my heart. Kicked and thrown around roughly, it became very, very worn. Standing on the veranda of the *Bhavishyath*, I could see the entire length of Chitpur Tram Road, full of hawkers, tourists, students, beggars, devotees, passers-by, rickshaws, autos, buses and trams; and I could see the red walls and white windows of Jorasanko Thakurbari from really close. As I stood there gazing at these sights and taking in the scent of one-hundred-and-twenty-year-old paper, I returned to the past without having to disperse into the five elements. Just when I was considering another visit to the inner spaces of the Thakurbari, Mano da returned, soaked in sweat. He wore a kurta with a frayed collar; his dhoti was pulled up on the right.

'Eesh! Aren't you Grddha da's daughter? Why are you here?' he asked, pulling his right leg up the steps like a heavy weight and throwing it into the door.

His large form filled the small doorway. His eyes evoked the interiors of the wild; his voice sounded like a distant roar.

'I want a job,' I put it to him straight.

Mano da had just fished out a piece of paper from his pocket and was putting it on top of the heap of books and papers on the table; he turned, startled. Silver strands fell on his forehead, over his glasses. He shook them off and guffawed. 'A job? For you? Here?'

'I can proofread . . .'

I wiped my face and neck with my dupatta. Greed filled my eyes as I peered inside. A sea deep enough and wide enough for me to swim about in at ease rippled inside that ancient building which hadn't had a fresh coat of paint in many years.

'Didn't your brother recently . . . ?' he asked, after a moment.

'It's been three days,' I said.

'I saw the news,' he said. 'The condemned man and the hangman's son in the same hospital. Your baba must have haggled with the channel fellows over that?'

An insipid smile creased my face.

'Anyway, good that it got postponed. What if you felt guilt about it later? That your hands had wiped out someone who might have become a good man had he been spared?'

His smile became brighter.

'I fear guilt,' I said.

When I stood before him, I felt courageous as never before. With his fair skin and ample cheeks, Mano da must have been a wonderfully handsome man in his youth.

'I have seen you only on TV.'

'But I have seen you since childhood. I used to peep in on my way

261

to school. I was delighted whenever I saw you inside the building or by the road.'

'But why?' he asked, astonished.

'Because Ramu da used to say that you are a tiger!'

'Hey, Nischol, did you hear?' He laughed heartily and called to the accountant.

The accountant raised his head from his book and looked at us. 'This time Piplu da paid the electricity bill. He wants it back . . . four hundred and fifty rupees.'

'Ha, don't change the subject, Nishcol! Whenever someone praises me, you always spoil the mood by mentioning unpaid bills and pending debts! Chetu! Tell me! Does this old man look like a tiger? Did you think so when you saw me?'

I rested my eyes on him and smiled. 'A tiger is a tiger for life.'

'Even if its leg is broken?'

'Even if it decides to keep a fast!'

Slapping me affectionately on the shoulder, he laughed again. I joined in too. A trace of a smile glimmered even in the eyes of the Tranquil One—Nischol da. Ramu da had used the prefix 'great' for Mano da. The first time I had heard that description was in Father's references to the male infant born to Dr Nishikant Basu in the now decrepit house that stood in the junction of Amherst Road and Harrison Street. I had never had a chance to see a great man, and so when Ramu da said, why, there is a great man living very near us, I stored it in my head and peeped into the *Bhavishyath* office every day on my way back from school. The story of Mano da's leg, broken by the police, gave me shivers of excitement. Even Ma, who never talked politics, became articulate whenever the Emergency was discussed. Father described it as the time when S.S. Ray replaced us, the hangmen.

'You are hired!' Mano da called out, sitting in the chair behind the table.

I sat on the doorstep beside Nischol da's low desk. Piles of paper covered all the furniture in the room. It was the best laboratory to study the effects of ageing on the colour of paper. The change wrought by time on all things is a topic I love to study. It may turn human beings into animals. Or animals into trees. How will it change Father, I wondered. It turned Ramu da into the five elements. A lamp had been lit at the head of the cot he used to lie upon. In the belief that until the soul leaves the earth, it returns to the place where its body used to be, Thakuma kept refilling the lamp with oil. It was precisely at the moment when Ramu da had merged into the cosmic dust that swirled between the planets and the stars, and thus become a part of time without beginning or end, that the thought of working at the *Bhavishyath* entered my mind. Like the bird that has experienced at least once the pleasure of singing on a tree, I simply could not return to roost within the four walls of our home, killing time teaching Champa and Rari their English and Bangla and maths. As long as Ramu da lay on the cot in our tiny room, my life had revolved around him. Helping him eat, sometimes helping to bathe him, powdering his back, turning him around, reading the newspaper and books to him, switching the TV on for him . . .

'You didn't ask about your salary?'

'Whatever you can give . . .'

'Oh, did you vow to work here without pay?'

'Lots of big shops are opening in Kolkata,' Nishcol da observed, without lifting his head from his work. 'They're looking for young women with some education and good looks to work there. There's no shop which doesn't have the board "Sales girls wanted". You'll get at least a five hundred . . .'

'I am happy with a job here.'

'Why, I ask?'

I smiled at Mano da, playing with my dupatta, twisting it like it were a rope with which to make a noose. 'I have wished for it since childhood.'

'So you wish to work with a tiger? Why not go to the Sunderbans? Plenty of tigers there.' His voice rang deep.

'Are there any tigers there whose legs were broken by the police?' I asked.

He stared at me fixedly.

'Tigers who canvassed for Humayun Kabir in the 1946 elections?'

His eyes welled up. But he rubbed them dry, taking off his glasses. Then dragged his bad leg and went inside. After a while, he returned. 'I was looking for a place where you can sit. Come in, I've found a chair.'

The doors inside the building were painted green. The white walls

263

were covered with dust and dirt and cobwebs. We reached a room by the side of what looked like a central courtyard. A black-and-white photograph of a man with carved lips caught my eye. With an inner shiver, I recognized Jatindranath Mukherjee's picture. Next to it was another image of Bagha Jatin stepping on a tiger. I had heard Thakuma tell the story of how Jatin had killed the tiger. He had gone to Koya village hearing that a leopard was troubling the villagers, but what he found was a gigantic Bengal tiger. It leaped on him but he faced it barehanded. Heavily wounded, Jatin finally pulled out a dagger and stabbed the beast in its neck. It died, struggling. Jatin had to be hospitalized for a long time because the wounds from the tiger's claws became infected. The Bengal government of those days, impressed by his bravery, honoured him and presented him with a shield inscribed with the image of a man fighting a tiger.

'*Bhavishyath* was begun by Jatindranath Mukherjee.' Mano da looked at me. 'I am a tiger by tradition!'

The helplessness and pain in his voice left me silent.

Dadu was summoned by the British when Thakuma was in the labour room, crying out in pain as she brought forth my father Phanibhushan Grddha Mullick. But Dadu was not at home when the summons arrived and so Thakuma's father, Triloknath Grddha Mullick, had to go. He was a disciple of Swami Vivekananda, a sannyasi in ochre robes with a long white beard that hung to his navel.

'I cannot even think of another person like Bagha Jatin. When an Englishman asked him how many men he could fell with his bare hands, do you know what he said in response? That he could not knock down a single innocent person, but if they were wrongdoers, he didn't mind any number!' Mano da smiled proudly.

Grandfather Triloknath was taken to Balasore. Bagha Jatin had been amassing resources for an armed revolt by plundering taxis and boats. While he was preparing to subvert British power in India with German help during the First World War, he was moved to Balasore by his friends after he came under police surveillance. The police surrounded them. Refusing to escape and leave his friends in the lurch, he fought hard and fell, wounded. He was admitted to the hospital; Grandfather Triloknath was brought there to hang him. But when he heard who the prisoner was, he burst out in anger: 'My noose is meant for criminals, not for tigers!'

The enraged British officer shot the unconscious Bagha in the chest and killed him. He then hanged Grandfather with the same noose meant for Bagha. Thus Triloknath, revolutionary and sannyasi, attained fame as the first hangman to be hanged for defying the government. He had snapped at the Englishman who was trying to hang him: 'Step aside; I'll put the noose around my neck.' He fixed the noose between the third and fourth vertebrae of his own neck, and told the officer, 'It is time!' There was no lever, no gallows tree. Behind the Balasore hospital stood a radhajhoola tree in full bloom with all its leaves fallen; the rope was tied on its branch. They had made him stand on a small stool. Grandfather looked at the sky with the noose around his neck, seeing it in hues of yellow. He repeated Swami Vivekananda's words: Amra jabo, jagat jabe . . . An Indian sepoy removed the stool. Grandfather let out a sound and then dangled in the air. The tree swayed with his weight and rained flowers on his dead body. Just when your Father was entering this world, his grandfather left it by his own noose, said Thakuma proudly. She described the shower of yellow flowers as if she had seen it with her own eyes.

Mano da opened a big window in a dark corner. There was a black table there and a chair with one of its armrests missing.

'There's no power now. Come on, you can sit here,' he said. 'You can do any work you like.'

'I can correct the proofs.'

He went in and returned with a bundle of paper. 'These are my memoirs.'

'Are they mostly about Jyoti babu?'

'If he is cut out of the story, what would remain of the autobiography of someone who's lived in Kolkata all his life? He had been a part of my life since I turned ten or so . . . though I was not present in his life later.'

I ran my eyes over the first sheet:

Dr B.C. Roy accused the communists of rewriting many scripts to fool the people. This led to a heated exchange between Roy and Basu in the legislative assembly.

265

Basu: Which drama script did the communists alter?

Dr Roy: I refuse to reveal it.

Basu: Why?

Dr Roy: Because their names should not be uttered.

Basu: No one should be like this in an open legislative assembly. You are behaving like Hitler, Dr Roy.

Dr Roy: Yes, Hitler is replying to Stalin's questions.

I laughed and so did Mano da.

'This should come after the story of the white woman. Pay attention to the page numbers . . .'

Suddenly, the room was filled with light and the ancient fan began to turn, grunting. The fourteen-inch TV in a corner of the room also came to life. Sanjeev Kumar Mitra's face appeared. Can't I live in this land without seeing him, I fumed silently.

'At the same time, the prime minister repeated after the cabinet meeting that Jatindranath Banerjee does not deserve to be pardoned. Jatindranath Banerjee has, however, been admitted to the hospital with an upset stomach.'

Sibdev babu appeared on TV next.

'Till three days ago, Jatindrananth was very confident. The hanging won't happen, I will escape, he kept repeating. But today he is very dejected. I won't escape, they will hang me, he keeps saying now. His illness is not fully cured but he does not care to eat any more . . .'

I folded the papers and got up.

'What happened, my daughter?'

'I feel like talking, Mano da,' I whispered involuntarily. He gazed at me for some time as though he were reading my heart.

'To whom?'

I was about to weep. Mano da was taken aback. Sensing some sorrow he did not know of, he placed his hand gently on my shoulder.

'Mano da, do you think the hanging will happen?'

He sighed heavily. 'Isn't it death? It is the most uncertain of things . . .'

He sighed again. My heart shuddered as I left, promising to return early the next day. My right hand shook uncontrollably. Suddenly, I felt the right edge of my dupatta. A noose I'd made hung there, ugly. It was a very bright day. I walked through the tram tracks, sad. Go some distance on this road and you'll reach Sonagachi, my heart reminded me. His home appeared in my memory. The memory of those lips painted red bothered me. After wandering about in front of the Jatrapara offices, I caught an auto rickshaw to Strand Road. As I walked home, I saw his channel's van parked in front of Nimeshwar Baba's small temple. My heart choked as joy and sorrow, anger and enthusiasm jostled there. Four or five buffaloes came down the road as a hearse arrived. There was a block in the traffic now. Feeling too impatient to wait it out, I found a small opening and entered the house through the saloon. Loud voices could be heard from Father's room.

'No, no, Sanju babu, no more compromises on this. The marriage first, and only after that your coming and going . . . .'

'Grddha da, why are you talking like Hitler?'

I lingered at the door of my room for a moment. The lamp at the head of Ramu da's cot was burning bright. The whole room smells of the graveyard, I thought. I went in and sat down beside Thakuma's cot, feeling worn out.

'Look, the marriage isn't what's important to both of us now. If you dawdle, things won't move! There must be pressure from your side to make sure that the President's decision is not adverse. As far as I am concerned, it doesn't matter either way. Your well-being, however, is important to me.'

'What are you proposing, Sanju babu?'

'The chief minister's wife and women's organizations are planning a major agitation. Chetna must take part in it. It is a great chance for her and your family.'

Father had become silent. Hitler was considering Stalin's advice. Nobody asked me a thing. All the things I wanted to talk about were largely to myself. But I had no language for this inner conversation. Maybe I didn't need one.

34

After Mayadevi died, Prajapati was mother and guide to Siddhartha Gautama. He left home at twenty-nine. Wandered in the world seeking the root of sorrow. When he returned after attaining Enlightenment, the two people who greeted him and accepted his Word were his father Suddodhana and his second wife, Prajapati. Later, many people were drawn to him and became his followers. But the Buddha did not offer spiritual advice to women. When men became his followers, many families were orphaned. Wives whose husbands left and prostitutes whose clients went away lost their livelihoods. They gathered together under Prajapati's leadership, shaved their heads and set out in search of the Buddha's camp. Crossing the desert and fearsome wilds, the procession of five hundred women finally reached the camp, their feet chapped and broken, heads covered with dust. They begged for mercy. Ananda, the Buddha's disciple, was touched. He went to the Master and pleaded on their behalf: Five hundred women wish to follow your path, please permit them to leave their homes. But the Buddha did not budge. Take the very thought away from your mind, he said. Why, persisted Ananda, is it not possible for women to do this? It is, responded the Buddha, but don't think about it. After strenuous efforts at persuasion and much begging, the Buddha conceded and accepted the women as disciples. However, he warned: With this, the life of this faith which should have stretched a thousand years has fallen by half. In our family, Annapurna, the wife of my ancestor Saubhadra Mullick, decided to follow the Buddha's way. But the Buddha did not allow her to give up her home.

The memory of Grandmother Annapurna surfaced in my mind when I witnessed the protest by almost a thousand women led by the wife of the chief minister at SSKM Hospital, demanding justice for the young girl murdered by Jatindranath. The Buddha had permitted only men to leave their homes and walk the path of Dhamma. He was convinced that women trapped in their perishable bodies that are eventually sapped by time require no extra enlightenment. The only prominent man in the whole protest was my father, I noticed from my place at the rear. Jatindranath sat glum-faced in the back of the jeep with the policemen.

I could see clearly the stubble-covered hollows of his cheeks, and his bleak, emotionless eyes. He was handcuffed to a beam inside the jeep. He looked straight into my eyes as I stood near the telephone booth with Mano da and instantly recognized me. The jeep was held up by the protestors for twenty minutes; all that while, he maintained that intent gaze. His face disappeared when the TV cameras and the press reporters pushed ahead. By then the women police had arrived and they began to remove the protestors. In the melee, I saw Sanjeev Kumar Mitra, in a green T-shirt and jeans, deep in conversation with a young girl in a black T-shirt and jeans, her hair bobbed fashionably like the film stars.

I touched Mano da's wrist. 'Let's go, Dada.'

He gave me a searching look. 'Heard that you and that reporter are going to get married. Is that true?'

I coloured. 'I don't know.'

'Sukhdev told me.'

'There was some such talk . . .'

He considered Sanjeev Kumar Mitra again. 'Is he trustworthy?' he asked no one in particular.

I had no reply. We were there only because the uncle of a child who had been found murdered had come to Mano da requesting his help for a post-mortem. The murdered child was my friend Amodita's daughter. Mano da used his influence to get it done. As we were coming out, the women shouting slogans and holding placards barred our way. The small tempo bearing the body of the six-year-old waited for the vehicle carrying the man whom the protestors wished to punish for killing a thirteen-year-old to pass. We stood by till Jatindranath's vehicle left, then the tempo went in, and the protestors dispersed. Mano da gripped my hand and walked ahead briskly.

'You told us you were not participating in the protest, Chetna.' Sanjeev Kumar Mitra surfaced out of nowhere.

'I didn't come for that.'

He shook hands with Mano da. 'How are you related?' he asked.

'She's my daughter . . . soul-daughter,' replied Mano da.

I smiled, eyes welling. Confusion glinted in Sanjeev Kumar's eyes.

'I heard of you the very first day I went to meet Phani da . . . but wasn't been able to meet you.'

'We're of the old sort, child. What was this protest for?'

'For these people—who else? If the death sentence isn't carried out, will they get work? Remuneration?'

'Isn't it the other way round? If the death sentence is carried out, don't you stand to gain more than the hangmen?'

'Say "for us", Mano da. Aren't we all the same, we press people?'

'No, we aren't. I can't understand you.'

'Ah, forget it! Come, let's leave together.'

'No thanks, we came by bus.'

'But does that mean you have a quarrel with cars?'

He had taken his glasses off. It seemed to me that he looked at Mano da not with respect but with sympathy.

'Where are we going?' Mano da asked.

'Let's get some tea and start an adda!'

He took Mano da's hand. Mano da raised an eyebrow at me. Like Annapurna, I had abandoned desires and needs, memories and obligations. Sanjeev Kumar didn't like Mano da asking me. The intolerance was evident in his voice when he said, 'Women can't take a decision!'

'Sanju babu, it is your age that makes you say that. At my age, you'll start leaving everything to the women.'

Sanjeev Kumar Mitra pretended not to hear what Mano da said. The moment she shaved her head and took to ochre robes, Annapurna was declared an enemy of the family and society. When Emperor Bimbisara's consort, Queen Khema, became an ascetic people accepted it, saying that she had attained Enlightenment in the course of her past births. When Annapurna sought to tread the same path, however, they asked: how could a woman become so heartless as to abandon her family and children to seek happiness just for herself? A woman's nirvana lies in her service to the husband and children, they ranted. Annapurna's three little children cried out for their mother. The people stoned her. I felt I was the woman who had declared two thousand years ago: 'My heart is fixed on bliss.' A smile bloomed on my lips.

'What's there to smile so much about?' Sanjeev Kumar Mitra turned around in the front seat of the taxi and asked.

I turned my gaze outside the window and continued to smile.

'Two thousand years back, women did not have the right to leave their homes,' I whispered.

'So who's giving up their home? You?' Mano da asked, bewildered.

Sanjeev Kumar Mitra said with a smirk, 'Don't pay any attention, Mano da. Chetna keeps saying these mad things. She lives in the past, really. The only thing that attracts her is history. She doesn't see the world in front of her.'

'Sanju babu, all that's in front of your eyes is but a repetition.' The pain in Mano da's voice was palpable. 'We don't learn anything from history . . .'

Annapurna's spiritual journey started when she began to smile to herself in the middle of unending domestic chores. It was her mother-in-law who first became anxious about the daughter-in-law who smiled for no reason. She beamed while doing the washing and the puja, while handing the rope to her husband when he set out for the palace.

'What's there to smile about?' her husband asked, feeling vexed when he sensed that she did so even in the darkness of the bedroom.

'I don't know. Bliss bubbles up inside me and flows out.'

'What has happened that you should feel so happy?'

'That is my soul's secret.'

Saubhadra Mullick jumped up and extended the lamp's wick. Annapurna did not leap up or try to cover her nakedness. She faced her husband in her femininity without feeling smaller.

'What happened?' she asked, calmly.

'Out with the truth! Who do you think of that makes you smile all the time?'

'The Tathagatha!'

She beamed again. Her husband grabbed his purse and set out for the courtesans' street. There he slept with the most beautiful woman he could find. She was much, much more beautiful than Grandmother Annapurna, but he found no pleasure. When he tried to have intercourse, the memory of his wife's smile pulled him down. He ordered her to stay out of sight when he set off for the gallows each morning after puja. His mother had been a widow since her youth. Tears and discontent reigned on her face permanently. My ancestor ordained that his mother should henceforth perform the Kali puja and the arti, and that she alone

271

should hand him the rope every morning. Not just him, but the entire Mullick family felt troubled by the woman who smiled to herself. What was behind that smile, they wondered—love, lust, scorn, sadness? No one could believe that a woman could attain bliss by means other than her husband, children, clothes and jewels. The news of the woman who smiled to herself constantly reached the royal court; the emperor heard of it. He visited her incognito. The radiance of her smile worried him too.

We stopped the taxi near College Street and got off. Raja Ram Mohan Roy, Raja Baidyanath Mukherjee, Justice Edward Hyde and the watch maker David Hayer had got together to establish the Hindu College during the time of Grandfather Devicharan Mullick. The college first began nearby, at the residence of Gorachand Basak on Chitpur Road. Once it shifted to College Street, innumerable bookshops sprouted around it. Young people milled around the shops that had completely taken over the footpaths, making it almost impossible to walk. There were girls everywhere—in sleeveless tops, jeans, short skirts that touched their knees, leggings. As we stepped into the Coffee House, the din of a hundred people chattering all at once left me deafened. Seeking a place to sit, we made our way forward. The conversations from each table reached all the other tables.

'Truly, this was a move that spoiled Thakur's name! The truth is that I didn't feel so bad even when his Nobel medal was stolen!'

'Do you know, most people still don't know that the medal is lost?'

'The government hushed it up . . . but surely, it is an insult to the whole country! Could this happen anywhere else?'

'This is the very depth of depravity. Such a university, world famous! The vice chancellor handing out an appointment to a woman with no qualifications! Selling land illegally!'

Many were venting their rage.

'No place to sit on the ground floor. Let's look upstairs,' Sanjeev Kumar suggested.

Dragging his bad leg, Mano da hopped up the stairs.

'Hey look—that's Sanjeev Kumar Mitra!' A girl's voice rose from the table behind us.

'Who's that female? Isn't she the hangwoman?'

'But she looks quite happy!'

'Right, if it were me . . .'

The statement remained incomplete. I wanted to laugh at that possibility: if it were me. One day, as she was serving Grandfather his food, Annapurna assumed the padmasana and entered into deep meditation. Serve the fish, Grandfather shouted. She didn't hear him. She sat up straight, eyes shut, the smile on her lips. All the loud yells, the shakings, the water that her mother-in-law poured on her, the children's loud wails—none of it could make her open her eyes or erase that smile. She came back from that world of bliss which she alone could enter only the morning of the next day. To the questions of others, she replied with her smile alone: I left my home and went to the Tathagatha. When this became more frequent, the rhythm of domestic chores was upset. I will buy you jewels if you stay at home, Grandfather tried to entice her. But I already have three jewels, said she—the Buddha, the Dhamma and the Sangha. All efforts to make her submit through angry words and blows came to naught. Grandmother has left her poem in the *Therigatha*:

My body dries up, crumbles, and joins the five elements in the Tathagatha's radiant presence. But my soul, it rises with great dignity and triumph into the infinite radiance of nirvana.

We climbed the spiral stairway. The asbestos roof of the ground floor was littered with used paper cups, plastic bottles and betel stains that looked like blood stains. When we sat down at a free table, an old gentleman in a dhoti and kurta came towards us, beaming. 'Manavendra babu, what a long time! Didn't I warn you that our bhavishyath, our future, was dire?'

Mano da's face lit up. 'Komal da, it is not the future that's dire, it's the present! What's the news? How are you?'

'Babu, what could be new with me? I go to Mother's place for the dying every morning, offer whatever help I can, come back. I hang around here after that.'

When the gentleman departed, Mano da told me, 'An old comrade of ours . . .'

'I've heard so much about you. I'll come over to your office one day. Let's do something on TV about—'

'No.'

Sanjeev Kumar Mitra tried to get a word in, but Mano da didn't let him complete his sentence.

'Only those who want to read the *Bhavishyath* need to know of it.'

'But a news item on TV can be good publicity, Dada.'

'We don't need publicity, Sanjeev babu. Leave *Bhavishyath* to its fate.'

There was a minute's silence. Sanjeev Kumar Mitra wiped his glasses and put them on again.

'Chetna works at the *Bhavishyath* now?'

'Yes, she is our proofreader.'

'Good. But we wish she had been prominently present at the protest today. That'd have given her greater mileage.'

'I am not a petrol car.' There was anger in my voice.

Sanjeev Kumar looked at me closely. But when I returned his gaze and found his eyes, blurred behind the smoky glasses, my body woke up again. The memory of our walks together came back. Aparajita and nilmani vines sprouted again inside my body, holding out their tender shoots. His face fell. The waiter brought the coffee; we drank it in silence.

'Portugal—I predicted that Portugal would win!'

'But you see, she is all alone in the cabinet . . . . what can a woman do when she is so isolated?'

'Look, this Grddha Mullick is very cunning. But what I can't understand is how our chief minister can justify the death penalty!'

Snatches of conversations billowed around me.

'Why are you smiling?'

I realized I was smiling only when Sanjeev Kumar Mitra asked.

'I feel happy,' I murmured.

'What's there to be so happy about?'

'Maybe that you have left my life?' I said.

Sanjeev Kumar's face went red as if it had been slapped hard. We were silent when we came down the stairway.

A man with a grey beard and sunken cheeks and a cloth bag on his shoulder accosted us at the foot of the stairs. 'Two rupees, just two rupees,' he said, holding out thin volumes with yellow covers.

274

'Two rupees? What is this?' Sanjeev Kumar turned to him.

'Poems, Babu, my latest ones.'

Sanjeev Kumar took one of the books, flipped through it and asked in mocking tones: 'What profit do you make selling these for two rupees?'

'The true profit is the pleasure of selling, Babu!'

'But counting the money, you stand to lose in the end.'

'Money is but a concept. On the same paper, if you print "five", it is worth five rupees; if you print "five hundred", it is worth that much.'

'Fool!' Sanjeev Kumar Mitra grimaced and muttered under his breath. He stepped out and hailed a taxi.

'I need to talk to you, Chetna.'

'Later . . .'

'Should I remove myself? Here, I take your leave!' Mano da smiled and climbed into the taxi.

I followed him, but Sanjeev Kumar Mitra stopped me roughly.

'Wait, wait—we need to talk about our wedding.'

I stopped.

'Let's go to that old house. It is close by, if you walk a bit through this way . . . the house, don't you remember?'

His voice was alluring. I closed my eyes and looked at him from within, smiling to myself.

'I am not interested.'

'What do you mean?'

'Weren't you talking to a girl in front of the hospital today? Your wife ought to be someone like her. We are completely different. Like my baba says, you can't twist a rope out of clay. Nor can you make a pot out of rope.'

'But your father's agreed to register the marriage at the earliest.'

'His decisions need not be mine always.'

'He's given me his word that you'll be thrown out of your house if you don't cooperate!'

I burst out laughing.

'Why are you laughing? Are you totally mad?'

I couldn't stop. I was laughing to myself. What a terrible loss, I realized; it had taken me so long to understand Grandmother Annapurna who fought for the freedom to abandon the home! If only the little girls who were dragged into the bushes could laugh loudly at their attackers. If they could, the life of the world's injustice would reduce by half. Anyway, this is the turning point you must take note of in this tale of death, suffocation and severed limbs: Henceforth, I smiled to myself, I cannot submit to the will of the father or the lover or the husband or children to come in the future.

35

Six-year-old Amolika's eyes had been gouged out. Her limbs had been hacked off. Her neck had been pierced with an iron rod. But since I had already seen her little body the previous day, I was able to accompany it with a hardened heart. Her mother, Amodita, had been my classmate in primary school. She was married before she turned fifteen. During the final exams in the ninth standard, I remember shutting the history textbook I'd been studying and going along with Ma to Amodita's house in the slum near the railway track to take part in the singing and feasting before her wedding. When her wedding procession and the carriage drawn by a white horse came along Strand Road, the hearses and the funeral cortèges gave way. Amodita looked like the pale crescent moon, not sufficiently nourished. In the days that followed, she waxed like the full moon; but in the next two or three years, she shrank like the waning moon. She lost two infants; her husband, a worker in a cotton mill, became asthmatic; her paralytic father-in-law needed full-time care. Soon she looked like an over-milked cow. I did not have the courage to look at Amolika's little body. It was hard for me to even believe that it was the body of a human being. The murderer was a neighbour, an eighteen-year-old. He had promised to teach her a song. He had sung the first few lines of 'Twinkle, twinkle, little star' for her but before she could sing along, he clamped his hand over her mouth and dragged her into the bushes.

'Chetu, hang him, please, please! Please hang her killer!' Amodita shrieked in pain when she saw me.

Her wail reminded me of Jatindranath who had gone back to Alipore Jail from the hospital. He was to be hanged for having raped and murdered a little girl. Because Amolika's corpse had been chopped to pieces, it had been cremated at the electric crematorium at Nimtala Ghat. They immersed her ashes in the Ganga. I stood on the steps of the Ghat while pyres burned on both sides. The smoke from the pyres spread everywhere like fog. A she-goat and two kids fed on the marigolds and stared at the pyres impassively. On the other side of the river, the factory chimneys emitted dark clouds of smoke. A passenger boat and another one decked for a marriage celebration passed us by. The waves lashed at those who were offering funeral oblations. Those who had already taken their holy dip in the Ganga crowded into the tea and snack shops all around. I moved to the pavilion built on the spot where Rabindranath Tagore had been cremated. The road, full of phlegm and cow dung and spit coloured with betel, was occupied by a steady stream of mourners, arriving and leaving. Amodita came up from the Ganga with wet clothes and hair, supported by someone.

'Chetu, she's gone, Chetu! Who's left now to call me "Ma"?' she wailed.

It reverberated all over the Ghat beyond Strand Road. I could respond only in two ways: either burst into tears or smile to myself. If only I could smile at her affectionately, I thought. Even if she had survived, Amodita's daughter would not have called to her, for her little tongue had been cut off first. When her body was found, it lay in a corner as a small, ant-eaten piece of flesh. The doctors didn't close her mouth fully, so she went forth from the world calling for her mother. Amodita and her wails disappeared into the slum behind the shops along with the ten-forty Prinsep Ghat train. The dust of seven decades had accumulated in the pavilion dedicated to Thakur's memory and turned into dirt over time. An emaciated man in a towel black with filth lay there sleeping, a black dog with oozing warts all over its body next to him, panting, its tongue lolling out. The place was littered with large Durga statues, abandoned after last year's puja. A sannyasi with a tangled beard and dreadlocks sat in front of Bihari Binod Mallick's shop, puffing hard at a cigarette. When a strong wind deposited on my head some ash from a pyre, I turned to go home.

'You don't have any TV programmes now, my daughter?' Gangadhar da, who was leaning on his wares—bamboo litters to carry corpses—and enjoying a bidi, asked me as I crossed the railway gate.

'Dada, isn't it better to wash one's hands before one's tummy becomes overfull?'

'Ah, right, I agree,' said he, drawing in the smoke. 'But it was a pity it didn't happen . . . you'd have been a star!' He smiled, seeing it happen in his mind's eye.

'Tell me truly—aren't you scared even a bit, Chetu, to kill someone?'

I tried to smile.

'If the fellow you kill is cremated here, that's some business for me too!'

I smiled again. The hottest selling stuff, no doubt, is the death of other people. As I walked home, what I had told Gangadhar da stayed in my mind. There must a dash of salt in your food, a little bitterness as well, and you must wash your hands before your stomach is full—that was written by a woman, Khona, who was a poet and an astrologer. They say she was Varaha's daughter-in-law; Thakuma claimed that she was Radharaman Mullick's cousin, the daughter of his father's sister.

'That boy's here!' Ma, who was waiting with water pots at the tap near the lane towards the Port Trust workers' quarters, hissed to me. 'You have to take a decision, Chetu. It's not good, these comings and goings of his.'

'Let him come and go, Ma. So many have come, and how many more are yet to come . . .' I answered her irritatedly.

When I went into the house after a bath I could hear his voice. My legs were still for a moment. My eyes were drawn to Ramu da's empty cot. To the wavering flame in the lamp that stood at its head. I sat cross-legged on the floor with a handwritten draft Mano da had given me to correct. It was a chapter from his autobiography, the chapter about the Emergency. Feeling uneasy at the very first sentence, 'When Siddhartha Shankar Ray returned from Delhi . . . ' I put away the manuscript. Khona filled my memory. My ancestor's sister and her husband gave her away to Anacharya who lived in Barasat, who adopted her as his daughter. She became a great scholar under Anacharya's training. Varaha, who was one of the jewels of Chandra Gupta Vikramaditya's court when it had just seven jewels, made a mistake when he cast his own son Mihira's horoscope. Though his lifespan was a hundred years, because of a mistake in calculating the birth time it appeared that the boy would live only for ten years. Fearing the pain of losing a child after having raised him for ten years, Varaha put the baby into a bamboo basket and set him afloat on the river. The tribal people of Barasat found the baby; they raised it and the child grew to become a great scholar in astronomy. Soon, Mihira met Khona and, impressed by her scholarship, he married her. Once he was convinced that he had mastered everything that was worth learning, he set out for the royal court with his wife. The tribal people sent a guide along to help them get past the jungle; they also entrusted them with palm-leaf manuscripts. The guide was instructed to test Mihira's knowledge on the way; if he failed, the guide was to give him the manuscripts so that he could study further. But if he passed, he was to bring them back. They saw a pregnant cow on the way. The guide asked, what will be the colour of its calf? Mihira calculated the position of the stars and said: brown. Khona predicted: white. They waited till it delivered. The cow gave birth to a white calf. They continued their journey and soon came upon a man who was gravely ill. What is his ailment, asked the guide. A stroke, Mihira concluded after his calculations. He's been bitten by a snake with a red mark on its hood, said Khona. Her answer was the right one. They went further and met a Brahmin on the road. Tell me, how many children he has, the guide demanded. Four, said Mihira. Six, said Khona. She won this time too.

'These manuscripts are for you. There is much more that you need to grasp in your studies.'

The tribal guide bid them goodbye after handing over the manuscripts to Mihira. If one's scholarship isn't complete even after so many years of hard work, what's the use of looking at some more palm leaves, asked Mihira, sorely irritated. In a fit of anger, he threw them into the Ganga. Khona jumped into the river and saved some, but the rest floated away. King Vikramaditya was hunting in the forest on the other bank of the river. Mihira went to see the king who, impressed by Mihira's scholarship, appointed him as his court scholar. When he saw Mihira, Varaha recognized the son he had abandoned in the river.

'There's nothing we can do about this. It is a battle between those who are for the death penalty and those who oppose it.'

Sanjeev Kumar Mitra was talking, munching something in between. I got up, displeased. He didn't seem to remember that a death had occurred in this house just a few days back.

'Raje raje juddho hoye ulughagraar praan jaaye . . . Haven't you heard, Sanju babu? When kings fight, it is the ulu bamboo that loses lives. Ah, Babu, what do you think? Should these fellows be killed, or should they be worshipped in captivity? How much money do we need to feed them in jail? Can't we save on that if a good many were hanged?' Father guffawed.

'Ask Chetna that question, Phani da. She's the one who speaks against the death penalty the most!'

'The sireless bitch! Let her raise her voice against me and I shall cut out her tongue!'

At that, I went up to the door. Standing on the doorstep, I smiled at Father. 'When did you come?' he asked, lighting the cigarette between his lips. Sanjeev Kumar's face grew hard, but I ignored it and gifted him with a broad smile.

'Chetna's been brimming over with joy for the past couple of days! What's up?' he said, taking off his spectacles, wiping them, addressing no one in particular.

'Happiness fills me . . .'

I beamed now.

'What's happened that has made you so happy?' His forehead furrowed.

'The hangman delights in death.' I laughed aloud.

Suspicion clouded his face.

Vikramaditya invited Khona to his court, claiming that he desired the company of good human beings. On the previous day, he had asked a question about the number of stars in the sky. None among the nine jewels of his court could answer. At home, looking at her husband and father-in-law who were helpless, defeated by the king's query, Khona laughed aloud. What an easy question! She then proclaimed: according to her, the number of stars in the sky was 100×10^{22}. The next day, Varaha bragged in court, what a question, even the women in my house can answer it! The king was astonished. He went to Varaha's home incognito and met Khona. She was no beauty, but her great scholarship made such an impression on him that he began to constantly desire her company. She was invited to his court as the tenth jewel.

'I've come to talk of the marriage. I'm not interested in prolonging this.'

I—smiling, lost in my thoughts of Khona—hurtled down suddenly from the stars to the earth.

'You will not marry me,' I said, still smiling. 'That's not your real aim.'

Sanjeev Kumar Mitra's face burned up.

Father took the cigarette off his lips and looked at me. I looked at both at them with an even more joyful expression.

'In your eyes I am the daughter of a beggarly chap who has no qualms about finishing off a man once in ten or fifteen years for a measly sum of a hundred and fifty rupees a month. Your eye is on the market, Babu, I know that very well.'

'What market?' He went pale.

I laughed again merrily.

'Like my family has knowledge of the different ways in which a human being may be killed, you have inherited the knowledge of the different ways in which a woman may be sold!'

Sanjeev Kumar Mitra leapt up. 'What do you mean?' he rasped.

Father kept looking at us in turn, not making any sense of our conversation. 'Sanju babu, has something happened that I do not know of?' Father's eyes reddened.

'Nothing!' He rubbed his palms together, deeply flustered.

'Tell us, Chetu,' Father said, angry now.

I kept smiling at Sanjeev Kumar Mitra, and that made him very uneasy indeed.

'Baba, please return Sanjeev babu's bangles and ring. I don't wish to be his wife.'

'Why then did you give me hope, Chetna? Why did you let me kiss you? Why did you come to my bedroom?' he attacked, knowing well that such questions would be hard for me to handle in Father's presence.

Father threw away his cigarette, jumped up and caught me by my hair.

'You bitch! Out to ruin the family name? I'll kill you . . . '

I was thrown but I turned towards him, still smiling.

'Have you included Niharika's name among the four hundred and fifty-one, Baba?'

He let go of my hair.

'If you haven't yet, then count me and Ramu da as well, and it will be four hundred and fifty-four!'

Father burned with anger and sheer agitation. I coolly set right the wet hair that he had disturbed, raised my smiling eyes to both of them once again. Father was very troubled. I went back to my room and sat down on Thakuma's cot. I looked at Ramu da's empty bed and smiled again. Father followed me there, pulled me up and slapped me hard repeatedly on both cheeks with the back of his right hand.

'You rotting corpse, you don't know how to keep your tongue! I'll pull it out of your head!'

'Better to chop it off . . . that's easier, Baba.'

I was still smiling. My eyes had welled, my cheeks were aflame, but when I tried to smile broadly, the pain vanished. Father looked daggers at me. I remembered Khona's line: The sorrows of the one who owns bullocks but does not till the soil never end. She was the first woman poet of Bengal. Mihira became jealous when Vikramaditya's eyes filled with longing for her. To secure her presence in court, the king set difficult mathematical problems about the land's slope and the moon's mass. Varaha and Mihira realized that if she found the answers to the king's questions, Khona's fame would spread throughout the world; they felt that it was better to commit suicide than to be known as a woman's husband or father-in-law. When Khona set out for the palace in the morning, Mihira knocked her down. He hanged her on the beam of the house with a noose. In agony, she thrust out her tongue. Varaha tore out her tongue, and Mihira let the king know that she had failed to find the answers and therefore had cut off her own tongue out of sorrow. The king could not love Khona without her tongue. She couldn't live without it, either. She died, bleeding from her wound. The son who Varaha predicted would survive only ten years lived to a hundred. When Khona died, he was just twenty-five. He did not dare look at the stars after that. For the seven and a half

282

decades that remained of his life, he dwelled in a closed room.

I walked out towards *Bhavishyath*. It was far, but I walked as if in a dream. When I reached the old mansion on which the banyan tree and many creepers grew, a taxi braked suddenly beside me. Sanjeev Kumar Mitra wanted me to get in. He was not someone I knew. The red stars etched on the broken-down wall behind me reflected in his smoky glasses, blood red. I wanted to laugh. The wall had begun to collapse. The green of the moss was spreading upon its red bricks. The stars had lost their shine. The moss had begun to creep over them too. I paid no attention and kept walking quickly. I was panting, but I would have liked to sing: 'Twinkle, twinkle . . .'

36

Radharaman's son Devadutta, born to Chinmayi Devi, was a bandit who roamed the banks of the Ganga. Once he met an extraordinarily beautiful woman there and made her his bride. Her skin was like the blue lotus; her name, Utpalavarna. She had been married once before. Only after her first husband set off to trade in the land of Vanga did she realize that she was pregnant. His family cast doubts on her chastity, and she had to leave home full-bellied. She gave birth in the middle of a forest on her way to Vanga. Leaving the infant in a leafy bower, she went to seek water. When she returned, it was missing. Crying inconsolably, Utpalavarna sought it everywhere for many days. She did not have the courage to face her husband without their child and so decided to go to her natal home. It was then that my ancestor Devadutta stumbled on her and forcibly made her his bride. He was obsessed with her; she submitted fully. She became pregnant again and gave birth to a girl child. Devadutta constantly feared that he would lose her and became increasingly suspicious; he began to quarrel with her every day. One day, in the middle of one such row, he pushed her down while she was feeding her child. The child fell on the floor and was injured. Seeing the pool of blood, she feared that the baby had died. Wailing loudly, she ran out, determined to kill herself by jumping into the Ganga. But she fell unconscious and the river carried her further down the bank, where she was rescued by a young man. Seduced by her beauty, he too made her his wife; she had no choice. The years passed. One day, her husband brought home a lovely young girl, still in her teens. When she saw that her husband had married another, Utpalavarna felt shattered. She considered the girl her enemy for she was more youthful and beautiful and began to harass her in all possible ways. She cursed and beat her; even tried to kill her. One day, she caught the young girl by the hair and was about to dash her head on the wall when she noticed a large scar on the back of her head. 'That mark was left when I fell off my mother's lap and was wounded. Mother thought I was dead. She jumped into the river.' The moment Utpalavarna realized that this girl was none other than her own daughter, the scales of ignorance fell off her inner eye, and she set off on a journey seeking the meaning of life, relationships and experiences.

Sanjeev Kumar Mitra had reached the *Bhavishyath* office before me and was waiting there. Sitting in his presence, my mind too was tormented about the meaning of life, relationships and experiences. I pulled out one of the dust-covered manuscripts from the table and began to read it. It was a piece of paper with the heading, 'Special Order of the Day on the Rumour of Surrender, 14 August 1945'. I wiped my neck and face with my dupatta and buried my face in that yellowed piece of paper. Gradually, I made out that it was a special order signed by Netaji Subhash Chanda Bose to the Indian National Army at Syonan.

'I have something to discuss with you, Chetna.'

Noticing from the corner of my eye Sanjeev Kumar's face flushed with either anger or shame, I continued reading.

Comrades, all sorts of wild rumours are afloat in Syonan and other places, one being that the hostilities have ceased. Most of these rumours are either false or highly exaggerated. Till this moment, fighting is going on at all fronts . . .

'Chetna, this is no joke. Tell me, what terrible wrong have I done to you for you to treat me thus? Is it because I got you the fame and money you enjoy today? Or that I helped with your brother's treatment? Or that I'm still exerting pressure on the government for your father?'

I say this not only on the basis of reports from friendly sources, but also reports given out by the enemy radio . . .

'I consider this my duty. Therefore I am not haggling.'

If there is any change in the war situation . . .

'I wished to improve your life, Chetna. It's my duty, I thought. Because I had decided to marry you.'

'If there is any change in the war situation, I shall be the first to inform you.'

Sanjeev Kumar snatched the paper from my hand.
'No, don't! It'll tear. It is old and falling apart.'
'Answer me. Didn't you want us to get married?'
'Desire and decision are different things.'
'Intense desires and decisions have the same result.'
'Desires that are based on mistaken ideas aren't valid. They can really be desires only when there are facts to back them up.'
'I'm not here to argue with you; all I want to say is that if the world today knows of Chetna Grddha Mullick, that's because of me.'
'You gained more out of my fame than I did. You made lakhs out of it and gave my baba ten thousand rupees. But what did I get? My status as the symbol of the self-respect of Indian women and all women of the world?'

My eyes smouldered and smarted. They were full of the moment when he had arrived with his cameraman at SSKM Hospital to film Ramu da. Instead of helping us, he had sold our wretchedness.

'Okay, okay, everything I did was wrong. Give me another chance to set things right.'

'Sanjeev Kumar Mitra!' I called him harshly. 'I just want to know one thing. What do you need from me now?'

'Chetna, you've misunderstood me terribly . . . .'
I picked up the paper and started reading again.

Therefore I want all of you to remain perfectly calm and unperturbed and carry out your duties in a normal way.

'Please, Chetna.'
Sanjeev Kumar Mitra's patience was wearing thin. The black telephone on the table began to ring. A few moments later, Nischol da appeared at the door.
'My sister's husband has passed away.'
'Eesh . . . where are they, Nischol da?'
'Maniktala.'
'You should leave immediately, Nischol da. I'll let Mano da know.'
Sanjeev Kumar left soon after Nischol da. I opened the window and looked at the red buildings of Thakurbari and saluted the invisible poet. Mano da said that Mrinalini's private kitchen could be seen from this window. Her personal cutlery and dishes had been stored there. I had heard the story of how the village girl Bhavatarani had been brought to the city where she'd become Mrinalini. Thinking of the vast, empty rooms of that mansion made me afraid too. It was a mansion of not just words and colour, but also of death. Thakur's older brother's wife Kadambari Devi had committed suicide somewhere within its vastness. The poor girl who entered Thakurbari at the age of nine could not win her husband's affection. She found in his younger brother a friend, poet and object of love. Her tragedy saddened me. Would she have cursed Thakur's bride Bhavatarini, like Utpalavarna? As I mulled over it, Sanjeev Kumar came in again and tried to press me to his chest crudely. Completely vexed, I pushed him off.
'What do you want? Out with it, fast! I have work to finish!'
'Work ? Oh—very heavy work indeed! I have made a request to the chief minister to give you a good job, Chetna. Didn't you know this government is interested in carrying out the death sentence? Wasn't Banerjee's act despicable? And besides, rapes are on the increase all over the country. Everyone in the cabinet feels that it is time to send out a clear and precise message.'

'I don't want to hear of it.'

When I was about to sit down again, he slipped into the small gap between the table and chair and tried to pull me out. I clung to the *Bhavishyath*'s ancient table and resisted him.

'I want you to perform that hanging, Chetna. You'll gain a place in world history. A man would not have received so much attention. Because you are a woman you'll become a celebrity, just wait and see!'

He was tempting me, but I said, 'I don't want to be a celebrity.'

'Just think—there's not a single woman in the world with this job. It's just you, you alone!'

I looked at him. The white skin of his neck was slightly bluish. The veins in his neck were tense. Suddenly, I remembered Maruti Prasad Yadav. The veins on his neck too had tensed when he held me tightly from the back. I tried to look intently into Sanjeev Kumar's eyes. Behind the darkness of his spectacles, his eyes glinted the colour of fire, like an animal's. His smile had now ceased to be charming. He took my hand in his and began to talk again. I pushed him away with my free hand.

'When I first saw you, you were barely a girl. Now you have ripened into a whole woman,' he said hoarsely.

'Betrayed girls grow up faster,' I said. Outside, a bhelpuri seller's bell rang. A passing tram's whistle followed it. Beats and sounds rose up from the shop that sold musical instruments in front of the *Bhavishyath* office. Sanjeev Kumar tried to pull me out again.

'Chetna, I never wanted to betray you. My only thought, then and now, has been to protect you. I missed you terribly in the days when we quarrelled and stopped talking. You never bothered to come looking for me then. Never tried to call me. I am no one to you—isn't that true?'

I looked at his palms. He wished to grab me with both hands, it was clear. I caught hold of his right hand.

'Sanjeev Kumar babu, leave me alone. Let me go and find a life.'

'Answer my question. Haven't you desired me?'

'I did desire you. Your love . . . your house where the aparajita blooms . . . your studio with its thousand lights . . . but none of it was real. It was my imagination. And so I've forgotten it. You too must forget.'

He fixed his eyes on me. Nearly said something, but swallowed it and retreated. The prayer bells and chants from the Shiva temple to the left of Thakurbari rang in the air. I came out from behind the table. But before I could reach the door, he pounced on me again, enfolded me in his arms roughly and tried to kiss me, pressing my body against the wall. I struggled.

'Move aside! And tell me why you are here again.'

'To see you. End your complaints.'

I laughed. I held him at a distance, pushing him back with my arms. 'That's just the means. Tell me what you are aiming for.'

A foolish expression appeared on his face. 'Let's go and meet the chief minister. He must be convinced that people support this.'

I pushed him away. 'Public support to murder a human being?'

'No ordinary human being. Someone who cruelly raped and murdered a young girl. Hanging him will be a great lesson to all criminals.'

I now laughed in scorn. 'Sanjeev babu, my father hanged four hundred and fifty-one criminals. For robbery, murder, dacoity, rape. But each day, the number of criminals continues to rise. New offenders take the places of the deceased instantly. No, not death, the punishment should be something else. '

'Chetna, you speak like this because you don't know a thing!' He pulled me close again.

'Tell me the truth, don't you love me? Don't you enjoy it when I embrace you like this? Aren't you happy when you are near me?' His voice sounded feeble.

I smiled sympathetically.

'Why do you keep smiling like this, with no reason?' His vexation was now beginning to show. 'Tell me truly, don't you love me?'

I laughed even louder. 'Till sometime back. Not any more.'

'Why?' His forehead wrinkled.

'I realized how small you are . . .'

He released me and moved away. 'What do you mean by that?'

'You are a weak man. You have no strength . . . no honesty . . . no stamina . . .'

Silence fell. There was just the sound of papers rustling. The sound of a mridangam or tabla wafted in from outside. We stood there looking at each other. Suddenly, he flew at me like a tiger and pushed me down to the ground. I thought he was trying to rape me. I remembered Amolika, and smiled again. Utpalavarna, who sought refuge in Gautama Buddha's hermitage, gained enlightenment one day when she swept the prayer room clean and lit a lamp there. As she sat gazing at the flame that burned there, she entered deep meditation and became enlightened. When the other monks and nuns wondered how this had happened, she wrote a poem as an answer to the nuns:

We, mother and daughter
We became co-wives
We saw the tragedies of worldly pleasures
I left my home for Rajagraha
And thus attained homelessness . . .

'Your blasted smile! I'll teach you a lesson,' he muttered, interrupting the poem in my mind rudely.

When Utpalavarna set out for the forest to meditate alone, a monk named Ananda, who coveted her, unleashed his lust on her. The other bhikkus carried her back to the Buddha's residence. Seeing the severely wounded Utpalavarna, even the Buddha who had overcome all the sources of the world's misery was sorrowful. He went to the king requesting that a nunnery be built in the middle of the city for devout women. Thereafter they were not permitted to go away to forests or lonely hilltops to meditate in solitude like the monks. For this utterly perishable body to be consumed by ants, termites and worms if buried under the soil—as Sanjeev Kumar Mitra's fingers tightened brutally around me and his body pressed down on me, I thought—how they were afraid of it. Not just the unlettered sinner, Grandfather Devadatta, but also Gautama Buddha who had left behind everything. When it struck me that it was a puzzle how one could attain nirvana without conquering fear, I chuckled aloud.

'Please gouge out my eyes, chop off my arms and legs, you must turn red with my blood,' I called out.

His force withered away.

'And most important—don't hesitate to cut off the tongue!' I said through my laughter.

289

'Are you mad?' he asked, disheartened, getting up and smoothing down his clothes.

The copy of the old *Bhavishyath* flew down from the table and fell a finger's length away from me. I picked it up and read aloud:

'We have to face any situation that may arise, like brave soldiers fighting for their motherland. Subhash Chandra Bose, Supreme Commander, Azad Hind Fauj, Syonan, 14 August 1945, 1500 hours.'

'Chetna . . .' His voice was now soft as if he had admitted defeat. 'Let's stop this tamasha now. You must come and see the chief minister. The death sentence will be carried out only then. If it doesn't happen, you'll never be worth anything.'

I stared hard at him. For a couple of moments, our eyes were locked on each other.

'What do you gain from it?'

He sighed. 'Not just me, but all the different media. We've never had such sky-high ratings as we've had these last few weeks.'

I felt as if I had been gazing at the wavering flame leaping from a lamp lit in a room swept clean. Women do not need much time to attain enlightenment.

37

'Phani da, did you hear, the central government has advised against accepting the mercy petition!'

I was busy correcting the proofs of Mano da's autobiography. I had just reached the part where he describes in detail how he went with Jyoti Basu to Sealdah on Direct Action Day and found smouldering corpses everywhere along the way. Sanjeev Kumar Mitra's cheerful voice disturbed me. He was shouting so that I would hear. Father called Ma to bring him some water. Ma gave the two glasses of water to me. Father and Sanjeev Kumar were waiting for me with beaming faces.

'What did you take me for, Sanju babu? Didn't I tell you that very day? That his name is on my list? But one thing's clear, no point building castles in the air until the President's made his decision. No one can predict death, Sanju babu—take it from someone who has hanged four hundred and fifty-one criminals.'

'But this time it is very unlikely to be aborted, Phani da.' Sanjeev Kumar Mitra threw a sidelong glance at me and took the glass, drank a mouthful, and caressed the glass which he held up. 'Because the home ministry's advice is on the decision to be taken regarding the mercy petition. The chances of its being rejected are very, very slim. That does mean Jatindranth's days are numbered, indeed!'

'Ma Kali! Bhagawan Mahadev! It was a terrible shame last time! After that entire hubbub, when it didn't happen, you can't imagine the misery that my family went through. It isn't like the old days any more, Babu. We are now famous because of your TV.'

Father lit his cigarette.

'If Banerjee's sentence is indeed carried out, your fame will double. I'll do everything I can. I've dug up the murdered girl's family.'

'We heard that they had consumed poison in a flat in Bombay?'

'No, that was a yarn spun by some reporter. They are in Delhi now, living with their son. But have apparently not stepped out of their house for the past ten years. If only we could get them in front of a camera . . . ah!'

Sanjeev Kumar drank up the rest of the water and handed the empty glass to me. Father had finished the other glass. I was about to leave with the glasses when Sanjeev Kumar turned to me.

'I need your help again, Chetna. We must restart *Hangwoman's Diary*.'

I paid no attention and walked off.

'I'll come, Sanju babu,' Father said. 'I have more tales to tell than her anyway.' He stroked his moustache and smoked his cigarette. 'Haven't I told you about Surya Sen's death? I still remember how they dragged him there. His teeth had been knocked out. His fingernails were bloody— they had driven nails into the tender flesh under them. They brought him to the gallows on a bamboo litter. We had to work very hard to fix the noose. I believe that he was brought there well after he had died . . .'

He pulled in the smoke.

'Are you interested in a controversy, Sanju babu? Here: I, Grddha Mullick, the hangman, say Surya Sen was dead even before he was hanged. Why, isn't that great stuff for news? But make sure I am paid well.'

Sanjeev Kumar Mitra was impatient. 'The demand of the hour is for Jatindranath Banerjee.'

Not interested in listening any more, I went back to my proofreading and began to flip through the pages. I was thinking of the widow, Savitri Devi, who hid Master da—that is, Surya Sen—when he lived in hiding in the Chittagong Hills after Jugantar and the Dhaka Anushilan Samiti merged to form the Jugantar Anushilan. The British forces were out to capture Surya Sen, Pritilata, and Kalpana Dutta. They surrounded Savitri's house. The three fugitives escaped, shooting the British officer Cameroon who came up the steps. The hills were combed for them but they continued to evade the British and carry out daring raids on their armouries. That made the British announce a reward of ten thousand pounds on Surya Sen's head. Lured by the prospect of so much money, Surya Sen's relative, Netra Sen, invited him home for a meal, after informing the police. When Netra Sen's wife was serving the food, the police surrounded the house and arrested Surya Sen. But Netra Sen was not fated to receive the reward. The next day, when Netra Sen was at his meal and his wife was serving him, a member of Jugantar crept in with a large chopper hidden behind his back and hacked him to death.

When the police asked Netra's wife if she knew who had killed her husband, she pulled the edge of her aanchal over her face, fixed her gaze on the floor, and testified: 'I saw my husband being killed with my own eyes. I was serving him his meal. He was sitting here, on the floor, and eating. I was sitting on this side, fanning him. The killer entered. My husband was taking up a ball of rice when the man raised the chopper. My husband started violently and the rice fell on the floor. Before he could get up, the killer had upset the dishes, stepped on the curries, and had him by the neck. He hacked him down in a second. Blood splattered everywhere; my head was completely drenched. But don't ask me who killed him. I won't utter the name.'

'Why? It was your husband he murdered, or wasn't he?'

'He betrayed the desires of a whole people. That moment, he ceased to be my husband.'

The British tried to intimidate and threaten her, but to no avail. She refused to reveal the killer's name. I remember how Thakuma would puff up with pride when she told us children this story: 'She was truly a woman!'

I was holding the page in which Mano da described going with Jyoti babu to Chittaranjan Avenue to rescue Bankim Mukherjee, Nirad Chakrabarti and Abdul Momin and his wife who were being held by a mob. He described very evocatively how they found a single Muslim sentry holding off an entire crowd by himself, how they had to struggle hard to rescue the four, and how the sight of burning corpses littering the entire way back made him almost lose consciousness. Tired of reading about death and faith, I turned the pages again randomly. That led me to the description of the mass murder of seventy farmers during the Tebhaga Uprising. I turned the pages again. But whatever I did, words like lathi charge, teargas, Naxal attacks, Emergency, the Bijon Setu massacre thrashed about in my eyes as if hung by nooses. Deaths, murders, mass killings, suicides. But the killings of Ananda Margis and refugees happened in the time of Jyoti Basu who had once sorrowed at the killings of farmers and activists. Feeling sick at heart, I set aside the manuscript and went into the kitchen. But seeing Ma and Kakima sitting with their backs turned to each other, cooking the same thing, reminded me of the description of Partition in Mano da's autobiography. I thought I'd walk to the Ghat, but the long free-food queue opposite the house put me off. I stood leaning against the salon's wall.

'Those days, it used to take till noon to finish work and get back home, Sanju babu. Many would be hanged by the same rope. My baba would stand by the lever, ready, chest out and muscles tensed. I used to tie the arms and legs, and put the mask on the condemned man. When Surya Sen was hanged, Richard sahib told me to leave . . . I can't remember his full name. But the face I recollect very well. Below his brows, there were two well-like cavities. You'd notice that they held two eyeballs only if you peered hard. His sepoy went up to Baba and said, when you get out, don't tell anyone about the condition in which the prisoner was brought to the gallows. Only say that he was laughing or crying.'

His voice was so loud, it could be heard from the Ghat. The road was unusually free of crowds; just a single hearse passed by. A very old man lay in it. His children and grandchildren held on to it reluctantly.

'If everything goes as we want it to, it will be a happy ending.' That was Sanjeev Kumar. 'Things have been very smooth till now. The chief minister's wife has taken a very strong stand.'

'Uh-hm. I've heard she is a very competent woman.'

'Her protest has created waves, Phani da. Two days ago there was a meeting where film stars spoke—what a crowd it was! People want justice to be done in this case. Only a few like Mahashweta Devi are against the death sentence; the general feeling is that he must be hanged. These meetings have all convinced the central government. We have also requested the Trinamool Congress to intervene if necessary. They are favourable too.'

'Ha—so the Trinamool and the government have finally agreed on one thing! Didn't I tell you, Sanju babu? That there should be a hanging once in a while to rejuvenate the land and the people? Isn't that how people get to know that there's a government in this country?'

'I say, if Chetna could come to the fore now, things would be more colourful.'

'Disobedient hussy! She's stuffed with pride! I'll kick her out if she doesn't do what I say! Then she will have neither this family nor this house!'

It was an awful night. CNC included a sentimental story about the sorrowing parents of the murdered Mridula Chatterjee.

'Aren't you keen on punishing the wrongdoer?' the reporter asked the deceased girl's thirty-five-year-old brother.

His tired face appeared on the screen.

'Why didn't you write to the President?'

'What has happened has happened. We will never get her back. What does it matter if they punish him or not?'

There was deep pain in Binoy Chatterjee's voice. I went to bed early that day. Outside, two lorry drivers drunk on locally brewed liquor created a ruckus. Thakuma went out, scolded them both and returned. Silence fell after a while. I sat up, unable to sleep. It seemed to me that there was no other sight as petrifying as that of a silently burning lamp placed under a cot just a little wider than a bench. Worries crowded my mind. A deep enmity towards Sanjeev Kumar Mitra surfaced. He controlled the death of Jatindranath Banerjee. As well as the lives of those who were to kill him—Father and me. Each person inside this house of ours, now crumbling to dust with age, was under his thumb. Rage smouldered within me. In the dim light, I imagined Jatindranath Banerjee sitting with a foolish smile on Ramu da's cot. Till now he had been but a concept. Now he was real. The noose with which Father had chosen to hang him sat coiled in a large iron box in one of the dark rooms of the prison like a cobra ready to lay eggs. After being appointed the hangwoman unexpectedly, I had talked and talked about death and my ancestors for a whole month, taming myself with words the way the hangman's rope is softened with banana flesh and soap. But the moment the hanging was postponed, I fell down into an unknown cellar. That had been a terrible fall. Someone who had lived inside me till then had died, and was reborn as someone else. In the yellowish light, like everything else—the stained walls, the cloth bundles that hung from the nails hammered into it, the old pictorial calendar, the mirror, the little statuette of Durga that resembled Niharika that I had carefully mounted on the small slab—I, hunched upon the bedding spread on the floor, too appeared to be but a shadow.

'Chetu, still not asleep?'

Thakuma sat up on her bed, shaking the betel on to her palm.

'Can't sleep, Thakuma.'

'Come here . . .'

I went up to Thakuma, who was sitting with her legs outstretched on the bed, and pressed my face on her wrinkled back, like I used to as a child. Her palm, little more than bones, stretched back and touched my cheek lovingly. If you pressed your ear to Thakuma's spine, you heard the *tham-tham* of huge waves breaking on rocks and shattering. That's Thakuma's heart beating, Ramu da would say. But now, when I listened, it sounded more like the cellar opening. Even the thought of the cellars inside Thakuma's heart drained me of all courage.

'Did you sleep with him?' She turned towards me, chewing the betel.

That was a blow.

'He looks like a man capable of making a woman love him and making her happy too.'

She sighed.

'A woman and man shouldn't be joined by heart alone, but by bodies too.'

295

She sighed again. I wilted in amazement—that she could discuss the body and sex in this room even before the lamp that was showing Ramu da the way to the other world died out.

'The body is a great burden. In your youth it is easier to tame and chain it. But as you grow older, the body grows weak, the mind becomes harder to hold in place. Whenever I saw him, I thought I knew someone who looked like him, and I remember now—he looks like Netra Sen.'

'Thakuma . . .' I was disconcerted.

Thakuma chewed her betel for some more time in the dark. Then smiled softly. 'I thought so because it occurred to me that you resemble that girl.'

'Which girl?' I was fully alert now.

'Netra Sen's wife . . . what was her name? Savitri? Sati Devi?'

I smiled again to myself. Savitri, or Sati, or perhaps Durga, and if not then Chamundi. I don't know what made me go seeking him again. Maybe it was that intense night. I served Sanjeev Kumar a meal, sitting on the floor in the grand mansion at Sonagachi. I sat beside him, waving a fan. And then seized the chopper I had hidden behind me and brought it down hard on his neck. Whom he had betrayed for me to kill him so, I didn't know. But when I woke up rudely, I knew. He had betrayed my love; my body that turned tender and vulnerable when in love. My soul which refused to leave him, like the yellow light of the dimly burning lamp. My desire, always unfettered.

38

It was in 1784 that Warren Hastings wrote to his masters that knowledge gained from close interaction with conquered people would be of great use to the colonizing power, and that it was essential to attract and appease these people, render their chains lighter, and impress on them feelings of gratitude and obligation towards their conquerors. That was one hundred and ninety-eight years before I was born. I remembered Hastings not just because Sanjeev Kumar Mitra had begun to frequent our house with small bottles of liquor stuffed in his pockets and some small change for Father. It was the newspapers and television channels that made me think of him. They poked into the sorrow and the anger of the murdered child's parents and her chronically ill brother. Everywhere one heard those who had loved her, those who had kept their memories of her, screaming as they fell into the trenches of the past.

To overcome my fear, I smiled and told jokes to myself, muttered words of consolation, and tried to sing songs from my schooldays. Have you lost your mind? Ma scolded me. Thakuma smiled kindly. 'A death has occurred in the house, hasn't it? And she was the most beloved to him. When the dead hold tight, not wanting to leave, living people can't find balance.'

I woke up screaming from my sleep. In the nightmare, Ramu da's soul which was lying on the cot grew a tail; it twisted around my neck and strangled me. Ma couldn't put to rest my thoughts about the tail the departed soul was likely to grow. The soul, in my dream, was smooth and shiny, as if it had been shaped out of the clay from the Ganga. His eyes and hair were red and his eyeballs white. His arms and legs flowed from the cot, spreading all over the room like a viscous liquid. It, however, was transparent like clear crystal and as flexible as molten wax. The thought that my sibling's soul tarried painfully in this room, in this house and at Strand Road, reluctant to leave me, made me weep for months after. The image of Ramu da returning from college, carefree and happy, swooping me up in his arms and twirling me, little petticoat and all, and then throwing me up and catching me in his arms, making me laugh, kept flashing in my mind. My heart broke to pieces.

'I caused Ramu da's death, Thakuma,' I sobbed, pressing my face on her thin, twig-like knees.

Though it was Sanjeev Kumar Mitra who started it, I could not get over the thought that the immediate cause of his death was my own cowardice. If only I had handed over the gold coin to Thakuma as soon as he gave it to me, if only I had told everyone that he had stolen it, it would not have been lost when Thakuma's bed was being made. Kaku wouldn't have been tempted to steal it and buy clothes and gold for his wife and daughters. Father wouldn't have beaten up Kaku. And Ramu da wouldn't have fallen on the floor without knowing who would win, England or Portugal.

'No one can be responsible for another's death. We can only be instruments.' She stroked my shoulder gently. Even at the age of one hundred and four, there was still the warmth and delicacy of affection in her shrivelled fingertips.

'Don't you feel sad at losing the coin, Thakuma? Wasn't it the proof of our history?'

'What use do the poor have of history, Chetu?' She sighed.

'Then why did you search for it over and over again?'

'I kept looking for it only to convince myself that I had lost it. Now I am sure I have lost it. Why grieve for it now?'

As I gazed at her I tried to imagine how those eyes and cheeks and lips must have been in her youth. I was overcome by a feeling of deep compassion towards her aged body that desired to stay in bondage to the earth by continually fanning a small spark of life and vitality into a tiny flame.

'And if I didn't know that it had been lost? I am old. How many days more, who knows? My soul would have hung back here, hoping that the coin would be found somewhere in the wooden box or the rats' nest in the attic. Just imagine, Chetu, me turning the place upside down, searching, and searching again, like Hastings sahib on his horse at two o'clock at night.'

When Thakuma opened her mouth, laughing innocently, I too smiled. That's how I chanced to think that night about Hastings sahib and Grandfather Vidyasagar Mullick who knew the finest details of the Englishman's life. He was the son of Grandfather Purushottam's sister Kantimati and could recite from memory the whole of Hastings's famous letter in which he argued that the knowledge of the conquered peoples' language, culture and lifestyle was very useful to understand their mental states and natural rights, and this would make the conquerors capable of assessing them by their own standards.

... But such instances can only be gained in their writings; and these will survive when the British domination in India shall have long ceased to exist, and when the sources which once yielded wealth and power are lost to remembrance ...

And then he peered into our souls with two shining eyes hidden in the forest of his long, tangled beard, abundant, shaggy eyebrows, and thickly lashed eyelids, and asked: 'Notice where his wily foresight lies? In the part which says ". . . in their writings"!'

Grandfather Vidyasagar was one of the few in our family who tried to get over the pain of poverty by immersing himself in knowledge. Ramu da used to joke that all references to scholarship left grandfather deeply perturbed because he had aspired to be a writer himself. Hastings made friends with nawabs; learned Urdu and Bangla and Persian. But what always floored me was his love story. For him, love always leapt up in the midst of the gravest danger and life-or-death situations. I was keen to imagine what he would have been like—this poor waif who grew up in an orphanage, joined the army for survival, and reached this new land, Kolkata, in the middle of the eighteenth century. Throughout his youth, he questioned corruption, but also made money and rose in the ranks. He had been one of the prisoners in the so-called 'Black Hole' about which British historians have made much noise, in which several British men were trapped during Siraj-ud-Daulah's campaign after the death of Nawab Alivardi Khan. He was nearly on his deathbed when he met her—the widow of one of the men who had died there, and a mother of two. I was intrigued by the woman who had rendered him helpless with love even in that terrible atmosphere of decay and death. Hastings escaped from the nawab's prison, to Fulta Island, and married Mary. Though he endeared himself to Lord Clive who led the British forces from Madras to defeat Siraj-ud-Daula, his misfortune did not end. The two children Mary bore him—a boy and a girl—died. But his horses continued to surge ahead. He became the Resident of Murshidabad. Those were the days of Mir Jafar, who bestowed upon him the title of nawab in return for his betrayal of Siraj-ud-Daula, and his son-in-law Mir Qasim. Hastings remained a faithful servant of the Company, but sold coffee and salt on the side and made piles of money. As a member of the Calcutta Council he roundly condemned corrupt officers of the Company but he himself became a contractor distributing bullocks for carts—and later, unable to tolerate corruption, returned to Britain. It was a little before his return that Mir Qasim began his campaign and our ancestor Atmaram Mullick became the nawab's trusted man and chief executioner. Thakuma used to describe with great gusto how the British camp at Patna was surrounded by Mir Qasim's troops and how Grandfather Atmaram put to death hundreds of British men before the Company troops came to their rescue.

I whiled away that night sleeping next to Thakuma, alternately waking and dozing. Must escape to Mano da's office as soon as I can, I decided. Our bathroom was used by four families. Narayan da's wife Sankari Devi was taking a bath. I waited by the road for her to finish. The six-ten Sealdah Mail passed by, shaking the very foundations of our houses. A mini-lorry bearing a herd of goats for the slaughter house beyond the cemetery—their eyes drooping, like those who had seen a lot of life—purred impatiently. The street was still dozing. Black smoke rose lazily towards the sky above the Ghat. The dirt and muck that lay very close to my feet, our rickety outmoded houses, their roofs dotted with patches of plastic, and the terrible ear-splitting sound of another circular train—all of it created the impression of violent death. Narayan da passed that way with his cart full of bamboo for the litters without noticing me. A rich brahmin, his chest divided in two by a wet black sacred thread, searched for his car parked somewhere near the Nimeshwar Baba temple, chanting 'Narayana, narayana . . .' aloud. He was probably with a group of mourners from a distant place. Rajkumari Devi, the mother of Swayambhu, who worked in the Port Trust, hobbled up in her frayed sari and torn blouse, and smiled at me. That was a smile that could appear only on the faces of those whose souls had reached the other world well before their bodies. Her husband Parameswar da must have come down with his bag full of ear cleaners and swooped her away with his crystal-clear, flexible tail.

'The Ganga has dried up,' she said, smiling at me. 'When I looked there this morning, there was no river. Just a road.'

Rajkumari di's greatest pleasure was to share the memories of her life in Mayadwip before Partition.

'Why did you come to have a bath so early? Did the water your Ma collected get used up so soon?'

Sankari Devi had come out and was now drying her hair with a towel, head thrown backwards and her big chest thrust forward. She was fifty, but her body was still shapely and her face very comely. Only her fair-skinned back bore lash marks, inflicted by Narayan da who suspected her of having affairs. This had been going on for as long as I could remember. I had my bath and came out; there was a row of men at the tap near the waste heap, all of them yellow with the soap lather on their bodies. Father too bathed there, when there was water in the tap, along with the others, wrapping the green-and-red towel around his waist, pampering his body with soap, and telling tall tales to co-bathers. Kaku refused to bathe in public, choosing instead to do so in our broken-down, mossy courtyard. I noticed the lash marks on his legs after I heard that he had picked up this habit in jail. Only then did I know that he had been jailed during the Emergency.

'He's turned up before daybreak today, that boy!' Ma told me as I stepped inside. I pretended not to hear and looked for a white dupatta to go with my dark green kurta. Thakuma put her legs up on the cot and drank her tea, blowing into it noisily.

'My girl has become reed thin in such a short while! It's her heart burning for him . . . all because of you . . . I had warned you early enough—we don't want an alliance from a non-hangman family. But you fell for the coat and the pants and the cash in his pocket . . .' Thakuma began to scold Ma.

'Everyone knows whose habit it is to fall for the cash in others' pockets!' Ma vented her anger. 'All I wanted was for my girl to receive a good alliance. Who knew that your son would sell her for cold cash on that pretext!'

Not waiting for Thakuma to finish her tea, Ma snatched the cup and marched into the kitchen. Thakuma wiped her eyes and smiled, winking at me. 'We don't get along!'

I smiled too as I combed my hair. It was hard for me to understand why she, who told us many stories of dire enmities, but declared that no enmity could be eternal, should treat Grandfather's beloved—my mother's mother—as an inveterate enemy half a century after she had died.

'Oh, what corruption, Grddha da, everywhere! Just everywhere—my blood boils!' Sanjeev Kumar Mitra's voice could be heard from Father's room.

'You're telling me about this, Sanju babu? Look, people have but one thought: money, money, money. Sometimes I think, get rid of the rope and the noose, get a gun and shoot all these buggers! This world can be redeemed only if we kill off some of these corrupt fellows!'

Father, clearly, was excited. I sat on Thakuma's cot doing my hair.

Hastings, who had come to India on a salary of five pounds, returned with savings worth thirty thousand pounds. He lived a life of ostentation in England and soon became penniless. Eager to make another fortune, he came back to Kolkata. He got off the ship as the governor of Bengal in a city ravaged by the terrible famine of the eighteenth century, in which one-third of the population had died and turned to dust, where houses made of bamboo leaves huddled together in misery. When he got on the ship, he was a widower. He fell in love again on the ship, with the German-born Marian Imhof. A married woman, she left her husband during the journey and joined Hastings. But she had to be released from her marriage in Germany. That took a long time— they waited for eight whole years to get married. He built for her the bungalow, Alipore Gardens. Later, he faced impeachment proceedings on charges of corruption. Though absolved of the charges, he left India and returned to England.

Hastings lived for a full twenty-four years more with his beloved in his residence at Daylesford, riding on Arabian stallions, trying to foster Indian plants in his garden, and acquiring Indian animals as pets. His death was due to unknown reasons. The day after he died—23 August 1817, or perhaps 7 September 1817; my ancestor Vidyasagar could never pin down the date accurately—at two o'clock at night, horse hooves sounded on the road in front of Alipore Gardens. The horse carriage Hastings had used drove up, its bells ringing, and stopped in the front garden of the bungalow. Taking off his hat, Hastings stepped down briskly and went inside. He climbed the spiral staircase of Kashi marble with quick steps and, until daybreak, kept searching for something in the rooms on the upper floor. When dawn broke and sunlight entered the city, the carriage became as transparent as crystal and, melting like hot wax, turned into vapour.

This, however, is not the relevant part of the story. After he had left for London, Lord Hastings had written to his friend Thomson that it pained him to remind Thomson of his writing desk again and again.

He complained that neither Thomson nor Larkins had given him any news about the matter. You have not been able to understand my anxiety about it, he accused.

Two years later, an advertisement appeared in the *Calcutta Gazette* that a rosewood writing desk owned by Warren Hastings had been stolen with two little pictures and some personal papers in it while it was being transported from his house in Esplanade to England. Or it had been accidently sold off with other items put up for auction. Mr Larkins and Mr Thompson offered a reward of two thousand rupees to anyone who could offer valuable information about the aforesaid writing desk.

I soon forgot Hastings and was about to set out for the *Bhavishyath* when Sanjeev Kumar accosted me in the little space between the salon and the moss-covered courtyard.

'I don't think you've come back to normal after Ramu da's death,' he said, taking off his spectacles and eyeing me. 'Things are only going to get worse if we go on like this. Chetna, return to the channel. We have thought of a special programme that you can handle. And I have a personal interest—I want to be near you all the time!'

I picked up the cloth bag I'd bought with Champa's tuition fee and smiled at him. But my eyes welled, somehow. My confidence was being broken by all the great male figures of history who sang of the memories of their love in inflated terms. I thought I could forgive Hastings all his evil: after all, he had survived lack of food and air by falling in love with a woman who was near him! Once, only once, if only Sanjeev Kumar Mitra could love me like that! I longed in vain.

As I moved towards the door, he stopped me. 'Chetna, don't abandon me like this! I am sorry for whatever wrong I have done to you. I couldn't meet you when you were grieving only because there were urgent things to be done at the office. I was shattered, Chetna. This programme about the death sentence has been the biggest thing in my life.'

I smiled again.

'Don't shame me like this, with smile after smile. Say something!'

'The death sentence was also an important event in Jatindranath's life.'

'Look, this is a hot discussion not just here but all over the country! Chetna, you are going to be famous nation-wide! Don't kick out the goddess of prosperity standing at your doorstep!'

303

'I have work to do, Sanju babu, please move out of my way.'

'Tell me, what is my great crime?'

I lost control. 'What is your crime? Ask yourself!'

'It's not as if it was I who killed your Ramu da!'

I was trying to laugh, but my eyes overflowed. 'You, yes, you—you *did* kill him! It all started when you stole Thakuma's coin!'

My voice broke and dissipated as tiny slivers. If, in that moment, he had held me close, whispered genuine apologies in my ear . . . a small part of my heart beat ardently for this, putting me to utter shame.

He bent down and touched my feet. 'Here, I'm begging your pardon. I did behave like a filthy person, Chetna. My fault, all of it. Please forgive me!'

I swallowed. For some time, it was hard to figure out how to react. 'I won't come to the channel's programme.' My rage returned.

'Okay, if you don't want to, then don't . . . but don't hate me!'

I swallowed again, taking him in. The heart, full of wounds but barely twenty-two years old, twitched in confusion.

'My family members will come here formally to propose marriage. Please don't shame me like this then, Chetna. You don't have to trust me, but you can trust them, can't you?'

I eyed him suspiciously.

'Our family doesn't care for caste and creed . . .'

My heart stopped melting and became frozen again. 'No, Sanju babu, I cannot trust you any more. You will never realize how I loved you.' My voice had suddenly become hard.

'But you too have not realized how much I love you, Chetna.'

He came closer and pulled out a little box from his pocket. He's going to insult me again with another ring or bangle, I thought. The moment he holds it out to me, I decided furiously, I'll either slap him hard on the cheek or throw a noose around his neck and end this nuisance forever.

'Look, I have brought back to you that which caused all the trouble.'

He opened the box and held it up.

'I cannot give back your brother's life. But I'll strive to give you the affection Ramu da gave you. And here is the history that you and your family cherish.'

My eyes nearly popped out. It was Thakuma's coin! I snatched the box from him and examined the coin, unable to believe my own eyes.

'Where did you get this from?'

He laughed triumphantly and put his spectacles back on his nose. The black hue of his shirt rendered them smokier still.

'You have always underestimated me. I need you, but you need me more. You know that well, and I know how well you know that!'

He caressed me lightly on my cheek and walked away. Like flames leaping up from beneath my feet, fear consumed me. Not because I remembered that interaction with conquered people was a way of making their chains feel lighter. I thought he was dead. But I had still lit a small lamp for his soul to make its way away from the earth. But he had used that light to come right back to me. Reaching out with a tail as flexible as molten wax, he had thrown a noose around my neck and pulled it tight once more. But that crystal noose was not of a clear hue at all. It was smoky, opaque. A mourners' procession that followed an expensive silver-plated hearse went by slowly. The feet of the corpse were red with alta—a married woman. I felt envious; Hastings must have loved Marian till his death and taken pleasure in her presence. The man who walked behind the hearse turned around; our eyes met. I was stupefied. It was Maruti Prasad Yadav. The first man who convinced me that I could be a hangwoman. It was an awful sight to see that man walk with his hands on a woman's funeral bier, turning around to look at me, finally disappearing from sight. My breath stopped when I thought of that woman who must have suffered the stink of paan masala and the reek of sweat, and his ignorance of the possibility that a woman could be taken without attacking her. Would she return to the earth as a soul with a tail and hold fast to her relatives? Sanjeev Kumar had melted away from sight. The hearse too. Yet the grating of its wheels resounded in my ears, bringing back the thought of the ghost of Warren Hastings. I saw him cross the oceans, climbing up and down the spiral staircase in search of some old letters and two pictures. But even then—what a pity—Lord Hastings looked just like Sanjeev Kumar Mitra . . .

39

When the condemned person falls into the cellar below, the noose tightens around the neck and breaks the spinal cord. The blood vessels of the heart close down. The vessels of the brain rupture. The neck is broken. At that stage most men ejaculate. In women, the reproductive organs are suffused with blood. In the momentary caress of Death the Lover, those mortals, doomed to eternal arousal, will retain their last dream of infinite joy and hurtle into the cellar of the next birth. And therefore, the souls of those who die violent and unnatural deaths will return to the world and continue to seek pleasure. Not that there aren't a few who stand firmly before death, not succumbing to its seduction. Like Khudiram Bose, hanged by Gauricharan Mullick, the paternal cousin of Grandfather Kalicharan. This was eight years before Father's birth. Khudiram was Lakshmipriya Devi's son. She tried to secure a long life for this son, the third born and only survivor, by selling him to her sister, symbolically taking three handfuls of grain—khudi. When he was eighteen years, seven months and eleven days old, Khudiram ascended the gallows. He walked to it as if he were approaching his own bed. He wore his death-hood calmly. When the noose fell on his neck, his heartbeat did not quicken; nor did his chest heave with deep breaths. When Gauricharan pulled the lever, the cellar opened. The body slipped down gently. It did not struggle even once. The rope did not straighten. The British doctor who examined the dead body wiped his eyes and whispered, it's like he went in his sleep. Gauricharan stood rooted to the spot, unable to lift his arm from the lever after the deed was done. No one in our family has ever witnessed such a graceful passing. If you die, die like that, praised Thakuma.

Khudiram's story used to make Kakima really mad. It's the stories of revolutionaries hanged to death that made Kaku stray, she would say. But Thakuma would retaliate, declaring that it was after he married her, twenty-five years his junior, that he turned into a useless, henpecked sissy. Kaku was constantly scolded: Father called him totally useless; a worrywart, typical of a fellow who doesn't touch a woman, said Ma; poor fellow, he's touched by fear, said Thakuma, it has snuffed out his brain. His obese body that shone as though it were a plastic sac filled with water, and small, childlike face that didn't at all suit the body made him a laughing stock outside the house too. Only Ramu da was kind to him when he mused that Kaku was not always like this. I was not old enough and so couldn't comprehend how he could have been anything but this: someone who slept till ten, bathed in our courtyard, ate heartily and doused himself with talcum powder before going off to the salon to cut people's hair, talking incessantly about Uttam Kumar and Supriya Devi.

When Sanjeev Kumar Mitra and Maruti Prasad disappeared in opposite directions, I stood there by myself for a while. The sun hadn't fully risen yet. Various kinds of humanity streamed along the road. Defying the deafening roar of the train to Dumdum, a cuckoo sang its first notes of the year from the banyan tree in front of the ramshackle quarters of the Port Trust workers. Both the fear of death that the thundering roar evoked and the hope of love in the defiant birdcall sent a shiver of excitement through me. The last coin from the bag that Grandfather Manohar received for serving in Gwalior became moist with the sweat in my palm. Inside the house, Thakuma was absorbed in the re-telecast of the series on Khudiram shown last night. She glanced absently at the coin, reluctant to take her eyes off the TV screen, then jumped, finally noticing it. When her eyes turned to me, a tear flowed down her bony cheek. She kept staring at it till the furrow on her cheek dried up and became a dark line dividing it in two. On the screen, Khudiram stood holding the bars of the cell, lost in thought.

'What use do the poor have of history, Thakuma?' I asked gently, kneeling beside her.

'Chetu, only now, when I have it back, do I realize its value.'

She laughed. Only women of ripe old age can laugh so.

'How did you get this back?'

'He gave it.'

'How did he get it? Didn't Sudev sell it?'

'Those who buy it keep selling it. And those who sold it keep buying it back,' said I, remembering Ramu da's words.

Khudiram was hanged eight years before Father was born. The magistrate of Muzzafarpur, Kingsford, ordered the caning of a young man, Sushil Sen. The punishment left him with serious injuries.

Enraged, his colleagues in Jugantar tried Kingsford in a people's court and sentenced him to death. The mission of carrying out the death sentence fell upon the shoulders of two young activists, Khudiram Bose and Prafulla Chaki. Thakuma would describe how they hung around the courthouse watching Kingsford, plotting to blow him up with a bomb, as if she had been right there. Her descriptions buzzed in my mind when I stepped into Kaku's room. His room was opposite the kitchen in our house which was like a rectangular box with its mouth open. When I went in, Kaku was lying on the double cot in their small room, rubbing his ample, hairless chest as he watched the series on Khudiram on the fourteen-inch TV mounted on their wall. The room was tiny; the double cot and the almirah filled it completely. The children's books and old toys were on iron shelves fixed on the walls.

After Ramu da's death Kakima and the girls rarely slept in our house. Kakima would come back after taking the girls to school, enter the kitchen, turn her back to us and cook for Kaku and herself, and serve him in their room. She constantly spoke to him in a reproachful tone. Then she would shut the door firmly. The men in this house have no sense of day and night, they see no difference between a house of mourning and a bridal chamber—Ma spat in disgust. Thakuma winked and smiled: I conceived him during the day.

Seeing me, Kaku sat up, took his gamchha from the head of the cot, wiped his neck and chest, and gave me a helpless, sad smile. I went up and sat next to him.

'Uh . . . you haven't spoken to me for so long, Chetu!'

I could recollect our last conversation exactly. One and a half months back, on 18 May. The day the governor rejected Jatindranath's mercy petition. That was the day when Kaku sent me off to get paan and I walked with a carefree bounce in my step before Sanjeev Kumar Mitra's camera. It seemed ages ago. My head whirled at the thought of all that had happened in my life since that day.

'I have had nothing to say after the decision to become a hangwoman, Kaku.' I fixed my gaze on his eyes. 'How did Manohar Mullick's gold coin reach Sanjeev Kumar Mitra?'

My question left him flustered. He was about to ask, which coin, but then, as if he decided not to, he took my hand and, caressing it, said, 'My dear, Kaku is an old man now, isn't he? Isn't he nearly sixty-five? Two little children . . . you know, don't you? They are still so small. What will happen to them if something happens to me?'

'My baba is eighty-eight, I have never felt afraid about what will happen to me if something happens to him. Do you know why, Kaku? Because I know that you will be there for me.'

When my eyes overflowed and my voice fell, heavy with sorrow, Kaku wiped my eyes wearily.

'Kaku is a good-for-nothing, unfortunately, Chetu. All of you have suffered nothing but loss and pain because of me. Anything I have ever done with the intention of protecting others has always damaged them. Isn't that why your baba keeps reviling me, calling me useless?'

He covered his face with both palms and lowered his head.

'I . . . this happened to Ramu because of me!'

The guilt in his words was unbearable.

'I think it happened because of me. But I didn't come here to tell you that. How did Sanjeev Kumar get hold of the coin?'

A wrongdoer's sheepish look dawned on his face.

'It wouldn't have reached him unless it was through you. I know that.'

He sighed.

'Syami told me that antiques sell for high prices. When I thought of it, I felt that Sanju babu might be interested. So I saw him . . .'

I kept looking at him steadfastly. I could easily imagine the moment when Kaku dragged his fat, sweaty body and stood before Sanjeev Kumar Mitra, panting. How did he respond when the coin was shown to him?

'He burst out laughing. And said, I'll take it, for any price you quote.'

I could hear him laugh too. A new noose fell around my heart. Every pore in my body shivered.

'It was wrong, Chetu . . . but when Syami insisted . . .'

When I was a child, he used to take me to school and bring me back. I thought of the mornings and noontimes we had spent going to and coming back from school on his bicycle. That was another Kaku.

'Old age had sapped my courage, Chetu. Not because I am old, but because of the children's faces.'

His voice faltered and tears flowed. I tried to quiet my heart and leaned on his shoulder.

'Like I am sure you'll be there for me if Baba is no more, you can be sure that I'll be there for Rari and Champa, Kaku!'

'But you . . . you are so gentle, and will be married off today or tomorrow. What can you do, my daughter?'

'Whether I marry or not, I'll always be there for Rari and Champa. Isn't that enough?'

My voice faltered and tears flowed too.

'I was never afraid in the old days, nor did I worry so much. I was ready to give myself up for the country, like Khudiram here. Death, the police, the army—I feared nothing. I laughed even when they beat me black and blue in jail. In fact, I hummed a song . . .'

'*Ekla* . . . ?'

'Oh, that was Mano da's song! Mine was *Aandhar shokoli* . . .'

He smiled through his tears.

'The policemen hammered nails into our fingertips, whipped us, branded us . . . but I never stopped singing. But now I am afraid to remember that self. I don't even feel I am myself any more. That old me can never be retrieved!'

'Kaku, you are the same Kaku.'

'No, my dear. Dada is right. I am not good enough to kill even a hen.'

He looked at his own hands.

'Huh . . . they killed me by half. In return, I tried to exterminate them. Wanted to be like Khudiram . . . ended up useless, not capable of finishing off even a fowl!'

His voice fell. His favourite childhood tale was the assassination planned by Khudiram Bose and Prafulla Chaki. They tried to kill the magistrate with locally made bombs and bullets. It had happened some twenty years before his birth but he always narrated the tale with such fervour. First, they decided to plant a bomb in the court. But since that meant other people might get hurt, they decided to strike when he arrived at the club. They bombed the magistrate's carriage, but only when they heard the cries of women did they realize their mistake. Kingsford wasn't in the carriage; it was the wife and daughter of a barrister. In the melee that followed, Khudiram and Prafulla fled in different directions. Prafulla reached Samastipur and took a train; a police officer in the same compartment began to have suspicions.

310

When it appeared that he was going to be arrested for sure, Prafulla shot himself in the head. Not knowing this, Khudiram trudged twenty-six kilometres to reach Samastipur. He was in a tea shop when two police constables saw him. He tried to escape but was soon nabbed by the crowd who checked his clothes—two pistols fell out of his pockets. He had enough ammunition on him to fire thirty-five rounds. He did not lose composure even with the crowd that kicked and hit him just for fun. Even as he was being led to the police vehicle, a keen look remained on his face.

'I was a fool, Chetu. I could never really see through our people and our leaders. I began to have my doubts when they tried to manhandle us at Baranagar in 1971. Those were Congressmen, but the communists supported them. I felt giddy when I looked at our attackers. We'd taken to arms for *their* sake. Right before my eyes, ten or twelve young men were beaten to death. I still see that horrible scene . . . the sticks, stones, bricks, the blood splattering at each blow . . .'

Kaku was jailed in 1973.When he got out in 1975 the Emergency was declared. He went underground, migrating to Bombay where he lived as a shoeshiner, a tea vendor and even a blind Muslim beggar, distributing George Fernandes' subversive letter written after he went underground. How he picked up the courage to do such things, I don't know even now.

The TV suddenly grew louder. The cell was being opened in the screen. Khudiram was being brought out by policemen. They stood him in front of the gallows, but it was time for the commercial break. Kaku got up suddenly and switched it off.

'There was no woman in Khudiram's life. If there had been, he couldn't have died with a cool mind and strong body. I tried to run away from women. Reached nowhere. So I decided to return to them. But still, I am nowhere . . .'

I did not move. His words made no sense to me. But I could see Khudiram's eyes on his face. Even when he was brought before the magistrate, he did not know that Prafulla was dead. To save his friend, he admitted to being the sole conspirator. As soon as he had testified, Prafulla's body was brought; Khudiram recognized his friend. But the British were satisfied only after they had severed his head and body, and sent the head to Kolkata. It was my grandfather who took it there, wrapped in a red cloth.

'Whenever I go to the foot of the gallows, I am filled with fear about myself. What am I doing? Protecting or punishing? When Dada pulls the lever, I shut my eyes tight. The lines of *Aandhar shokoli* ring in my head. Each of those deaths was my own. Dada hanged *me* all those times,' he kept mumbling in pain.

'Don't cry, Kaku,' I pleaded sadly.

'Had forgotten it all . . . now, it is back. I've had enough, Chetu. How can one get rid of all these memories?'

Unable to sit there any further, I got up slowly.

'I have to go. I've found work at the *Bhavishyath*. Let me leave now.'

'Forgive me . . .'

'Don't say things like that.'

'No one speaks the truth. And even when they do, the truth is always incomplete.'

He began to tremble. When I came out I was covered in sweat as if I had been inside a burning furnace. So, Sanjeev Kumar Mitra had managed, once again, to make me all the more weak and helpless. I went towards the door and saw Thakuma standing at the doorstep. She turned to me. A small procession of mourners passed by.

'Oh, these children!' Thakuma exclaimed without emotion. 'Today also a child's been playing with the noose.'

I went right back in and sat down on her cot. In this Kolkata of ours, it's impossible to pass a day without remembering someone from the past or stepping on the clods of history. The TV channels hadn't made a story of Belu and Benu's game inspired by the sight of Khudiram walking up to the gallows and putting the noose around his own neck. I felt drained thinking of Benu looking up at his sister dangling from the noose. At that moment, Father came hurrying in with an angry yowl. His feet were hardly on the floor. Ma caught hold him just as he was about to fall and carried him back to his room. She came out after a while.

'So, today it begins early.'

I didn't ask, but Ma told me anyway. 'Didn't you understand? They are finding new lawyers for him, it seems.'

Ma was referring to Amnesty International arranging a group of

lawyers to fight Jatindranath's case. They would argue that he was
mentally unstable. I sat motionless on Thakuma's cot. They sentenced
Khudiram Bose to death. But a group of prominent lawyers volunteered
to fight his case for free. Khudiram changed his testimony under their
supervision. They split hairs over the law, but the death sentence
was confirmed. It apparently brought a smile to his face. The judge
was puzzled. Maybe he heard the judgment wrong, he thought. But
Khudiram said, give me some more time, I will teach you how to make
a bomb. He went to the gallows with his head held high. My ancestor
Gouri Charan was old and wizened, but it was the first time that he
met a condemned man who greeted him with a smile as he put the
death-hood on him. After the hanging, Grandfather Gouri Charan broke
down. The cold feel of the coin lingered in my palm. Sanjeev Kumar
Mitra sat somewhere, shaking with laughter. I got up in a hurry and
slung my bag on my shoulder.

'Where to?' Ma asked suspiciously.

'Nowhere in particular,' I murmured, since the truth must be told
but not all of it. Probably the cuckoo from earlier cooed with sarcasm.
A circular train dashed in the opposite direction. The caress of Death
the Lover aroused me too. What if I do not realize ultimate joy in this
world and have to leave with an unquiet body to the other world? With
that perturbing thought, I hailed an auto rickshaw. The days were flying
past. Time was running out. If I had some more time, I'd teach him to
make a bomb too, though that meant one of us would be annihilated.

40

I flew through Madan Mohan Lane like a bird with wings on fire. The
song *Aandhar shokoli* clung to my lips like a burning spark and singed
tongue. The song that Kaku sang when they hung him upside down
in the police cell—I simply could not stop humming it. I walked by
the Batliboi bookshops through the busy moss-covered road towards
Bhavishyath and daydreamed that a dreamy-eyed young man was

standing in one of Thakurbari's imposing red buildings and singing this song. The anguished eyes and lovelorn face of the young man walking down the stairway, saddened by the absence of his muse, pierced me so. I always pictured all women who commit suicide as dangling statues. They hung, heavy forever, at the tip of the rope stretched tight like a violin string. I thought of the woman who produced music when her devastated lover touched her lifeless body. *'Chhalana chhaturi aashe hridaye bishaado baashe,'* I hummed, as I entered the *Bhavishyath* office. Mano da, who had been joking and laughing with someone on the black telephone, stopped laughing and looked at me in surprise. He became glum all of a sudden. He ended the conversation, put the receiver back and smiled sadly at me.

'Your kaku used to sing magnificently. That song . . . when he sang when they hung him upside down, all of us would forget our pain, close our eyes, and keep rhythm. Oh, what a song it is! Who else but our Thakur could write such a song! But the funny thing is that it was one of the songs banned then. You see why? It begins with a reference to darkness, right? *I look into the dark to see when you will arrive, but I do not see you.* The state interpreted it as: There is Emergency everywhere, when will democracy arrive, I try to see! But, hey democracy, I do not see you! So Siddhartha Shankar Ray found politics even in the poems Thakur wrote for his Lady Hecate!'

I smiled, so did the statue-like Nischol da.

'Don't laugh, Chetu, this is no joke! All poems with words like darkness, sorrow and pain were supposed to be banned. Even phrases like "the barriers will be overcome" or "barriers will not last" would invite instant proscription! What else is there in Thakur's poetry other than darkness and sorrow and pain?'

'Tomare dekhi na jabe . . . tomare dekhi na jabe . . . ' I hummed involuntarily, *I cannot see you*. And when I replaced Kadambari Devi with democracy in my mind, my heart grew lighter.

'At first this was a great shock to me. Thakur was Indira Gandhi's guru, after all. She studied in his Shantiniketan. There she was apparently fond of dancing. But Nehru would not permit that. How do we comprehend the fact that a woman who'd declared that her happiest years were at Shantiniketan went on later to ban Thakur's songs? But later, it ceased to be a mystery. She banned the words of the Father of the Nation and even those of her own father! Why, even parts of her own speeches were proscribed! What honesty! Only women can do such a thing, Chetu! You women, I swear on my own mother, you women are extraordinary creations!'

'*Chhalana chaturi aashe hridaye bishaado baashe / Tomare dekhi na jabe, tomare dekhi na jabe . . .*'

I smiled and continued to hum. *Betrayal enters with élan, it fills the heart with dejection.* The television and the fans came to life when the power outage ended and suddenly I could hear Sanjeev Kumar Mitra's voice.

'So the issue before us, Advocate Kulkarni, is this: It has been more than ten whole years since Jatindranath received the death sentence. Someone who receives a sentence for an ordinary murder case would normally be out by now.'

I lost my lines and looked at Mano da. He peeped in and went back to the papers on his desk. I went in and sat in my chair. I wanted to turn off the TV but couldn't bring myself to do it when his face appeared. It is a truly unique experience for any hangwoman to witness a discussion about the legal arguments that the lawyers appointed to save the prisoner—who is to die by her hand—hope to take to the Supreme Court. My head grew heavy thinking of this blindman's buff we were playing—Jatindranath, I who had been deputed to kill him, and the lawyers attempting to save him.

'What you said is true, Mr Mitra. The delay on the part of the government in forwarding the relevant documents about Jatindranath's sentence was the main reason why his mercy plea was rejected. So, in a way, the state government is responsible for his present plight. That's what we are trying to point out. What happened in Punjab in 1983? The condemned convict Sher Singh remained on death row for two and a half years. He submitted a petition. The court opined it is one thing to receive a death sentence, but quite another to suffer the agony of waiting for it interminably. His sentence was reduced to a life term. Compared with that, Jatindranath ought to receive compensation from the state government! Not a year or two. Eleven whole years spent waiting for death! Is this permissible in any civilized country?'

'Your point is very relevant, Advocate Kulkarni. When a citizen's freedom and life are to be taken, shouldn't they be taken in a fair, just and reasonable way?'

Mano da who came in, asked me, seeing Sanjeev Kumar Mitra's bubbling enthusiasm: 'Tell me, is this lover of yours truly against the death penalty?'

I kept silent.

'Isn't he the same chap who went whining behind that child's brother yesterday?' He laughed outright. 'The truth, Chetu, is that these days my respect for Einstein is on the rise. How right he was—everything is relative! This earth and its position, its speed, why, even the distance between you and me—everything!' He stopped briefly. 'But then, why do we need measurements at all? I don't understand!'

The sparkle of his rapturous smile was contagious—I smiled too. The state, when it decides to take the life or freedom of its citizens, will do so only after ensuring that any measure to this end is just, fair and reasonable. That too was a strange day. I realized that when hung upside down, those who have a heart can sing only of dead loves. Like the sea trapped in a pot with its mouth shut tight, the soul surged fruitlessly. Everything inside the *Bhavisyath*'s office seemed to rise and fall. The leaves of the ancient fans which looked like the sails of a sunken boat, the multicoloured sheets of paper flapping in the hot breeze, Mano da's silver locks, Nischol da's fingers—all of it was boiling and bubbling. Outside, the sky was dark with menacing rainclouds ready to burst.

'Chetu, I was thinking—why not attack the prison and finish off this Jatindranath?' Mano da had hobbled in to hand me a few papers on his encounter with Charu Majumdar. 'This bother will be over and done with! Right now it's: Will he be hanged? No! Will he be let off? No! '

'This man is the government's prey. It won't like anyone else taking his life,' I said.

'Ooh, so what is this government? A Bengal tiger? That it should be so insistent to knock down its prey by itself and maul it to death?'

His lovely mischievous smile came on.

'Jyoti babu once asked Feroze Gandhi, do you know why your wife has turned out like this? You know what his reply was? He said, if you live in that house, you'll see for yourself the submissiveness that

Congress leaders and freedom fighters keep showing . . . any girl would turn arrogant there.'

He smiled again.

'Like I turned into a hangwoman!'

Mano da looked straight at me.

'Chetu, are you capable, really, of hanging someone?'

The question infuriated me enormously. The same belligerence and fury that overtook me when Maruti Prasad attacked my body, and Sanjeev Kumar my soul, re-emerged with a vengeance. Without stopping to think, I pushed back my chair, pulled off my dupatta, looped it lightning fast into a noose, threw it around Mano da's neck and pulled the other end through the bars of the window. Mano da was taken completely unawares. Though he was quite tall and well built, he was only as heavy as a baby bird for me then. Before he knew what was happening, his thin right leg stuck out from under his dhoti and banged on the table and his eyeballs bulged and popped dangerously. I let go. Hearing the sound of Mano da falling on the floor, Nischol da came in running but stood rooted to the spot, unable to even cry out. I removed the noose just as I had made it—speedily—rubbed his neck and soothed it, and helped him into a chair. At the brink of losing consciousness, he coughed and spluttered and looked at us in turn. When Nischol da went up to him, he stroked his neck and chest, pointed his finger at me and tried to say something. I poured him a glass of water from the earthen pot there and stood leaning against the table as if nothing extraordinary had happened. After he drank it and took several deep breaths, and calmed down somewhat, he looked at Nischol da and said, 'Give her a hundred-rupee raise!'

Nischol da stood there as still as a statue. 'Who'll give us that money?' he asked after a couple of seconds.

'Look at him, how he is!' Mano da said, coughing. 'What keenness to insult the capitalist in front of the proletariat! Hey mister, I am going to dismiss you!'

Nischol da left with an unsmiling face. I, unable to face Mano da, went back to the proofs of his autobiography. Sanjeev Kumar Mitra's voice came back after a break.

'What other arguments do you intend to raise in court?'

'Mr Mitra, the next question is whether Jatindranath's mental condition renders him fit for the death sentence or not. We say, no. A group of experts . . . doctors . . . must be appointed to examine him.'

'That too is a vital point, Advocate Kulkarni. But tell me, why should we worry so much about the mental condition of someone who is about to die anyway?'

'Because of the possibility of paribartan, transformation. Isn't transformation everything in the world? Does not the death penalty bar the possibility of transformation forever? A life sentence can be converted into a death sentence, Mr Mitra, but not vice versa. Any kind of punishment that cannot be reversed is best avoided.'

I switched off the TV, went to Mano da and, kneeling, put my head on his shrivelled right leg. He smoothed my hair affectionately. 'Interesting. This experience of death is interesting!'

'Killing too is interesting,' I murmured. It had now become evident to me that none of the hangmen in our family, beginning with our earliest ancestor Radharaman Mullick—none of those who had become the arm of the state and the intoxicant of the crowd—had undertaken this work for material gain. Over and above money, there are two gains to be made in murdering another. The first is fame. More than the desire for money, it was the thirst for fame that drove Father. The fruition of his desire for fame as an actor was satiated only by the gallows. The second is a connection with the powerful. That drove my grandfather Purushottam Grddha Mullick. For Kala Mullick, it was the delight of delivering before a crowd of his betters and superiors the crazy pleasure of witnessing death. Grandfather Bhisma took satisfaction in performing his inherited dharma with precision and dedication; it was revenge that fired Pingalakeshini. And for Grandfather Kalicharan, it was the chance to demonstrate his aesthetic talents. But the true force that drove all these individuals was something else: when they woke at the crack of dawn, took a dip in the Ganga with eyes still sore from sleep, offered Ma Kali and Bhagawan Mahadev red-coloured flowers, liquor and blood from one's own thumb, prostrated themselves at their parents' feet, and set off with the readied rope to the foot of the gallows, their chief gratification came from the knowledge that they were thereby proving that they possessed the ability to perform the most difficult of human acts. I did not believe even for a moment that justice would be done if Jatindranath were hanged to death. But the very thought of putting the noose around his neck and pulling the lever made my hair stand on end. The rage that Mano da's question produced taught me that I too was driven by the need for such gratification. That possibility sank its teeth into my body. Time was running out fast. I, hailed as the symbol of the strength of Indian women and all the women in the world, *had* to do it. When I put the mask on his face, Jatindranath would look directly into my eyes. My hands tingled to break into the prison, as Mano da suggested, and strangle him to death.

At noon, Mano da and I went out to a bhelpuri seller, bought some bhelpuri, and stood munching it in front of Thakurbari. A garlic seller sat on his haunches by its grand arch, silently watching passers-by, waiting for buyers.

'*Esho esho, premamoy, amrito hashiti loye*,' I hummed again. *Come, my darling, with that honey-filled smile . . .*

Mano da gave me a surprised look and asked, his mouth full. 'Are you really in love with this Sanjeev Kumar Mitra?'

'Sometimes I want to kill him.' I was chewing too. I didn't look at him when I said that.

He looked at me carefully and rubbed his throat. 'Where is he from, really?'

'He has two houses here. One is a ruined mansion, with trees and creepers growing in it. The other is in Sonagachi, with spiral stairways and pillared verandas and marble floors.'

Mano da looked at me, alarmed.

'He also knows a south Indian language. His father hails from the south. His mother is Bengali. That's all I know of him. He claims that the ruined mansion was bought by his great-grandfather in the eighteenth century.'

When we were back in the *Bhavishyath* office, Mano da found the book *South Indians in Kolkata* by P. Thankappan Nair, opened the third chapter, and held it out for me to read.

There was contact between Calcutta and South India in the 18th century as the city was the capital of British India from 1774 to 1912.

319

The Maharaja of Cochin State used to send his trading vessels to Calcutta in the 18th century.

I ran my eyes through the pages, confused. I had heard the story of how our ancestor Jnananatha Grddha Mullick had met one of the Malayalees in 1793. He had accompanied Captain Andre Barthalomeo D'Cruz in a trading ship which made its profits by buying rice from Bengal and transporting it to Ceylon. That memory broke through the moss-covered layers of my mind.

The assistants of the rich merchant Kunhi Pokki used to visit Calcutta for trade. The *Calcutta Monthly Journal* reports a robbery that took place in the house of one of these representatives.

Mano da looked at me.

'If Sanjeev Kumar Mitra is the descendant of one of those Malayalees who came here then, oh, some coming that was, Chetu!'

I shut the book, turning to look at him. My mind was a void. The absurdity of romance between a trader and a hangman made my soul rant and rave again. Nischol da came in and turned on the TV. All the channels were airing the same news story.

'The family of Mridula Chatterjee writes to the President . . . The family of the murdered Mridula Chatterjee has written to President A.P.J. Abdul Kalam requesting him to reject Jatindranath Banerjee's mercy petition.'

'See? The matter's going to swell now. This is democracy—the people decide. Not all, but some.' Mano da leaned back in the chair. The void widened inside me. I watched the news for some time and then got back to Mano da's manuscript. The din of the trams outside made my heart beat faster. My ears ached for footsteps at the door. He would come, I was sure. I had got out of the house early today just to see him. That's why I waited patiently till he arrived at the *Bhavishyath* office, make-up and clothes intact.

'I have been waiting for you at your house for quite a while. What's keeping you here?' he asked brusquely.

'I was waiting for you.'

I picked up my bag, shut the doors noisily and turned to him.

'Let's go.'

'Where to?'

'To your house. I've no peace till I finish what I've started.'

Sanjeev Kumar Mitra did not know what I meant. Our eyes met. Behind their smoky cover, his eyeballs rolled like two black marbles.

'Your great-grandfather reached Kolkata by ship from Cochin, didn't he?' I asked.

Confusion reigned on his face.

This time, I walked in front. He followed. I stopped a cycle rickshaw and got in. He obeyed me when I gestured to him to get in.

'Go straight and . . . ' I gave directions to the rickshaw-wallah. We passed the tabla and tanpura shops and moved by the tram tracks past Jatrapara.

'Where are you taking me?' he asked me warily.

'To your house!'

I hadn't completed what I had begun, I remembered again. I leaned my head back on the ragged red seat and sang the rest of the song:

Esho esho, premamoy, amrito hashiti loye
Esho mor kache dheere ei hridaya nilaye
Chadibo na tomaye kabhu janame janame aar

Come, my darling, with that honey-filled smile,
Come with soft feet, I will never let you leave me,
I will never let you leave me from birth to birth, never.

'Who is this darling? Me?' he asked.

I looked at him tauntingly. And then, my tongue in searing pain, continued, '*Tomare dekhi na jabe, tomare dekhi na jabe . . .*'

41

Manasa was a goddess but she was an orphan, and wretched. The king of snakes, Vasuki, had been sculpting an idol of his mother's form. Lord Shiva who was passing that way was seduced by its beauty. But Chandi, his wife, called to him and he had to hide his erection; as it happens with men in such circumstances, he ejaculated and the divine semen fell on the idol. The idol was impregnated by it and Manasa was born. That was Thakuma's version. She was called Manasa because her birth was the result of sex that had taken place in Shiva's mind. The terrified Shiva tried to hide his blunder by leaving the baby girl in a snake pit where thousands of eggs were hatching. The baby snakes protected her from the cold and the heat, clasping her with their tails. But the fluids from the sharp scales protecting their tender underbellies seared her skin and made it slimy. And so she turned a bluish black, as though she had swallowed venom. Only the tribals were willing to accept the black, orphaned goddess. The illegitimate daughter of the God of Destruction thus remained in the backyard of the Hindu faith as the untouchable goddess of the dark-skinned and the poor.

We passed the stately homes in the area that spread over Cornwallis Street, Bowbazar and Maniktola from Chitpur Road, and reached the white-painted bungalow. Sanjeev Kumar Mitra was, by this time, fairly squirming with unease and distrust. The place was just like it had been the last time we visited. Men, some of them in a chauffeur's uniform, stood chatting beside the parked cars. The nine pillars of the front veranda rose to the sky as before. The grand entrance at the head of the steps opened out into a central courtyard reminiscent of the Jorasanko Thakurbari. In the courtyard, as before, three middle-aged women, head covered and nose decorated with heavy studs, washed dirty dishes. Like the other day, the sounds of dance, music, conversations and peals of laughter, and the scents of various kinds of food, wafted in from the many rooms in that mansion. Sanjeev Kumar opened the door on the right side of the second storey. The blood-red satin sofas and paintings with gold frames drew me in swiftly, like powerful magnets. The red coverlet and the carved bed with its large frame too were the same.

And once again I felt that rats were frolicking on it. A thousand snakes stuck out their icy tongues from within my body. My cells became their snake pits. The fluids oozing from the sharp scales on their underbelly seared my skin and turned it slimy. Sanjeev Kumar rested his hand on my shoulder and tried to study me, anxiety and wariness evident in his face.

'Why did you say you wanted to come here?'

I beamed. 'When is Nagpanchami this year?'

'Uh, who knows? There's no Nagpanchami where I come from,' he said, discontent writ large on his face.

'Every place has it.'

'Actually, I don't even know what it is!'

He moved away from me and went to sit on the bed. I ran my fingers over the carved image of the snake coiling up its leg.

'That's the festival of Devi Manasa.'

I went up to him and sat down beside him, but he didn't try to touch me. He had propped himself on his arms. I took off his dark glasses and looked at him through them. His fair yellow-tinged skin looked as though it had received a coat of blue washing. Through the dark lenses, the red bedcover looked like clotted blood and the black wood of the rosewood bed looked like the alluvium from the banks of the Ganga. That was an interesting sight. Only the golden tongue of the statue of Durga at the head of the bed was a deep yellow.

'Tell me, what is the connection between Nagpanchami and your visit here?'

'The goddess of Bengal is not Durga.'

I put my hand on his shoulder and caressed the soft white skin of his throat with my index finger. He squirmed as if my touch tickled him, then firmly held my finger in his hand. Though she may be unarmed, be wary of the woman who comes into your bedroom of her own will—that is what men learn from the world. Thakuma said if the prey who should be running away in terror decides to turn around, raise its head and walk straight back to the predator, that will scare away any beast, no matter how menacing.

'Doesn't the whole world celebrate Durga as the goddess of Bengal?'

'That's because they fear Devi Manasa.'

I took his hand in mine and began to stroke it gently. He took fright and shrank into himself. A thousand tiny baby snakes of fear and suspicion began to uncoil and writhe all over him; those green eyes revealed that helplessly.

'Ah—say, what made you bring me here?' He withdrew his hand slowly.

'I haven't had an iota of peace,' I told him truthfully. 'It's like someone threw a noose around my neck the last time I came here, and has been pulling the other end hard since.'

He smiled weakly. 'No escape from the noose for even a moment!'

'What to do, can't help it—am I not of the hangman's blood?' I sounded powerless. 'I wanted to see you. I wished to talk to you, wander about Kolkata with you, see all the streets and roads I've seen only on TV with you. I want to experience them with you.'

Sanjeev Kumar's brow furrowed. The cord of suspicion was tightening further. I enjoyed the unease and anxiety on his face.

'Sanju babu, I am a poor girl from an ordinary family. People like me—we don't have the right to even see this world. That's reserved for people like you. What, then, are people like me to do?'

'Why are you putting yourself down? Surely you are no ordinary girl?'

Fearing that he would start lecturing me again about womanhood and self-respect, I pressed my lips to his. He was thoroughly confounded.

'Hey! What're you doing?' He jerked away from me.

The snakes raised Manasa after her father abandoned her in the snake pit and ran for his life. They carried her out of the snake pit and bathed her in the Adi Ganga. They fed her; became her cradle and her swing. Black, white and red snakes became her ornaments. Their tails became her garments. Seven black cobras with priceless nagamani jewels encrusted on their hood formed her diadem. When she perspired, venom-coloured blue sapphires fell off her forehead, breasts and navel. When she came of age, Vasuki took her to her father, the god Shiva. Not recognizing his own daughter, Shiva first tried to marry her. When she opened her third eye to curse him, he realized who she was. Her dazzling beauty made Chandi apprehensive. She began to conspire to drive her away, while Manasa tried hard to win the love of her father and stepmother. However, all her efforts were in vain. It was she who saved him from the deadly venom he swallowed during the churning of the Ocean of Milk, but Chandi was so envious of her beauty that she even stabbed her in the eye when she was asleep. Later, when Chandi kicked her to the ground, Manasa turned her into a statue with a single intense look from her one eye. Shiva begged her to revive Chandi but soon after, he abandoned her again under the shade of a bael tree, ordering her never to set foot in her father's home. When the tears of anger and hatred that filled his eyes fell to the ground, Netra was born. He offloaded the job of caring for Manasa to Netra and vanished. From then, Manasa, who had been gentle and loving, became a fury, always quarrelsome and vengeful.

'You didn't show the least interest in our wedding plans. Why this sudden burst of love?' He moved away some more.

'This is not love or any such thing.'

'Then?'

'The pain I felt when you mangled my body—it is still there. How can any woman love a man who has not offered her a loving touch?' I touched my left breast as I asked him.

He drew back as if bitten by a snake with slow-spreading venom. Then, rubbing his eyes, he got up, as if looking for his glasses, paced around the room and returned to me.

'Chetna, you have only misconceptions about me.'

'From the day I met you, I have lost track of what is right and what is wrong. One day you pass the death sentence, the next day you order that the person who carried it out be killed . . .'

'Kill, kill, kill! Is that all you can think of? You are mentally ill!'

'The most dangerous of contagions: mental illness,' I laughed quite merrily.

'Why do you laugh like this infernally?'

It was too much for him to bear.

To get rid of Manasa, Shiva fixed her marriage to a venerable sage, Jagatkaru. The envious Chandi promised her wedding clothes and jewels, but did not keep her word. As the appointed hour drew close, poor Manasa worried about how she would cover her shame. The snakes consoled her. They became her ornaments. Thinking of Manasa in the sage's mud hut in the middle of the forest, adorned from head to toe, gleaming in the light of a stone lamp, made my heart ardent and tender. Snakes in hues of black, white, blue, red and gold in place of jewels. Instead of flower garlands, black cobras with brilliant gems on their hoods. But Chandi's envy knew no bounds. The moment Jagatkaru stepped into the bridal chamber, she sneaked in some frogs. Manasa's snakes got distracted; they slipped off her body and went for the frogs. Seeing snakes emerge from his bride's body as if from a snake pit, Jagatkaru took fright and ran away. Poor naked Manasa broke down crying in the little hut. Shiva had to threaten and persuade Jagatkaru to return. The venerable sage approached his bride, trembling, his eyes closed. He was loath to touch her. To be absolved of his duty, he created an infant, a son, Astika, using the powers he had acquired through his penance, dropped him in Manasa's lap, and fled. Once again she was left alone. The wrathful Manasa sat on a blooming lotus beneath the hoods of seven black cobras, the snakes swirling and sliding on her body. Manasa could never forgive those who did not respect her precisely because she had weathered insult, betrayal and insecurity. I could see that.

'Come, come, sit near me,' I called. 'Do you remember, the day before the hanging was postponed, the two of us were here . . .' I smiled confidently at him.

His kiss, the way his moustache brushed on my neck and cheek, like the fine strands at the end of a moist rope . . . I lay back on the bed and looked at the statue at its head. Poor Durga's tongue hung out. Her lovely wide eyes were fixed on me.

'Don't you want to fuck me at least once?' I asked, trying to hide my laugh.

'Your voice brims with hatred, Chetna.'

'Aren't you men sick and tired yet of women who give in meekly?'

'I'd really wanted to marry you . . .'

'I have no such desire, but I do want to know how you are going to fuck me at least one time. My soul needs to know. I want to know what the man I loved, whose love I wanted, is really like. What if I die before I know that?' I laughed. 'Just think of it, me, going round and round in this room of yours, with a long tail clear as crystal, soft as molten wax . . .'

He raised his eyes, not able to make sense of what I was saying.

'Everything is wrong at the office,' he murmured. 'In truth, the only thing blocking our marriage . . .'

His face was so handsome. How I wished to turn into a serpent, slowly slide towards his feet, slither up his body, higher and higher, raise the jewel-clad hood and thrust my forked tongue at his face! His green eyes would roll in fear. The red of my nagamani would be reflected in them. After that, there would be no need to get married; nor would it be pertinent. But the thought of a bridegroom who feared me, who threw me a child shutting his eyes in fear, was disgusting indeed. Manasa needed worshippers and so she tried to turn everyone into a devotee. Even the Muslim ruler Hasan became one, but not the Shaivite Chand Sadagar.

'How did your ancestor reach Kolkata?' I asked.

'Who knows?' he replied, puzzled by the sudden change in the topic of conversation.

'Okay, let me help you understand. He came by ship. He came to purchase stocks of rice for Ceylon. Around 1773 or '74.'

He looked at me, even more puzzled. 'How do you know that?'

'When he arrived with gold coins jingling in his waist pouch, there was a river here called the Adi Ganga.' I sighed heavily. 'Bahula was swept away by that river.'

'Bahula? Who?'

'Lakshminder was her husband.'

'I can't make head or tail of this!'

'You know no history, no legend!' I was scornful.

Bahula's husband Lakshminder was the son of Chand Sadagar, who was an ardent Shaivite. He worshipped only Shiva and Durga, and ignored Manasa. Rather, he reviled her as the deity of the untouchables and tribals. Furious, Manasa vowed to make him bow to her. Six of his sons died of snakebite. His trading ventures collapsed. Despite these misfortunes, Sadagar was determined to bow only to Shiva. He boarded a ship to expand his trade to other lands. When the ship returned with loads of wealth, Manasa unleashed a terrible tempest and lashing rain. Durga went to his rescue; but Manasa urged her father to call her back. Sadagar's ship sank. Manasa let him swim to shore where her devotee, Chandraketu, lived. He too urged Sadagar to adore Manasa, but Sadagar was adamant that he would rather die than bow before a daughter abandoned by her father and a wife forsaken by her husband. He had now lost all his material wealth and became a beggar. Manasa thought of a new way to make him submit. She let him reach home and begin efforts to rebuild his shattered life. Then, at her suggestion, Krishna's grandson Aniruddha and his love Usha left Heaven to be reborn as Sadagar's son Lakshminder and his friend's daughter Bahula. They grew up, fell in love, and their families agreed to the match. However, when they examined Lakshminder's horoscope, it was revealed that he would die of snakebite on his wedding night. The two families fell into deep sadness. Many well-wishers advised Sadagar to pray to Devi Manasa, but he refused. Instead, he went ahead with the wedding and built a bridal chamber which no snake could enter. But a snake did enter, and the groom did die of snakebite. In those days, those who died of snake venom were neither cremated nor buried but placed on a bamboo litter and set afloat on the Ganga. Unable to see her beloved go thus, Bahula too jumped into the river. For six whole months, they floated on the river, the young girl and the decaying body, from village to village, until they reached the village of Manasa's foster mother Netra. When she saw the young girl accompanying the decaying corpse, she swam into the river and brought them ashore. At her request, Manasa appeared to Bahula and promised to give Lakshminder back his life if Sadagar became her devotee. Sadagar had to admit defeat before his daughter-in-law's entreaties and his son came back to life. He began to worship Devi Manasa on the fifth night of the new moon in the month of Sravan. But he turned his face away when he bowed before the inferior-born goddess of uncertain paternity, and when he offered flowers, he always did so with his left hand.

Sanjeev Kumar was pacing the room, totally lost. The training he had received from this world as a man reminded him that coitus was important in such circumstances. But he was afraid to take a woman who had walked into his bedroom of her own free will. When the forty-two-year-old man who came to buy rice with gold jingling in the pouch at his waist got off the ship in Kolkata in 1773, the Adi Ganga in front of Kalighat was not the pond it is today. It was a youthful river full of vitality. It broke with playful sounds against banks thick with the avid black of alluvium. Bamboo rafts, sailboats and canoes spread on its bosom. Human beings swimming in it and offering oblations made it come alive.

'Do you know what happened to your ancestor?' I asked.

He tried to smile. 'Who knows? I've heard that my grandfather came here in search of him. Or was it my grandfather's father? Don't know ...'

'But I do.'

Disbelief was writ large on Sanjeev Kumar's face.

'He was hanged.'

He looked as if he had been slapped. A fantastic serpent, blue-black as fate itself, slithered through the cells of my body, making them burst into a pleasurable tingle like grass sprouting from soil.

'Wh-what for?' he stuttered.

'For robbery. For stealing gold from a merchant from Talashery.'

'Chi! Utter rubbish! Gross lie! Don't vent your anger towards me with this nonsense, Chetna!'

'It's the truth!'

'How the hell do you know?'

'Of all the many thousands dispatched by my ancestors, only he came back to tell us what death feels like.'

I wanted to laugh. He looked at me incredulously. I liked his face at that moment. There is great bliss—even in these days of democracy—in receiving devotion, even if it is expressed with a turned face, and in receiving worship, even if it is performed with the left hand.

42

The appropriate reply to Sanjeev Kumar's question—how come you Grddha Mullicks alone store up such frayed, old memories—was surely in the pamphlet that George Fernandes, that hunter who was eventually trapped in his own net, brought out on 15 August 1975 while he was still underground. He wrote, if three people each tell the same story to just three others, in eighteen operations, taking, say, eighteen hours, 38,74,20,489 people will have heard it. Yes, in other words, the entire adult population of the country. Unknowingly, Father, Thakuma and I propagated this formula of 'three raised to the power of eighteen'. We exerted ourselves to swim towards our origins so that we may survive. If each memory would lay three eggs and the three memories hatch into three philosophies, the lives of the entire adult population in this world would become eternal through the equalizing wisdom of death and desire, like the river, the sea, the earth and the sky. As I lay back on his red-covered bed with a freedom I did not actually enjoy, I stirred with unease, thinking of the shattering of the networks of three, of words rendered infertile, of words castrated, and of the earth turning barren as blood flowed over it. I felt nothing but derision for Sanjeev Kumar.

But it was useless to blame him. Narayanan, who attained considerable knowledge in Sanskrit in Nagercoil, was penniless. He went to Talashery and married the daughter of a wealthy rice merchant and thus became rich. The tale of what took place after Narayanan boarded the ship to Kolkata would sound unbelievable to people like Sanjeev Kumar. Only those who know of eighteenth-century Chitpur and Kolkata are capable of understanding and appreciating it. How could he imagine the adolescence of Chitpur—the gushing Adi Ganga, the Hooghly, the royal tigers that came out of the Sunderbans to sunbathe, the slaves auctioned off at Ahrtala and Nimtala, the little huts thatched with bamboo, like grey mould on white bread? Behind the grand mansions that lined Chitpur's main road, aptly described as its major artery, tiny paths twisted and turned like small veins, uniting and separating, giving life to liquor dens, dancing halls and brothels, and then slithering like snakes towards the banks of the Ganga. Like Devi Manasa, the city made them her ornament and weapon. What tests may have awaited the scholar from a distant land?

'When my forefather set off for Kolkata, his son was but a young boy. He went there in search of his father after many years, but could not find any information. If he had been hanged as you say, wouldn't he have gleaned the news from someone?'

There was a note of accusation in his voice.

'Hangings were very frequent those days. Every day almost, corpses hung on gallows set up in market places. Many a time my ancestors had to split the work among themselves to ensure that justice was being done all over town.'

I ran my fingers along the shiny smoothness of the bed. Men are like tortoises, with hard shells and soft bodies inside. When the shell breaks the helpless creature inside trembles in fear. I was elated at being able to hurt him so. But what I had said was the truth. There used to be gallows trees in the present-day Bara Bazar, on Fancy Lane behind the Raj Bhavan and the junction near the Lal Bazar police station where Bentinck Street and Chitpur Road meet. Many were the bodies that were hanged on these gallows, concrete manifestations of the kind of justice handed out by my ancestors.

'No, no, impossible! You can't be talking about my ancestor—he was a great scholar and thinker. He must have gone to Kashi or Gaya and attained moksha or nirvana there,' he protested further, having thought for a while.

'Just as hanging is my family profession, stealing is yours, Sanju babu. No wonder caste is such a glaring reality in this country even now.'

I threw yet another noose around his neck with a beatific smile. He struggled hard in it, not able to even think of fucking me at least once though I was there, in his bedroom, unarmed and helpless. The pleasure Pingalakeshini had felt dawned on me now. Sanjeev Kumar paced the room, totally disturbed and arguing with himself.

'So, even if we concede he was hanged to death, it can't have been for robbery. Maybe it was for murder. Yes, there's a chance that it happened that way. Suppose someone attacked him—yes, he must have retaliated in self-defence—and the aggressor must have lost his life. Or let's suppose he did steal. But he wouldn't have been hanged for that! What you say has too many holes in it, Chetna!'

I laughed. 'When you steal without the owner's knowledge, you steal only his wealth. But when you steal after threatening him with a gun or knife, you steal not only his wealth but also his sense of security, and his faith in other human beings!'

'You are raving mad!' He lost his temper. 'Another word about my ancestor, Chetna, and I'll lose control!'

That was a truly honest statement. So I was not provoked. For those who have nothing to hold on to, only the greatness of their ancestors remains.

'It is easy to create darkness by shutting one's eyes, Sanju babu. But what has happened has happened. I can't say if he really stole or not.

But he was arrested for robbery; there are documents to prove that.'

Once, the day before two Musalmans, two Europeans and four Bengalis were to be hanged for robbery, my ancestor Dharmaraja Grddha Mullick's paternal uncle Satyanatha Grddha Mullick dreamt during his siesta that the noose around the condemned man's neck would not tighten. After offering the puja and the sacrifice to Ma Kali at night, he set out from home, handing over three of the six neatly coiled and readied hangman's ropes to his younger brother Jagannatha and carrying the other three himself. The two travelled in the horse carriage sent by the deputy commisioner of police in the dead of night. The carriage ran fast through the area then called Shimulia (and later called Shimla) for its abundance of Shimul trees, bells and hooves resounding. There was a sound of rippling water, and then, suddenly, someone jumped in the way of the carriage with a blood-curdling scream. Hand me all your belongings and run for your life, he ordered. Grandfather Satyanatha picked up the burning torch that hung over the wheels of the carriage and held it up to the intruder's face. He was still brandishing the sword that was wet with blood and pressing down the wheel with a single muscular leg.

Grandfather spoke kindly to him. 'Chorer mayer kanna, ugar baaro noi, phukar baaro noi . . .'

The attacker was a bit taken aback, but rebounded, pressing the sword against Grandfather's neck and yelling: 'Making fun of me? Me . . . who set out after a blood sacrifice to Chiteswari?'

'Son, do not tell stories of animal sacrifice to the hangman!' Grandfather Satyanatha smiled. Jagannatha Grddha Mullick, who had been crouching inside, quickly tied a noose and threw it around the robber's neck, shouting to the driver to take the horses forward. The horses bolted like lightning and the dacoit was dragged all the way down. 'Stop, stop,' called Grandfather Satyanatha. The driver stopped. Grandfather hopped down, pulled out the sharp knife he carried at his waist, and cut through the noose around the man's neck, setting him free. His pulse had stopped. Grandfather massaged his neck and beat his chest to revive him. Helping him up, he gave the dacoit a drink of water, made sure that he could walk, and then continued on his journey. But in the melee, he had lost the copy of the chief magistrate's order confirming the death sentence. The policeman guarding the gallows had to ride to the chief magistrate and inform him of the loss. The chief magistrate had been getting ready to witness the hanging with his family; the news made him very angry. Slapping the policeman hard, he rushed to his desk and, taking his quill, rewrote the order from memory: 'On the tenth of June, let them be taken from jail to the place of execution, which place the sheriff directed to prepare as near the house of the slain victim Sushil Mohan, as may be convenient, and there let the said Madhu Datta, Mir Ali Muhammad, Anderson, Healy, Ishaq, Subrato Datta and every one of them be hanged by the neck . . .'

Sanjeev Kumar kept staring at me. The contempt and scepticism on his face made me yawn. I got up, bored.

'You had requested, right, that you want to fuck me at least once? I came so that you could do that. But you are only capable of saying such things, not doing them. Like Jatindranath's noose, this too keeps becoming longer and longer. You are never going to fuck me!'

I took out the purse from my cloth bag and looked for change.

'It's hard to get out of this place after dark, especially for a well-formed young woman like you.'

I gave him a sidelong glance. 'Why? Do some real men come to the red street occasionally?'

His face revealed that each of my words wounded him. Pretending not to hear, Sanjeev Kumar repeated, stubborn as a child: 'No, my ancestor was a rich man. He had no motive to steal . . .'

'Did you steal Thakuma's coin and those diamond studs because you were in need?'

He wasn't even listening. 'This city makes the rich poor, and the poor rich. All in a trice.'

Thakuma had so many stories of European sailors arriving with fat purses of gold and ending up in the Maidan, forced to sleep in the open, suffering mosquito bites. There even used to be a big gang of white thieves in the city—'sahib chor'. My Grandfather Satyanatha hanged to death first the English sahibs, then the Bengalis, and finally, the Musalmans. When he put the noose on the last Musalman's neck, the condemned man said in a failing voice: 'If you hang me, the sin will pursue you till the Last Judgement. I am innocent.'

My ancestor's hands shook. The rope was actually shorter than what was needed. It was also frayed, having been dragged along the road. But he closed his eyes, thought of Ma Kali and Bhagawan Mahadev, and fixed the noose. The man had been made to stand on a high stool. The magistrate dropped the red kerchief when it was time. Grandfather pulled the stool away. The man dangled in the air, struggling. The crowd which had witnessed the other five hangings shouted in fascination at the sight. His neck bones must be broken, my forefather thought. But just then, to the great surprise of everyone, the rope snapped and the man fell to the ground. There was a moment's silence, and then everyone rushed to pick him up. Grandfather slid the noose off his neck. He screamed and writhed, and was then still.

That day Grandfather Satyanatha also had to punish two slave girls who had run away from their master's home. They were little girls, sold in the monthly slave market, which used to be just next door from our house in Nimtala Ghat. Their master was a merchant. The judge awarded them fifteen lashes each. When the cane fell on their thin black backs, drops of blood spattered on his face. The sweeper who had sold empty bottles thrown away from her master's house was also given the same punishment. She and the shopkeeper who had bought those bottles were both whipped and paraded around town tied behind an ox cart. But all the hallowed justice that Grandfather Satyanatha meted out that day was rendered meaningless because of the snapped rope. Upset that he had brought infamy to the goddess of justice, he went to the Chiteswari temple, fasted there for a day and night, and meditated. The dacoits and thieves and robbers who had come there to offer animal sacrifice ran away, seeing him. When daylight spread, he made his way home through the thick foliage that surrounded the temple, watching out for snakes while making a vow to Devi Manasa. All of a sudden, he found his way barred by a robust young man with a bluish mark on his neck, like Bhagawan Mahadev himself. He held a piece of paper and began to read aloud from it: 'On the tenth of June, let them be taken from jail to the place of execution, which place the sheriff directed to prepare as near the house of the slain victim . . .'

'Who are you?' asked Grandfather Satyanatha, deeply surprised.

'Naren dakat.'

'I've heard of you—so you are the one who gives away stolen wealth to the poor.'

'All lands need some such people, otherwise the land will be ruined.'

'Why are you here?'

'Yesterday's incident . . .'

'Work, my son, is God.'

'Work, Mahashai, is indeed God.' He folded his palms.

'I feared that you had died . . .' Grandfather said looking at Naren dakat's body, bruised black from being dragged on the road.

'The fear of death? In a hangman?'

'Son, not one of those who have been sent off with nooses made by us Grddha Mullicks have come back to tell us how it felt.'

'I have come. I will come again.'

There are two views about how our Chitpur got its name. Some say that it was named after Chiteswari Devi; others say that there was a dacoit who lived here, Chitte dakat. Naren dakat set out to rob after offering a human sacrifice at the Chiteswari temple. Ma Kali, the goddess of death and justice, is also the goddess of robbery and dacoity. Naren dakat, who had risen to fame after Chitte dakat, was hanged by Grandfather Satyanatha, just as he had predicted. He lived at the end of Gopal Kristo Lane in Tantapada, on the road that goes to Nimtala east of Beadon Street, but none of his relatives, except his mother, ever saw him. He was saved by the poor when the police tried to catch him, but was betrayed by a fellow robber. He was caught while looting the house of a merchant from Talashery, and sentenced to death along with three accomplices. When Grandfather Satyanatha set out to execute the sentences, one of his coiled ropes broke the cords with which it was bound, straightened as if it were alive and fell on the floor, and its free end caught fire. That was the most evil portent possible! He was terrified and put out the fire with his bare hands, singeing his palms. As he walked towards the gallows Grandfather's heart thumped like never before, like a war drum, and his fingers grew cold. The police officer read out the order when the condemned convicts were lined up. Grandfather silently promised three goat kids to Kali for strength. Contrary to their usual eagerness, the crowd this time wept silently.

'On the 14 August let them be taken from the jail to the place of execution, which place the sheriff directed to prepare, as near the house of the slain victim Kunjali Mappila, as conveniently may be, and there let the said Naren dakat, Hari dakat and Ali dakat, every one of them be hanged by the neck . . .'

Hari dakat's and Ali dakat's hangings went smoothly. When it was time to tie up the limbs of Naren dakat who watched the proceedings emotionlessly, he murmured, 'There is a mistake in that order. I am not Naren, I am Narayanan.'

To Grandfather who was looking at him uncomprehendingly, he said, 'I come from down south.'

'Should never have . . .'

'My mother Vasundhara Devi thinks that I am her long-lost son . . .'

'Why did you do such a thing to that poor woman?'

They could not speak further. The noose was fixed in its proper place. When the magistrate let the kerchief drop, Grandfather pushed away the stool mechanically. The man struggled on the rope. Grandfather shut his eyes and waited a second. Then, with a colossal sound, the gallows tree came crashing to the ground. People scattered, screaming. Naren dakat lay thrashing on the ground. Grandfather went up and cut the noose off his neck. He writhed again and screamed in pain. Grandfather helped him up and gave him water to drink. The deputy police commissioner and the judge left to prepare a fresh order. Narayanan dakat opened his eyes on Grandfather's lap.

'True, you have come back,' Grandfather whispered warmly.

'You shouldn't have cut the noose . . . I had begun to find my way . . .'

'Those who set out never come back, son,' Grandfather said, smiling.

'But I speak the truth. I know what death is like . . . maybe I came back to tell you about it.'

Grandfather tensed. He swallowed.

'First, I felt the pain from the noose tightening. Though outwardly smooth, I found out that the noose contains many thousands of sharp spikes; besides the terrible pain when they pierce the tender skin of the neck, I also felt the entire weight of my body on the neck. The body separated very rapidly, like fat in curdled milk. A sharp dart of pain, as if from a strung bow, shot up my spine, piercing all my organs, passing in a straight line through the heart and the brain, reaching the skull. Before my eyes, a tongue of flame flew out, like a bird released from a cage. That moment, all pain ceased as if pulled back sharply. At the same time, the sensation of being caressed with a feather from the feet upwards enveloped me. The calm body felt delicate, without the skeleton's hardness. I felt weightless. I was below a mountain. I began to climb it, my feet not touching the ground, with no effort at all . . .'

His eyes were full. Struggling for air, he told Grandfather. 'Death is climbing a mountain. Believe me!'

Just then the judge's carriage returned, its bells ringing. The deputy police commissioner's black stallion kicked up the dust near Bara Bazar. The fresh order was ready. They took Grandfather and Naren dakat to the gallows near Fancy Lane. The hangman and his victim took a shaky ride together towards death in the same vehicle.

'Why did you become a thief?' Grandfather asked him, truly grieved.

'The question was whether I should become a white thief or a black one. I chose to be black . . .'

A short while later Naren dakat's dead body dangled from the gallows tree on Fancy Lane. Grandfather wept after he had delivered justice. He took a hundred and eight dips in the Ganga to rid himself of sin and started for home. At the top of the steps that led down to the ghat he found a woman waiting for him. She had covered her face with her aanchal.

'Who are you?' asked Grandfather.

She raised her tearful face to him.

'Why do you cry?'

'Chorer mayer kanna, ugar baaro noi, phukar baaro noi . . .' she said. The undeniable yet impermissible tears of the mother of the dacoit.

'What did they do to him?'

Grandfather stood before her like a guilty man. The hangman did not get to know much about the victim after he had hanged him and taken his wages.

'They didn't return his body, not even a piece of bone. Why, have they eaten it up?' she burst out. 'Give me a piece of his bone at least. I will break it in thirds and make three Narens from them. And if each of them creates three Narens, Mahashai, I will gift to this world Narens too numerous to wipe out even if all those dogs, your white and black masters, get together.'

Staggered, Grandfather stayed silent. Across the centuries, my body tingled in excitement.

'The story's taken a lot of time, Chetna. I have to go,' Sanjeev Kumar looked serious and glanced at his watch.

'I need to talk to you.' I refused to get up.

'You should not be talking to me, but to the world . . . and you are not prepared to do that.'

'I did love you . . .' My voice congealed. He looked at me carefully.

'Did love you—what does that mean?'

'I believed you would love me . . .'

He tried to smile without giving me an answer. 'I wanted to marry you. But you and your baba, did you both not insult me? But I have no ill will, only that you must obey me.'

'Who do you take me to be? Prey or slave?'

'Who did you take me to be?

'My mate . . .' My voice could go no further.

Destroying all efforts to smile, the tears pushed through. With all the helplessness and sense of inadequacy that marked me at the age of twenty-two, I stood, head bowed, before a man. He could have held out his hand to me. Or rejected me. He did neither. Instead, he turned me into an object for sale. Sanjeev Kumar's phone rang then. He took the call and walked a few paces, relieved.

'Great achievement, Harish babu!' His face lit up. He turned to me, looking triumphant. 'They have agreed to write to the President!'

'Who?'

'Mridula Chatterjee's family. They are requesting him not to set aside the death sentence. Now things are going to heat up!'

My heart grew dark.

'They were not in the limelight all this while. Till now other people have been screaming; the victim's kin were quiet. But the rules of the game will change now!'

He became cheerful.

'Did you hear Harish babu ask: "How did you manage this?" Truly, Chetna, I don't know how. I don't know how they changed their mind.' He sighed.

'Three raised to the power of eighteen.'

He didn't grasp it. Someone knocked at the door. Sanjeev Kumar became alert. He opened the door; a shadow crossed his face. The girl I had seen on my last visit peeped in.

'Didi asked who came in with Sanju babu?'

'Why does she want to know?' he barked tersely.

'She wanted to see, she said.'

'Tell her I'll show her when it is time.'

She stood for a moment, not knowing what to do with those harsh words. After she left, he began to hurry. 'Chetna, you must leave. I don't have to tell you . . . this isn't a good place.'

He got ready to leave, glasses back in place. I didn't want to stay back any more. I went down the steps, downcast. I was interested in his history. But he didn't share it. Like any ordinary fish in the river or sea, he lived locked inside the present. I felt a deep sense of loss about Narayanan dakat's bones. If only Vasundhara Devi had got a piece, if only she had broken it in thirds and created three Narayanans, if only each of them had created another three, and thus within an hour, the entire adult population of a country!

I was disappointed.

43

Ramnatha Grddha Mullick was the grandson of the sister of Satyanatha Grddha Mullick who had put Naren dakat to death. It was he who made our bodies shiver and our minds fill with sourness at the mention of the courtesans of Sonagachi. He was just sixteen; a poet, musician and orator like my father. At the time when Grandfather Satyanatha had first met Naren dakat, he was with Wajid Ali Shah, the exiled king of Oudh, living with him as a trusted attendant and disciple. Whenever

Father put on a laundered kurta and dhoti and set off for Sonagachi, Thakuma would warn him: don't forget the tale of Ramnatha Grdhha Mullick. Though he had seen, since childhood, his grandfather and father and brothers put to death many criminals, when Ramnatha actually witnessed a murder, he was shattered. Thakuma also cited his story to prove that none of us could kill without the vital signal—the magistrate dropping the red kerchief.

Ramnatha used to sing beautifully the sad song *Babul mora naihaar chhooto jaye . . .* which Wajid Ali Shah composed when he was exiled from Oudh to Calcutta in 1856. A picture of the nawab, with his childlike face and belly that was as round as a small hillock, resting his knee on long cushions and enjoying the music with his eyes shut, has been preserved in a contemporary oil painting. Thakuma claimed that the picture showed clearly the tears flowing down the nawab's cheeks. Whenever she heard Saigal sing the same song on radio or TV, Thakuma would shed tears, raise her arms and fold her palms together, saluting the ancestor she had never seen. When I stepped out of Sanjeev Kumar's apartment the same song drifted in from some room in the upper storey of the mansion. I stood in the veranda for a second. The song was of a bride taking leave of her father, but it really referred to death.

O my father, I am leaving home.
Four bearers lift my palanquin . . .

We Bengalis have no difficulty fathoming the sorrow of a small ruler powerless to defend himself, leaving his crown and sceptre behind to live as a refugee elsewhere. Hearing the woman's soulful rendition of the song, my eyes grew moist too.

I sang along silently as I went down the steps. If only he would call me back, I yearned inside. I knew it was not because I loved him but because, selfishly, I wanted myself to be loved. And so when he dismissed me with a cold 'Okay, Chetna, I am busy,' it didn't offend me. The sweltering breeze blowing in through the courtyard tried to console my sweaty body. Twisting the strap of the cloth bag on my shoulder, I walked down with an empty heart. The peal of anklets could be heard from some room; the sounds of an ektara and a sitar too. *Babul mora . . .*

sounded above them; I walked slowly so that I could catch the whole song. But then one of the women who were washing dishes in the courtyard slipped and fell while carrying a very large cooking pot, hitting her head on the floor. I left my bag on the lowest step and rushed to her just as the other woman, who had a bad leg, was trying to lift her up.

'Didi, be careful,' I told her. Blood trickled down her forehead.

The other woman, with innumerable lines on her forehead and the bad leg, went back to washing the dishes.

'My head spins . . . water . . .'

I looked around. The woman with the bad leg pointed towards the kitchen. I helped the injured woman out of the courtyard. Grasping my arm with one hand and bracing herself against the pillar with the other, she stepped up on to the veranda. There were two other women in the kitchen, which had large pots simmering full of vegetables, meat and fish. As we passed that way they looked warily at me.

'What's happening here?' I asked. 'A wedding feast?'

'Isn't there a wedding here every day?' she complained, stroking her forehead. She led me to a row of small tin sheds in the backyard off the kitchen. I got her some water from the earthen jar in the veranda there and wiped her blood off.

'God bless you . . .' she said passionlessly, sitting on the bare floor and sipping the water.

I wet her forehead, dabbing the wound with my dupatta to dry it.

'What is your name, Didi?'

'Just right for this house—Sushila!'

There was bitterness in her laugh.

'You aren't from Kolkata, are you?'

'Jellingham . . .' she sighed. 'I had fifteen bighas of land there. I was thirty when the ship factory came. They took four hundred acres. My land too . . .'

I could connect the rest of the dots easily.

'I am old now,' she looked at me harshly. 'It's your time now.'

I was stupefied.

'Fix your mind on it and you can find first-class babus! All the fellows who come here are big, big ministers, politicians, rich kids . . . Catch hold of a good one and you can live well for the rest of your life!'

Feeling amused and insulted all at the same time, I glanced around without looking at her. It was a large compound. Behind the shed was a house that revealed the nakedness of its red bricks within the crumbling concrete. A sari hung out to dry in the balcony rose in the breeze like the sail of a ship. The holes in it were magnified.

'Don't trust old men, they don't value a woman's love,' she continued. 'The young fellows of sixteen or seventeen . . . catch one of them and your life is fulfilled! If the first girl is a smart one, they won't have the guts to seek another one at that age. The older chaps aren't like that. They want to sample more and more . . . several . . . different things . . . all in a short while. They are never happy, nor will they make anyone happy!'

Her voice gashed my heart like a sharp-edged knife. Hers was a terrible face—reddened eyes, a large hole in one nostril left by an absent nose stud, clotted blood on her forehead. I felt afraid and so I tried to imagine her as a busy housewife in Jellingham, moving deftly between chores in a house with cows, hay and a heap of grain. But even that left me very afraid.

'Or, if you are more interested in cash, look for thirty- or forty-year-old fellows, householders. They are worse than dogs. Have no clue how to love a woman or understand her. But if you can learn to argue and get your price, your purse will swell for sure.'

On one of the upper floors *Babul mora . . .* continued. My eyes were moist. When they met hers, hers grew wet too. I ran my fingers gently on her slowly balding head. Her eyes grew warm. 'Go, go to your work. You can make some cash only at this age!'

'I have another job, Didi.' I wiped my eyes and tried to smile.

'What job?'

'I am a hangman!'

I said that dramatically. Almost like Father, when he thumps the desk and tries to console people who come to the tea shop after the funeral rites and sit with bowed heads and heavy hearts, declaring, 'Look, as a hangman who has dispatched four hundred and fifty-one people, let me tell you, death is not in our hands.' This is what probably made her sit up gaping in surprise.

'Hangman? You? Why are you here?'

My tongue slipped right back in. I wanted to tell her that, for

342

generations, so many in my family have come to Sonagachi seeking their desires. It was at the age of sixteen that Ramnatha was brought here by the nawab's servants—it was known as Sonagaji then—to learn the intricacies of intercourse with a woman. It was full of red-brick houses, big and small. He walked through the labyrinthine network of paths with a beating heart and perspiring palms. Finally, he reached the interiors of a two-storeyed house. In the glow of the gas lamps mounted on the walls, a beautiful woman, past forty, entered seductively. She became the first and last woman in his life. In the supreme pleasure he experienced that night, he fell in love with her and decided to marry her. Listening to the young chap with the barest trace of a moustache on his face, the woman laughed. But he was determined indeed. He told her about his relatives near Nimtala Ghat. When it was dawn, he started out, promising to return at night; but no sooner had he stepped out of the room than a young woman, her nakedness barely covered by her sari, rushed out of another room and fell at his feet. Before Ramnatha could even move, the man she was running from caught up and stabbed her viciously. Pausing long enough to make sure that she was gone, he bounded into another room, looking for someone else. The young woman lay on the floor, bleeding from her last struggle. Her large eyes bulged towards Ramnatha as she breathed her last in his lap. Ramnatha collapsed; for a whole day, he wandered the streets, forgetting the way back home. In the end, he reached home and fell grievously ill. He was feverish for weeks together in the memory of that terrible incident.

'Why did you come here? Why should a hangman come here?'

The woman, Sushila, was clearly angry now.

'I came with Sanjeev Kumar babu.'

'I know that. But for what?'

'He said he'll marry me,' I tried to joke.

She gaped again with surprise. 'Sanju babu?' She considered it. 'That's not possible. Don't believe him.'

I didn't respond. I was thinking of the young man who had murdered a young girl, Bidhu, in Sonagachi. He was an innocent villager who received a proposal to marry a rich widow's daughter in Kolkata, and was invited to see the prospective bride's home. He and his relatives were impressed by the huge mansion in the city, filled with great luxury. But the biggest lure was the girl's dazzling beauty. The wedding ceremony was held in the bride's home and presided over by venerated brahmins; afterwards, both families set out for the bridegroom's house. All his relatives in the village and from other villages came in their best clothes and finery to greet the bride. There was a grand feast and payesh was served, and all those who ate the payesh began to fall senseless one by one. Unaware of this, the bridegroom waited in the bridal chamber. The bride entered, beautifully decked in jewels. When the bridegroom placed his hand lovingly on her shoulder, she looked at him with contempt. Pulling off his clothes, she sneered at his nakedness, 'So you are a man, are you?' Spitting scornfully in his face, she walked out, leaving the young man speechless with shock. He fell asleep, weeping, and was roused at dawn by loud and piteous wails. All those who had come for the feast had been robbed of their clothes and jewels. The young man sought his bride and her family among those who rushed to cover themselves somehow. He ran over a long distance following the wheel marks of their carriages. Finally, he went to Kolkata in search of them, but found that the grand mansion had actually been rented by the woman posing as the rich widow for a few days. Having lost his money and his honour, the young man decided not to return to his village. He went about from house to house in Kolkata, looking for the girl and her mother; in the end he reached Sonagachi. Bidhu did not realize that the client in her room was the man she had married some time back. Seeking revenge for his humiliation, he ravaged her body through the night. When she tried to escape, unable to bear the terrible pain, he hunted her down.

'Leave now, it is getting late.'

Sushila di shook me back into reality. 'Why did you tell me not to trust Sanju babu?' I asked her in a circumspect tone. *He probably has a wife and children back home*—Ramu da's words rang in my ears.

'He will never marry anyone.'

'Really? Why?'

'Don't you know what this place is?'

'Avinash Kaviraj Road . . .'

Hearing someone call from the kitchen, Sushila di drew her aanchal over her head, slowly extended her knee, got up and went into the house with a weariness too early for her age. She completed the address as she went in: 'Number 15, Aparajita Apartments.'

I didn't understand. I followed her back through the kitchen and into the courtyard. Picking up my bag, I prepared to leave.

'Stop!'

I spun around. Two women were coming down the staircase. One of them was the wizened old woman who had sung for me the song about the kite when I had come here the first time. The other woman was a beautiful middle-aged woman in a red silk sari. I could not tear my eyes off her face. But neither could I look long into her eyes.

'Have we met before?'

The middle-aged woman came over and fixed me in her stare. I looked at her like a fool. Her face was familiar but I couldn't recall where I had seen it. Her form, radiant as a goddess, the scent of blooming jasmines all around us, the sweetness of her voice and the intensity of her eyes left me scared and weak. It was she who had been singing before.

'Why did you come here?'

'To see Sanju babu, Di,' Sushila di answered, from the courtyard.

'Why?'

Her brow furrowed. I looked her intently. She had Sanjeev Kumar's straight hair and his long, regal nose. My body tingled.

'Didn't you hear me? What were you doing in his room?' Now her voice was harsh.

'Talking,' I said.

'Isn't it enough to talk in the studio? Do you have so much to talk that you must come here? What were you talking about?'

'History . . . the history of Sanjeev Kumar Mitra . . .'

Her eyes lit up with a smile.

'What history? Let me hear too.'

'His ancestor was a dacoit. In the eighteenth century he was hanged to death by my ancestor Satyanatha Grddha Mullick. He was the only man who came back to tell us what death feels like.'

She looked at me disbelievingly. 'Eesh!' she exclaimed. A few more moments passed.

'Come, have a cup of tea.' She took a deep breath and invited me in.

'No, I am in a hurry.' I was feeling strong again.

'Stay for a while before you leave,' she urged me.

'I don't know who you are.'

'Trailokya Devi, that's my name.' That's all she said. I yearned to hear more. But she didn't tell me anything more. 'Why, have you heard the name before?' She looked at me intently now.

I was amused. 'Have you heard the story of my ancestor Ramnatha Grddha Mullick's first visit to Sonagachi?'

'Tell me. I love to listen to stories, especially true ones!'

We eyed each other cautiously. I felt like I wanted to be with her, always. I began to tell her the story and we went towards her room on the upper floor which was far more beautifully and tastefully decorated than Sanjeev Kumar Mitra's. She bade me sit on the bed covered with a red silk spread. A place prized, traditionally, by Bengali housewives— they wept and laughed, played cards and shared sweets, all sitting on their beds.

After that first experience, Ramnatha was a shattered man. Whenever he remembered that night at Sonagachi and his first woman, he thirsted to return there. But the memory of the bloody incident always deterred him. He would lie hunched up on his bed, weeping and laughing in turn. The months went by. Then, one day, news appeared that there had been an attempt to murder a woman from Sonagachi. An acquaintance, another woman, had taken her to a nearby pond and tried to drown her in it. On investigation the police discovered that five other women had also been drowned there; their bodies were recovered. The police also found out that the same woman was apparently behind all five killings. The woman who had lured her victims, all of them women she knew, with false stories and stolen the gold jewellery they wore at the time, was sentenced to death on 4 September 1884. She kept protesting her innocence till all her appeals were rejected. On the eve of her execution, she finally confessed her misdeeds to the chief investigating officer Priyanath Mukhopadhyay. She confessed to conducting false marriages by setting up the girl Bidhu as a bride, and to luring women to the pond, promising to introduce them to a sannyasi who could increase any amount of gold by five times. She also told him her last wish. 'I want to see once again the boy Ramnatha of the Grddha Mullick family.'

346

Priyanath Mukhopadhyay arranged for that. She held Ramnatha's hands through the bars of the prison cell, and with love in her eyes, murmured: 'I will never forget you. If only all men would submit to a woman like you did . . .'

He listened in silence, his heart splintering.

'Don't forget anything that I taught you. I have taught you everything that you need to know about a woman.'

He bowed his head, weeping at the memory of that night.

'I have a wish. Will you fulfil it for me?'

He was still wordless.

'You said you would marry me—will you do it?'

He looked at her, thoroughly amazed.

'Not today, tomorrow . . . on the gallows. You must put the noose on my neck. What can be the hangman's marriage garland if not the noose?'

Ramnatha broke down. She reached out from behind the bars to stroke his young face gently. He felt weak, worn out with sadness at the thought that they would never spend a night together again.

'Why, why did you take those five lives? You who gave me a lifetime's love in a single night, how could you ensnare and kill five people?'

She had stroked his head.

'I have an adopted son. I did it so that he won't suffer. So that he won't spend his life on the verandas of whorehouses guarding them. I gave back to the world what it gave me. I give back to you what you gave me.'

When the jailer announced that it was time for the meeting to end, Ramnatha gripped the bars of the cell desperately and blurted out the question: 'Your name . . . you didn't tell me your name . . .'

'Trailokya.'

'Who gave it to you?'

'I gave myself that name. There are three worlds, the world of Desire, the world of Form, and the world of the Formless. I am of all three.'

She went away without a single tear in her eyes. Ramnatha requested that he be permitted to perform the next day's execution; Grandfather Satyanatha agreed. And thus, Ramnatha Grddha Mullick carried out his first and last execution.

'Tonight you must sing that song in my memory,' she told him when the noose was placed around her neck.

He promised.

Immersed in grief, he sent her to her death. The bones in her neck snapped easily, without the least struggle, like a leaf falling. The whole night after, he sang the nawab's song, lost in her memory.

When I finished Trailokya di let out a deep sigh. So did the other woman.

'You speak sweetly.'

'And you sing marvellously, Trailokya di.'

She smiled easily and broadly. 'I didn't know my name had so many dimensions. Thank you for telling me.'

The girl I had seen earlier came in with tea and sandesh wrapped in a banana leaf. The sandesh was truly exquisite; it made me feel very happy, suddenly.

'Trailokya di, where is your home?'

She gave me a kind look, went over to the tanpura at the head of the bed, played a note on it, came back to me, and said cryptically: 'For the past six generations, this has been our home. I am an Agrevali.'

She smiled effortlessly. The radiance and power on her face were such that age could not dim them. It made me feel a bit afraid.

'Do you know what an Agrevali is?' She got up again and walked towards the balcony. 'The belief is that we were born in the race of apsaras.'

I listened to her keenly. It was then the meaning of that mansion with white walls, red windows and nine stairways dawned on me. For the Agrevalis, prostitution is a matter of pride, like execution is for my family.

'The worst sinners are those who die without experiencing the true pleasure of sex. They are reborn even crueller and wickeder. The gods sent us to the earth to prevent such sinners from being born.'

I went red, but she was undeterred.

'We came to Kolkata from Agra. We were the dancers at the Mughal court.'

I went up to the balcony and looked out. Sonagachi seethed and bubbled. Dark, besmirched, dilapidated buildings spread out everywhere, forming a labyrinth. Female bodies set up for sale since noon still waited, sweating profusely. A bunch of sneering young men

348

chewing paan walked by, swinging their arms. A group of women who had found no clients pursued them, fighting amongst themselves. Wherever I looked, I found women with dark skin and lips painted red, like the statues of the goddesses in Kumortuli. 'Aren't all these women like that?'

She came near me, looked out, and closed the red window curtain. 'No. Not all of them. We Agrevalis do not sell our bodies, we only share our souls.'

I was flummoxed.

'No one who steps out of this place can ever hurt a woman with his body or mind,' she said firmly.

I smiled scornfully. 'But that's not true, apparently, of a man who lives here!'

'Do you mean Sanju?' She sighed. 'He didn't grow up here. He grew up in his father's place. He can never understand the culture of this place. His mind is hard—it can never be happy at the happiness of others. It is narrow. He doesn't know how to take pleasure, and what he recognizes as pleasure is not that at all. His father was the same . . .'

Her voice fell. I had no response. She took up the tanpura and ran her fingers on its strings. We were quiet for a few minutes.

'Trailokya di, how are you related to him?' I wet my dry lips.

She looked at me surprised, 'He's my son! Why, can't you believe that?'

'He told me that his mother was no more.'

She burst into peals of laughter that brought tears into her eyes. Her head shook so; her fair neck and cheeks turned a pale red. The girl who had peeped into Sanjeev Kumar's room came up and stood there silently. Trailokya Devi got up.

'Who can tell how someone will die, Chetna? You can go now. We will meet again.' She turned to the girl and said, 'Tell one of the drivers to drop Chetna at her house.'

I got up, my heart weakening when I bid her goodbye. Walking down the steps with the girl, getting into the car—it all felt like a dream. As I passed through the streets of Sonagachi full of cheaply made-up women in stale garments, men stinking of betel, bidi and cigarettes, and the smell of fish and meat frying in oil, both my anger and my desire for

Sanjeev Kumar frothed and raged. I wished to drain him further with the story of Sankaran, Narayana Asan's son, who came to Kolkata in the nineteenth century when the canon fired in Fort William for the change of guard at five in the morning and nine at night.

I met him many days later, after Ramu da's last rites. He came home. He who never bore the weight of what had passed, who was always cheery and optimistic, he walked into my room freely.

'Did you hear, Chetna, three people were executed in the Gulf on 31 May?'

I shook the water out of my hair.

'The video is marvellous. It would make a great programme.'

I gave him a sharp look.

'Why don't you say something? Are you cross again?'

When he came up to me again with those words, looking deep into my eyes, with the innocence of a carefree teenager, I wanted to make him entirely mine, so fully that he would never touch another woman in his life. I stroked my long curls which fell on my body like Manasa's serpents.

'Your mother is a beshya, isn't she?' I asked that question slowly, carefully.

He shuddered in shock. I watched keenly as his face and eyes turned a flaming red, and he began to rub them hard as though his blood pressure had shot up. He ran out of the house, then came back in with a turbulent face, and then went out again only to return once more, to pace about the narrow rooms.

'Your mother is an Agrevali.'

'Yes,' he muttered after some time, as if admitting defeat.

'All the girls born in that house will have to take up that profession? Just think, if you marry me, if we have girls . . . .'

I thought he was about to hit me. Instead, he turned away sharply, eyes welling as if he had been hit. I was anguished as I saw him grip the prison bars he had erected around himself, head bent in sorrow. How I wished to reach out through those bars, stroke his face, kiss his palms gently. Ramnatha—who sang *Babul mora . . .* the whole night after Trailokya was hanged to death—came to my mind. He never had another woman after her. Not because of his excessive love towards her, not because he had lost the sexual urge. But because each time he tried to have sex, he felt in his body the writhing movements of the girl who had been stabbed before his eyes. He lived for a year after her death; he hanged himself at the age of seventeen. The night before he killed himself, he sat on the Ghat, singing the nawab's song till dawn. I hummed the rest of the song.

'Stop! That's the song my mother sings!' Sanjeev Kumar blurted out, agitated.

'So?'

'It hurts me.'

'Then I'll sing it all through the night!'

'Why do you wound me so? What do you want?'

I smiled at him. My body trembled and sourness gushed up in my mind.

'I too must fuck you at least once!'

I tried to smile, but wept instead. His face blanched, but his eyes were wet too.

I felt gratified. Like Trailokya, I gave back to the world what it gave me.

44

The big turns in this story took place on 11 and 12 July. The first was actually not so eventful. But the incidents on 12 July were connected to some things that happened the day before. I didn't go to the *Bhavishyath* because it was a Sunday. The big news of the day was about the villagers of Paraspur who lost their land when the Padma changed course. They were blockading a minister in the state's cabinet and the legislator in the West Bengal legislative assembly from Paraspur. Fifty-four houses had been swept away. But what really affected me was seeing Mano da. I heard his voice in Kaku's salon that evening and quickly went over.

Kaku was cutting his hair, squeezing himself into the little space beside the board that said 'Hair cut: Rs 15; Style cut: Rs 30', and so on. Meeting him unexpectedly, my heart that had been wound tight like a coil of rope became a bit loose and relaxed. When I went up to the old, battered chair where he sat covered with a dirty towel, Mano da moved his eyes and smiled naughtily at me.

'When I see this Sukhdev's face, I remember the story of his going off to Siliguri to hunt somebody's head! Ooh, I am always scared when I sit here covered with a towel! Do you know—I have seen him chop off someone's head! I leapt up instinctively and caught the sword, but do you know what he told me? Dada, don't be afraid, there won't be a drop of blood; in the olden days, we Grddha Mullicks used to also decapitate wrongdoers!'

Moving his scissors through Mano da's hair, Kaku let out a deep breath. 'Her father says I can't even kill a fowl—and that's true!'

Cheap shaving cream smelt funny, like spoilt milk. The smell pervaded the air of the salon. On the long, narrow stand on the wall was an old brown shaving brush which had lost quite a few of its bristles in encounters with innumerable men. The two mirrors on the wall behind the stand reflected the asbestos ceiling as though it were slanted. On the other side, a small, toy-like TV silently played a song sequence from an Uttam Kumar movie. Kaku had decided to start a salon after trying his hand at many other kinds of work. He had been a rickshaw driver, a shop accountant, a cotton millworker. He could not stick on anywhere. Watching his fingers move on Mano da's white head, I thought of Wajid Ali Shah. In the room's silence, Mano da's white locks fell softly like rain falling on the river.

'You don't know, Chetu, those were strange times. Thinking back now, I don't know if it was really us who did all that . . .' Kaku looked at me, rolling his eyes. 'It's as though I can still see Jyotirmayi.' Mano da turned and looked at Kaku.

'Who?' I was eager to know.

Kaku sighed again and examined the hair tips with his fingers.

'It all began with Jyotirmayi . . . It was she who noticed that there were shoe prints on the mud paths of the fields, from the fields to the road.'

He was telling the story of what had happened in the Terai village.

I did not wish to recall the tale of Kanu Sanyal, Charu Majumdar and Jangal Santhal who called forth Spring Thunder with the bow and arrow. But Jyotirmayi's story was interesting. She, while looking for her father who had not come back from the fields, noticed the shoe prints and alerted the villagers. When workers began to go missing, she went from hut to hut and got the women together. They went to the field before daybreak and hid. They saw policemen surround workers in the middle of paddy fields and bundle them away, gagging their mouths. The womenfolk stopped the police and would not let them leave. When they were told that the police were arresting the tenants who hadn't paid the rent arrears, the whole village rose up in anger. The police ran away but returned with a stronger force. That was when the arrows sped out of the bushes towards the police. Police inspector Sonam Wangdi was felled by Jangal Santhal's arrow.

'Oh Chetu di, you should have seen the police flee the day Wangdi fell. They threw away their rifles and their boots too!'

'She learned to shoot using that rifle!' Kaku sighed.

'How sharp her aim was!'

When the police returned with reinforcements, the villagers picked up whatever they could and prepared for outright war. Some of the women who carried their babies in slings on their backs beat up the police, but were crushed beneath their feet.

'Nine women and two infants.'

'Jyotirmayi?'

'No, she . . .'

Kaku was weeping. 'Because her body was never recovered, Chetu. Until that happens, there is no evidence to prove that she is dead.' As he shook the towel he had used to cover Mano da's chest, the tears in Kaku's right eye flowed freely. He had been in love with her. My head grew numb as I stared at this man who had loved Jyotirmayi, waged war against Indira Gandhi and lived in mortal fear of Syamili di.

Mano da examined himself in the mirror; satisfied with what he saw, he nodded his approval. I stepped on to the pavement with him. He looked at the buzzing humanity on the road for a few seconds. 'Did you think I came here to have a haircut? So late? I made some inquiries about that boy. Some phenomenon he is—a Naxalite father, a sex-worker mother, and the son is a journalist,' Mano da guffawed.

I lunged back as if taking a blow.

'Naxalite? Who?'

'That fellow's father. His name was Mitran. He used to hang around here in 1967. In Calcutta University, studying English literature, I think.' He smoothed my curls and smiled. 'Let's get some tea?'

'From her father's shop?' Kaku came up behind, cribbing like a child. 'I don't want it. Dada hasn't spoken to me in so long! What did I do, to be accused and ignored thus? No, no, I don't want even a drop of water from this house!'

'Okay, okay, from somewhere else then, if not from here. Let's walk a bit.'

We went over to Komal da's shop opposite the railway crossing, to the left of where Sircar mama used to ply his trade. There was no place to sit, so we stood there sipping from our mud cups. A luxury boat passed by on the river. Green, yellow and red lights flashed from it; we could hear music—a guitar and drums—from inside the boat. Father: Naxalite; mother: sex worker—the drumbeats seemed to tell us.

'Mano da, is that true? How did you get to know?' I asked him when we were going back.

He held my hand gently. When we reached my house, he placed his hand on my shoulder, looked straight into my eyes, and said, 'Don't I have the responsibility to find out about the man who's going to marry you?'

Tears sprang into my eyes.

'His father was a revolutionary. When the revolution failed, he left this place. Took a girl with him. After four or five years, she came back.'

'Very mysterious, Mano da!' I whispered.

'Let him be whoever . . . my worry isn't that. Will Jatindranath's death sentence be carried out or not? Is it easy to kill, my child?'

I sighed. Kaku, who was lagging behind, now caught up.

'Mano da, I will definitely kill the person who is meant to die by my hands.'

'You know what taking a life is only when you raise your hand to kill. There is someone inside you, someone you take everywhere with you. He will stop your hand at that moment. You will have to kill him first to kill another.'

354

He paused to look at Kaku and me.

'It's not like you think. The fellow who leaps out of you is much stronger than you can imagine.'

'It will be a woman who leaps out of me, Mano da!' I tried to joke, but he continued, sadly. 'But that's the saddest thing. Even the Creator cannot stop some women.'

'You're saying that the execution will be stalled if she is stronger?'

'No, only that if it happens we will lose Chetna forever!'

His voice was calm. I did not understand then that it was necessary to convince him there was more than one Chetna. That night too was a sleepless night. I kept thinking that death was crouching somewhere in the room with a camera. It was lapping up my movements. I tried to think of something else: Kaku. I thought of him with wonder. I remember him moving into this house permanently in 1987, when I was five years old. He put down his bed and other belongings with a big thud in the room which Ramu da had been using till then. Then he opened his trunk and gave me several dolls and balloons. He spent till evening cleaning the room and then stepped out after a bath. It was about ten when Hemu da banged on our door. I jumped awake.

'Oh Didi, very bad! Phani da and Sudev da are fighting!' he yelled.

'Ma Kali!' Thakuma jumped up and ran out.

I rubbed my eyes and ran after her. As we waited for the body of a very old man to move on the road, we could hear them grappling on the ground where the sweet shop stands now, in front of a cycle repair shop that was there then.

'I'll kill you today, you bugger!' Father's booming voice resounded on Strand Road.

The bored young men who had come with the corpse turned around again and again keenly, and cracked jokes. Kaku, who was trying to wriggle out of Father's grasp, could not be heard in the din. When Thakuma, followed shortly by Ma, rushed there, separated them, and took them back home, Father was still yelling in fury: 'Shameless fellow! I am ashamed to call him my younger brother!'

'Why? What happened?' Thakuma asked.

'Why are you beating up this poor fellow? Are you mad?' asked Ma, and his fury turned towards her.

'Do you know where he was?' Father raised his hand to slap Ma. 'In Sonagachi!'

'Eesh,' said Ma and withdrew, drawing her aanchal over her head.

But Thakuma smiled as if it were nothing. 'Oh—so that's the big thing! Well, isn't he a man too? Where should he be going?'

'Chi! See how the mother who gave birth to him speaks!' Father was wild with anger.

'But, Dada, you were coming out while I was going in. How come I alone am at fault?' Kaku said with a whine as he came out with a bit of talcum powder on his face.

That started Father off again. Thakuma smiled in disdain.

Kaku rubbed the talcum into his face and went to Ma: 'Didi, I know that none of you want me. I know, you don't think very highly of me . . .'

When he went away into his room with his eyes full, everyone fell silent. Ramu da shut his book and went and stretched out on his cot. Thakuma started chewing betel again. Ma, flustered, caught hold of me and snapped, 'Off to bed, child!'

'Thakuma, why did Baba beat Kaku last night?' I twirled the edge of my blue-on-yellow frock and asked Thakuma in a low voice the next day.

'Chetu, the evil spirit from Darjeeling must have got into him!'

I remembered the pain in Thakuma's voice. Only after I joined the *Bhavishyath* did I know which evil spirit it was— the one from Darjeeling that had got into him in 1987. That he had remained with Jangal Santhal who had drowned himself in booze after his release from prison in 1979, continually racked with want. He had constantly moved with Jangal Santhal from one place to the next till Santhal's death in 1987. The thought of Kaku's life filled me with pain at twenty-two, just as it had when I was five. I slept off in that ache and 11 July passed out of my life.

The following day, 12 July, however, was very eventful. The rusty old ambulance that carried the body of the young woman who had been found in the Maidan, strangled with her own dupatta, broke down right in front of our house. Some retired policemen came out of it, asking Father, what news, Phani da. Father was pleased; he took the gamchha off his shoulder and led them into the tea shop respectfully. I was going to take a bath and caught a clear glimpse of the bluish bloated face inside the ambulance. For a moment it seemed like Kaku to me. The swollen eyelids, the blackened face and the hair sticking to the skull left me fearful. When I came back after my bath, I saw it again. There was a white worm wriggling over the checked coverlet on the body. The policemen and Father were coming out after tea.

'Not one or two, but six whole weeks! No point keeping it, worms have begun to appear,' one of the policemen said.

'Wasn't there an inquiry, Babu?' asked Father.

'The only lead was a name—Sujoy. We looked everywhere possible. Really sad . . . seems like a really nice girl.'

My mind became dim as I went in and dried my hair. My body remembered the unbelievably intense pain you experience when the man whom you love and trust suddenly thrusts his hand out to wring your neck. It was with a heavy heart that I changed and had breakfast. I put Mano da's proofs into my bag and was about to leave when a woman showed up at our door.

'Chetu di, do you remember me?'

It was Sushila di, from Sanjeev Kumar's house. This was unexpected. Before I could ask her why she had come, Trailokya Devi stepped in through the door.

'Everyone knows the hangman's house is on Strand Road!' Her sweet voice rang in the house.

I did not know what to do. 'Come in,' I invited, somewhat ashamed of the house.

'Thank you for inviting me in, Chetna. Come, Sushila.'

She walked in gracefully, like an empress, and sat with ease on Ramu da's cot. Thakuma was shaking the betel on to her palm—her eyes almost popped out. I ran into the kitchen and told Ma that Sanjeev Kumar's mother had come.

'Mother?' she asked, flabbergasted.

I ran back without replying.

Trailokya Devi was looking around our house.

'It's an old house,' I said quickly.

'This part used to be the cowshed or storeroom of our house during the days of the maharajas,' said Thakuma, stuffing the betel in her mouth. 'Did you know, there were eighteen flowering trees here—for Wajid Ali Shah's white doves?'

'Sanju babu didn't come?' Mother asked mindfully, bringing her some water.

'No, I came to perform a puja at the Ghat. Today is my husband's death anniversary.'

'Sanju babu's father?'

'His real name is Shambu,' she smiled. 'But his father didn't like it. You Bengalis have two names each, and likewise, two natures, he would complain.'

She looked at me with a smile.

'He was a good man, scholarly, brave, never reluctant to sacrifice his life for others, but . . .' She put down the empty glass and looked at me as if sending a warning, 'the wife is not permitted to do it.'

'Do what?' I asked, involuntarily.

She gave me a cold smile. 'To sacrifice herself for others!' Kindness and pain mingled in her expression as she looked into my confused eyes.

'Call your father! Where is he?' Thakuma urged me. She had forgotten that the woman before her was the mother of the man who had stolen her gold coin.

'Don't bother him please. I will come again.' She got up to leave.

As if it was reluctant to let her go, the room held fast to the scent of roses she had brought in. She turned to me when we were outside: 'Come, Chetna, I'll drop you at the office.'

I was mesmerized by her; she made me feel strong. I followed her, bag on my shoulder. When she turned left from our house and walked towards the expensive car parked near the transport station, many who were working on the road and in the shops raised their heads to look at her. The car turned left from the Nimeshwar Baba temple. Sushila di, sitting in the front seat, bowed as we drove past the front of the temple. The woman in the back seat, by my side, leaned back against the seat and hummed, 'Babul mora . . .'

'Can't take a step on the Ghat! Too many beggars!' she said then, looking at me, eager for conversation.

'They began to appear in Kolkata in the eighteenth century,' I said. It started with the farmers who had lost their land when their villages had been taken over to create Kolkata. They began to collect a paisa each from the shops which stood on the land that had been theirs once.

Though the shopkeepers paid up at first, later, when trade prospered, they decided not to pay the farmers. The beggars who lost their livelihood filed a complaint in court.

'How do you know?' She was amazed.

'The complaint filed by Jeebandas Bairagi, Basudev Barmarchari and other beggars was written by an ancestor of mine.'

'Oh!' she smiled slowly.

'At that point, Sanju babu's ancestor Naren dakat had not yet come to Kolkata.'

I cast a sidelong glance at her. Her eyes grew wide. History is the most potent of weapons. Falling prey to its sharp points while off-guard can weaken one's entire nervous system. By the time my ancestor met Naren dakat, the beggars in Kolkata had grown so numerous that one of the richest men in the city, Krishnachandra Ghoshal, and his son Jainarayan were compelled to conduct a census of beggars. They counted some five hundred blind, crippled, ill, orphaned, widowed, elderly beggars including aged prostitutes. The beggars all died in almost the same manner—run over by speeding horse carriages! Did any of the people who sat inside those carriages which dashed along the city roads fast enough to knock down and kill people care to show any feeling of fellowship with those who were killed thus? I doubted it.

When the car reached the Jatrapara offices, I touched the driver's shoulder.

"I'll get off here. I can go on my own.'

Trailokya Devi leaned forward.

'Pawan da, don't stop. If it is not a bother, let's go home, Chetna. I need to talk with you.'

This time, it was I who looked at her sharply.

'What do we have to talk about?'

She leaned back against the seat and looked at me affectionately. 'It is wonderful to talk to you. Look, I am fifty-three now. At this age, it isn't food or medicine that one needs, but someone with whom one can talk freely.'

Those were honest words. As the car waited for the gates of Aparajita Apartments on Avinash Kaviraj Road to open, I noticed that the street was quiet and empty save for a lone schoolchild and a fortyish man in a suit who crossed each other. The car went in; when I stepped into the house of nine stairways as the guest of the lady of the house, my eyes searched for Sanjeev Kumar Mitra. We climbed the stairs to the same apartment. She went in and turned on the air conditioner. Leaning against the bolsters on the bed, she called me to her side. I sat on the edge of the bed, feeling shy. There were carved lotuses blooming on each leg of the rosewood bed.

'You looked really familiar, you know?'

I waited a moment as she changed channels on the TV with the remote.

'Maybe you saw me on TV?'

She got up then, walked towards the wall near the northern window, and stood before a large mirror, looking at herself.

'No,' she said, 'not there. Here, in this mirror.'

Because she sensed that I was nonplussed, she came over and placed her hand on my shoulder.

'When I look at you, I feel that I am looking at my own face as it was many years ago.'

She smiled. I could not.

'He's never told you anything about me?'

'Only that his mother is no more . . .' My voice grew weak. 'I don't know why he said that. Could any son say his mother is dead when she is alive?'

A smile bloomed again on her face.

'No one can tell exactly how someone died, Chetna.'

She sat on the bed.

'Swami Vivekanada died in meditation. There were drops of blood trickling down from his nose and mouth, and seeping from the edges of his closed eyes.'

'Mahasamadhi,' I began my counter-argument. 'Maybe the soul broke through the brahmarandra centre of the skull and flew away.'

Our eyes met.

'That happens only when death occurs during meditation. When a person is hanged, his soul escapes through the nine openings of the body. Like water being squeezed out of a plastic bag with holes in it.'

I stopped to enjoy the expression on her face, and continued.

'The flow of life splinters in many different directions. Thakuma says that the victims of the gallows search desperately for the pieces of their own self in the cellar below. Some lie scattered there. Some are crushed under the feet of those who get down there to take the body out.'

She looked unwaveringly at me for some time.

'He was a great man for cracking jokes. His father was a Madrasi; they are known for their sense of humour.'

She picked up the remote.

'Especially when it is about women and others, people they think are lower!'

Casting a brief glance at the scene that appeared on the screen, she turned to me. I liked this woman whose whole demeanour was gracious and dignified. Instead of possessing the self-hatred and inferiority of women who rent out their bodies to men, she was as energetic and joyful as a girl of sixteen who was constantly courted and constantly in love.

'Chetna, what did you talk about with him? Why not tell me his history as well?'

'I don't know a lot. There are records only about his ancestor Naren dakat.'

I related that story. There was amazement on her face.

'You are probably right. It is true . . . thirty years later, Sankaran alighted in Kolkata as a young man from Kollam seeking his father. He was a great merchant . . . he wrote about his arrival in Kolkata.'

I drew in a deep breath. When the guns sounded the hour of nine inside Fort William, the employees in Writers' Buildings wrapped up their work, extinguished the lamps, and left for home. At the same time, a twenty-year-old young man arrived in the city with a wooden box and a rolled-up mat. He gazed awestruck at the grand mansions lit up with fancy gasoline lamps as he searched for a place to rest. The silence was broken now and then by carriages with black or brown horses that came dashing down the road. The doors and windows of the beautiful mansions with balconies and terraces surrounded by decorative cast-iron railings were shut by then. When he crossed into Sobha Bazar through Chitpur Road, suddenly the road came alive with people and sounds. He stood among the bela flower sellers and the vendors of chilled sweets with his box and mat, and watched the nightlife with amazement. Then, not knowing that this was Black Calcutta and that the nightlife went on till dawn, he picked up his box and mat and began to walk through Garanagata Lane. On the way, Sonagachi lay waiting, like a bloodthirsty ghoul decked up as a beauty.

She burst out laughing when I described how he ran through Pathuria Ghat towards the Hooghly to escape the pimps and prostitutes who tugged at his belongings.

'Sankaran took rice from here, brought cardamom and pepper from there. He became very rich, he owned many grand buildings in Kolkata. His grandson married me after selling one of those.'

'What about his son?' I sat up, now interested.

'He was a kalari expert. He took the initiative to begin a gymnasium in Kolkata. He was active in Subhash Chandra Bose's Indian National Army. No one has seen him since he left for Germany to work under Bose. He went back home just before leaving the country and got married. His son was Sanjeev's father, Mitran.'

She seemed engrossed in some memory.

'He came here to join Calcutta University. The right time to come! Jumped into the revolution as soon as he came. We met in college . . . I liked him at first sight.'

'Trailokya di, did you go to college?' I was indeed astonished.

'I was the topper in school, but I couldn't complete my degree. Mitran was in jail by then. After he came out, he took me straightaway to Kerala. Our son was born there.'

'You came back . . .'

'Yes.'

She sighed again. I listened to her spellbound. Love ended the moment marriage began. Her lover was not a mate any more; he was a sentry, guarding her all the time. All the lessons that her ancestry had taught about winning and keeping a man's love fell to naught. Mitran was afraid of his wife. Of her voice. Of her body, her courage, her happiness. So Trailokya Devi returned. He didn't let her take their son, nor did she try to seize him. Mitran died when their son was eighteen. That was when Trailokya Devi invited her son to Kolkata. He came because he had no other option. He lives here because he still has no other option.

Her face had turned glum. We were silent for a while. I was sketching in my mind the road he had traversed.

Trailokya Devi wiped her face vigorously and became pleasant again. 'Forget all that. Whenever I hear "hangman", it is Phanibhushan Grddha Mullick's face that appears in my mind. He's so often on TV and in the papers!'

She paced about the room slowly, as graceful as a dancer revealing the beauty of her body. She came up to the carved bed and, caressing the lotus at its head, looked at me. This big room and the cool floor and the shiny rosewood furniture, and me—nothing seemed real then. When I turned my face casually to look at the wall behind me, I was surprised to see a picture of Devi Manasa. Serpents, eager to fly, made a halo of light around her face as she sat with her infant.

'Won't you feel fear when you kill?' she asked lightly.

How is anyone to say exactly how one may kill another? Just as I was about to speak, Sushila di interrupted us. She had run up the stairs and was panting heavily when she exclaimed, 'Didi, someone has come looking for Chetna!'

'Looking for me? Here?'

'Chetu!'

I heard a cry. As I hurried out, there was Mano da hopping up the steps, pulling along his bad leg. He lurched desperately even as he neared, a film of tears clouding his vision. He stumbled as though he were blind. I looked at his face, and the whitish worms sank their maws into my cold feet. I knew it without his telling me. Someone dear to both of us had died.

45

There are sixteen hells that await human beings after their death, said Thakuma as soon as she saw me, as if nothing special had transpired. Eight of them are hot, the other eight cold. In the first of the cold hells, the Arbudanaraka, the karma of each soul is amassed as mustard seeds in sacks. It is like a large plateau in the middle of two infinitely high mountains. Each soul that enters shivers in the constantly blowing cold wind that makes the skin prickle. The soul must remain in that hell till the last of its mustard seeds have been counted—at the rate of one seed per century. After having enjoyed the fruits of fulfilled karma, it has to return to accomplish the unfulfilled. But more frightening than this, to me, was the idea that each soul that fell into this hell had to carry all the memories of the full-grown body, vulnerable to the heat and the cold, like an enormous cloth bundle. That Thakuma could speak about souls and hells on 12 July, when a crowd gathered on Strand Road, this street of death, was truly extraordinary, and even the corpses peeped into our ancient dwelling—where the glory of our bloodline lay. The sight of Father, who, since his nineteenth year, had been the greatest merchant of death tales, and the biggest guardian of justice, sitting in this old room so familiar to television viewers and documentary audiences, smoking uneasily, and Ma collapsed in a corner, weeping feebly, looked like a scene from a television show. In the courtyard of our house a blood-soaked chopper lay inside a circle of chalk. The blood that had splattered from it seemed to be rolling on the green moss, like drops of molten wax.

'It was Emperor Ashoka who built a hell on earth. But it isn't enough to build it, right, Chetu chotdi? Doesn't it have to be run properly? That's where I say, no ruler in India could have survived without us!'

Thakuma's cackling voice rose high. A policeman walking by, puffing at a beedi, looked our way. He grinned, showing his stained teeth. Ashoka's hell too had sixteen cells. All the terrors after death must be suffered in life, he insisted. He had ascended to the seat of the empire after eliminating ninety-nine of his stepbrothers born to his father's ninety-nine wives.

'Only you can spout history at such a moment! No wonder you have been left to decay here bit by bit even after crossing a hundred!' Blowing her nose and wiping her overflowing eyes, Ma got up and scolded Thakuma loudly.

Seeing me standing beside Thakuma with no emotion on my face, she became even more furious. She gave me a tight slap on my cheek. 'What are you staring at, eh? Have you caught the same bug as your old devil and his hag of a mother? Don't you have the decency to shed a single tear?'

I rubbed my cheek and tried to smile. It will take Ma many more years to realize that after 18 May I simply cannot cry in the face of death.

'Smiling? You heartless wretch!' She gave me a searing look.

'Stop your strutting right now!' Thakuma's voice rose. 'Her blood is that of the Grddha Mullicks. Do you know what it takes to be a hangman? Presence of mind! She has it. She will spread our fame even further.'

I never failed to be amazed by the power and energy that resonated in Thakuma's voice, emerging as it did from a body that had shrunk to barely a couple of metres. What world will she leave for after death, I wondered. When one entered the mountain path of the Nirarbudanaraka, the cold would re-emerge with sharp fangs and tear at the bodies of the souls, causing the gooseflesh of the Arbudanarka to burst and for blood and pus to flow out. But they would turn solid as ice that very instant, adding to the terrible throbbing pain. The cold can burn more intensely and cruelly than fire. Each soul must cross the Nirarbudanaraka after learning that lesson. Each soul has to spend a period twenty times longer than what it spent in the Arbudanaraka. Ignoring the women of the neighbourhood who had gathered there, I pushed my legs through the front of the kitchen and from there, into Kaku's room. The boot prints of the police were evident thanks to the blood that had pooled there. Falling into a cold hell while alive on the earth was, in a way, a completion of incomplete karma.

'Chetu di!'

Ten-year-old Champa ran out of the kitchen, blood smeared on her cheek, and clung to me. Don't cry, don't cry, I tried to tell her, but then I began to weep.

'Where is Rari?' I asked, as I held her close.

She pointed towards the kitchen. Our dilapidated kitchen had been taken over by the press. At their head was Sanjeev Kumar, shooting questions. Maintaining full dignity as she faced the cameras, five-year-old Rari was earning for herself a distinctive place in the world of grown-ups. My body trembled from top to toe.

'When Ma came in Jethu ran to her and slapped her. Baba got in between, but Jethu hit Ma again. Ma shouted at him . . . and then Jethu . . .' Stopping to make sure that the reporters had the time to jot down her words, she continued: 'went to the kitchen and got the big chopper and slashed Ma in the neck . . .'

That was the moment when I noticed how unpleasant it feels when goose pimples of fear spring up on the body.

'Didn't your father Sukhdev Grddha Mullick stop him?'

'Jethu is very strong. Baba fell.'

'Tut-tut-tut,' said Sanjeev Kumar.

He has entered the Attattanaraka, I surmised, enraged. The hell of Attattanaraka is climbing up a high mountain. The hell of Haahavanaraka is in descending it. The Attattanaraka is so cold that the chapped and broken wounds from Nirarbudanaraka give out the sound 'tt . . . tt . . . tt . . .' And when souls fall from Attattanaraka into the Haahavanaraka, the sharp chilly wind that always blows in the opposite direction to the soul's path makes the soul scream 'haaa. . .' in sheer agony. The next, the Huhuvanaraka, is a frozen pond. The souls make their way on the slippery ice, but sometimes fall through crevices into the waters beneath. It is so cold that the souls cannot even open their mouths; all they can do is groan, 'hooo . . .' Beyond it is the Utpalanaraka, where the naked bodies of the souls turn bluish in the unrelenting snowfall. Then they pass on to the Padmanaraka, where instead of snow, large blocks of ice come down like hail. Last is the Mahapadmanaraka, where the body shatters into pieces and everything inside comes out. I wanted to ask Thakuma how Emperor Ashoka, who built all these hells in the human world, would have fared in his life post-mortem. Emperor Bimbisara, who was a follower of the Ajivaka cult, married Subhadrangi who was also a follower of the same cult. The ministers and Chanakya prevented them from having intercourse for a very long while, said Thakuma. In the end, after waiting for many years, a baby boy was born to Subhadrangi, who took him up in her arms and declared, 'He ends all my shoka'—that is, sorrow—and hence the name Ashoka.

'He was a bastard. Not that I didn't love him. I had to do it . . .' Father's voice rang from inside.

'Susmita, what did your baba do then?'

When I heard Sanjeev Kumar ask again, I left Champa in the courtyard and went into the kitchen.

'Stop!'

I pulled away those who were crowding there; they turned to look at me.

'Aren't you ashamed to ask such questions of a child?' My voice choked with anger. They were taken aback for a moment, but they left Rari and turned towards me. Sanjeev Kumar pushed everyone aside in half a second and was beside me, holding out his mike.

'Chetna Grddha Mullick, what do you say about this tragedy that has struck your family?'

I did not utter a single word; merely looked hard into his eyes. There was a crowd milling around us. Someone stepped on Rari's foot, and she cried aloud, 'Haa . . .'

'Chetna Grddha Mullick, please say something! What happened? Is your father really guilty? What is your view of this incident as a hangman?'

They were like the crowd that gathered to watch Grandfather Kala. I ignored the questions and tried to take Rari away from the crush.

'Why can't this woman open her mouth and say something!'

I closed my ears to all sounds, and pressed my lips on Rari's cheek.

'Why didn't you answer, Chetu di?' Rari asked me.

I held her even more closely and kissed her on the cheek again. Her eyes filled with tears.

'Excellent visual . . . get it . . .' I heard someone say. When a pot that Ma had hung in the kitchen fell and some aluminium pots and pans rolled on the floor, there was another round of pushing and shoving in our kitchen. I became exhausted; there was nowhere we could hide in the house from the lights and sounds.

Then, Mano da's voice rose from outside: 'What is going on? Have you not a shred of decency? Get out, everyone!'

'Tell that girl to open her mouth and say something, Mano da!' A press reporter begged him. I heard laughter too. Sanjeev Kumar Mitra moved towards me through the crowd and hugged me by the shoulder. I was holding Rari. He stroked her shoulder. His expression softened again to that of a friend or lover.

'Chetna, you must issue a statement now. This is an opportunity.'

He waited for a response for a second.

'Your job is hanging in the balance now—don't you see that?'

He brought his face close to mine. Not knowing whether it was the cold hell or the hot one, my body shuddered. Rari hugged my shoulders tightly.

'This is an excellent chance—God-given! You must stay on the side of the government.'

The first of the hot hells is Sanjeevanaraka, I wanted to tell him. Because it revives the shattered bodies of the souls who get past the Mahapadmanaraka, preparing them for greater ordeals. Grandfather Agnimitra Mullick, who was deputed to set up the hells on earth by Emperor Ashoka, enjoyed this hell the most. He greeted the shivering souls emerging out of the Mahapadmanaraka by poking them with flaming torches. Leaping up in agony, they had to run over a smouldering hot floor. Emperor Ashoka chose the Sanjeevanaraka to finish off his brothers. They had to run on smouldering coals for ten yojnas; they perished on the way, turning into ashes. Thirteen years later, Ashoka experienced a change of mind after the battle of Kalinga and proclaimed himself to be the father of his subjects. As a father, he desired the well-being and happiness of all his children. If souls are capable of carrying a sense of humour along with the memory of their mortal bodies, then these ninety-nine souls, in some world above or below Jambudwipa, must have burst out laughing hearing this proclamation.

'Chetu, come out.' Mano da made his way in with difficulty and grasped my arm. 'These fellows will smother you to death.'

'What happened, really, Mano da, tell us something!' Sanjeev Kumar caught his arm and looked at him beseechingly.

'Two children have been orphaned.' Mano da gave him an acerbic look.

'Not that, Mano da, why did someone like Phani da do something so cruel?'

'Ask him.'

'Shouldn't there be a reason? To save the honour of the family, he said. What does he mean by that?'

'Sanjeev babu, ask him!'

'Dada, there's no point in getting angry with me. Did I create this situation?'

I clasped Rari to my shoulder and turned towards him.

'Yes! You! *You* have brought this upon us!'

'Me!' He gaped at me. 'What did I do? I just wished for good things to happen to you—that's all! Even the other day, I was trying to get you a better house. I'd just recommended to the minister—a permanent job for you and a pension for your baba!'

I couldn't help feeling that it was Ashoka standing before me. The police entered, with some neighbours from the Port Trust quarters bringing in the bodies. I squeezed my eyes shut on seeing Kakima's partially covered body, her mouth open as if in an eternal scream.

'Ma . . .'

Rari thrust her arms over my shoulder and called desperately. She heaved once, about to cry—then, realizing its fruitlessness, fell silent. Champa pressed her face into my side and burst into tears. When they brought in Kaku's body, I held them closer, so that they would not see him. But I looked at his body again. His eyes were closed. There was blood on his large, bloated body like an unreal coat of paint. When the police and the crowd left with the bodies, I took the girls and went over to Thakuma. She raised her hand and caressed Rari on the shoulder. Thakuma stroked my cheek gently. 'Did it hurt? She was actually slapping your baba!'

I made Rari sit on my lap and held Thakuma close. The policemen's footsteps could now be heard from Father's room. I had known that sound from childhood but it was hard to believe that today they came seeking not the hangman but the wrongdoer. Hearing noises from the room, Ma got up with a sob and ran there. The din increased—they were taking Father to the police jeep, I guessed. Thakuma and I sat still as statues. In seconds, our ancient house became empty and silent. Thakuma caressed Rari. But within a few minutes, Sanjeev Kumar Mitra's face appeared again at the door. 'Chetna, one moment . . .'

I hesitated, then put the child on the bed and went up to the door. He moved towards the kitchen. 'Is it true that the deceased Grddha Mullick was a Naxalite?'

He asked as if it were some deadly secret.

'Chi! What a pity! Would have made a great story when he was alive! I didn't know of this when we were doing *Hangwoman's Diary*! What a loss!'

I had no response.

'I've been thinking of how we can save your baba. As far as I can see, it can be done if you issue a statement that Sukhdev Grddha Mullick was a Maoist!'

I didn't get him, not one bit.

'Ah, there is record of his Naxalism as he was jailed as a Naxalite. That makes it easy to identify him as a Maoist.'

'Oh!'

'If you cooperate a bit, Chetna, we can save Phani da easily. Declare that Sudev was a Maoist, that's why your father murdered him and his wife. And with a good lawyer . . .'

Until then I had been more or less tearless. But when he proposed this, Kaku's face rose up in my mind and the song, *Aandhar shokoli* . . . I felt the tears come. He must have paid for all his karma in the hot and cold hells S.S. Ray set up, like Ashoka, during the Emergency.

'Think about it, Chetna.'

I went back to Thakuma, distraught. Rari was lying on her lap.

'His wedding proposal—how is that going?' she asked.

My voice refused to emerge.

'Uh-hm! How will it work now, Chetu chotdi? How can he marry you now? You are not an ordinary woman, but a hangwoman! You can't be married to an ordinary man.'

She stroked my hair proudly.

'Are you human, woman?' Ma, who had come back in, snapped. 'One of the sons you gave birth to in pain is dead, his neck broken—and listen to her talk! One son is dead, the other in jail! But does she have a single tear to shed?'

'I wept a long time ago.' Thakuma opened her mouth and smiled innocently. 'Now there are no tears at all, girl. I am so old! Is not all life alike? Is not each death the same? What is there to cry about so much?'

But Ma went to Father's room, still scolding. Neighbours and acquaintances kept flowing in and out. Why did he do this, they all wanted to know. When Kaku's and Kakima's bodies were brought back late that night, the house filled up with people. They went through all the rites, same as Ramu da.

'Why did Baba do it, Ma?' I asked Ma while we were preparing

Kakima's body—bathing her, putting the sindoor on her forehead, and dabbing her feet with alta.

'Only your baba knows. Syamili ran in sweating and your father came running behind her, shouting at her to stop. He caught hold of the poor woman's hair and dragged her down. She spat on his face . . . then he went and got the chopper . . .'

I felt the noose tightening around my neck again. As I walked to Nimtala Ghat once more for the ceremonial dip, I couldn't but help admire Father. How the man clung to his resolve never to tell a story fully! Like the soul which has to return to the earth to complete unfulfilled karma even if it has gone through all the sixteen hells, he would come back, I felt, with a newer set of tales. I left the Ghat soaking wet, holding Champa and Rari; it was very late. We waited in front of the timber mill for the traffic to ease. CNC's news bulletin was audible from inside the timber mill.

'And the biggest anticlimax has been the arrest of the famous hangman Phanibhushan Grddha Mullick, who boasted of having executed four hundred and fifty-one criminals, for double murder. He has been remanded to custody. If sentenced, he may have to share the same premises as his prospective victim, Jatindranath Banerjee. But if Jatindranath's mercy petition is rejected, then his execution will have to be carried out by Grddha Mullick's daughter Chetna Grddha Mullick, all by herself. The whole country now waits eagerly to see whether she will be able to accomplish this without her father and her uncle. From Alipore Jail, this is Sanjeev Kumar Mitra, along with Atul Kishore Chandra, only for CNC . . .'

I knew how it felt to have your skin prickle and for the prickles to swell with pus, for teeth to clatter, the body turn bluish, and the flesh fall off piece by piece. When the girls called my name, I started to walk again. Mustard seeds, I reminded myself. Too numerous to count.

371

46

'Grddha da, why did you do this?'

'I had my own reasons, Babu.'

'Is it true that you are deluded?'

'Which beggar said that?'

'But think of it . . . of hacking down one's own sibling!'

'It happened. I grieve for him.'

'Won't they reduce the sentence if it was done in a deluded state of mind?'

'Babu, I am eighty-eight years old. My whole life has been devoted to carrying out justice. Should I now subvert it?'

'But will not an act like this from someone like you send a wrong message to society?'

'I should not have done it. But I have done it. The only message I can send society now is that of my bowed head.'

'This is a double murder, Grddha da. What if they send you to the gallows?'

Since morning all the channels had been airing the scenes of Father speaking to the reporters as he sat in the police jeep, and each time I heard the question, my heart quivered. But my wonder at the way he dealt with the questions was endless. He raised his eyes to the crowd with the same dignity he wore on his face while performing the role of an emperor on the azar of the jatra.

'I hope for the gallows! Babu, I hope so because sending someone like me to the gallows will be a very good message for society!'

The jeep began to move. The regal expression on his face as he turned once more to look at the crowd was one only he could summon. He was looking at me, I felt, and asking, 'One thumping line, right?' My only consolation was that he wouldn't be passing through the many hells when he lay all alone in some prison cell. Having to go through hells while still in the body was the worst punishment any soul could receive.

'Look, look, does the man have even a twinge of regret, an iota of hope, even a trace of conscience?' Ma saw him on TV and screamed in deep agony.

'He did what he did. Now you want him to weep like a child for what he did?' Thakuma, who had been enjoying his performance, hit back, opening her mouth in a big smile.

'Uh-hm! Yes, yes, that's all you'll say, mother and son! Do you have a heart? Don't you feel the slightest anger at a man who hacked your own son to pieces?'

'What's the use of being angry now? Didn't I also give birth to Phani in pain?' She was unfazed.

'So you don't grieve Sudev's death at all?'

'What is the use of sorrowing, girl? Will he come back? Girl, this is a family which has executed not thousands, but lakhs of people over generations. The blood of the Grddha Mullicks cannot hate death; it can only love it. Poor Sudev, he's gone. But well, he didn't come to stay in this world forever. He had to go, someday. He went by a single slash—lucky fellow!' she said coolly.

'Thakuma!' I called out, alarmed.

She turned sharply to me: 'Why, Chetu, are you afraid? Chetu, are you not my grandchild? You ought to laugh loudly in your mind when you hear of death. Irrespective of whether someone dies or is killed, it's all fated . . . only fate . . .'

Fear was slowly filling each of my pores.

'Oh fate, indeed! Do evil and then justify it all, fate indeed!'

'Tell her the story of how our ancestor Upendra Mullick created the Ajivaka cult, Chetu!' Thakuma ordered angrily.

I looked at her, empty-faced. She firmly believed that the Ajivaka cult was founded by our ancestor Upendra Mullick. Once, when he was about to behead a young man, the victim looked up and addressed him as 'father'—only then did Upendra realize that it was his own son, born to a courtesan. It put him in a dilemma—he was duty-bound to execute his son but could not bring himself to do it. When he aimed the sword at his neck, his hand shook and the sword slipped, missing its aim. This was all due to the anger of the gods, proclaimed the king's spiritual advisor. The king released Upendra's son. But the infirmity still plagued Upendra's hands—they kept shaking. The realization that he could never raise a sword ever again shocked him. He began to think deeply about the accidents and twists of fate in life. He pondered at length about life, death, relationships that transcended life and death, and the reasons and causes of karma. He rationalized having to raise a sword to his own son's neck as the result of his former karma—as the prevailing thought of the Buddhists and the Jains suggested. But what karma that was, he wasn't sure. Was it that he had sex with a courtesan? Was it that he gave her a son? Or was it that he was a hangman? He struggled to think it through. One day, as he was lost in thought under a mahua tree beside the Adi Ganga, a branch of the tree broke and fell to the ground, bringing down with it a bird's nest with three little chicks. One of them died on the spot, its neck broken. The other fell into the river. The third clung to the nest still on the branch and survived, only to be gobbled up by a fox within moments. The dead chick with the broken neck was eaten by a vulture. The one in the river was snatched up by an eagle. But it fell out of the eagle's beak, and straight into Grandfather Upendra's lap. He dried the little creature with his garment, put it back in the nest and restored the nest to another branch. And then the chick said to him: So we meet again. He was stunned. The chick continued: Three births before, you owed me a debt of life. Fate brought you back here to repay it. Don't be proud of it or sad. This made him think and wonder at the long path he had had to traverse, past three whole lives, to reach this spot beside the river and sit there lost in thought, so that his gratitude to another creature could be repaid. That's how the Ajivaka creed, which decrees that all series of karma are determined by fate, and that all living creatures are but pawns on a large chessboard, came into being. Grandfather Upendra believed that human beings did not suffer the fruits of their karma; rather, human beings were determined by karma according to the larger designs of fate. Later, he passed on his discovery to the slave Mankhali Gosala and, descending into the Adi Ganga, completed the cycle of life.

It worried me when I considered the possibility that it might be all a play of fate: Father, who boasted about sending four hundred and fifty-one people to their death, ending up in the Haldia Sub Jail. If so, then I too could be just another character with him in the same play, and maybe such strange vicissitudes awaited me as well. What worried Thakuma more than Father's going to jail was his going to the Haldia Sub Jail. She retold the stories of the five prisons the British had opened after taking over those of the nawabs, sultans and maharajas. I recalled then that my ancestor had met Naren dakat in the Bara Bazar Jail. This debt being repaid when Satyanatha Grddha Mullick's descendant met Naren dakat's descendant—in which birth had it originated? Whenever I shut my eyes, I saw Father in the prison cell. His face looked swollen as if he had been drowning. In the olden days, at Harinbadi Prison, they laid out the dead bodies of prisoners—who used to die almost on a daily basis—on bamboo rafts, and set them afloat on the Adi Ganga.

'God, what a life,' whined Ma to the world in general. 'What did I do to suffer so much! Why did I have to lug around a fellow like him? There hasn't been a single day of happiness in this life. I haven't heard a single warm word!'

'Your lack of talent, girl,' Thakuma raised her head and taunted her. 'Look at him, still a fit man. He can have any number of women even now.'

'Oh yes, he can, he can—he's *just* eighty-eight!'

'At least one person in each generation of our family lives till a hundred. In my generation it is me. In the next, it is going to be Phani!'

The arrogance that rang in her voice drove Ma mad.

'Yes, even if everyone else in the family dies, you'll cling on till hundred or two hundred! How awful! Are you a woman? Shamelessly praising a cad who hasn't the slightest regret about murdering his own brother!'

'If he killed Sudev, there must've been a reason!'

'What reason?' I asked, anxious.

'I don't know what it is . . . but if he killed without the signal of the magistrate's red kerchief, there must have been a good reason.'

After this confident declaration, Thakuma turned on the TV to see whether they were showing Father. Kaku had brought the girls back from school. Kakima said that she would return to take them with her to Budge Budge. I racked my brains but still couldn't see what Kakima could have done to make Father attack her in such a mad frenzy of rage. The only people who came to see us after the hustle and bustle of the first week were Mano da and Sanjeev Kumar. If Mano da came with little things we needed in the house, Sanjeev Kumar came to find out what was new.

'Chetna, aren't you going to the jail to meet your father?' he asked me, during a flying visit to our house the day Father was remanded to fourteen days in custody.

Mano da who was been sitting on Ramu da's cot and chatting with me, raised his mischievous eyes towards him. Sanjeev Kumar's make-up was still intact.

'No.'

That flustered him.

'Wouldn't it be good to meet your father?'

'Yes, yes,' said Mano da, laughing heartily. '"Hangwoman Daughter Meets Hangman Father"! Marvellous!'

I liked the sharp point of his humour but refused to laugh.

'Don't tease, Mano da, we can't do these days without some such thing! If Chetna goes there today, that will be big news.' Sanjeev Kumar wouldn't let go.

'But Sanju, what's in it for you? Won't all the channels cover it?'

His face lit up. 'Well, we do have a contract . . . That all of Chetna's trips and visits will be exclusively for CNC.'

'That contract became void the day the execution was postponed.' I spoke with complete confidence.

Mano da agreed with me and turned to Sanjeev Kumar with a pitying look, 'Yes, yes, what a shame!'

But a new glimmer of hope now lit his face. 'No, no, we can think about it. But on condition that we will decide what you do in the coming days.'

'Which means?' Mano da frowned.

'For instance, we will decide that it is better for Chetna to go to Kalighat and perform puja, rather than go to the jail. We will follow her and shoot all her activities.'

'Brilliant!' Mano da laughed disdainfully. I couldn't laugh, though; I kept a watchful gaze on Sanjeev Kumar.

'Baba said that no one is to visit him in prison,' I said. 'And he knows my face has value for TV channels. It won't be proper to reduce its value.'

Mano da looked a bit taken aback but when he looked at me, the naughty smile came back. He nodded vigorously. 'Yes, yes, very true. Don't step out under any circumstances, don't reduce your star value! If they need it so much, let them buy it for a hefty price! After all, you have to live too, my daughter. Two old women in the house, and two little children! Aren't you the one who has to carry the burden of the family?'

Sanjeev Kumar left without continuing the conversation; Mano da gave me a sympathetic smile.

When Sanjeev Kumar came back after a week to check whether I had changed my mind, Mano da was visiting us again.

'Ah, Sanju babu, we'd heard that you're going to marry this girl? When is the wedding?'

A sheepish look spread on Sanjeev Kumar's face. 'Wedding, Mano da? In this mess?'

Mano da gave him a broad smile. 'Son, all creatures in nature know when to hold a hand out to one's mate.'

'In the earlier days, when horse carriages had to travel long distances, some drivers would fix a stick over the heads of the horses and hang a bunch of green grass at its end. The horses would run faster to get at the grass. They never knew that no matter how fast they ran, they wouldn't get to the grass . . .' I sighed involuntarily. 'Our wedding is like that bunch of grass.'

Sanjeev Kumar's face blanched. 'No, never! Don't question my sincerity, Chetna. As far as I am concerned, our wedding has already taken place. It happened that day when I jumped down after you into the cellar. That was the first time my body mingled with a woman's. Mano da, I accepted her as my bride many, many years ago!'

'Even before you met her?' he asked mockingly.

'Yes, even before I saw her. I knew that someone like her would be waiting for me somewhere . . .'

'The hangman's daughter?'

'No, but someone's daughter, somewhere,' he said determinedly.

'In truth, Babu, didn't you make a certain forward calculation in the case of your life's mate?' Mano da's voice was very calm.

'Uh-uh! For each generation, a different standard!'

'Have you given up the plan to set up Kaku as a Maoist?' I wanted to change the subject.

'Why did you ask that? See, Mano da, this is why I can't get along with Chetna! She tears down all that I do to help her. And she's always criticizing me and making fun of me.' He jumped up and left in a huff.

Mano da smiled. 'Since Sudev is no more, what does it matter to him what he is made out to be? Let's make him a Maoist according to Sanju babu's plan. Just for a joke . . .'

Because I could sense the depth of sorrow in his tone, I did not reply.

'The dead are dead. Don't you have to think of the living? If it helps Phani why not think on those lines? They can even say that it was Sudev who killed that woman in Imphal! It has market value.' He laughed. I couldn't help laughing with him.

When Sanjeev Kumar came again after three days, I was alone. That made him more confident.

'I am telling you this for your own sake: this new image will suit you better than marriage at this moment. See, if you get married now, your whole image will change. But if you want, you can be not just the symbol of the self-respect of Indian womanhood and of women everywhere, but also the symbol of love for the nation.'

'The followers of the Ajivaka cult believe that every life is divided into eight phases, Sanjeev Kumar babu,' I said, trying to stay calm.

'Ah, there we go—old tales again!' He got up, irritated, and began to pace about.

'We have to do something . . . when Grddha da gets bail, will the two of you come to the studio?'

'No.'

'But Chetna, there has to be an answer to the question why he did it!'

'Ask Baba.'

'He won't reveal it.'

'Investigate and find out.'

'Look, that'd have been easy if it were big fish, but people like you . . .'

'Small people are harder to crack?' I sighed.

'I'm in no mood to argue. For the time being, let me put to you something that'll help your family and you stay alive. Or become irrelevant.'

He got up as if he was finished.

'Sibdev babu tried his best to make Phani da say that it had happened in a moment of delusion. But no, your father didn't yield. If this is your attitude, I can't help you.'

'If you accept the fact that we don't decide who helps whom, then half the problem is over.' His confusion made me want to laugh again. Despite his persistence, I didn't go to the prison. Father came back on the twenty-first day once he secured bail. A press reporter and a couple of channels were already waiting in the tea shop. I held Champa and Rari close, and sat in a corner of the kitchen. Sanjeev Kumar bounded in.

'Chetna! Where is Chetna?'

I didn't bother to answer.

'If it's about her baba, we know that he's been let out,' said Ma, returning with cleaned fish from next door. The police had taken away our fish chopper.

'No, not that. Where's Chetna?'

I went out to meet him. He ran up, smiling, unable to contain his excitement.

'Chetna, great news! His mercy petition's been dismissed!'

'Vidhi!' I murmured.

'Yes, yes, what excellent judgment!' He was brimming over with enthusiasm. 'Watch—my game starts now!'

He rushed out with that declaration. I felt sorry for him. By 'vidhi' I meant fate, not judgment. When I thought of the lanes through which my life had travelled since 18 May, it struck me that it had a curiously distinct method in its madness. This world pulled me into its huge noose by accident. When I closed my eyes I saw Kaku, Sanjeev Kumar's mother and Maruti Prasad Yadav. I remembered how the printer's ink in Yadav's press stank like menstrual blood. In the nights in which I tossed and turned sleepless beside Rari and Champa, who were completely senseless to the world while they slept, I yearned to walk back through those lanes. Fate, which worked like a country's founding constitution, something that determined well in advance everything in the lives of the innumerable living things—how, when, where things should happen—and, like my father, could find its own reason for everything that happened . . . how I wished something like that existed.

47

The day Jatindranath Banerjee's mercy plea was rejected again, the last hearse was passing by when Father got back home from the jail. Looking at the expensive silver-coloured vehicle, he said, 'Ah, a blessed soul!' and came in. I tossed and turned as usual. An old cow mooed inexhaustibly near the railway crossing. The loud jokes of the lorry drivers hanging around their vehicles near the transport company, and the noisy chirping of the mynahs that had been rudely woken in the banyan tree near the Port Trust quarters kept flowing in. Father didn't seem worn out by his stint in prison. When he finished speaking at length to the reporters who had been waiting for him, he went into his room and changed, and Thakuma went up to his door. I saw him tie the lungi around his waist, and drape the gamchha on his shoulder after rubbing his chest and face with it. He then sat down on the cot and lit a cigarette.

'His mercy plea's been rejected again,' Thakuma told him, holding on to the door frame.

He made an affirmative 'Hm,' focusing on his smoking without looking at her.

'Will you be denied the job because you are now a murder convict?' she asked him in a worried tone. 'If the hanging is postponed for want of a hangman! Bhagawan Mahadev, the land will be ruined, Phani!'

'Will you please go to bed now, Ma? Only the mercy petition has been rejected—so many more hurdles to be overcome. It could get upset at the very last minute!' He spewed the words out, sorely irritated.

'Surely, a question that must be asked when the elder son who's murdered the younger arrives home on bail?' Ma, who went in with a glass of water, put it down noisily.

Both Father and Thakuma looked daggers at her as she left the room; they didn't say word.

'I don't wish to live in the house of such a horrendously evil man for another moment! But what can I do? I have no place to go. Those wicked men! When they cut the country in two wasn't it my home that got lost? Oh God, forty bighas of paddy which grew gold—who knows who's farming it now?' Ma complained in the kitchen.

'Where is Chetna? Call her,' Father said loudly.

I picked myself up, and went to the door. He looked at my undone hair and tired face.

'Are you strong enough to care for this family hereafter?' He let out some smoke.

Thakuma intervened. 'Marry her off to a man capable of continuing our family's profession, Phani. One of my grandfather's brothers went off to Mumbai—why not search them out? Or, forget that. There are other hangmen in this country; let's see if there are smart young men among them?'

'Ma, we can't live in these times just following the family trade—don't be funny!' Father said gruffly. He then said seriously, 'Your wedding must happen soon. Who knows how much time I have left? The death penalty may be banned in the country any time. If that happens, our family trade will itself become extinct.'

'Though we can't feast three times a day, we aren't starving. I work day and night,' Ma ran back once more from the kitchen, glowering. 'I'd like to sell at least some rotis, a bit of bread besides the tea. But there should be some surplus, no?'

'She's started again,' mumbled Thakuma as she got up to go back to her cot.

I put one foot into Father's room. He lifted his face up towards me: 'Uh?'

'Why did you kill Kaku, Baba?'

The question unnerved him a bit. He just sat there head bowed, like a guilty man. Then peered into the nearly smoked out cigarette. 'I didn't intend to kill him . . . he got in the middle.' He sounded honest.

'What did Kakima do to you?'

An immense rage spread on his face. 'If women turn to vice, the family decays. This is no ordinary family. There have never been thieves, murderers, or loose women who besmirch the bloodline. And I won't let that happen now!'

'Loose women who besmirch the bloodline? Who is that?' I went up to him, anxious and eager.

He drew in the rest of the smoke, stubbed out the cigarette and lit a new one. He raised his hand against further questions. 'Don't ask anything more. Let the dead sleep in peace.'

I wilted.

'What Ma said makes sense—you must be married soon. I can then die in peace.'

He wiped his naked chest and shoulders with the gamchha and, swinging his legs, became thoughtful. His eyes were on the iron beam. My eyes followed his. I saw Niharika's body dangling from it. I left his room and went and sat on Ramu da's cot. Champa ran in and switched the TV on. It came alive, popping and wheezing. A woman's voice on CNC declared, 'In the meanwhile, Jatindranath's family has decided to approach the Supreme Court again . . .' Champa was going to change the channel, but hearing the name, she looked at me and pulled her hand away. 'This is to request that the hanging be postponed as Jatindranath is mentally unbalanced. The organizations that oppose the death penalty have decided to launch a door-to-door campaign to generate public opinion against the hanging. CNC's special correspondent Sanjeev Kumar Mitra reports that the follow-up procedures regarding that have not yet been clearly identified. Sanjeev, can you tell us what is going on at Writers' Buildings?'

Sanjeev Kumar appeared in his dark glasses and a blue shirt. 'Anindita, the central ministry for home affairs has not yet formally communicated its decision about the death sentence to the West Bengal government. Once it is received, the government will approach the high court to fix a date. The ruling government and the ruling parties have expressed their approval of the rejection of the mercy plea. The chief minister's wife has appealed once more that people should desist from representing Jatindranath's crime as a minor one. The jail authorities have increased the number of policemen guarding Jatindranath in Alipore prison from ten to twenty upon learning that his mercy petition has been rejected.'

'What has been his response to the rejection?'

'I hear that he is most dejected. He learned of it through the radio. The jail authorities say that he has not eaten anything since, nor is he talking to anyone.'

'Is there a chance that the hanging will be further delayed?'

'We can't say anything about that, Anindita. This is the President's second rejection of the plea. Jatindranath's execution has been fixed twice before, but both times, it was postponed. A month back, it was postponed just hours before the hanging, taking into account his family's appeal. The President had sought the opinion of the home ministry in this regard. The ministry's response was that he deserved no mercy. They highlighted the fact that there were sixteen wounds on the body of the young girl he murdered. At the same time, a group of twenty lawyers have come together to defend Jatindranath. It is reported that they plan to approach the Supreme Court.'

I switched off the TV because it made me tremble. But Father came in and turned it on again. Sibdev babu's face appeared.

'Yesterday too he ate as usual. For lunch he had rice, dal, vegetables and a piece of fried fish. He had six pieces of bread, butter and a glass of milk for breakfast. He bathed as usual at noon. The guards were on alert outside the bathroom. It's not like I can run away from here now, he protested. Not because of that, I told him. For your own good. So that you don't slip in the bathroom and break your leg.'

'Sibdev babu, there is news that he is mentally unbalanced?'

That was Sanjeev Kumar's voice.

'A big lie. The jail doctor Bimandev Mukherjee examined him. He's certified that Jatindranath is physically and mentally fit. In addition to that, we are seeing to it that he doesn't catch the tiniest of ailments,' he said, a mild smile on his face.

'Sibdev babu, have you spoken to him since the rejection of the petition?'

'Yes, he was pacing up and down the cell. He tuned the radio, and then came to the bars and asked if he had any visitors.'

'Did anyone visit him recently?'

'No.'

Sibdev babu's face reappeared.

'His brother Kartik had come a little earlier, but Banerjee did not want to meet him.'

'Is he expecting someone else?'

Sibdev babu smiled. 'Maybe. Aren't human beings unfathomable? How can we say what anyone wants? He does ask if there are any visitors, but doesn't care to meet his family members when they come.'

'This man who knows that death is now at the door to his cell even though the date has not been fixed—whom is he waiting for? Is it for death itself? We are not sure . . . From the Alipore Central Correctional Home, this is Sanjeev Kumar Mitra along with Atul Kishore Chandra, CNC . . .'

Father stroked his moustache and looked at me. 'Said nothing substantial, these fellows!'

The news that followed was about the death of a woman in Imphal and the consequent protests. Jatindranath was a security guard who had killed a young girl and was now behind bars, awaiting his punishment by death. The security forces of the country had done the same in Imphal, yet people had to rage in the streets to get them punished. How immensely strange!

48

When Queen Saba decided to visit Sulaiman immediately after he threatened to wage war against her people if they refused to accept Allah, the Only God, it was because she wished to rescue them from humiliation. All kings, faithful to God or not, are like that, she told her ministers. They seize the land, contaminate the soil and the water, and turn the wisest of the wise into slaves. And so, to save her people, she set out for Sulaiman's palace. The king was adamant that when she reached his court, she ought to be able to sit on her own throne. So he bid some of his slave djinns to steal it from her palace and bring it to him. When she entered his court, the king pointed to the throne and said, please sit down, will this throne suffice? Seeing her throne in the enemy's court, Saba was silent. It is only a chair now, she said, if it is to be a throne, my people should bow down to it. Sulaiman fell in love with her and took her to a marvellous crystal palace. When the sun's rays entered the rooms through the pure crystal roof of the palace at dawn, they split into the seven colours of the rainbow. The very first day, when the queen opened the door of her chamber at dawn, she saw the king at his morning prayer. He was clad in pure white garments and seated on a white floor mat; innumerable globes of light in the seven colours of the rainbow danced around him.

I was narrating the story of Queen Saba to Rari when Sanjeev Kumar came to tell us that the date of the execution had been fixed. He was in a state of high excitement. I had been trying to get Rari to stop playing with the water Ma had collected from the tap the night before. Maybe because one still *had* to retell this tale though it was some two thousand years since it was first heard, it always made me afraid.

'A good date—14 August!' he said, ignoring Rari who was hiding shyly from him. 'Chetna, it will happen this time. It has to! That's why they are not allowing time for yet another mercy petition or court intervention.'

I looked at him with all the irritation of a storyteller interrupted midway.

'He is still hopeful. Because it did get postponed at the last minute last time. But I see no such possibility this time. Even if it does we will get a few days' respite.'

I dried Rari, tied the same towel around her waist and sent her in to change. Then I dealt with him.

'Why do you think so?'

'We have to plan something for these intervening days. Chetna, could you please come with me to the prison once? If we can create a story about you visiting the jail to console and comfort him, it will do you good, and him too.'

'What good is it to the man who is to die if the person appointed to kill him offers consolation?'

'You can console him, can't you?'

I couldn't help laughing.

'That has big news value, Chetna!'

'All I hear in this house these days is about killing and dying. And see what's happened—there's nothing left in this house except killing and dying. Can you please let human beings give up all this, escape from it all and live in peace, Babu?' Ma came in and scolded him, having changed Rari into dry clothes.

His face grew callous. 'Ah! So I've outlived my usefulness! Maybe someone's made a better offer and you want to get rid of me?'

'I just can't keep on accepting help and more help from you, that's why . . .' I too didn't flinch.

'I have always tried to do good by you. Only for your well-being.' He

385

moved away, throwing me a disgruntled look. 'Cooperate some more in the following days, Chetna, it will be very advantageous for you. Don't worry about the expenses and money. I'll take care of all that.' Then, hesitating, he continued, 'If it is about the wedding . . .'

'Don't speak of it any more!'

'Why, have you found someone else?' He frowned.

I lost control again. 'Anyone will do. Must be a man, that's all. Anyone with the qualifications to become a hangman can marry a hangwoman. Must be a man; should have presence of mind—that's all.'

'You don't know how much pressure I had to put to change that rule,' he whimpered.

'You reaped the greater benefit from it, anyway.'

'I don't want to argue with you. Don't challenge me. If I decide to do something, I know how to get it done.' He challenged me.

'Excellent!' I shot back.

He walked out. But I was perturbed.

'Chetu di, what happened to Queen Saba?'

Rari, who seemed to have been waiting impatiently for him to disappear, came running and pulled my dupatta. Champa too joined us. I continued with the story.

The king prepared a fantastic feast for Queen Saba—with pepper and cardamom from south India. He expressed his wish to marry her, but she said, don't insist on marrying me. Then he set a condition, don't take anything valuable from the palace without my permission.

The girls' faces lit up with interest.

Saba was fabulously rich and did not need anything expensive. So she went to bed peacefully. At night, moonlight filled the crystal palace. The stars shone on each crystal and they multiplied in many reflections. When she shut her eyes and tried to sleep, Saba felt thirsty. The spice in the food she had eaten made her feel all the more thirsty.

'And then?' Rari's little eyes sparkled with an eager smile that made me remember Kaku; I felt pain.

But no sooner had Queen Saba sipped from a glass of water she had poured herself from the golden jug beside the bed than the king jumped into her room! You have broken your word, he shouted. She told him, I have taken nothing valuable. But he let out a loud snort of laughter and said, what is more valuable in this world than water? The queen admitted defeat.

Rari's face clouded with thought. 'I will never eat spicy food!' she said. 'And never go to any king's house.'

I patted her head.

'But I'd like to see the palace full of rainbows! Is it still there, Chetu di?' Champa asked.

'No, it fell to ruin, a long time back.'

'And what happened to Queen Saba, Chetu di?'

Before I could answer, I saw Sanjeev Kumar outside the house. I felt irked by his presence.

'You haven't left yet?'

'Don't think I'll leave so soon,' he smirked. 'The police have come searching for you.'

There was a triumphant lilt to that. I went to Father's room and opened the front door. Two policemen stood there.

'The copy of the court order.' One of them held out an official envelope.

'Baba is not at home, Babu.'

'This is for you,' he said, then pulled out a packet of paan masala from his pocket, tore it open and put the contents into his mouth.

I took the envelope with trembling hands and checked the address.

To
Ms Chetna Grddha Mullick
Official Hangwoman

I held it in my hand, unsure of what to do.

'You've to come and meet the IG. The jeep is here.'

'Baba is not at home.' I swallowed hard.

'They don't want your baba any more, Chetna. He is a murderer. The government could never appoint a murderer as a hangman.' Sanjeev Kumar Mitra chuckled.

I had no response to that.

'The jeep is here,' the policeman repeated. I looked at him and Sanjeev Kumar. It didn't take much time for me to decide. As the lowest link in the chain of law and order, I was duty-bound to obey the summons. I went in, changed, asked Ma for something to put in my purse.

'You'll go alone in the jeep?' Ma asked, at a loss.

'Don't be afraid. I'll be back soon.'

'Ma Kali! Protect my child!' she prayed, raising her eyes to the sky. A thin ray of sunlight entering the room through a tiny hole in the asbestos fell on Ma's silver hair, making a rainbow there.

As I sat in the jeep, I saw the CNC vehicle follow us. The policeman sat opposite me in the back of the jeep. His eyes roved on my body as he chewed the masala. The fingers of my left hand twisted around my dupatta. The fact that he had forgotten I was a hangwoman about to hang a man who had raped and killed a young girl did rankle me. I peered at him closely; the bones in his neck stuck out.

'Uh-um?' he asked.

'The bones in your neck stick out,' I said.

He rubbed his neck on impulse. 'So what?'

'You'll be finished in a second with a noose.' I smiled sweetly.

His face dimmed. When he looked at me again, not lust but fear shone in his eyes. And then he stopped looking. Sanjeev Kumar's vehicle reached the Writers' Buildings ahead of us. As I walked to E Block, through the front of the red-painted building, his camera followed me, pointed like a gun. I paid no attention to him and entered the lift with the policemen. We reached the fourth-floor room which bore the sign I.D.G.P. and I.G. (C.S.). The policeman went in, asking me to wait. Sanjeev Kumar hurried there after us.

'Are you scared to meet the IG?'

'Chakrabarti babu?'

'No, this is a Srinath Mullick. Accused in two custodial death cases. Take care!'

I didn't reply. My heart beat calmly. Half an hour later, I was summoned. When I stood at the door and said, 'Excuse me, Babu,' a pair of round eyes in an unattractive face of about fifty looked up at me.

'Chetna Grddha Mullick. So is it you the government has appointed as the hangwoman?'

I took a few steps in and stood with my head bowed.

'Very young! Your old man didn't come?'

'No, Babu.'

'Are you brave enough to go to the jail on your own?'

He got up to come and stand directly in front of me. A young man in plain clothes who sat by the computer in a corner of the room averted his eyes in fear.

'Do you have the guts to hang a man?'

'Yes, Babu.'

'What's the guarantee?'

'If you allow me, I can show you, Babu.'

He picked up a wooden ruler from the table and extended it towards me. Startled, I took a step back. He reached out and raised my dupatta with the ruler and surveyed my chest.

'Let me see . . . your condition . . .'

My legs froze. But my blood boiled and my hand tingled. The man in the corner of the room stooped further, utterly revolted.

'Huh, good!'

His eyes bored into mine. I could not pull away mine either. We stood there for a while, like fighting cocks, locked in each others' menacing gaze. There was ten times the arrogance and dominance of Sanjeev Kumar in this man's gaze. I felt utterly nauseated.

'How many times did you do Chakrabarti?' He came closer.

'What?' My voice changed.

He laughed aloud contemptuously and I knew what he was hinting at. I felt sorry for Maruti Prasad Yadav then.

'Babu, I could leave if you'd just give me the papers.' Controlling myself, I tried to manage a smile.

'I need to see you again. I will send the car this evening.'

I looked at him unwaveringly for a few seconds, and then laughed. The man in the corner looked at me in disbelief. The IG opened a file, pulled out some papers, signed them and handed them to me.

'Hm! Leave now!' He muttered an obscenity. 'The car will come by evening, okay?' he called out.

'I will be waiting, Babu.'

When I stepped out of the room, Sanjeev Kumar came up to me. I smiled sweetly this time. He came closer with an apprehensive look.

'Don't you have to see the superintendent?

389

'Uh-hm.'

'May I come too?'

I didn't say yes or no. He came out with me. As usual, his cameraman buzzed around me like a bee. I remembered the tale of Shah Ismail Khazi who was deputed by Sultan Ruknuddin Barbak Shah of Bengal in the fifteenth century to extend his kingdom by conquering Kalinga and Kamarupa. He conquered Kalinga but had to admit defeat in Kamarupa. King Kameshwar of Kamarupa decided to execute him. His executioner was my ancestor, Nathu Grddha Mullick. Ismail Khazi requested him to let him pray before the execution. The king allowed it and Ismail Khazi began to pray to God, Most Gracious, Most Compassionate, on a white sheet laid on the raised dais of the gallows platform. The king raised his eyes to heaven, following Ismail Khazi's eyes, and was dazzled by light which had split into brilliant slivers the colours of a rainbow. They pierced the king's eyes, and he trembled. What is your last wish, the king asked Ismail Khazi. Take me, said Khazi, but do not harm my soldiers. King Kameshwar felt a deep affection for him. He cancelled the execution, and in his company, the king embraced Islam. But Barbak was envious of Ismail Khazi's popularity and had him assassinated and his head and body buried in different places.

Barbak Shah's grandson and heir was mentally unsound and so after his death, Barbak's brother Jalaluddin Fateh Shah ascended the throne. He was killed by one of the palace guards, Shahzada Jaluddin, an Abyssinian descended from Queen Saba. Jaluddin seized the throne, but another Abyssinian, Saifuddin Firuz Shah, a faithful aide of Fateh Shah, overthrew him, and claimed the seat of power. But he too was killed before long. His son Mahmood Shah was only three years old. Both the toddler sultan and the regent Habish Khan were murdered by Shamsuddin Musafar Shah. But in just a few years, Shamsuddin was hacked to death by his own accountant who revolted against him. Thakuma said it is Ismail Khazi's curse that has befallen us. When he was being overpowered, he cursed Barbak Shah: May you forever feel the terrible pain of your breast being cleaved in two. That's why our land has been cleaved thus, she said.

When the jeep stopped at the Judges' Court Road near the prison, I got out and walked ahead briskly. Sanjeev Kumar and the cameraman had to run to catch up with me. I stepped into the jail yard, which was shaped like the letter A, with confidence. Sibdev babu greeted me sadly. Sanjeev Kumar followed me in.

'I thought Grddha da would come too?' he said as he signed the papers.

'Baba is not at home, Babu.'

'Will you be able to handle this by yourself?'

'I think so, Babu.'

'You can ask some of the policemen to help you tie the condemned man's arms and legs.'

'No need, Babu.'

There was determination in my voice. Sanjeev Kumar and Sibdev babu looked at each other.

'I will do all that myself. That is very important to me.'

'Okay, as you wish. Shouldn't you examine the rope?'

'Yes, I'll do it.'

I chose the Manila rope from Buxar Jail. I did not sneeze this time when I took it out of the iron almirah.

'I can do the first test hanging if we can find a sack and sand,' I offered, as if I'd been in this business for many years.

As I walked ahead, passing the government press and through the schoolyard in the jail, I forgot not just Sanjeev Kumar Mitra but the whole world. The convicts who were cleaning the front of the welfare office looked up at me, passed some comment and laughed. I noticed the cell which had been occupied by Netaji. I then went towards the gallows platform, turning left from Netaji's cell. Sanjeev Kumar gazed at me, wonderstruck. The sack which Father had used to do the test hanging lay there soggy from the rain and bleached by the sun. I had it filled again and tested the rope. The prisoners clearing up the yard stopped working to look at me. I heard them say something. But my mind did not dither, nor did my hands shake, not even for a second, when I put the noose on the sandbag and got up on the stool to tie the rope on the hook.

'Will it rain today?' I asked, looking at the sky.

'It rained heavily yesterday. Many places are flooded and waterlogged,' said Sibdev babu.

'If it rains, it will have to be taken down. If not, let it hang like this for a while.'

'Okay, I'll see to that. You can go now if you wish. I'll get someone to do it.'

'No, Babu, I'll take it down myself. That's my job.'

'So you'll wait till then?'

'Yes.'

'In that case, there is one more thing. We usually ask the condemned person his last wish. We've managed to get whatever he asked the last couple of times. But this time he's asked for something different . . .'

I was all ears.

'He wants to meet you and speak with you.'

Not just I, even Sanjeev Kumar and the two policemen there were taken aback.

My tension eased after a moment. I smiled. 'I don't mind, Babu.'

'Come, then.'

He moved to the right, to the side of the condemned's cells. I read their numbers clearly: 1, 2, 3. He went up to cell no. 3 and waited for me. My steps were slow. I waited on the veranda on which there was some sunlight still. A man sat inside, a radio to his ear. He got up and came towards the bars. We looked at each other. He was not wearing a shirt. The bones stuck out prominently on his thin chest.

'It'll happen this time, won't it?' he asked.

I looked at his yellowed face and sunken eyes.

'Nothing more unpredictable . . .' I couldn't complete the sentence.

'Chetna di, you are an executioner. Will anyone marry you?' he asked.

Because I hadn't expected him to ask such a question, I was silent.

He raised his hands and held the bars. 'Ever since I first saw you I've been thinking: can't you marry my younger brother, Kartik? He, the brother of the executed, you the woman who executes. You two won't find better matches!'

Losing all capacity for words, I looked at him. By the time she came out of the crystal palace, Saba had embraced Allah as her Supreme God. Was it for water? Was it for her people? She did not say. I thought, perhaps it was to sustain the colours in the palace of love built of clear crystal? When I turned back, far beyond the high walls behind the gallows tree, the sun, sapped by age, began to fall off like a head severed by an invisible noose.

I stood before Netaji's cell for a moment. Sanjeev Kumar caught up with me.

'What did he say, Chetna?'

I smiled at him. 'I accept your offer. Ten thousand rupees.'

'Why the sudden change?'

'From today, each moment of mine is yours. You must follow me everywhere with that camera of yours.'

'Great!' He smiled.

I walked out, telling him to follow me. The touch of the wooden ruler on my breasts when it raised my dupatta hadn't faded.

49

If women want to stand up straight they should be willing to bend occasionally, Thakuma said. That's the first lesson women ought to learn. I kept murmuring it in my mind as I sat in the CNC studio with Sanjeev Kumar Mitra. He was not in a hurry because the show was not going to be telecast live. The stress of having hauled up a sandbag all by myself stayed in my arm. There are plenty of stories in history of people bending because they were unable to stand straight, I fumed. Even the 'Bankim' of Bankim Chandra Chatterjee's name means 'a little curved'. When Sri Ramakrishna Paramahamsa teased him, 'What happened, A Little Curved?' he replied, 'Because of the kicks from shoe-clad feet.' He served the British as a deputy magistrate and sang 'Vande Mataram'. It was my ancestor Narottam Grddha Mullick who prepared the rope for Muzzafar Khazi Choudhury who wanted a noose to commit suicide, refusing to bend before the British. The same Narottam worked under Khazi Choudhury's son who was ready to bend before them. When the junior Choudhury hunted with British officers Narottam joined the group of servants who made loud banging noises to flush the prey out of their shelters. Later, when the choudhury's daughter Faizunnesa became the choudhurani, Narottam protested against accepting the authority of a woman, that too a Muslim woman. He returned from Tripura to our family home and its incessant succession quarrels. At that time, the choudhurani's husband, Muhammed Khazi Choudhury, approached Narottam and bought his loyalty. He then tried, till Muhammed's death, to help men who wanted to seduce the choudharani.

'No, I have no hope that crimes against women will end with this hanging,' I declared, sitting as firmly as I could in the old chair in the studio.

The currency notes I had demanded and got, correctly counted, writhed inside my purse.

'Banerjee is going to be executed for having raped and killed a young girl. Even the chief minister has declared that this will be a strong message to those who offend women's honour and dignity.'

Sanjeev Kumar looked at me with a victorious smile. I experienced, all over again, the pain his hand had inflicted on my left breast, and the agonies he had showered on me in the cellar. A sourness invaded my mouth.

'Yesterday, before I went to the prison, a police officer poked my breasts with a wooden ruler. He threatened to send his car to my house this evening. If I go where he wants in that car, I will be raped too, for sure. Will the chief minister punish a police officer like him? What is the guarantee?'

Sanjeev Kumar looked utterly shocked. He sat up. 'Unbelievable! That a senior police officer dared to behave thus to a woman in this democracy? Why didn't you complain, Chetna?'

'If I complain, will you assure me justice, Sanjeev babu?' I looked intently at him.

'Can't you reveal the name of the police officer who did this to you?'

'I will, most surely, if he repeats it.'

'Why do you try to protect him now?'

'I hope this sends out a strong message to him.'

'But being a senior officer, can't he trap you easily?'

'I believe in people's goodness. I want to give him a chance to become good.'

'But you deny that chance to the man who is to be hanged, Jatindranath!'

'Not me, it is the state that has denied him the chance.'

Suddenly, Sanjeev Kumar pulled the mike off and rushed to his superior's room. In a minute, Harish Nath came out running.

'Chetna, what we are recording now will be telecast in two hours. What you said about the police officer—that's a political bomb. If you can give us more details, we can put it on the nine o'clock news as a special bulletin.'

'What for?'

'Shouldn't the guilty be punished?'

'There are other names in the list of the guilty, in that case. For instance, you, Sanjeev Kumar Mitra.'

'What! I don't like this over-smart preening you're doing! There's a saying back home that one should not stretch too tall, unmindful of the hump!'

'My Thakuma says, one bends in one place to stand up straight elsewhere!'

I twisted Thakuma's words a bit to let him see what a strange relationship he and I shared. Harish Nath and Sanjeev Kumar exchanged helpless glances. They tried to bring me around for some time. I faced them both with a broad smile. After some time they found it unbearable. When Sanjeev Kumar sat down again, suppressing an angry obscenity, I really wanted to laugh. But I was still worried as I went home in the channel's car. What will be the culmination of this constant repetition—of taking refuge in him and then running away, wounded? The Hemant Kumar song *Pather shesh kothai, ki aache shesh pather* . . . filled the car. The hangman's rope from the jail, which I had brought with me according to the custom, sat inside an old sack on the seat beside me. I held on tightly to it. I felt a deep affection towards it, coiled inside the smoothness of the plastic sack like the root of some ancient tree. At the end of the ride, following a large crowd and a hearse that moved at a snail's pace, I practised in my mind the acts of tying the rope on the hook and pulling the lever. By the time I took the hangman's rope to Father's room and placed it under Dadu's picture, I was a changed person.

'Where were you?' asked Father.

'At Alipore Jail. Then at the channel. I agreed to renew the contract.'

Maybe it was my fearless tone, but Father's eyes bore into me.

'So you have become able enough to make all the decisions yourself?'

'The policemen didn't let me ask for your permission. They won't let you be the hangman because you're the defendant in a murder case.'

'Who says that I can't be the hangman? In so many countries, it is such people who work as hangmen!' He was angry.

'Anyway, that's not allowed in this country.'

'It's allowed in many places!'

'But I don't decide these things, Baba.'

His eyes grew redder. 'You should have threatened to leave the job! Your rash, disobedient act will affect us all. You think hanging is simple? That you can do it all alone?'

'Baba, haven't you been doing it alone?' I asked, my voice calm.

'Huh! Listen to that! Haven't I been doing it alone! I am a man whereas you are a mere woman!'

'But Baba, you yourself said that I am the symbol of woman's power for the women of the entire world!'

A towering rage gathered on his face.

'Huh! One has to say many such things for the reporters and their audiences. That's just politically correct talk! Not practically correct, though. The fact that you are a woman and hence have many limitations is the practically correct thing!'

'I have no limitations now that will affect my ability to carry out a hanging, Baba.'

Because I had begun to pant, he stared at me incredulously.

'I went to meet the jail minister,' he let me know in a disenchanted tone. 'I have asked to be allowed to come with you as an assistant. If that is allowed, I'll be able to make sure that you don't make a mistake. The fact that you've never done this before makes me very afraid.'

'I am not the least scared, Baba,' I assured him.

That was true. My breasts had grown hard as stones. The pain I had felt when Maruti Prasad grabbed them from behind, when Sanjeev Kumar wrung them, when the police officer touched them with his ruler, had vanished. The urge to kill frothed at my fingertips. I need to kill a man, I decided, stubbornly. My fingertips must feel the last throb of his life's breath. That will be my message to the world, I thought. When I came back after a bath, Father was waiting for me.

'Really, if you hang someone, who will marry you? Just calling oneself a hangman is very different from being one. That bothers me as each day passes . . .' His voice choked. 'Chetu di, listen to your baba. Tell the IG babu and the minister that you can't do this without your baba. They must say, let him be present there as an assistant. Only then can we make use of this chance.'

He came over and placed his hand on my shoulder. Father's effort to appease me made me laugh.

'No, Baba. That won't work.'

Astonishment spread on his face.

'Don't be crazy, Chetu, if it goes wrong, our entire bloodline will be tainted!'

'It won't go wrong,' I stated, firm and clear. 'I want to do this by myself. Even if you simply stand beside the gallows with your arms folded, Baba, no one will believe I did it. The hangman's daughter. His mere assistant! Besides, what right does a man who chased a woman and hacked her to death have to hang another who raped and murdered a young girl? I make the ideal executioner for Jatindranath Banerjee. I want the status of the hangman, not of the hangman's daughter!'

When Magistrate Douglas recommended that the British government confer honours upon Faizunnesa Choudhrani, Queen Victoria offered her the title of begum first.

'I am already a begum,' she told the Resident Sahib who came to give her the news. 'It's no use becoming a begum again. If the empress would like to acknowledge my abilities, then I should be given the title of nawab. I will accept nothing less.'

'But, Choudhurani,' the Resident Sahib began, 'that title is for men.'

'That's because women haven't been given a chance to be rulers.'

In the end the British gave her the title of nawab. Thus she held court and discussed the affairs of government with her ministers, travelled the country, and went hunting in her veil. She lay on her bed—one half of which remained unoccupied—which was covered with the soft pelt of the Bengal tigers she had hunted, and wrote her autobiography, perpetually troubled by the eternal war between organized religion and the woman's body.

'Okay, okay, what do you plan to do now?' Father asked, as if throwing a challenge.

'I performed the sandbag test today,' I said. 'It was a success. I will go there once again tomorrow. Before that, tonight, I will smoothen the rope. Then I will discuss the condemned convict's health status with the jail doctor. Speak about other things with the IG babu and Superintendent babu. After that, I'll sign the papers. I'll tell them that I will want the remuneration right then, and in cash.'

Father kept gaping at me.

'And then?'

'I know what to do, Baba, don't worry about me.' I sounded vexed.

'Okay, okay, how much did you get from the channel? Give it to me; I need to meet the lawyer tomorrow.'

He held out his hand. I continued to sit there, holding him fully in my gaze.

'Stop sitting there pop-eyed! Hand me the cash!' He leapt up, scowling.

'Tell me first why you killed Kakima.'

He didn't expect that. 'You needn't know that!'

'If I need not know that, then don't harbour hopes about the money I earned!' My voice became louder.

Father squirmed as if he had been hit and stood glaring at me. 'What did you say, you arrogant—'

'I'll give you the money if you tell me why you killed her.'

He got up and went into the house, then rushed out in a frenzy and hauled me up by the neck. I thought he was about to strangle me but I didn't struggle or fight back. I knew by then that I had not just the urge to kill but also the urge to die.

'Baba, I need to know!' My voice was unforgiving.

He released me then, weakly, went inside, had a drink and came back. Ma came in with a pot full of water on her hip. Seeing her, he grew weaker and more helpless.

'Why, what's happening here?' Ma placed the greenish pot in the courtyard and hurried back into the room.

'I asked Baba why he killed Kakima. He hauled me up by the neck.'

Ma's voice was lethargic. 'Who knows? Maybe he grabbed her forgetting that she was his brother's wife?'

'Chi! You beast!' Father lunged forward, caught Ma by the neck and shook her head hard. 'I'll kill you too, you fool! I killed her so that I won't have to grab her! I can't accept a cheap whore as my sister-in-law!'

Ma freed her head. Father beat his head with both his hands and looked at us, trying to control his panting.

'I saw her at Kalighat . . . in a place where she shouldn't be seen . . .'

I stood still, overwhelmed.

'Do you think I will suffer that?'

The room was filled with quiet.

'She went there to make money to take Sudev for treatment to Madras,' said Ma, without the slightest hint of bewilderment, untying her hair and tying it up again. 'Treatment here would have cost three lakhs. There, it'd cost only one and a half. That's why she . . .' Ma's voice choked. 'If I were in her place, if it were you who suffered, bloated up, in pain, not able to pee, I'd have gone there even now, in my sixties. Or taken this girl to sell. What else is left in this house to sell? Your family history from four hundred years before Christ?'

When Ma stepped out of the room, laughing loudly, Father's eyes bulged and his mouth opened and shut desperately, as if he were drowning. A veritable lake welled up in his eyes. He hobbled to his cot and stretched out on it. Ma and I stood near the door and looked at each other. We heard a sound, like that of a very, very old clay idol falling to the ground and crumbling into dust. Ma rubbed her chest and went into the kitchen. My wet hair dried instantly from the heat of my body.

Thakuma returned with little Champa and Rari. She had brought prasad from Hemu da's temple. She came in, rubbed a little ash from a pyre on my forehead, and daubed some sindoor paste made with the blood of a sacrificed fowl. 'Everything will go auspiciously,' she said to no one in particular.

I hugged Rari and Champa, and sat on the cot. 'Chetu di, when you kill him, will his eyes pop out?' Rari asked.

'Will he cry out?' Champa wanted to know.

'No.'

I held them closer and laughed. Champa was beginning to ask something else when a loud knock was heard at the door.

'Grddha da, open the door!'

That was Sibdev babu. When Father opened the door, I too got up.

'You've got into a fine fix, haven't you? What all did you blab on TV?' he asked, deeply perturbed, seeing me.

Father and I were both equally perplexed.

'The telecast is still on. Before it ends, the reporters are all going to mob you here. Whatever you say, it will affect the government badly! We have orders to remove you quickly.'

'To remove her! Where to?' Father's voice boomed.

'For the time being, to the jail. Till the hanging is over, no one from the press is allowed to have any contact with her!'

I stood there, dumbfounded.

'Bring enough clothes for two days, and the rope, of course.'

'Babu, she is a child. Will she be able to do it alone?' Father's voice was feeble.

'Grddha da, you should have thought of that earlier!' Sibdev babu lost his temper.

'Better do it well . . . remember, the chief minister and his wife and many other important people are coming to watch it!' Father said.

I didn't even know what to think.

'But Babu, to take a girl like her to a jail where there are only men . . .'

'Don't you worry about that, Grdhha da. She will not come to any harm in Alipore Jail. No one will utter even an indelicate word! I assure you that. Chetna, quick!'

I went mechanically to my room. Ma, Rari and Champa watched, electrified. I gathered my clothes into a plastic bag, and then Champa and Rari came and hugged me tightly; I kissed them. After I had soothed them both, I opened my purse and took out five thousand rupees and gave the money to Ma. Thakuma held me by the shoulders and kissed me on the forehead. I then hurried to Father's room to get the rope. When the sack was opened, Thakuma came in and lifted it effortlessly towards the pictures on the walls, closed her eyes and prayed. She then placed it on my shoulders. I stood up straight, like a young warrior bound for battle with the bow on her shoulder.

'Bless me, Baba,' I whispered.

'Stop.' He wiped his eyes, lit the sandal incense sticks, and waved them before the images of Ma Kali and Bhagawan Mahadev. I folded my hands in prayer. When he gave me the sticks and told me to place them before Dadu's image, his eyes welled up again. When I moved them in front of his face, I looked sadly into his eyes which were still moist with the memories of his lost love. Father then fished out the liquor bottle from behind Dadu's picture, poured a little into its cap, and held it out to me. I did what I had seen Father do: think of Dadu and our ancestors and splatter a few drops three times. After having made the offering, I looked at Father, who was watching me with hands folded, and Sibdev babu, and poured the rest into my mouth. Everybody gaped. Like Faizunnesa who wore the veil and went off to the jungle to hunt, I too felt the urge to declare, I am not a begum, I am a nawab. When the grating taste of the liquor seared my tongue, I said to no one in particular—I am not the hangman's daughter, I am the hangwoman. There was a distance of just hours between me and that status; fifty-four hours, to be exact. When the rope, worth just one hundred and eighty-two rupees, which lay on my shoulders, poked my arms and breasts and gave me pain, I thought: This too is a man. Till then I had thought otherwise. I had the wrong idea that the rope, which lay bent, waiting for a chance to straighten its spine, was a woman like me.

50

Sibdev babu found a space for me to make a bed in the welfare office of Alipore Jail. It drizzled all night. The dust-covered files and the papers that rustled in the breeze from the fan overhead reminded me of the *Bhavishyath* office. A young woman constable, Kadambini Ghosh, had been deputed to keep me company. Whenever Sibdev babu moved away, she chatted joyfully on the cell phone with her boyfriend. I found the delicate smile that bloomed on her lips as she looked at the cell phone both attractive and irritating. I could never create the fantasy of such a man; nor could I claim for myself that smile which made a woman exquisitely lovely. Therefore, when they chatted, I threw open the windows on the left side wall of the office. I saw, immediately, Netaji's cell in the yellow light, like a sunken ship. Behind it towered the gallows tree. Late at night, I woke up to the sounds of a wrestling match somewhere nearby. Kadambini Ghosh was fast asleep on her back, hugging the cell phone to her chest. I went to the window and looked out. Below the gallows tree, two old men were locked in mortal combat. One of them was about seven feet tall, and heavily built. His skin was completely wrinkled, like the folds of a bag; it was impossible to guess his age. When he stepped up and moved away, when he raised his leg or attacked his opponent with his fists, his flesh could be seen crinkling inside his infirm skin. The other was a middle-aged man, much shorter. One of them wore a blue loin cloth, and the other a red one. I knew their faces well but could not recall where I'd met them. After some time I heard someone mutter from just below the window, 'Today Mosh will throw Grddha.' 'If so, let's call Agnimitra,' someone else opined. 'It's time to draw a black curtain between a red and a blue, Satyanatha,' said a woman's voice. Women? Here? I was flabbergasted. 'Pingalakeshini, where is Ratnamalika?' asked another very roguish voice. Suddenly light dawned in my brain—they were my ancestors. I had only heard of them and so could not recognize them by sight. My hair stood on end; this was simply unbelievable. I was assailed by waves of heat and cold simultaneously. I woke up with a start to find myself standing beside the same window. The yellow light burned bright behind the gallows. I could see cell no. 1 and no. 3 vaguely. I felt someone stand holding its bars. I went back to bed breathing hard. Even when dawn arrived the heavy breathing had not left me.

'IG babu is here.' Sibdev babu hurried into the welfare office at nine, when the police convoy reached the jail gate.

'Don't argue with him,' he said, 'he is a difficult man.'

'He is a Mullick. So am I.' I tried to laugh.

'Don't laugh. He is angry enough to kill you. Just wait till the hanging is over and I'll teach her a lesson, that's what he bellowed when he saw your show on TV. He's surely going to give Grddha da a hard time.'

That didn't scare me at all. Before long, Srinath Mullick entered, followed by some policemen, anger and embarrassment written all over his face. Our eyes met when he reached the office; his were fiery with rage. But that didn't affect me even a bit.

'It's time to examine the gallows. The hangman should come along.'

He gave me a severe look. I went down the steps smiling at him and walked, in no apparent hurry, towards the gallows. My eyes darted towards cell no. 3. Jatindranath stood there looking at us, pressing his face on the bars. As I set my dupatta right and got on the gallows platform, I felt that I was stepping on a theatre stage. A group of prisoners from the two-storey wards came out to watch. I pulled off the plastic sheet which protected the rope from the rain.

'The noose! Where is the noose?' The IG addressed me wrathfully.

'Babu, the noose is knotted just before the hanging,' I told him humbly.

I tied the end of the rope and hanged the sandbag. The sandbag which had soaked up the night's showers weighed heavy on the rope and turned round and round. Suddenly, it looked like Father's body. I broke out in a cold sweat.

'Babu, it weighs more than seventy-five kilos. One and a half times the convict's body mass,' Sibdev babu stepped up and told him.

'How much does the rope weigh?' he asked.

Sibdev babu looked at me.

'3.2 kilos,' I said, after a moment.

'How are you so sure?'

'Familiarity. From seeing it all the time; hearing about it all the time.'

My smile provoked him further. In truth, that smile had become a part of my face.

'You talk too much. I will teach you a lesson!' he said, as though throwing a challenge.

I laughed again. He stormed off towards Jatindranath's cell. Sibdev babu threw me an anxious glance and hurried after him. I could hear him ask something when he reached the front of the cell; in the strong breeze, it wasn't really audible. After speaking with Jatindranath, he spun around and walked back towards me with large strides; he looked like an assassin approaching me. Sibdev babu had to run to catch up with him.

'Babu, as his last wish, he asked for three inland letter cards,' he told the IG.

'Uh-hum?'

'To write to his wife, brother and father.'

'Will they come to receive the body?'

Sibdev babu's voice grew as heavy as his face. 'No.'

'Is anyone from his family coming to witness the hanging?'

Now we were face-to-face. He fixed his eyes on me while talking with Sibdev babu.

'Two male relatives can witness it. Haven't you told them?'

'Yes, but they are still hoping that the President will intervene.'

'Seven hundred and seventy people have applied for permission to witness it!'

He glared at me steadily.

'If she slips up before that huge crowd, I won't let her off easy!'

'There won't be any slip-ups, Babu,' Sibdev babu said in an appeasing tone.

'She will be here all of today, right?'

He stroked his face, mad enough to butcher me alive, surveying me from top to toe.

'The order from above is that she should stay here till the hanging takes place at four in the morning day after tomorrow.'

'I want to have a special meeting with her after that.'

He gritted his teeth. The only thing that worried me was my own lack of fear. After the IG and his group left, I went back to the welfare office. As I went up its steps I glanced towards the gallows once more. Another wrestling match was on—between Grandfather Mosh and a relatively young-looking person, with skin as dark as rosewood. Only when I saw him get on the sandbag I'd hung up and sit there, swinging his legs, did I recognize Grandfather Kala! I shut my eyes tight. The termites of memory were boring into my brain.

'This Mullick is a devil. The earlier one, Chakrabarti babu, was so good!' said Kadambini, coming to the door. I went in, sat down in a wooden chair, and looked out. The doorways of the two-storeyed wards in front of us lay open. In the days when Grandfather Satyanatha Grddha Mullick had met Sanjeev Kumar's ancestor Naren dakat, jail meant

Harinbadi. It was the largest gift Europeans gave Kolkata—Harinbadi prison, next to the Maidan. But by my grandfather's time, the splendour of Harinbadi had dimmed. The city had just three main prisons. Dadu preferred Presidency Jail near the Maidan; but Grandfather Kalicharan liked Alipore Central Jail. My uncle Nagbhushan, however, liked the women's prison at Bhawanipur best of all. I blankly watched the freshly bathed convicts sit down in a row for food. The scent of woodsmoke and spices rose from the kitchen on the right. Two ageing convicts hobbled towards the seated rows carrying large pots of food, with pieces of wood attached to their handles. The convicts who hung around the kitchen and the veranda observed us, two women, closely. Two people went over with food towards the condemned cells. Then, Sibdev babu called, asking me into his office.

He was having his breakfast in his room. 'You haven't inherited your father's best quality,' he mused, while chewing a large piece of luchi, gesturing to me to take a chair. A constable came in with plates and served us luchis and aalu. They reminded me of death and our house on Strand Road.

'Chetu di, learn how to speak with the big people. You will reach nowhere if you try to challenge them and make them feel small instead of trying to please and appease them.'

He poured himself some water and drank it. And then completed what he was saying: 'Don't forget, you are a woman.'

'I'll remember that, Babu,' I tried to smile. There was nothing further to do, and so after the food, I went to a corner and sat there, leaning against the wall. Sibdev babu was busy sending off someone on parole and readmitting someone who had returned from parole. Time passed sluggishly. Sibdev babu's phone rang. He picked it up and smiled at me. 'This is he . . . your . . . the other fellow,' he said affectionately.

'Uh . . . uh . . . yes, yes, she is here . . . but, sorry, till the fourteenth, not even a fly in this world can speak with her. The mess last time! A full day of shooting, the quarrel; didn't you fly at each others' throats?' He laughed good-naturedly. It made his gentle face brighter still.

'Oho?'

He held the phone a little away and looked at me.

'The President's response to Jatindranath's brother's mercy plea will come soon.'

The news didn't touch me the least.

'Will it be postponed this time too?' Kadambini, who was sitting in the other chair, leaned towards me.

'No . . .' I murmured.

She looked at me in surprise.

'I can see the signs of death on him . . . his neck has turned bluish.'

I was amused to see her rub her neck at that. Outside, the convicts were out with hoes and other implements to clear up the yard. Three of them were talking together; suddenly one pushed down another. The third tried to intervene, but he got into a fight with the second. It went on till a policeman ran up and started lashing them with a cane. Sibdev babu put the phone down, came over, and sat down beside me.

'See, there's a lot of hard work to do in jail,' he pointed out.

'I've heard that in my ancestors' time, it was khanidhaana,' I said. This was the practice of extracting mustard oil by employing prisoners, bound hand and foot with iron rings, to operate an oil press.

Sibdev babu was about to say something when a policeman came up and whispered something to him. He stood up, put on his cap, and looked at his watch. 'It is Kartik, Jatin's brother. Let me take him to meet his brother. You can go back to the welfare office.'

Not long after Kadambini and I had reached the office, a policeman came to fetch me.

'Where to?' I asked him, 'Cell no. 3?' My heart beat faster.

'He says his last wish is to marry his brother to you.'

'He has no right to wish so,' I retorted, disturbed. I went reluctantly to Jatindranth's cell.

Jatindranath stretched his neck out from behind the bars. 'Chetu di, meet my younger brother, Kartik. Please won't you marry him?'

The young man and I looked at each other. He was about thirty or so; want and sorrow had marred his face. I recalled seeing him with Kokila Banerjee in the studio. He looked far more exhausted now.

'I don't plan to get married now,' I said seriously.

'So the only plan you have is about my neck?' Jatindranath asked.

His smile had faded. He crept back in, disappointed. Then we heard a Saigal song from in there.

'He's been like this recently. Gets very sentimental quickly. Any reference to death makes him distraught,' Sibdev babu said.

Jatindranath's brother went out, head bowed, after standing there silently for a few minutes.

'Will no one else come from home, Kartik?' Sibdev babu asked.

'No, nobody else . . .'

'Jatin's wife?'

He shook his head in the negative.

'He's signed papers to donate his organs.'

'Very good, we have no objection.'

'But according to the law, he can be brought down only after half an hour. By that time it will be too late.'

'He's an unfortunate one,' Kartik said to himself.

I stood there with Sibdev babu even after he went away.

'I have done everything else Jatin asked for . . .'

'He behaves with me as if he's known me for a long time,' I said.

'I can't understand him. When we asked about his last wish, he said, I just want to see her.'

I turned around and walked slowly.

'Do you hope that Sanjeev Kumar Mitra will marry you?' he asked.

'I don't think it a great piece of fortune to hope for!' My voice was rough. Suddenly, a terrible scream rent the air. A horrid wail, a man's—it came from cell no. 3. I saw, as if in a dream, Sibdev babu bounding back, the police and convicts rushing there. I was calm; somehow, I felt no special anxiety or fear. The wail, strong enough to shake the sky and the earth, tapered off gradually, like a long-echoing prayer. All the sounds from the printing press and the jail school were submerged by Jatindranath's immense cry of desperation. When it stopped, a strange quiet filled the jail yard. I stood watching Sibdev babu and the policemen open the cell and go in. They came back after a while, locking the door of the cell.

'The petition's been rejected,' Sibdev babu let me know, his face very dull. 'The news is being read on his radio.'

I continued to stand, like a statue. We both stood there for a while.

The heavy sobs from cell no. 3 followed me. When I looked at the gallows, a burning sensation flashed inside me and disappeared. In the end, after centuries, I too had ended up here. Unbelievable! I saw all my ancestors. When I closed my eyes tight and opened them, I saw Grandfather Jnananatha with his black curtain behind the gallows, making his calculations on it. When the curtain swayed in the wind, I saw Ratna Begum sit behind it, predicting the future. I feared I was losing my sanity.

The hours passed by quickly. The policemen told me that Jatindranath had neither got up, nor spoken, nor eaten, that night. I could not sleep, either. At six, I heard the puja bells ring. I opened the window and looked at the gallows. A small crowd was waiting impatiently on its platform—my ancestors. I looked towards cell no. 3. Some convicts and ten or twelve policemen were gathered there. Kadambini came inside.

'He's performing the Kali puja there. Wants to meet you after.'

I felt like seeing him too. I bathed quickly and changed. When I reached cell no. 3, the puja was over. He handed out the prasad. I got a guava. I took it with folded hands; he went back in and returned with a radio. 'I don't need it. You can have it.'

I accepted it with numb hands. He kept his gaze on my face.

'I went to jail just four years after I got married. Haven't been with my wife since then,' he said in a low whisper. 'I don't remember the happiness of holding a woman close to my body at all . . . Would you please embrace me one time?'

I jumped back, shocked.

'I don't know how to persuade a woman to hold me. What do I lack?'

I couldn't pull away my gaze from his. Before my eyes his face became that of a child. A child who had lost the game, an injured child. I was filled with compassion. Making an effort, I moved forward. I tried to raise my arms towards him. He smelt bad, like mouldy bread. When he held me close, tears pricked my eyelids. We were almost of the same height. He pressed his face on my shoulder. I shut my eyes tightly; his overflowed and my shoulder became moist. He then looked at everyone and smiled.

'I can go happily now . . . all my wishes have been fulfilled!'

The convicts and the policemen looked truly shocked. Jatindranath

408

kept smiling at someone he alone could see. When they served breakfast, he was still smiling. When he was done with the tea, tender coconut and the lassi, Sibdev babu held out a glass of glucose solution to him. He downed it in a single gulp. He went back to do another puja. Gave out prasad to everybody. This time I got a piece of dried grape. I held it along with the guava. He folded his hands and asked Sibdev babu, 'Can Chetna be here? I would like to keep looking at her.'

'You donkey, she's here to kill you,' said Sibdev babu. He obviously pitied the man.

'So what, isn't she very pretty?' He laughed heartily.

I didn't know whether to laugh or not. But I sat cross-legged on the floor in front of his cell, still holding the prasad and his radio.

After some time, he came closer to the bars and told me: 'Be careful when you tie my arms and legs. The skin's delicate from getting too little sun. If you tie the rope too tight, it'll break and bleed.'

I stayed quiet. At one o'clock, the welfare officer Hari Ray, Sibdev babu and some policemen came. They laid a table and some chairs before cell no. 3, and had their noon meal.

'I'd asked for ilish shorshe,' he smiled at the officers. When the ilish was served, he picked up the serving dish, brought it close to his nose and took a deep breath. 'The last hilsa of this life!' he laughed to himself. I put back into my plate the ball of rice and dal. My eyes darted towards the gallows below which my ancestors from the earliest times waited. I could not eat my food. It was unbearable to witness a man eat his last hilsa.

At two o'clock, he came back close to the bars again and smiled. 'Are you bored? No one from home is going to visit me here. You are now my relative and my foe! What a joke!' He went inside without waiting for a reply.

At four, Sibdev babu brought him tea and biscuits. After we drank our tea, he washed his mouth and sat down to Kali puja again. As I sat there keeping him company, the policemen standing on guard looked at me and tittered among themselves. My body has his mouldy smell too, I thought. During the course of the day, it had merged with the fruity scent of the guava.

At eight, the jail authorities brought him dinner, but he didn't eat.

Better to travel on a light stomach, he said.

'Hey Jatin, have a little bit, fellow?' Sibdev babu insisted.

'Okay, do you want mishti doi?'

Sibdev babu handed it to him; he wolfed it down and looked at me with a smile. 'This life's last bit of mishti doi!' He licked his lips and turned towards Sibdev babu. 'In a way, this is much better, Babu. This is the first time someone has asked me what I'd like! No one's ever asked me even when I was a child . . . till I came here. The truth is that I became aware of what I liked only when the death sentence came close each time.'

'Be brave, Jatin!'

He laughed and went in. Sibdev babu looked at me. 'You'll continue sitting here?'

I got up and followed him. When we came close to the gallows, it began to drizzle. The hot raindrops fell on my face as if they were being flung down. I did not see any of my ancestors under the gallows.

'Be up sharp at two. The hanging is at four-thirty. Don't oversleep.'

My body tingled. I couldn't sleep. For the first time, I was able to imagine a man's form dangling in the air. Outside, it sounded as if a whole sea was rolling. I woke up at two, and did the final Kali puja the way I had heard Father and Thakuma speak of it—with flowers, liquor and blood. Then I walked to the gallows. I untied the rope and tied it back firmly on the hook. I made sure that it was secure. I heard the door of cell no. 3 creak open. As I watched, Jatindranath Banerjee stepped out in new white garments. A whole group of men stood before him: Srinath Mullick, Sibdev babu, the jail magistrate and some others. Sibdev babu read out something in Bangla. I could hear it only vaguely. He and the jailer declared loudly that the Jatindranath Banerjee mentioned in the order was indeed the person before them. They moved forward, Jatindranath in the middle, the policemen flanking him. I closed my eyes and saw him approach the gallows. Slowly. His very last footsteps.

51

The last drizzle of his life; the last dawn; the last smile. I saw Jatindranath Banerjee's sallow face and sunken eyes clearly even in the dim light. As with all the women in our family, in moments of deep crisis, my hands were doing and undoing nooses on the hangman's rope. My nervousness doubled when I realized what I was doing. In my determination to be ready before he reached the gallows, I looped the rope twelve times; it moved twelve times like the cord of a garland of invisible flowers. By the time he came up the steps my noose was ready with its thirteen beautiful loops. Its perfection and strength was alluring even to me. When he walked towards the small circle drawn in white in the middle of the planks, a cold wind blew. My pores tingled with the delight of the beloved being embraced for the very first time by her lover. I wished to be embraced thus and to hear the sweet assurance of love: I will be with you until death. The magistrate, the IG, Sibdev babu and others stood in a row. If only Sanjeev Kumar Mitra could have joined them. The jailer came up and held out a coil of rope to me. The moment the condemned man reaches the foot of the gallows, tie his arms together and fix the leather strap on his legs within a second—Father's words rang in my ears. He always said, 'If you take too much time, the condemned man might collapse out of sheer mental tension. Sometimes he'll go weak and his bones will cave in, and the body will flag. That makes the hangman's job quite hard.'

While I was tying his arms, Jatindranath turned around and looked at me. 'Someone is speaking . . . who is that?' His voice was calm.

'My ancestors . . . maybe yours too!' I whispered.

'Why do you tie up my hands?'

'An open and outstretched hand is a formidable weapon.'

I tested the knots hurriedly and held out my hand for the leather strap for the legs.

'In our childhood we thought the palm was a great instrument,' he said, opening and closing his palms within the knots on his wrist.

I put the leather strap around his calves.

'Are feet weapons too?'

'The feet are the wheels of the soul's vehicle. If they are not together, the journey won't be smooth.'

He sighed deeply; his feet seemed to echo it back. I finished, and stood up. The next task was to put a death-hood on him.

'Jatin, pray if you want to,' said Sibdev babu, patting him on his shoulder.

'I don't want to pray now, Babu,' he said, '. . . please say something to me before my time is over!'

Not able to meet his tranquil eyes, Sibdev babu lowered his gaze.

'I feel greedy for conversation, for laughter . . . I haven't heard enough of both. I didn't realize that till now. The real pleasure of human life is hearing other human beings, experiencing their presence. Who knows if I'll get those where I am going? And if I'll be able to hear them? Chetna di, say something. Your voice is so sweet . . .'

This was the greatest test in a hangman's career. I didn't know what to tell the living body now barely moments away from the 3.2 kilo Buxar rope knotted with thirteen loops, hanging from the hook. What would have Father done in my place, I tried to think nervously. If Kala Mullick, or Grandfather Mosh, or Grandfather Kalicharan were forced to tell a story to gladden the person about to be sent away, what would they choose, I searched my mind.

'What did you eat this morning?' I asked, wiping my perspiration.

'A piece of sandesh,' he said. 'I didn't want to go without tasting it again.' A smile appeared on his face.

I drew my breath in and began to tell a story. Sandesh was Satyajit Ray's favourite sweet. His great-grandfather Ramsundar Majumdar crossed the Meghna over to East Bengal and lived by the Brahmaputra. But what happened? During a great flood which swallowed up the village, the family ended up split in two, one on either side of the river!

I looked around. Everyone stood still, frozen. My voice panted and wheezed like an asthmatic's. I didn't have much time to tell him the whole story. I told him how Knowledge and Wealth in that family were thus separated; Knowledge went to the branch of the family on one side of the water while Wealth stayed with the branch on the other side. Then Ramakanta Majumdar was born; it was his habit to eat for breakfast a whole basket of rice and a hefty jackfruit. One afternoon, he was resting in the veranda when a big black bear strolled towards him. He caught it by the scruff of its neck, hit it with his slippers, and sent it right back to the forest. As I said this, Jatindranath laughed happily. My chest ached when I realized that this laugh which lit up his sallow cheeks would be his last. It was impossible to believe that he was a criminal, if you saw him laugh like that.

'God! What a loss it'd have been if I had left without listening to this tale!'

If you asked Ramakanta's oldest son anything, he answered in perfect rhyme and metre. His third son became a scholar in the Persian language. His second son Loknath gained great fame as an expert in Sanskrit, Bengali, Persian and Arabic. He could read aloud in Persian or Bengali a book written in Sanskrit or Arabic, and vice versa! Within a year of his marriage Loknath turned to tantric yoga. His parents were terrified. Fearing that he would become an ascetic, they threw his books into the river. Loknath was shattered. He went on a fast for three days and attained samadhi. But he called his wife and son to him before he died. He blessed the boy by placing his hand on his head and, kissing the child's head, told his wife, you have only this child now, but a hundred will be born from him.

Jatindranath's face lit up with interest. 'How right he was! Now tell me the story of a woman.'

'Shall I tell you the story of Rokeya Hossain's *Sultana's Dream*?'

'No!' The IG's voice was inflexible. 'It is time. Jatin, we are sorry.'

The smile faded on Jatin's face.

Sibdev babu moved closer and asked, 'Jatin, any last words?'

'The government has killed me four or five times earlier. I am glad this is the last.'

Sibdev babu looked at the IG; he looked at me. His stare, like that of a hungry tiger, hit me hard. When Sibdev babu whispered my name and handed me the hood, I went up to Jatindranath again and stood in front of him. We looked at each other. His body weighed fifty-five kilos. Loss of hair had widened his brow. He had thick eyebrows, and below them, like two bottomless pits, were his eyes. Upon his sallow cheeks lay the pallor of long years in a sunless room. And then his neck, from which the bones stuck out. In his eyes there was no fear, but pity for me, or someone else. I closed my eyes, focused my mind on my ancestors. I thought of Thakuma, Dadu and Father. I folded my hands holding the hood. I had heard that Father always did this. And I begged forgiveness: 'Dada, tumi aamake khomaa koro.' Brother, please forgive me.

I tilted his face sideways and kissed his cheek. He smelt like the lal champa. He smiled. 'Tomar bhalo bhobe.' God bless you.

'Four-thirty!' the IG called.

I forgot that this was my very first hanging. I was not myself, I was an executioner. Only an executioner. The hood stretched between my palms like a black pillowcase. I put it on his face easily. He kept looking at me till his eyes were covered. The black head, which had no eyes, nose or mouth, upon the white-clad body continued to look at me. A thunderbolt passed through me that moment; I staggered. Something pierced my bones and flesh hard. That was just the beginning. A thousand streaks of lightning pierced me like arrows. My blood seethed and boiled. The bones and flesh quavered hard. Through each pore of my skin, a thousand souls entered. I realized how true Father's words were as I stood there—that it will feel as though you were on the azar. I too went through rehearsed steps, as if I were merely a character in a play, present to satisfy somebody else's sensibility. I looked at Jatindranath Banerjee once more. He stood like a statue with an unfinished head, arms tied, legs tied. That his heart was beating like a rubber ball bouncing in well-defined intervals was evident from the frame of his chest rising and falling inside the new white clothes the government had gifted him for this journey to the other world.

I checked the noose, made sure the knot was strong. Then I pulled the rope and passed the noose over his head and fitted it perfectly in the precise spot between the second and third vertebrae, as if I were offering flowers to a deity. I let out a deep breath.

'Tomar bhalo bhobe,' he whispered from inside the hood again.

I reached the lever in a flash, placed my hand on it, and looked to the left. The magistrate, the IG and the others were lined up behind the gallows. Their faces were unclear; they were all still. A red kerchief was dropped. The lever's ancient cold spread to my palm. My heart too bounced like a rubber ball. Someone stirred in my blood and emerged into the open, shooting out through my flesh. This presence tried hard to wrench my hand from the lever. It was like a tug o' war between us. Just when I thought I would fail, I saw the kerchief, and its deep red blinded me. I pulled the lever. The planks below moved away with a thunderous noise. Like the sky falling, Jatindranth's body fell straight in. My eyes were glued to the rope. One, two, three, four . . . someone was counting inside my head. Twenty! The rope became still.

My hand stayed on the lever. I felt nothing special. A man had died. The noose tightened on his neck. The vital blood vessel between the second and third vertebrae snapped and the blood flow to his brain ceased. His blood pressure rose dramatically. His heart stopped beating. The bones of his neck shattered in a way that made it impossible to stretch the spine. His eyes bulged inside the hood and his tongue stuck out. His new white clothes were stained with shit and urine. The blood rushed into his sexual organs and he had had an erection for the very last time.

'Chetna!'

It was Sibdev babu, running up and holding me by my shoulders.

'Are you all right? Lie down a bit if you want. There'll be some tension . . . it's only natural . . .'

He couldn't see that I was struggling to pull my hand off the lever. My hand was stuck hard on the metal rod, that primordial symbol of power. A sense of power surged through my blood when I held it. It became clear to me why my ancestors bore such pride, even arrogance, in their profession. I looked at the rope dangling from the gallows tree. Jatindranath's body had disappeared into the cellar. The rope was stretched fully; it looked more like an iron rod fixed to the ground. The sky had begun to turn a pallid white. A terrible silence pervaded the yard. The magistrate, the IG and the other employees—they were all like mannequins, silent and still. Suddenly, the six o'clock siren blared. Sound waves fled through the silent, wet, heavy air, shrieking like hunted and wounded birds. The morning bell inside the prison sprang to life. Like a town immobilized by an evil spell in a fairy tale suddenly coming to life, the jail woke up. The thud of a falling sandbag reverberated beneath my feet. The rope, which stood stretched so grandly, rose to the sky like a severed lizard's tail, and drooped, helpless, bereft of all pride. The drizzle began again. A policeman ran up from the cellar below.

'Twenty seconds . . . declared dead!' the magistrate announced loudly.

My body was tense and overwrought, like a stretched rope. All the souls that were stuffed into my body began to fall away in ones and twos, like grains of sand from an old, torn sandbag. I felt hollow and light, like an empty sack. Raindrops and sweat mingled and flowed from my head to the ground. Everywhere I turned, I saw nothing but a deep red. Dr Bimal Mukhopadhyay climbed the steps of the cellar and approached me. His white face looked so red that it was as if he was back from Holi.

'Just twenty seconds!' His trembling voice rose. 'Perfect hangman's fracture. The break in the C-2 vertebra was precise, simply beautiful. Like a seashell splitting open.'

I stared like a fool into his eyes; they were filled with approval and sheer awe.

'No one would even guess that you were hanging someone for the first time! Chetna, I was really tense, to tell you the truth. The slightest error, and the government would have been in deep trouble.'

'It's not right to express such satisfaction about taking someone's life, but I can't help saying so—you were excellent!' Sibdev babu came up.

'Are you all right?' the doctor asked.

I rubbed my palms together, wiped my face and neck with my dupatta, and let out a deep breath.

'You've cut at the very root of the male race, my dear girl,' said Magistrate Harinarayan Chatterjee. The approbation was evident even in the eyes of the policeman who was holding the umbrella over his wigged head.

'I observed each of your movements closely. How effortlessly you tied his arms, put the leather straps on the legs, put the hood on him, and pulled the lever—all in a flash!'

'Her baba Phanibhushan needs thirty seconds, usually,' Sibdev babu reminded.

'Ah! So, there goes the job of killing—to women now! Poor men, what do they have left? Sibdev, has anyone come to receive the body?'

'His younger brother is here, but he's not willing to take it. We will have to handle it, Babu.'

'Never mind. Isn't it our last opportunity to spend for him?' the magistrate joked, and moved ahead.

Sibdev babu and I looked at each other. His face was full of kind concern. 'Are you thirsty? Do you want something to eat? Tell me what you want.'

'Can I take his body?' My voice broke and sounded as if it weren't mine.

He started, and then smiled mildly. 'No, child. That's not needed. That's the government's responsibility.'

'His soul should not wander without peace . . .'

'Soul! You believe it exists?'

'It may or may not exist. But if it does, it should be given peace.'

He smiled regretfully. 'Let's think about it. Come to the office now. Don't you want the money?'

I rubbed my hands against each other. I felt as though death clung to them like a viscous film. It would be impossible henceforth to make a ball of rice and eat with these hands, I feared. The smell of mouldy bread would cling to me all my life.

Hemant Mullick's bhajans rang inside the jail. Kadambini brought me my bag. I walked as if I were floating above the ground. Jatindranath's brother Kartik was standing in front of the welfare office. My steps became heavy again. Sibdev babu patted him on the shoulder and went ahead.

When I neared him, he thanked me. The effort to smile made his face look ugly.

'What for?'

'You didn't hurt Jatin da even a little bit.'

He wiped the wetness of the raindrops off his face and stroked his stubble. 'I was really scared. That he may struggle in pain, cry out . . . I felt choked and breathless . . . but it was all over so soon, in the bat of an eyelid. I can't thank you enough.'

'Forgive me, I am but an instrument.' My voice faltered. I pulled out Jatindranath's radio and held it out to Kartik.

'All of us are somebody's instruments. Jatin da surely was. And I, as well.'

He turned the radio over and over, looking at it sorrowfully.

'He liked you. Told me to marry you.' He smiled, suppressing a sigh.

'Our land is dry. No guarantee that one can reap if one sows. You need credit every year. You get it, hoping that you can repay it the next year. And it goes on like that . . .' He stopped. 'It takes a very strong mind to live in our villages these days. To be able to farm your land, you need a mind strong enough to kill a man!'

I kept my eyes on him.

'The water has to be drawn up from a well four hundred rungs deep. It won't come up however hard you pull. You have to be very patient.'

I noticed that he swallowed what he was about to say. He tried to smile again.

'Ah, what was that story you were going to tell Dada?'

But before I could reply a policeman called me and I had to leave him. I was panting hard when I reached Sibdev babu's office. I saw IG Srinath Mullick sitting in the chair only after I stepped in. But he did not raise his head or look at me. It seemed to me that I had hanged Jatindranath Banerjee but actually killed Srinath Mullick.

'The CM called. He's declared a reward of fifty thousand rupees for the woman who accomplished this task. He's sent the signed cheque.'

He didn't meet my eyes but said in a tired voice: 'There is another ten thousand as remuneration; sign for that as well.'

I too was exhausted. If I wasn't, his attitude would have made me laugh aloud. I signed the papers and then, picking up the ruler on Sibdev babu's table, held it out to him: 'Don't you need this, IG babu?'

Though I was worn out, my voice still had enough steely derision to strike him hard. His face went red. 'Don't take it badly. We policemen live in such tension . . . sometimes we lose control. That's part of the job.'

'Tomar bhalo bhobe,' I said.

I went out with the money and the cheque. Sibdev babu came out with me. 'Before you go—there are more prizes to come! The chief minister is going to visit you today at noon. Go home and spruce up.'

'Why, why is he coming?' I asked, rather taken aback.

'Who knows? Maybe to make you a minister!'

He smiled and so did I. But it wasn't really all that scary. It is easier to hold the lever of the ruling machine than that of the gallows. I had learnt it at the age of twenty-two.

'Go out by the back gate. The vultures won't let you live if you go out through the front,' he warned me. 'You probably don't know about it—Judges' Court Road has been packed for the last two days. Some there are for the death penalty, and others against. And on top of that a

418

whole phalanx of TV crews and reporters from newspapers! BBC and CNC and even the cable channel fellow from Burkina-Fasso!'

Sanjeev Kumar Mitra's face appeared in my mind. I was a tiny bit regretful that he hadn't seen me carry out the hanging.

'His funeral rites will be at Harkat Tala, but we told the media that the funeral will be in his village in order to avoid them. Are you sure you want to go?'

'Yes.'

I had no doubt at all. They took me out secretly through the back gate. Right behind us, in a police jeep, was Jatindranath's body.

Kartik Banerjee was waiting for us at the Harkat Tala Ghat. Water trickled out from the hole in the pot he carried while circumambulating the body of his brother. The body was then burnt in the electric crematorium, and the ashes consigned to the Ganga. When he came up after dipping himself three times in its waters, he looked like an ascetic.

'I had no money for a proper funeral. That's why I didn't take the body. Sibdev babu said this is better . . .'

I had no reply.

'Thank you, once again.'

'Again? What for?'

'For everything. For saving him so quickly, for making him happy with a story, and for coming here to see him off.'

He left in his wet clothes. I got back into the police jeep which had brought me there. The policeman in the front seat gave me a broad smile. The jeep moved slowly through the traffic. I leaned against the seat and dozed off. In my sleep, I saw Jatindranath Banerjee read out in a different language a book written in some other language. Which book is this, asked Kartik. *Sultana's Dream*, I answered. The three of us were in the cellar below the gallows tree. Jatindranath wore the cut-down rope like a garland around his neck and lay on his back, straight and stiff. I could smell the stink of mouldy bread and the acridity of wet ashes from the pyre. We were lost in the pleasure of reading together, when someone called out, 'Chetna, hearty congratulations! Wake up!'

I was hesitant to open my eyes.

'Chetna, wake up!'

Someone shook me awake. I could make out from the voice who it was. My eyes opened of their own accord. Sanjeev Kumar Mitra loomed through the mist of my sleep, a triumphant smile on his face.

'Welcome, Miss Chetna Grddha Mullick, India's first official hangwoman!' he proclaimed loudly. My sleep vanished. I rubbed my eyes in dread and looked around. Yes, the same man. The same Sanjeev Kumar Mitra. His same old glasses. The same old smile. The same old studio of his. I yawned deeply and then sighed. Streaks of lightning travelled again through my body. The slimy feeling returned to my hands. All of it was old, I saw with a beating heart—I, alone, was new!

'For the time being at least, the only one in the whole world, you!'

So what if there's just one now, the ancestors in the cellar laughed. A hundred will arise from this one!

52

So he had betrayed me again, greasing many palms to get me to the studio; I, who had sent a man to the other world in just twenty seconds. My hands tingled for a rope. We were in the conference hall of CNC. They were congratulating me. I sat seething in the black velvet chair beside the oval glass table. In the TV screen on the wall, Jatindranath's life story and his pictures tumbled together. The captions 'Jatindranath hanged' and 'Hangwoman Chetna on CNC at 10' pushed their way through the images and sounds. 'Chetna is India's first hangwoman,' 'Chetna is the daughter of Phanibhushan Grddha Mullick, a hangman since the days of the British,' some reporter screamed. The image of me on 18 May when Jatindranath's mercy petition was first rejected, caught by Sanjeev Kumar's camera, appeared on the screen. On a road crowded with hearses and ambulances, Kaku stood once again in front of our dilapidated house. He spoke to me, handed me ten rupees from his pocket, and pointed to Hari da's shop. I walked again to Hari da's shop with the carefree lightness of a twenty-two-year-old woman who had never been in love, joyously swinging her long arms. It was on the seven o'clock news that day that I had first noticed Sanjeev Kumar

Mitra. He had stood proud then, mike in hand. Now he sat in the chair next to the owner of the CNC channel, Biswajit Ray, all bent like a slack rope on which washing is hung to dry. Ray congratulated them; he said that the coverage of Jatindranath's case was a huge achievement for CNC and that the team deserved full credit for introducing Chetna Grddha Mullick to the world. Biswajit Ray was about sixty, with a face as smooth as sandesh. By then, Jatindranath who had dissolved in the Ganga must have entered the Arbudanaraka. Would his soul carry the memory of sandesh? The thought disturbed me. The garland I had put on the glass table lay there like a sliced tongue.

'It's clicked, Chetna!'

When Biswajit Ray sat down, Harish Nath stood up.

'You are a phenomenon now, a big role model for today's India!'

He turned towards Biswajit Ray.

'I am not bluffing, there's evidence—eleven children played hangman yesterday and died.'

I froze in my seat.

'What does that indicate? That this hanging has created a huge impact among people. Which means your name is etched forever in the mind of lakhs and lakhs of Indians!'

Something exploded inside my head. My heart splintered like a discarded earthen cup that had been flung away. Sparks flew around my eyes like flies announcing the sign of death. I saw clearly, from across a glass wall, that I'd reached the gates of the hot hell, which looked like the ancient and dingy entrance to Nimtala Ghat. The dead Gautam Deb and the lightning-hit Rabia Khatun, with bodies transparent as crystal and tails soft as molten wax, ran around Biswajit Ray, Harish Nath and Sanjeev Kumar, playing tag. On the table, three children with black bodies lay dead with blood marks on them. Which explosion killed them? I asked myself in utter panic. I ran my fingers on my cheek and found a large black mole burning my skin and spreading fast. Let me not go mad, I prayed.

'The death toll may go up to fourteen. One child is critical in Midnapore. Another from Purulia has been admitted to SSKM Hospital with a broken neck,' Sanjeev Kumar added.

'Yes, yes . . . but more than that, Sanjeev Kumar Mitra, who's been

421

tirelessly pursuing this story since Jatindranath Banerjee's mercy petition was first rejected, deserves hearty congratulations! With this, CNC has gained a clear lead over its rivals. Well done, Sanjeev!'

Harish sat down. A beautiful forty-odd-year-old woman with stylish short hair got up.

'This story does show that if we put our minds to it, we can pull up the ratings and maintain quality as well. For me, the most exciting thing is that a woman has rewritten history. My hearty congratulations to Chetna!'

Sanjeev Kumar was next.

'I want to thank for the success of this event, first of all, Harish babu and Ray babu who encouraged me in all possible ways. Besides, both Phanibhushan Grddha Mullick and Chetna have extended their complete support to CNC since the beginning. I hope you will all continue to support me in all my future ventures. Let me congratulate Chetna for her great achievement. Well done, Chetna! Let me ask you, from where did you amass such presence of mind and strength?'

He was clearly on the azar, mouthing dialogues in costume. I was revolted. I rubbed my neck as all of them looked intently at me. My tongue felt glued to my mouth. I tried to smile at the painted faces around me. 'My Thakuma has often told me: If you want to stand up straight, you will have to bend occasionally. Thank you.'

They clapped. They didn't get it, of course. They were too busy celebrating. When Biswajit Ray patted Sanjeev Kumar's shoulder, the latter's face showed elation. They chattered excitedly with each other, offering mutual congratulations. Sanjeev Kumar's humble, simple avatar looked as distant and unreal as a TV serial. I was not disturbed any more by the vagueness of his feelings for me. The paths his forefathers had taken did not arouse my admiration. I was still standing at the foot of the gallows. My hands were slimy with death. The memories that stretched back two thousand years in the past lay tied up in knots in my brain; they were being pulled from all sides. I decided if my name and my life were to become undying in India and the whole world, it should not be in the name of this wretched love which may be realized only through spilling either my blood or his.

'Okay, let's leave after tea,' said Biswajit Ray, holding out a cup from the tray which a uniformed waiter had brought in. 'The show begins at ten o'clock. I will be there at the studio with a friend.'

His voice was modest but resonated with authority. Everyone lunged at their tea. Plates full of snacks went round the table.

'I am sorry I couldn't see your performance. The chief minister and his family were expected to witness the hanging. But they changed their minds at the last moment. I would've been there, in that case.' He gave me a friendly smile. 'Have some tea, Chetna.'

'No,' I said.

'The hangman does not eat without having a bath and conducting the puja at home, isn't that so?' The short-haired woman looked at me with interest. I didn't disabuse her. The cups were soon empty, the celebration was over, and everyone went back to their respective places. Only Sanjeev Kumar and I and the gaping garland were left.

'They are talking about you everywhere. You've become a star overnight,' he smirked. Even when he submitted himself to the make-up man's ministrations in the new make-up room that had mirrors all around, he had the same smirk on his face. My mind wavered like a kite, not knowing what to do. Get off the azar, end this drama, someone inside me said urgently. Someone else became greedy for the experience of making a noose and holding the weight of a body with a single hand. Sanjeev Kumar smiled at me. My fingers moved rapidly; the fringe of the dupatta became little nooses and tightened around them, breaking the skin. A strange woman with the vulture eyes of the Grddha Mullicks looked straight at me from the mirror. Her reddish bulging eyes scared me. Her face was burnt dark. There were shadows under her eyes. Her plaits had come loose and her long hair snaked downward to her breasts like serpents with slender necks. I saw Devi Manasa in the mirror. I was afraid to open my mouth; what if someone else's blood dripped from it? The stink of mouldy bread spread on my body; my hands felt greasy; the sourness of the bile from someone else's intestines filled the hollow of my throat. I felt nauseated.

'Don't forget me in the end, okay? Don't say I never told you how many strings I had to pull, how many I had to please,' Sanjeev Kumar said.

The gold coin gifted by the king of Gwalior to Grandfather Mosh

423

who sent off each condemned man with loving advice, and who went straight to his fields after each hanging, was stuck in my throat. Around my head, Ramu da's translucent body buzzed like a fly with its wings plucked. His eyes rolled like two footballs caked brown in the mud of the Maidan.

'Shall I give you some more happy news?'

When the make-up man went out, Sanjeev Kumar glanced at me, at the same time enjoying the sight of his own good looks in the mirror.

'Both the CPM and the Congress will invite you to join politics. Make your decision only after you discuss it with me. I say this because I know your old man so well. Make smart moves, and you may even become an MP! It's good that you didn't get married. Your market value would've fallen greatly.'

As I looked at him, the old sensation of a worm wriggling inside my left breast came back. My breast felt like it did the day he had assaulted it, all swollen and aching with pus.

'Get ready soon. It's time for the show. After this, it'll be impossible to see you . . . every TV channel in the world is running madly in search of you all over Strand Road.'

He was wallowing in the pride of having captured me for his own, of making a fool of everybody else. On my finger, an invisible ring tightened. The broken pieces of bangles tore the skin of my arms.

'That police jeep—how did it come to your studio?' I tried to hide the woman inside and smile.

Sanjeev Kumar smiled again. 'Who can't be kidnapped in this country if you hand out the cash?'

'Whom did you pay? Sibdev babu?' My blood boiled.

'That's a trade secret—who was paid and how much!' He laughed merrily.

I felt breathless. I remembered my fall into the cellar in Alipore Jail. I remembered the way he bruised my body to brand himself on me, like a dog marking its territory.

'Putting up with you is really hard sometimes, Chetna. Your talk— you completely forget your position and your condition when you talk. But I still like you very much. Even now, if you can moderate your behaviour a little, we'd get along really well.'

Just then Father appeared on TV. I sat up, alert. The camera panned down from the yellowing news report from 1960, the first one about him, on our wall, to where Father sat looking at his watch, smoking his cigarette slowly.

'At the same time, Phanibhushan Grddha Mullick who was earlier the chief hangman of the state, said that he was proud of his daughter Chetna for her flawless execution, as a father and as a citizen of this country. Grddha Mullick was excused from his duties as a hangman as he faces trial for the murder of his younger brother and his wife.'

The newsreader tilted her head and waited for him to respond.

'My name and life have been rendered eternal in Bharat and the whole world. I can now die in peace.' He exhaled slowly.

'What if the court sentences you to death, Grddha da?'

'I will tell my daughter, Chetna, let the length of the rope be precise. When you put the noose around my neck, it should fall right on the hollow of the throat.'

He contorted one side of his mouth and smiled as if he were challenging the questioner.

'You haven't said why you killed your brother and his wife?'

He sucked on his cigarette again. 'That's a long story. I have plenty of stories to tell. Why don't you come at leisure, and I'll tell you.'

I began to feel sleepy. When the make-up man came near me and asked, 'Didi, shall I apply your make-up?' I jumped awake. Sanjeev Kumar had left. 'Make-up? For the hangwoman?' I teased him and got up. My hair was now fully undone. The thick, wavy strands shone like live black serpents. I went to the studio. In the studio beside Sanjeev Kumar who was rehearsing his smile—meant for viewers—there were two chairs. In one sat Kartik Banerjee. My legs stiffened.

'All of us are instruments, didn't I tell you?' he said, smiling affectionately when he saw me. 'Perhaps the money I get for this will settle one of our smaller debts . . .'

I could not find the courage to look into his shining eyes. Behind us, against a black-and-grey background, a gallows tree had been raised. A coil of rope hung from its hook like a serpent on a tree. My heart writhed.

'Remember this? We got this ready last time? You know how much money it gobbled up? Luckily, we now have an opportunity to use it,' Sanjeev Kumar said. I sat in the chair, barely able to believe myself. I wanted to run out but the woman inside stopped me. My fingers twirled the fringe of my dupatta again and again.

'Yesterday we did a survey in schools: whether death by hanging was necessary. You won't believe it, Chetna, two hundred and seventy out of the three hundred children surveyed said it was necessary.'

He stopped, pulled off his glasses and looked into my eyes with those green eyes in the way only he could.

'Ninety-three percent of the girls said that they want to grow up and be Chetna Grddha Mullick and punish criminals.'

As I looked vapidly at his face, I recalled that this was the man for whom I had had such intense feelings. I tried to love, like before, his green eyes, his attractively styled hair, his bluish neck. It pained me to think that he would never have a chance to experience a woman's love from me.

'Okay Chetna, we have two guests today, be ready.' He began to hurry when he got the signal from somewhere through the earphones.

'This is not live, but the telecast will happen in just about half an hour. So think of it as a live telecast. Another thing . . .'

His voice, however, broke suddenly and his eyes bulged desperately. His face blanched as if he had seen a ghost. The merriment faded; instead, anger and pain and humiliation and helplessness flashed on his face. My eyes darted to the door. Harish Nath was leading in Biswajit Ray through the glass door; he turned around and made way for a woman in a red silk sari. She sauntered in gracefully and sat on one of the chairs brought in especially for them. Crossing her legs at the knees, she placed her arms lightly on the armrests of the chair and smiled at us. It was her. Hair tied up, a large red sindoor mark on her forehead, red paint on her lips. Trailokya Devi.

I was amazed. Sanjeev Kumar wilted. He busily searched for a piece of paper; ran his fingers on the keyboard of the computer; looked here and there in deep unease. He split apart beautifully, like Jatindranath's vertebra, in a precise fashion, like a seashell opened. Then, like a character on the azar, Sanjeev Kumar cleared his throat and tried to play his part.

'Welcome to CNC once again, Miss Chetna Grddha Mullick, the first and only hangwoman of India!'

I observed him. He was hanging on a rope that was fraying. Strands of the rope were breaking one by one. He became weaker by the minute. I leaned back in my chair.

'Chetna di, today a woman touched, all by herself, the lever which has been operated only by men all through the history of independent India. This is a great achievement for all the world's women. What do you say about that?'

His voice went hoarse. I looked at him with pity.

'We women never achieve anything by ourselves. Our lives are bound to each other like the links in a chain. One completes what someone else has begun in some other time. The one who begins does not ever complete it and those who complete it, do not begin it.'

I made sure my voice was gentle. His tremor was truly piteous.

'Kartik Banerjee, you are here after seeing your own brother being hanged. How were his last moments?'

Sanjeev Kumar turned towards him with empty eyes.

Kartik sighed deeply. 'Dada wanted to listen to a couple of stories. Chetna told him one.' He smiled at me. His voice had an unexpectedly dignified tone. 'They didn't let her tell him another.' Kartik turned to me again. 'What story was that, Chetna? The last story Dada would have listened to in his life?'

That was a story written by Rokeya Sakhawat Hussain who started the first school for girls in Bengal. 'One evening, I was lounging in an easy chair in my bedroom, thinking lazily of the condition of Indian womanhood . . .' it began. It frothed up on my tongue. Thakuma's brother Jaganmohan Grddha Mullick had run off to Bhagalpur to meet her after reading her story 'Pipasa', published in 1902. When she was born in 1880, Grandfather Kalicharan was nearing seventy-five. His heartthrob Binodini Dasi had appeared on the stage for the first time six years ago. The son who had come from the southern tip of the country in search of Naren dakat had become a rice trader and was also running a gymkhana. The year before Rokeya was born, Begum Hazrat Mahal, who had waged war against the British and lost, had died in Nepal. It had been two years since Kadambini Ganguly-Bose passed the entrance exam to the University of Calcutta.

'Yes, yes, what was the story? Let us hear it,' Sanjeev Kumar was apparently in a hurry to finish the show.

His eyes flew towards the door now and then. Biswajit Ray's arm was thrown around his mother's shoulders. I tasted the sourness and viscosity of blood in my mouth. I was thirsty.

When the narrator of *Sultana's Dream* went for a walk one evening, she met a friend, Sister Sara, and left with her for an unknown land. Because she saw only women in the markets, during daytime, she asked Sister Sara where all the men were. Only then did she learn that she was in a strange country where all the men were shut up in purdah inside their homes and the women went about their tasks in the outside world. On hearing this, Sultana was astonished. It is exactly the reverse in Kolkata, said she, and her friend exclaimed, how terrible that gentle and mild women are locked up in the house, and men, who are indeed dangerous, are allowed to roam outside!

Hearing this, Sanjeev Kumar let out a burst of utterly false laughter.

'Great, Chetna di, a story that truly suits this day, the very first day of your hangwomanship! All right, tell us then, how were Jatindranath's last moments? Can you demonstrate for CNC viewers? Here, we have readied for you a gallows tree and a hangman's rope.'

He got up and stepped towards it. In my ears, the hoof beats of eighteen stallions thundered. A bear-faced woman came riding a stallion with a golden mane. Behind her, Protima di and Kokila Banerjee sat, holding each other so that they did not fall off. In the middle of the city, through the mud paths on the fields by which the portia tree blooms, village women ran with rifles. They lined up on both sides of the corridor parting their red-painted lips in a smile, placing their hands on their hips, revealing their breasts from which milk flowed freely, looking like statues put up for sale. One of them, surely, was Kakima. Because the bloody chopper was still wedged in her neck.

I followed him, slowly. He handed me the coil of rope which seemed to be biding its time, like a serpent about to lay eggs. It was actually not a hangman's rope, but it felt so heavy! A fully naked woman stood under the gallows tree with her long, thick hair flowing down her back, testing its strength. On the piece of wood on which the hook was fixed, an ugly housewife sat, tuning her tanpura. That was Kalicharan Grddha Mullick's wife. A young girl, still a teenager, tested the strength of the hook. When she opened her mouth to laugh, the blood that had collected inside from her severed tongue began to drip. She raised her fingers in the air and wrote 100×10^{22} in the air, and a six-year-old girl with wounds all over her body ran into our midst screaming, 'I, Khona!' A woman in a veil pointed her gun and fired it. 'Nawab!' someone sneered.

'Look, it seems pretty strong. You can actually hang someone if you want,' he said as he stood under it.

'If who wants?' I asked, looking one by one at all the human forms I alone could see.

Sanjeev Kumar paid no attention and faced the camera.

'Viewers may be eager to know how Chetna hanged Jatindranath Banerjee today. How it took place and where, and what she did. Here we will recreate the experience for you!'

He tried hard to retrieve his confidence, but could not manage it.

'Come, Mr Kartik Banerjee, show our viewers clearly what your brother must have gone through today.'

Petrified, I watched Kartik get up and come up to the gallows, stand inside the white circle below the rope, and stick his neck out obediently. He smiled at me. 'If we pay off the debt, the land will be ours again, that's what this drama is about . . .'

It was either a dream, or I was going mad. I broke into cold sweat; many nooses tightened around my neck. Eighteen stallions pulled me in different directions.

'Tell me a story, Chetna, one that'll make me happy?' Kartik gave me a naughty wink. 'I like to listen to love stories.'

'Quick, Chetna, we have no time, we have to continue the discussion.'

A completely naked woman with loose hair leapt out of my body. She pushed me aside and snatched the rope from me. She was immensely strong. Her body burned like a forest on fire. The cells of my body melted. A thousand serpents fled in different directions from the top of my head. She knotted the noose. Smiled at Kartik. Do not fear, Kartik da, she comforted him. His smile became broader. His eyes were filled with love, mine with peace.

'The length is not right for you, it won't suit you.' My voice was calm. Kartik moved out of the white circle, looking very disappointed. 'Cut! Cut!' said someone, and the lights went off.

Sanjeev Kumar became impatient. 'What's going on, Chetna, please be quick!' He came up to me, his face red with impatience.

'Sanjeev Kumar, this rope actually suits you better,' I declared. My long curls were in total disarray. Fire shot through my veins. The lights came on again. Someone called out 'Start!' I looked towards the door. Trailokya Devi's chair was empty. The first thunderbolt passed through my body. My hands knotted the first noose. Suddenly, the scent of herbs and ghee-soaked medicinal pastes filled the air. A woman's cool hand suddenly took charge of my fingers, knotting noose after noose, as though she were helping a child write its first letter. I learnt to make the noose while having all my ten children, a blast of air hummed in Chinmayi Devi's voice. There is actually a seven hundred and twenty-eighth way to hang a person, Pingalakeshini reminded me, mussing my curls. Elokeshi . . . Niharika called loud and long. Careful Chotdi, suggested Thakuma. Come, she called, come into the world of bliss! I smiled and displayed the noose of thirteen loops my hands had forged, to the world. When I brought the other end of the rope through the hook, the noose gaped—its tongue, too, had been chopped off.

'Sanjeev Kumar babu, will you please step a little closer?'

I lured him with the noose as if it were the marriage garland. When he came closer, the memory of the ruined mansion where the bankalmi, the ramsar, the angulilata and the chehurlata stood blooming rose up in me. My body broke into new shoots once more. I ached for his embrace. My ears yearned to hear him say: 'I will be with you till death.'

When I took the glasses off his nose, I whispered, 'I want to fuck you at least once . . .'

He turned pale.

'Babu, take off that tie, please?'

He undid it with trembling fingers. I tied his hands behind his back with it. It was I who undid the first two buttons of his shirt. I touched the hollow of his bare neck with a finger. His face became piteous. I saw Trailokya, Utpalavarna and Annapurna. I saw his mother's henna-tipped fingers and Kakima's alta-soaked feet. In the land of women that Sultana saw in her dream, there was no such thing as war. The tiniest bit of earth which belonged to another, the smallest jewel that was another's, even if it were more valuable than the Koh-i-noor, and another's seat, even if it were more precious than the Peacock Throne, were not to be coveted in that world. The women there sought only the pearls that nature had fashioned in the bosom of wisdom. They lost themselves in the pleasures of nature.

'Here, this is where the noose tightens. The C-2 vertebra should break,' I announced loudly as I made him wear it.

Our bodies were so close, they nearly touched. Forgetting that we were surrounded by strong lights and the whole world, I looked into his eyes with desire. The man I had loved. I saw his long eyelashes, his fair cheeks, the innumerable veins in his neck. I remembered the streets of Kolkata where I had wanted to walk with him, the history I had wished to share with him. The blood of the hangman coursing in my veins cried out greedily for his life.

'Do not be afraid, Sanjeev Kumar Mitra,' I whispered like Grandfather Mosh. 'There is nothing, really, to be afraid of.'

His eyes were trapped in my gaze. Fear filled his; love filled mine. The aparajita vine with its blue flowers sprouted and grew through my veins. Slowly, I tightened the noose. Then, lightning fast, I pulled the other end of the rope. Sanjeev Kumar rose to the ceiling with a stifled moan. He weighed about seventy kilos.

'Come back, as your forefather did, to tell us what death is like,' I teased, tying up the end of the rope to the gallows tree. The noose tightened on his neck and he screamed 'Amme!' Ma, mati, manush, I answered. His legs danced in the air. Like a plastic bag filled with water being pressed hard, his life force tried hard to escape through different routes. His eyes rolled like balls. His tongue stuck out. His hands stuck closer to the body and scratched his thighs in sheer agony. I beamed into the camera, pulled off my mike and threw it down. Picking up my old bag from under the table and slinging it on my shoulder, I walked out. What the world gave me, I returned to it. I kept moving like the ilish swimming into the Padma, passing Sanjeev Kumar's desperately thrashing limbs, the people who had run up to hold him, and the numberless television screens all around. Nobody stopped me. Outside, Sanjeev Kumar's mother waited for me. I saw her and felt puny. Children,

I sorrowed. My hands are slimy. Never mind, she said, kissing me on the head and handing me a small cloth bundle full of soil.

'The statue of Durga is made out of soil taken from the beshya's doorstep. That is because the ego of the man who crosses it unravels and falls on the ground there.'

Just like at the gallows, I burst out laughing. The grains of sand made a grating sound inside the silk cloth. I held it tight with hands slimy with death. Thus my name and my life became undying in Bharat and the whole world, in the name of love, soil and death. I knew well that no one would stop me. Rain, soil, light and history stood waiting for me. *Jodi tor daak shune kevo ona ashe tobe ekla chalo re*, I hummed as I began my journey to the future, to Bhavishyath.

Acknowledgements

Ever since *Aarachar*, the Malayalam original of *Hangwoman*, appeared, I have received a flood of compliments—in person, by post, by phone—almost every day. The question that arrives inevitably after the compliments is: How long have you lived in Kolkata? I have written short stories set in Spain, England and France, but writing a novel in which the narrative takes shape through the eyes of a protagonist born and raised in a place completely unfamiliar to me—I never even thought I'd attempt that. However, writing a novel that explores the place of women in India was a dream I had nurtured for long. For many years, I sought a satisfactory backdrop—finally, the spark came when I saw Joshy Joseph's documentary *One Day from a Hangman's Life*.

My first visit to Kolkata was in 1999, on my way to Jamshedpur to receive a coveted national award for journalists instituted by the People's Union of Civil Liberties. Having seen Bengal only through Satyajit Ray's movies and the Malayalam translations of Bengali novels, I'd thought until then that all Bengali men and women were fair, slim, tall and good-looking. Bengal in my imagination was pristine, elegant. What I saw was just the opposite. Rusty old Fiat taxis riddled with holes. Roads full of spit and phlegm and poverty. Humans with teeth blackened by betel and ancient buildings with facades blackened by dried moss.

When I began writing a novel set it in Kolkata, it was Dileep, my husband, who first read the opening chapters. He read a few pages and said, 'It's good, but there is no Kolkata here. Let's visit the city again.' So we went to Kolkata again. The place had changed. Instead of Fiats, the taxis were ramshackle, rusty Ambassadors. Many huge concrete buildings had risen by then. McDonald's and Kentucky Fried Chicken outlets and various pubs had made their appearance. The city welcomed us bathed in red, yellow and blue lights. Large vehicles jostled for space with dust-covered buses and emaciated cycle rickshaws. There was no dearth of child beggars. Gangs of them surrounded vehicles that stopped at traffic lights. I had no idea what I was going to write but I was overwhelmed with the joy of anticipation. I saw that no better backdrop than Kolkata could be imagined for the story I wanted to write—the Indian woman's her-story.

Subhajit Das Bhoumik, photographer and director, took me everywhere—to Kalighat, Sonagachi, the Ganga, to Bengali homes. I wandered all over Kolkata with my cousin, the well-known sculptor K.S. Radhakrishnan. When *Aarachar* was ready for publication, DC Books suggested five different covers, two of which were his designs.

I returned home, only to be buried in books that told Kolkata's story. The more I read, the more confused I became as to where the past ended and the present began. It appeared to me that the experience of European colonial rule and that of corporate colonization were not too far apart. The stories of those who ruled and those who fell were the same. What left me astounded, however, was the presence of women—rendered completely invisible throughout history. Within decaying tombs in the ancient cemetery of History were the women who had revolted inside and outside their homes, the women who had dreamed of new worlds, the women whose tresses continued to grow long and longer even when their skulls had crumbled to dust. Those who did not seek them out would never know that they had indeed lived.

The theme I chose to work upon is such that some characters may remind readers of people and incidents in the real world. This resemblance is purely coincidental. A true incident is gestured at as the broad setting of this work but the characters are all purely fictional. Except for a few incidents and historical facts drawn upon to render the narrative believable at certain moments and to maintain its aesthetic balance, everything in this novel was entirely forged in my imagination.

I began writing *Aarachar* only because of the constant encouragement from P.K. Parakkadavu, editor of the weekly *Madhyamam* and a distinguished short story writer himself. I remember here with much warmth and immense gratitude historian P. Thankappan Nair who helped me find valuable historical material, K.K. Kochu Koshy of the

Central Reference Library, Kolkata, DC Books, the publisher of *Aarachar*, and my Malayali friends in Kolkata.

Nisha Susan, writer and journalist, called to tell me that she liked the stories of *Yellow Is the Colour of Longing* and asked if I would contribute to *Tehelka*'s 2012 fiction special. Thus the first chapter of *Aarachar* was published in English, translated by Sajeev Kumarapuram, even before the novel as a whole was published in Malayalam. The day the *Tehelka* issue was out, R. Sivapriya, my editor at Penguin, emailed me, eager to commission the English translation of the novel. And to my excitement, J. Devika was willing to translate it. She made the time to work on this long novel. T.T. Sreekumar read through her early drafts carefully and offered many useful suggestions. Putting down in a few meagre words the great appreciation I feel for these friends would be to squander away those feelings. Therefore I choose to consecrate my feelings for them in my heart forever.

I am not a Bengali. I have never lived in Kolkata. I am not even confident about my Hindi. I am an ordinary woman, born and raised in a village in Kerala, in a middle class family. I became a writer only on the strength of my wayward dreams and my crazy ability to have genuine faith in those dreams. Writing, indeed, is my *Chetna,* and also my *Bhavishyath.* Truly.

K.R. Meera
April 2014

Translator's Acknowledgements

At the end of translating a book like *Aarachar*, I know exactly what swimmers who take up the challenge of swimming across choppy seas and treacherous straits feel when they emerge triumphant from the waters. Besides the exhilaration, they know with unprecedented intensity that the feat would have been impossible without the active support of many people.

I have many such people to remember, but of all of them, I value the contributions of three: R. Sivapriya and Shatarupa Ghoshal of Penguin, and my friend T.T. Sreekumar. Sreekumar, who is a well-known social scientist and literary scholar in Kerala, went carefully through my early draft keeping in mind the Malayalam original and made very many useful suggestions. It is no doubt the common love of Malayalam literature that drew us both to this extraordinary novel; and surely it is the same passion that gave him the energy, made him find the time, to plunge into it. The painstaking, difficult task of polishing the translation was taken up by Sivapriya first and Shatarupa later, and with great sensitivity to the novel's eccentric narration and its aesthetics, mixing up all sorts of familiar binaries and chronicling our times which seem to have generated a new *rasa* appropriate for itself—out of *jugupsa*, revulsion. I know from experience that working on a translation with others will be fruitful only if they are all equally infected with the rhetorical intensity of the text. I think the four of us did experience that great pleasure alike and at the same time, and so I do not know whether offering thanks is the best way of acknowledging Sreekumar, Sivapriya and Shatarupa.

I also want to thank Amit Shovan Ray and Vidyarthi Chatterji who read the chapters and whose enthusiastic response was a valuable source of encouragement.

Most Malayali readers are exposed quite early in their lives as readers to very competent translations of Bengali novels and many Bengali authors are as familiar to us as our own writers. But it is K.R. Meera alone who could craft Malayalam's ultimate gift of love to Bengal, in the form of an astonishing novel, *Aarachar*. It, perhaps, is not a truthful representation of Bengal—I am however sure that it is our Dream Bengal, one that has sunk deep roots in our imaginations. I thank her for the enormous effort, and for holding my hand and being there as I crossed these strange and turbulent waters, her creation.

J. Devika
May 2014

A Note on the Type

Dante was the result of collaboration between Giovanni Mardersteig, printer, book designer and typeface artist, and Charles Malin, one of the great punch-cutters of the twentieth century. The two worked closely to develop an elegant typeface that was distinctive, legible and attractive. Special care was taken with the design of the serifs and top curves of the lowercase to create a subtle horizontal stress, which helps the eye move smoothly across the page.